MYTHBORN IV

Litany of the

Cypher

by

V. Lakshman

For more information please go to:
www2.mythbornmedia.com

NOTE TO READER
Please FOLLOW and LIKE us on:

We hope you enjoy
Mythborn IV: Litany of the Cypher
If you'd like to learn more about Mythborn,
please go to:

www2.mythbornmedia.com
or
www.dawnslightmedia.com

Contents

FLIGHT

Princess Yetteje Tir sat in the crook of Arek's arm, her amber eyes sweeping the cloudscape below. It spread out like a blanket of cotton blooms, small tufts of white and pink colored by the setting sun. In Arek's other arm lay Silbane's body, now small and fragile in death. It was still surreal, the idea that he was actually gone. Though Yetteje had only spent a short amount of time with him, the master's presence had been a source of strength and steadiness. He seemed to magnify the better parts of each of them whenever he was near. Like the sun behind clouds, his warmth wasn't missed until it was gone. She took a deep, cleansing breath, her gaze slowly crawling up to Arek's face, her forehead and eyebrows pulling up with concern. How would Arek fare with the loss? Arek himself had assumed the form of his bonded Aeris, giant war angel, Azrael.

Their group had dwindled since arriving here. Along with Silbane the other master from Meridian Isle, Kisan, was dead. Worse, Niall had thrown his lot in with Valarius Galadine, now highlord of the elves he had created after being banished from Edyn. She searched Arek's face, hoping to see some sign that the merging with Azrael meant the fight against Sovereign could continue, but the young adept continued to stare at the horizon, no doubt lost in his own thoughts about the past few days and the tumultuous turn of events when facing Valarius.

Thank Lilyth for that, thought the princess. The demon

queen had used them to open a way to the elven city of Avalyon under the pretense of rescuing Duncan Illrys, archmage and one of the Old Lords. Duncan was steeped in magic forgotten by most, like blood magic. He was also responsible for the deaths of thousands, perhaps tens of thousands, in his maniacal effort to reunite with his murdered wife and fellow archmage, Sonya, in the demon realm of Arcadia. Amongst those whose deaths were on Duncan's head were Yetteje's father and many of the people of EvenSea. Duncan also was, if it was to be believed, Arek's true father. This presented the princess with no small amount of conflict: the sins of Arek's father were hard to reconcile with Arek's current allegiance to Yetteje and her allies.

One thing not Duncan's fault, however, was the consequences of his own rescue. Their entry into Avalyon had used a lens and opened a gate for Lilyth to use, and she hadn't hesitated. Wave upon wave of her Furies had flooded in from this, her realm of Arcadia, into Avalyon, setting Valarius's elven tree city afire and attacking its people. Even now it burned, a blazing fire curling a tail of black and gray smoke that wound downward in the slate dusk sky. Avalyon looked like a falling leaf, twisting its way down to oblivion in the sea of clouds below.

So much loss, and for what? Though Yetteje didn't agree with Valarius, his elves were no different than anyone she'd met on her travels. They were fiercely loyal to their country and king, as were the Galadines to Bara'cor, and her own family to EvenSea. She glanced back at the burning city. It was a small orange dot now, spiraling downward in a descent that would end with the deaths of anyone left.

Yetteje thought back to meeting with the shade of her father in Lilyth's realm of the dead. He was a good man, yet a part of her felt that catch on her innate sense of morality, like a hem snagged on a burr. Noble houses had to be decisive, ofttimes under ostensibly defensible causes to secure their own borders and provide their citizens with safety.

That's necessary, she reassured herself. People want to be secure and safe, and the noble houses provide that.

That some had to be forcibly taken for their own protection was normal, wasn't it? Part of her wondered what her father would say, and yet she knew the answer. Power, won through diplomacy or force of arms, was still something exerted over people. Under that scrutiny, she had a difficult time approving of the noble houses' actions, whether EvenSea or Bara'cor. Were they simply tyrants, using convenient laws and royal decrees to hide their greedy expansion?

She'd walked through this strange realm half-blinded by grief at her father's death. Speaking to him again, even here where his death had been confirmed, had relieved some of her sadness. She'd had closure with him—and now Lilyth offered the chance at life for him again—if they followed the demon queen's plan. Why not take criminals who'd be executed and give men like her father life again? Was possession under those terms so horrible?

The thought suddenly made her wonder, was Silbane truly dead? Could he come back, just as her father had in Lilyth's castle? The hope sputtered as she thought of the cleansing argent fire that had washed through Arek's body. She knew in her heart the master had made a great sacrifice for such a feat. Whether or not he could return from that act was doubtful, but she made the decision to not raise false hope with Arek. Especially now with the wound still so raw. It suddenly felt like an invasion of his privacy to stare, so she turned her gaze out to their left, toward the silver-and-blue armored figure of the firstmark, Ash Rillaran, flying in formation beside them.

Yetteje had to admit that Ash looked majestic in the armor of his bonded Aeris, Orion, the sunlight dazzling blue and white off its polished surface, making her both squint and smile. That he'd always feared heights was now difficult to believe, for the man flew with his wings outstretched as if trying to catch as much air as possible. He smiled once at something evident only to him. Whatever it was, it made him happy, and that gave Yetteje a modicum of peace. For all they'd been through, it was good to know her companions were still able to find joy, if even in these small moments.

Something pulled Brianna's eyes up from her compass to meet Yetteje's own. The dwarven healer gave her a brief smile of reassurance from her perch tucked in Ash's arms, a quick half lift of her mouth. The fact that they were still alive was almost a joke in and of itself. Yetteje shook her head and smiled back. It was unbelievable when one considered they had faced Valarius, Sovereign, and the dark nephilim. She thanked whatever gods watched over them for their fortune, only to stumble in midthought as she remembered Helios, his sunburnt armor flashing carmine and orange as he erupted in a deep laugh.

They had not escaped Avalyon unscathed. The Watcher had fallen trying to save Orion, who in turn had given his life to save Ash through Ascension. Yetteje's eyes wandered back to Arek. Two stalwart companions were now gone, as well as masters Silbane and Kisan. Tej wondered again how their losses would affect the group. Her time at the Tir Combat Academy taught her much about leadership. Would they bond, becoming an alloy stronger than any of their individual traits? Or would they break at the flex, a fault hidden deep within their group's mettle giving way to fear and worry? She didn't know about the others, but her own confidence felt unshakable, like the stones upon which a mountain sat. If it were up to her they would stay together, stronger than before.

"Look!"

Yetteje's focus snapped at the healer's shout, looking where Brianna pointed. The isle of Lilyth had come into view, but something had changed. She could feel Arek slow, his wingbeats faltering at the sight ahead. A wave of doubt flooded through her. Something was fundamentally wrong. Then she saw it. Olympious, the City Eternal, was gone.

The pyramid that made up Lilyth's stone fortress had vanished, leaving behind a gouge in the mountainside like a giant hand had reached down and scooped it away. Nothing was left except exposed roots and rubble and what looked to be the remains of the surrounding city, desolate and silent.

They quickly spiraled down to the nearest edge of the crater. Both Arek and Ash changed form once their passengers had disembarked and the body of Silbane had been laid gently beside Duncan's unconscious form. Yetteje's eyes scanned the opposite rim, looking for any signs of life.

"What do you think happened?" Ash said quietly. Then he doubled over, gasping as pain lanced through him. Arek also stumbled, looking a bit sick, but not as much as the firstmark.

Yetteje went to Ash's side, her eyes wide, "What's happening?"

"Gods, I knew it would be bad, but this is terrible!" Ash said. "I saw Silbane…" He gritted his teeth, looking up at her through eyes watering with pain, "Price… for holding Orion's war angel form." He slowly tried to straighten, his face contorting between a smile and a grimace. A halfhearted

5

attempt at a chuckle sounding more like a whimper escaped as he managed to stagger to a mostly upright position.

She looked back at Arek, who seemed better off. "You okay?"

Arek nodded but remained silent. His pale eyes swept the city. Then he said, "He'll feel it less as he gets used to it." Then he turned and looked out over the chasm where the massive pyramid once sat. Motioning to the others, he moved to the lip cautiously, sliding lower to the ground. Once he'd found what looked to be a good vantage point, he looked back at Yetteje. She followed suit, moving up on her belly until she lay next to him, close enough to feel the heat of his body. It was a strangely heady feeling, as if Arek's very presence gave her energy and clarity. It was a feeling she didn't want to lose.

The devastation wrought upon Lilyth's abode was incredible. The foundations of Olympious had dug deep, and still the land had been ripped open by a beast. The gash was so violent that parts of blue sky showed through, gaps where the earth of the floating island had simply given way and fell to whatever lay below.

Within this wasteland figures moved. Arek's soft touch on her arm directed her eyes to the walls opposite them. She could see the slinking and feral shapes of mistfrights, their low gray forms moving randomly, sniffing the ground as if trying to find the scent of their missing home.

Arek looked back at Brianna and whispered, "Your kapsool ... how far is it?"

Brianna looked down at her wrist, taking a quick measurement from the glowing tattoo there, and said, "It's about halfway down on the right, near that broken arch."

Yetteje could immediately see what the healer meant. A stairwell had survived. It stood coiled around nothing, withered and broken, a curled hand of white bone around an invisible cup. A chill ran through her, raising the hairs on her neck and arms. This didn't feel right.

"It would be pretty quick to fly down, grab the kapsool, and return," offered Ash simply. Yet to Yetteje's ear, he seemed to defer to Arek.

Arek rolled onto his back, putting a forearm over his eyes. It seemed to Yetteje he was assessing something the others could not see. Then he raised himself up. Though he looked at Ash, his gaze took in the entire group. "How'll we carry all of us and the kapsool?"

Brianna moved over to them, her bulk making it hard for her to conceal herself. Still, she managed to stay below the sightline made by the cliff's edge. The doctor knelt and said, "I don't need the capsule, just what's inside."

Arek looked back at Ash. "We can't leave Silbane and my father."

"If you take Brianna, I'll take the rest," offered Ash.

Yetteje shook her head, "You can't carry three of us. I'll go with Arek. He can take Brianna and me. You stay with Arek's master and... the red mage."

If Ash noticed the princess's distaste at even mentioning the man who'd killed her father, he didn't show it. Ash simply replied with a quirk of his lip. "No matter what I say, it's going to end with you going, isn't it?"

Yetteje got up and crept away from the ledge, unshouldering Valor, the storied bow of the Galadines. "I'm glad we're getting to understand each other better, commander."

Ash's sigh only received raised eyebrows from Arek, who clearly had no desire to intervene on the firstmark's behalf.

Instead, Arek said, "I'll move in quickly and stand guard.

If worse comes to worst, we'll retreat. We can meet there." He pointed at a distinctively shaped island floating not too far away.

"Don't take any chances. We've made it this far without her gear," cautioned Ash.

Yetteje observed that the firstmark apparently still eyed the dwarven doctor with distrust, a sentiment the princess could empathize with even though she didn't agree.

Arek sighed and said, "Not really," his gaze flicking to the gun holstered on her belt. The weapon had killed Kisan, saving Arek's life.

"Her past is important to our fight against Sovereign," Arek said. "If whatever's in there will help her remember, I think it's worth the risk." He looked around and sighed.

"Lilyth didn't wait for us, so if we're going to get any answers, finding her is our best option." He waited a moment, as if waiting to see if someone would challenge him. When that didn't occur, he awkwardly added, "We need any advantage Brianna's equipment might bring, agreed?"

Ash frowned, then pulled Arek to one side. Yetteje suddenly felt herself pulled along by Arek's grasping hand, like a drowning man grasping at a cork ring.

When the trio were out of earshot of Brianna, the firstmark said softly, "You're in charge."

"Yeah, I guess…"

"He's right," Yetteje said. "Don't you see it?" She tried her best to connect with him. "Stop looking for approval from any of us."

"I'm not," Arek said, his face flushed.

Ash shrugged.

"It is what it is," he said. "People fall into line behind someone after battle's end. If it's not obvious yet, that's you." His gaze flicked back and forth between the two, his expression reminding the princess of that look old people got when they thought they knew something you didn't. It was slightly annoying.

He continued, "You can't treat this like a democracy."

Well, that's hard to disagree with, thought Yetteje, her mood mellowing.

The commander looked back at Brianna, who had turned her attention to Duncan's prone form. The archmage had still not recovered from the battle in Avalyon and Silbane's sacrifice to give him the dragonsight.

"You're in command because you defeated Kisan, not us. While we're stuck here, you're our leader. I'll follow until we're back at Bara'cor. For the sake of our small group's morale, be decisive."

He paused, then added, "If you don't want to… or can't… I'll take over."

That last part was delivered with a bit of ice. Yetteje had heard it a hundred times at court: the offer that was really a veiled threat. Ash wouldn't let things fail, regardless of the entire group's sympathy for and allegiance to Arek.

Arek's pale gaze met the firstmark's blue one as the silence stretched. Finally, Arek said, "I understand."

"Good," the firstmark said. He tilted his head. "Are we okay?"

"Maybe," Arek said, his eyes downcast and brows furrowed in thought. "What if I order you to free my father?" He raised his gaze, looking up with a half smile, though there was a hint of defiance behind it. Ash had sworn to bring Duncan to justice for his crimes against Bara'cor and the other fortresses of Edyn, crimes that had resulted in thousands of dead.

The firstmark turned and stared at him, then countered, "What if you decide to do what you did with Brianna's torc and free him from its power?"

Arek looked around, his eyes searching the landscape, or perhaps Yetteje thought, something within himself. Then he said, "I can't."

"What do you mean?" asked Yetteje. "I saw you do it."

Arek nodded, "That was before... Silbane gave himself to cleanse me."

Suddenly Yetteje understood. The blackfire was gone, and with it any chance Arek might undo the torc. "So that thing is really stuck on him?"

Arek looked at them both, then nodded slowly and said, "There may be another way to release it, but I'm not sure yet. Still, the firstmark's question is a fair one." He turned now to face Ash and said, "If I choose to let him go, it will be because we need his strength to get back to Edyn."

Ash paused, now his eyes searching Arek's. Finally, a small smile came to his lips but didn't reach his eyes. He looked more dangerous now than he had when confronting Arek over his leadership. Yetteje felt the leather-wrapped hilt of her blade in her palm, her grasp tightening around it. When had that happened?

Ash nodded his chin toward Brianna and the unconscious form of Duncan. "I'm following your orders, for now. We agreed a trial would settle things. You saw the death and destruction he caused... he killed thousands... for his wife?" The firstmark paused. "Is freeing him noble?"

"For his wife and son," Arek said, with a flicker of anger.

Ash sighed and finally raised his hands, saying, "If we need him, I'll agree. As long as your orders, beyond that, don't conflict with bringing Duncan to justice. Can we agree on that for now?" The firstmark held out his hand, waiting.

Heartbeats went by, then Arek slowly raised his own and took Ash's arm in a warrior's grip, forearm to forearm. "Just don't get yourself killed going after that damn kapsool," Ash said with a sigh.

"I don't die easy, Firstmark," replied Arek, and though he might have meant it as a joke, it came out sounding like a threat.

The commander hesitated. "No doubt." Then he pumped Arek's hand once and laughed, trying to break the tension. "Good. I can't carry all of us." He clapped the adept on the shoulder and made his way back to Brianna and Duncan.

"He'll be conscious soon," the dwarven doctor said, "but probably not useful. Give him this." She handed him a small square piece of clear paper.

Ash looked at it, confused, until Brianna explained, "Just place it in his mouth. It will dissolve and help him stay alert."

He nodded and looked at Yetteje. "Good hunting. We'll see you soon." The firstmark changed form, suddenly towering above them. He then scooped up the two motionless forms and took one last look at the princess.

To his last-ditch glare, Yetteje replied evenly, "I'm going."

Ash sighed in frustration, then leapt up into the sky, his wings catching air as he sped off toward the floating isle. She watched the sunlight glint off his armor as he wove his way to their meeting point. Her attention turned to Arek. Yetteje saw his nostrils flare. Maybe he drank in the air, now colored with the smell of charred wood and soil. Or maybe he was just angry.

"We are the hunters," he said.

"Yeah." She smiled at him. "You know we'll figure this out, right? Don't give up hope."

Arek ignored that, turning his attention to the sad creatures roaming the devastated rim of Lilyth's City Eternal. "They are the prey."

Yetteje smiled. Now that was more like the Arek she knew. She pushed herself back from the edge and motioned to Brianna. "You ready?"

"Do I have a choice?" she replied. "I can't get to my capsule without you."

Yetteje smiled. "Welcome to my world. Nothing happens when you're ready for it."

"So comforting," quipped Brianna, the hint of smile pulling the corners of her mouth and softening her eyes.

Yetteje could feel herself respond in kind, the corner of her eyes crinkling as her smile grew. "You must know the boys will have a difficult time if we don't act the part of princesses."

"Ha!" Brianna laughed, shaking her head and clapping Yetteje on the shoulder with an oversized hand. "No doubt we need to be more helpless."

"Hey! Can we get moving?" Arek said impatiently.

Both women tightened their belts and secured their equipment. Yetteje squeezed Brianna's arm, gave her a reassuring smile, then made her way over to Arek. "What's our plan?"

Arek changed, his form flashing into the gargantuan war angel, Azrael. Even when she'd thought she'd become accustomed to it, the sight was more than impressive. The adamantine armor of Azrael surrounded Arek, a combination of blinding white edged with azure blue. She looked up and saw his familiar face, giant-sized, behind a visored helm.

"Run in, fight hard, run out."

She smiled. "That simple?"

Arek pointed toward the area they'd infiltrate. "The landing area is small and looks unstable."

Yetteje heard a *snap* near her face. She turned, only to realize it was Arek getting her attention, his eyes making his meaning clear.

"I've got to change forms quickly to make room for us, which means you've got to exit fast. Watch your step."

"Got it."

He picked them both up and jumped. The sudden sense of downward velocity sent her stomach up into her gut, but the exhilaration took over. This was where she was meant to be.

Yetteje could feel the ground nearing. It was like a sixth sense. She felt the air thicken in response to Arek's wings beating. Before he asked, she'd grabbed her bow and prepared to leap from his arms, her eyes trained unerringly on the spot she intended, hopefully, to land.

ALION DEFT

Queensmark Alion Deft winged low across a plateau, signaling her Furies to land. She followed them down, landing lightly as her membranous wings spread to catch air. As they folded on her back, she cleared a space and then withdrew a lens. Holding it up, she said, "Lady."

The air in front of her shimmered and solidified as Lilyth's face appeared, floating a few feet from Deft and her party. "How is your progress?" the image asked.

"We have tracked them to an island not too distant, my Lady," answered Deft. She looked at her team and added, "We are ready." Behind them orange clouds sat against a pink sky. If one did not know the nephilim were consuming the Way, it was hard to tell this world was dying.

Lilyth looked at something Deft could not see, then back at the undead magehunter and said, "I know this is hard, but I want you to hold your attack."

Deft cocked a head but said nothing. Though her heart burned for vengeance, the Lady could not be disobeyed or ignored. Cursed to serve the Aeris queen, the knight once dedicated to exterminating every vestige of magic in the world now found herself the very master she once would have hunted down. The tale that brought her here was convoluted at best, so she did what every officer did and shut up, a mask betraying none of her inner turmoil.

"The final phase of the fall of Arcadia is at hand. Dawnlight, the mountain that exists across time, has been brought by me to a location near Harmagedon. These dwarves are my gift to my Aeris. There should be hundreds, perhaps thousands for the taking. Possess them and the East Gate will allow you to join me in Edyn." Dawnlight Mountain was one of the few places in the world that served as a nexus between planes. It could exist in Arcadia, Edyn, and perhaps a thousand other multiverses in between.

Deft nodded and asked, "These gifts are for every unbonded Aeris?"

Lilyth smiled, "Of course, and certainly for you and your Furies. Take them and join me. I will not stop you from facing Duncan but marooning him here is the same as death."

"Perhaps," answered Deft, "but less satisfying, my lady."

Lilyth nodded, "You will gather Aeris from where my Eternal City once stood and meet with Zafir. Your goal will be to possess the builders and escape through the gate at Harmagedon."

Deft's eyes narrowed and she asked, "But you will not forbid me to exact my vengeance upon the red mage?"

Lilyth, seemingly happy to share her thoughts, said, "No, I will not. However, you may find more joy in possessing a builder and remaking yourself into whomever you wish."

"It's not the same," snarled Deft. "The curse of rot he gifted upon me will not be cleansed."

Lilyth raised a delicate eyebrow.

"No, it will not. However, I have seen greed for revenge kill just as quickly as the quest for justice. Does it matter if you can use the builder's body to hold the rot at bay?"

"And Duncan?" Deft asked, emboldened by Lilyth's answer. "What price will he pay for the centuries he's tortured me?"

"Where will he go? He'll die in Arcadia, eaten and possessed before the end by the nephilim his son unleashed.

I cannot think of a more fitting end." The queen of the Aeris paused, then said, "Do as you will. Zafir has agreed to let our forces pass through in return for his own share of builders to possess. Aid him however you see fit. You go with my banner behind you."

Deft bowed once. "As you command, my Lady."

Lilyth's image vanished as Deft put away the lens. Then she turned to her men and said, "We will go to Olympious and gather the Aeris. From there, Harmagedon and revenge await us." She vaulted into the sky, followed by ten dark arrow-like forms as they became an echelon, the point orienting itself directly for the last location of the Eternal City.

Soon, thought Deft, the red mage will know what pain really means.

FLASHBACK:

LANDFALL

C aptain Serene Talaris looked at her chronometer, the setting sun painting its face in a transparent rainbow as the UV filters scattered the light across its surface. Clear blue eyes stared out at an ocean colored the same, and her lean face was framed by hair so dark it shined iridescently under the bright sun.

"The controls must be around here," she said.

"Maybe," opined the woman next to her. "Or all the silicate in the mantle is screwing with us."

Talaris raised an eyebrow at that and asked, "No kaffe, Firstmark?"

Her second-in-command shrugged and smiled. "Worse than none. It tastes like seaweed."

Talaris smiled. Firstmark Dawn Petracles could be a stick-in-the-mud when she was upset, but there wasn't another officer Talaris wanted more on this mission. Petracles was both practical and insightful, a rare combination.

Talaris looked over the vista spread out before them. Their ship lay felled like an enormous pine tree, over a kilometer long and broken in two. The hull was in pieces, fractured with the prow nose-down into a cul-de-sac formed by the crescent-shaped ridge poking its teeth just above the waves, the remains of a marine caldera. The aft section was shattered into multiple cylinders trailing east, out across the wide-open expanse of blue ocean, like a broken exclamation mark separated from its accusing point.

They'd suffered the constant pounding waves until their nans had become fully integrated with the local flora and fauna, finally allowing the crew to safely exit their ship to reinforce parts of the sea wall and forge shelters where they could tend the injured. That they'd been marooned near this pseudo-shoreline was fortuitous. Still, the *TEC Sovereign* hadn't fared well in the exchange. As was tradition with all TEC ships, the male pronoun was used. Therefore, the captain thought of *TEC Sovereign* as 'he', and so lamented the fact that his spine was broken, and their options extremely limited.

"Come on, then, just another day in the Commonwealth. No sense in wasting seaweed on complaints." She picked her way forward, not waiting nor watching to see if her firstmark followed. Their destination was on the other end of the island, where the long line of wreckage from the shoreline pointed at their final resting spot, as if the wreckage itself wanted to ensure no one forgot the crew was to blame.

"Hey, Cap," Dawn asked from behind her, "how long will the reserves last?"

Talaris knew her commander knew the answer. Her reason for asking was nakedly clear and it ruffled her feathers just a bit. "Longer than you will, asking stupid questions."

She could almost feel the woman's eyebrows rise and knew exactly the expression on her face. Rather than have Petracles bring up her mental state with the Sovereign, she continued, "We're not sure how much is being used. Depends on the sunlight."

"That final directive—"

Talaris turned, coming face to face with the firstmark. "I don't want to have this discussion again. Clones are decanted in situations where senior crew could come to harm. The four of us can't be out here risking our lives at the same time."

Petracles sighed and said, "Okay. Just seems harsh, even to clones."

"Stow it. It's our duty... and the others don't need to know." She said this last part with a surreptitious look around for anyone in earshot, then met and held Dawn's eyes until the commander acquiesced with a nod. After a moment, in an effort to recapture some of their sense of adventure, Talaris asked, "The real question is, why were we assigned only one RAI?"

The commander's mouth quirked into a half smile. "Let's ask." She gestured and said, "RAI-10, why only one of you?" The air coalesced into a man-shaped figure, his body clothed in a dark gray bodysuit covered with what looked like scales. Instead of a face, the figure had no mouth or nose and only a black slit for eyes.

Its voice, distinctly boyish, replied with deference, "The majority of Sentient AIs have been allocated to recovery. It was determined only one Reactive AI was necessary for this survey." Without facial features it was hard to read the RAI, so Talaris didn't try.

Still, they seemed woefully undermanned, thought the captain. She couldn't stop her eyebrows climbing in disbelief. Instead, she replied with a one-word question, "Really?"

"Early activation," supplied Petracles, explaining the lack of features on the RAI. "They're supposed to mimic indigenous life. We've just not been here long enough for an imprint to take hold."

"Your competence has never been questioned, captain," replied RAI-10 in what sounded like a child admonishing an elder. "Sovereign remains confident in your ability to terminate the Phoenix protocol and remote pilot the secondary core to our landing zone."

Captain Talaris scanned the long line of wreckage and said, "We're calling this a landing, now? You make it sound almost normal." She sighed, then asked, "If the Phoenix protocol was initiated, that means the secondary core will come online and wipe Sovereign's database. We can't let that happen. Do you have a location yet?"

The figure tilted its head up and said, "If you mean the secondary core, it's in low orbit. However, since the protocol was initiated from a location approximately five hundred meters down and three hundred meters west, it seems logical that is the location of the ejected piloting module. Do you want me to go first?"

The secondary core was a complete backup of Sovereign and designed to come online in case the *TEC Sovereign* suffered any catastrophic incident. That decision was normally made by the Phoenix protocol, however the Sovereign had countermanded his own replacement and instead created this away mission to locate the piloting module and guide the secondary core down to their location. His intention, it seemed, was to strip it of components to repair himself. Captain Talaris could feel her skin itch at the disregard for the Phoenix protocol, but hers was not the place to question the Sovereign's orders.

"No," stated the captain flatly. She looked back the way they'd come and let loose a short, sharp whistle. In response, two figures emerged carefully picking their way across the sharp rocks and shale.

"I don't trust you RAIs when facing a Phoenix.

Simulations show you both think what you're doing is right, and that usually means a fight. I want other options." Talaris looked at the commander and added, "Nonlethal options."

"Understood," Petracles replied. Once the other two officers—Commander Sahana Tir and Lieutenant Jenna Illrys—had joined them, the firstmark said, "RAI-10 says the module is about a half klick below. What are our options"—she looked at the captain sidelong— "to preserve the Phoenix? Any other SAIs available?"

Commander Tir spoke up. She was a study in opposites, with dark hair tied back into a tight ponytail framing a face the color of warm wood. Sapphire eyes focused on her commander as she replied, "Limited. We know the Phoenix protocol has been activated. We'll have to find a way around it—without dying," she added with a wry smile.

"Funny," remarked the captain, deadpan. "This is all a joke to you, Commander?"

The good-natured vibe disappeared like smoke in a cold breeze.

"No, sir. I was just—"

The captain waved her off and addressed the lieutenant. "What's the bottom-line risk assessment of going down there? Can the Phoenix protocol be circumvented or deactivated?"

"The Phoenix has been activated, and that means the Sovereign's main core is compromised," answered Lieutenant Illrys. She paused, then added, "I'm still trying to understand why following his orders makes sense, given the Phoenix protocol overrides the chain of command. She's going to protect herself until the Sovereign is offline." She paused, then added, "We're literally dealing with two sentient AIs fighting for control over the ship and more importantly, the revival of ten thousand colonists we have in stasis. Talk about being between a rock and a hard place." This last part came out more softly, as if Illrys worried Sovereign could hear her even out here.

Two command AIs were strictly forbidden to coexist without the strictest protocols. Time and again the devastation wrought by ignoring that simple rule had resulted in entire colonies being wiped out. Talaris didn't relish the idea of her crew getting caught in a war between two sentient AIs, each thinking itself in charge. Thankfully, because of their computational speed and accuracy, picoseconds were an eternity to terraforming ships like the *TEC Sovereign*. Whatever it had decided had already been through a half a million simulations or more. If the Sovereign said recovering the secondary core to repair himself was the best chance for the colonists to be revived, then this was the best chance. Of that, she was certain.

RAI-10 chose that moment to say, "Willful transgression of the First Laws will result in immediate termination." He didn't seem angry, or even particularly threatening. He was just stating a fact. His brevity, delivered in a boy's voice, made evident his artificiality in a very literal way. Though sentience was recognized in machine lifeforms and having sentient AIs run society had been proven predominantly effective, it was in these moments that the gap between artificiality and biology felt painfully clear.

"Let me worry about the First Laws," the captain replied. "If there's a price to be paid for keeping our colonists alive, I'll pay it with a smile."

Nothing further needed to be said, so the group sat silently, waiting for Jenna to formulate an answer to the captain's initial question. Finally, Lieutenant Illrys said, "You said nonlethal? Then LIL-8 is our best choice."

"She's experimental," cautioned Petracles. "Love the

idea, though. This could be a live test run."

"Nothing like real conditions," agreed the lieutenant. "Forcing Ascension may stress the matrix enough to spark unpredictable behavior, though. The question is..." She trailed off somewhat lamely, as if she didn't want to ask about short straws and volunteers in a group where everyone outranked her.

"Don't worry, Jenna," the captain said. "This isn't a democracy. I'll decide."

"Then the question is–who?" Petracles said.

Talaris pondered the thought. Their AIs were designed to self-improve, using experience to adjust their responses. Sentience wasn't a question, but Ascension... that got stickier. The moment an AI combined with a host, the theoretical result was a stable construct capable of using their nans to change the environment and their bodies. She'd released the nans the night they'd crashed, overriding the safety protocols and ordering them to save the crew. While that had gone better than expected, the nans were spreading, by the trillions. Without a fully integrated Sovereign to govern their growth, they were evolving in unpredictable ways. Still, her crew would've died here if she hadn't acted. Now they needed to restore Sovereign's capability to rein in the nans or they'd take over this world's ecosystem and biosphere.

"Keep in mind," the lieutenant offered, "that Ascension with the Linked Intelligent Lifeform isn't too much of a problem. The new LILs are primarily designed for female brain and body chemistry." Although there was no outward change of expression, she must've felt the firstmark's unvoiced approval, for Jenna's confidence grew stronger as she continued, "Because females have proven better at integrating with SAIs, we get the best of both worlds—nans, plus crazy-fast computational capabilities."

"Crazy fast?" asked the firstmark, half-jokingly.

"Technical term," replied the lieutenant with a smile before realizing she was addressing her superior officer. Her face fell. "Sorry, sir."

"I'm kidding," Petracles replied with exasperation, but Talaris realized it was her own stressed attitude affecting the normal interactions of her crew, not anything her officers had said.

"That would explain why an all-female command crew was detanked," Petracles added thoughtfully. "Maybe we're guinea pigs?"

The captain arched an eyebrow. "I'd like to think we're better than that. And if this was the plan, why didn't Sovereign just order it?"

Jenna shrugged. "RAIs often want us to come to a conclusion without their help. I've heard it increases our compliance by a significant percentage."

The captain took that in, then went back to mull the problem over. Combining the LIL's intelligence and control over the nans with a person's emotional and instinctual awareness was tempting, despite the danger that the AI would take over the human host. Possession by an AI was the worst-case scenario.

If it worked, someone integrated could theoretically perform feats considered by most to be magic, such as terraforming without the need for large, fixed infrastructure. Their biology powered the nans, allowing them to act for long periods of time. People, it seemed, made excellent batteries. Now it was up to the crew and potentially two AIs to find the piloting module and guide the second core to a safe landing near their crash site.

The Sovereign intended to strip what he needed from the

backup and repair himself. Through whatever zettaflops of calculations he could perform, he'd decided this was a better choice than just taking himself offline and activating the second core. He'd also determined these four women, RAI-10, and LIL-8, would be the ideal mix to bring the mission success. The captain thought Jenna was probably right: he knew something they didn't.

In truth, the ship couldn't have picked a better team. Lieutenant Illrys was a genius at SAI development. Commander Tir knew the command protocols of their AIs like her own face, and Firstmark Petracles was a down-to-earth survivor. They meshed well as a team, and if anyone could get past Phoenix and remote pilot that core safely down, it was one of the three people standing before her.

She regretted cutting Commander Tir off. If they were going to get past the protective protocols, they needed someone like her to act without inhibition. She reached out, catching the commander's eye, and asked, "Can LIL-8 get down there?"

Tir edged forward, peering past the rocky edge and down to the sharp cliff below. The rocks were poised above the open blue waters like teeth made entirely out of sharp volcanic shale. "Depends on how integrated the nans have gotten with the local stuff. If they're in, she's got the ability for line-of-sight transport." She met her captain's gaze and, clearly trying to make up for her earlier lightheartedness, simply finished with, "Yes sir, shouldn't be a problem."

Talaris nodded, then considered their options. The cove they'd fallen into was fine and as she'd noted the prow of the ship was buried nose-down inside a horseshoe shaped cul-de-sac. The crash had opened the caldera's west side, destroying it and letting the water flow in. Unfortunately, the aft section and the majority of their supplies lay strewn across a few miles of ocean, separated by the eastern wall of the crescent-shaped ridge. The wreckage included almost ten thousand colonists and a million more held in vitro. They needed to restore power to the Sovereign, or those people would die and whatever chance they had at a future here would die along with them.

She motioned to Jenna. "The firstmark asked about reserves. Does using the new protocol change any of our assumptions?"

The lieutenant thought about it, then answered carefully, "Reserves don't matter as much when it comes to SAIs like LIL-8, sir. They're able to pull energy from the host and the environment. I'd be more worried about compatibility. We're not going through normal pair bonding."

"The Sovereign chose us because we're compatible," stated the captain with the kind of certainty she knew the crew needed. "We got assigned for a reason."

RAI-10 put in, "Short term compatibility with the experimental protocols should not be a determining factor. Your safety margin is several days."

Talaris smiled, "Well, there you have it." She clapped her hands together, "Volunteers?" She couldn't help but bark out a short laugh in answer to the sudden scowl that flashed across Jenna's face. "Just kidding." She paused, then diverted her look to Sahana and said, "You know it has to be you."

Commander Tir nodded. "Yeah, I figured."

"You're best equipped to deactivate the protocol. We'll make our way down and join you."

Tir smiled and shook her head; "Forget it. I can take all of us, sir."

Talaris looked at her for a second before replying. "Still, I'm going to assign Jenna with you. I'll come down with

RAI-10 and the firstmark separately."

When Jenna looked puzzled, Tir nudged her elbow and said, "Redundancy, LT. If we go splat, they can still finish the mission." The commander clapped the lieutenant on the shoulder, commiserating with her sickened look with a grim laugh.

"At least you won't feel a thing."

HERITAGE

B rianna fought not to scream, the downward fall pushing her stomach into her throat. Worse, Arek fell as if pursued, gaining speed rather than slowing. The plummet continued for what seemed an eternity. When she was sure it was too late, his wings snapped open. They braked a few meters above the landing, and suddenly she felt Arek let her go. She panicked, falling awkwardly into what was surely free space, but then she hit the ground with a bone-jarring smack, tumbling to one side. The wind got knocked out of her, but otherwise she felt more ashamed than hurt.

In contrast Yetteje hit the ground in a smooth roll and came up with Valor drawn, pointing into the black maw that was the tunnel behind the broken arch. The glow of her arrow lit the scene in a surreal yellow pallor, as if the light brought to life sickness and disease hidden from their mundane sight.

The sight of Arek landing lightly beside her in his normal form told Brianna he must have transformed midair to fit into this cramped space. If he noticed her mistake of not clearing space, he didn't mention it. He simply took stock of his surroundings, his pale gaze finally coming to rest on her.

Brianna took a halting gasp as she tried to catch her breath, simultaneously cursing herself for missing his point earlier. This landing area was truly smaller than it looked. Clearly her enthusiasm at the prospect of recovering her equipment had overshadowed any idea of keeping the ledge clear. Luckily, Tej had understood and acted.

"You okay?" he asked Brianna, concern in his voice. His eyes scanned her as if he could tell without her needing to reply.

Perhaps he could, she thought, her mind racing back to the particles she'd seen through Silbane's gifted dragonsight. Arek had that gift now, so who knew what he could or couldn't glean from a mere glance? She nodded apologetically. "Sorry, I'm fine."

Arek stared at her a moment longer, then gave her a quick smile before moving in to support Yetteje. She knelt with bow drawn, using the light to peer as far as she could into the dark opening that led below.

"See anything?" Arek asked.

Yetteje shook her head. The place looked abandoned. "Those mistfrights won't stay put." She looked up the walls to the heights above, and Brianna followed her gaze, noting a few dark shapes already flitting from rock to rock. "We should keep moving."

Arek nodded and motioned to Brianna, who staggered to her feet and shuffled in behind the two. She consulted her wrist, then pointed, "There, in that direction." Her locator indicated a spot below them and past the tunnel entrance.

Arek patted Yetteje's shoulder, and the princess moved forward with a dancer's grace. She raced along the landing, her movement making her a living shadow, flitting from wall to wall until she sat crouched behind a column, broken and lying awkwardly against one side of the tunnel entrance. The rough stone pillars were in sharp contrast to the shattered rock and debris from above. She looked back and waved. At her signal, they both moved up to join her.

"Aren't you worried about those cat-things?" asked Brianna, looking behind her again.

"Not in ones or twos," replied the princess, "but they can

overwhelm us with numbers." At Brianna's puzzled look Yetteje added, "An experience I'd rather not repeat."

Arek gathered the group and said softly, "Lead us to your kapsool. Tej will go first but you stay right behind her. I'll bring up the rear."

A small tremor of fear ran through the dwarven healer. When had she become so scared? Perhaps the fight with Kisan had affected her more than she knew. Brianna shook the feeling off, though it was like trying to get rid of a smell that clung to you. She couldn't will her fears away, so she did the next best thing and stuck close to Yetteje and her drawn bow, as Arek suggested.

Yet her hand, as if it had a mind of its own, slowly crept up to unsnap the guard on her holster. Though she remembered the horror of shooting Kisan, fear was now a more powerful force, overriding her medical ethics.

As soon as they entered the gloom, her eyes adjusted, a quick wash over her vision that dispelled the darkness. Yetteje's bow was a yellow searchlight, so she put herself into the shadow of the princess's head.

"How far?"

She nearly whipped around at the sound of Arek's voice, his question startling her more than she expected. What was wrong with her? She took a calming breath, then looked down. The locator indicated a place further ahead. Luckily the tunnel seemed to be descending, which was a good sign. "About a hundred meters." At Arek's look of consternation Brianna added, "Meters are like paces."

At his nod of understanding, she turned back to Yetteje and said, "Down and right at the next fork."

The princess didn't answer. Instead she just nodded and moved out, her steps silent. They slowly made their way around a bend, the carefully laid stonework of the tunnel now torn and rent by whatever cataclysm had made Olympious disappear. Whatever had happened to Lilyth's city had brought devastation and destruction to the area. Water from some unseen source trickled through the stone, lending a cool dampness to the area that also didn't help.

Despite this they moved at the steady pace Yetteje set. The girl didn't show any signs of the fear that ran through Brianna. If anything, she seemed more resolute, more focused. The healer found herself envious of the composure the princess showed and tried her best to emulate it. Still, as they ventured farther into the tunnels, she could feel her jaws tightening and her skin turning cold.

They rounded the bend. The capsule lay there, sitting askew across a rock. It looked to have fallen from above, through a hole in the ceiling that let both light and rivulets of water stream through. Brianna's eyes automatically compensated, her entats reconfiguring her vision quickly to maximize details in the strange play of light and darkness that cut diagonally from above.

She barely noticed as Yetteje and Arek took up positions to either side of her. Instead, she moved forward and placed a shaking palm on the reader, waiting for it to scan her. A moment later the top slid aside with a small hiss and system lights went on, showing her a diagnostic of the capsule's condition. Everything looked good, except for the power. According to the readings, the recharging systems had been damaged badly. It was doubtful if even direct sunlight would help. Brianna sighed, mentally establishing priorities.

First things first: health and safety. She touched a corner and to her satisfaction, every panel on the capsule slid open. No sense in running out of power and leaving supplies locked away. Inside one of the largest chambers was a backpack, which she grabbed and donned. The pack adhered to her automatically, the nanoweave fiber adjusting itself so that its weight was distributed most efficiently.

She grabbed a small medical case and touched it to her belt, where it also attached itself. She grabbed a second smaller gun and holster, then turned to Arek. "This is a backup weapon like my gun," she patted her holster. "Because of the torc, Duncan can't protect himself without a weapon. He could use this."

Arek's eyes swept across the gun and then up, considering the light falling through the hole in the ceiling. "Agreed. Bring it."

Brianna nodded, then grabbed something from the medical pack, adorned with a symbol of a horizontal and vertical line within a circle. Lifting it out, she displayed it to Arek. It was a clear liquid held inside a glass vial. The healer took the vial and attached it to the end of the tube she'd used earlier when trying to revive Duncan.

"What is it?" asked Arek.

Brianna took a breath and then answered, "Do you know what a microscope is?"

Arek nodded, "We use them on the Isle to study the structure of small things." While his answer was straightforward, Brianna got the distinct impression he thought she was slightly daft for asking something so basic. Clearly, he did not realize how strange the mix of technology and what they thought of as magic on this world looked to an outsider.

"Nans are microscopic machines that will repair damage within my body. I want your permission to inject myself."

"It will heal you? But you're not hurt."

"Not on the outside," Brianna said, "but my memory is still gone. These nans might fix that and give us a better chance."

35

Arek looked her in the eyes, searching for something. Then he gave a small nod.

Brianna nodded back in thanks, then gave herself the shot with a quick jab to her thigh. She could feel warmth spread from the injection point as the nans spread through her entire system, carried in her bloodstream. Soon they would be in every part of her body, integrating with her at a cellular level. Perhaps then she'd clear the mental block that kept her from remembering. Ever since awakening here on this strange world, Brianna had been searching for a way to unravel the mystery of who she was. It was clear she was a healer of some sort, though the instruments she used were of a magic they'd never seen before. Worse, she acted through instinct and could not remember where she'd learned their use. Perhaps these nans would gift her back the memories she'd lost.

"What now?" questioned the princess, her amber eyes scanning the surroundings like predator on the hunt.

"Do you have everything you need?" Arek asked, looking at the kapsool with curiosity.

Brianna shook her head and pointed at a symbol on the capsule. It was a slowly pulsing arrow floating above the screen and pointing up and back the way they came. "This says there's a power source about six kilometers away."

"How far is that?" asked the princess.

Brianna queried her entats, then did a quick calculation and replied, "About six thousand paces." She waited for Arek to respond.

The young adept took a pace, inspecting the inside of the kapsool, his eyes seemingly taking in everything. When he looked up however, he answered Brianna with a short nod. "Let's get out of here and rejoin the others. If we're going to make that kind of trek, I'd like to revive my father. We'll need him."

Together, the party retraced their steps carefully, making sure to keep quiet. Yetteje took the lead again, her amber eyes sweeping across the tunnel passage. The journey back seemed much quicker, although the rocky outcroppings and light from Yetteje's bow cast shadows that bent and jumped, as if they had minds of their own.

As they rounded the last bend, Yetteje extinguished her arrow and raised a hand. They all stopped, crouching behind a large rock. She turned to Brianna and carefully pointed to the entrance. There, the dwarven healer could see four-legged shapes sniffing at the tunnel mouth, black shadows shaped like feral cats, but much larger. One turned its yellow eyes toward them, and they quickly ducked.

Yetteje found their eyes and whispered, "The gun won't work." She pointed to Brianna, clearly meaning it would be up to Arek and her if this became a fight.

Arek nodded, then took a deep breath and carefully tried to switch places with Brianna. Unfortunately, she wasn't ready and stumbled back a bit, her boot scattering small stones whose smattering of taps echoed up and down the passageway, somehow sounding even louder to her shock and embarrassment.

Yetteje's eyes widened. Then, without hesitating, she stood and drew Valor, preparing for the expected onslaught of mistfrights. To Brianna's surprise however, the creature standing at the tunnel entrance yelped once and scurried away. The sounds of scrabbling stones and debris outside told her many other creatures did the same, fleeing instead of murderously attacking.

Arek had followed the princess in a combat stance, but now he just looked puzzled.

Yetteje looked at him and shrugged. "You can get up,"

she said to Brianna. "They're gone."

Brianna nodded and gasped, realizing she'd forgotten to breathe. The appearance of the mistfrights had shaken her to her core, and she found it hard to quell the debilitating panic rising from her gut.

Arek put a hand on her shoulder and said, "Relax, Tej is right. They're gone."

"With Lilyth gone, perhaps they're leaderless for the first time," opined the princess. "Let's get out of here, though. Hopefully, they won't regain their courage."

A warm feeling flowed through Brianna where Arek held her, calming her breathing and slowing the hammering of her heart. Was he using his power to calm her? She tried to swallow but her mouth was still dry from fear, so instead she made eye contact with him and then jerked out a nod. "I'll try."

They fell into line again, picking their way forward. When they finally appeared, only silence greeted them. There was not a single mistfright in view. It was as if they'd all taken cue from the ones who'd fled the tunnel entrance and disappeared.

Yetteje looked back at them and smiled. "I'm not going to complain."

Brianna was inclined to wholeheartedly agree, and almost said so until she caught Arek's eyes looking up, one hand shading the sun from his pale eyes. Something in that gaze brought back her fears, as if he saw threats all around them that they did not.

When Arek finally spoke, he said, "Let's get out of here," and changed into his angel form.

Brianna couldn't help but wonder what Ash was running into as he made his way to the rendezvous. She hoped his luck would hold.

ASH

sh watched the ground fly by, details as minute as blades of grass and insects jumped into clarity, as if they were an arm's length away rather than hundreds of paces. Given their situation he sought a safe place to land. It needed to be secluded, yet distinctive enough to capture Arek's attention. His fears rose when he considered the circumstances when the boy returned. Would it include the safety of the princess and the doctor, or pursued by enemies? The latter thought made him sick to his stomach, for he had already failed once to protect the princess.The girl had become something akin to a sister to him; despite her ability with weapons and her burgeoning independence, he worried for her.

His sharp eyes picked out a spot not far from his current location and he dipped a wing, angling toward it in an inverted swoop. Not too long ago a sudden move like this would have caused him fear and nausea, but since acquiring the form and strength of the Watcher Orion, he thrilled to the feeling of descent.

In a few moments he flared his wings and touched down, flexing to compensate for the weight of the two men he carried. He laid Silbane's body down with reverence, then moved over a bit to deposit Duncan against the trunk of a tree so that he lay supine, his back against the trunk. He stared at the unconscious man; his revulsion balanced by his word to Arek that no harm would come to Duncan. It would be so easy, he thought, to bring justice to all those this man had killed in his quest to reclaim his wife. He mentally ticked off the names of those whose blood had been shed because of Duncan Illrys: Jebida, fallen in the mission to save Silbane; Yetteje's parents, killed when EvenSea had been razed by this madman's army of nomads and barbarians; and Bara'cor, which had suffered catastrophic casualties when the Gate to this realm had been opened. He switched form, feeling the sudden drain on himself, though not as bad as before. His hand caressed the hilt of his blade. One slice and justice would be served.

"He's Arek's only chance." A voice from behind him said. It was a woman's, and one he had come to know despite his short time here.

"Silbane was Arek's only chance," Ash replied. "This man is a murderer and a coward."

"You judge him so harshly, yet you ignore what every king has done to take a throne. Are the Galadines you serve so blameless?"

Ash stood slowly and turned, coming face to face with the shade of Sonya, the mother of Arek. Duncan's obsession with her had driven him to enter this realm. Ash tilted his head in half greeting and half admonishment, "You stood by Valarius, a butcher and despot. Don't preach to me about lack of judgement."

"I also led you to Arek so you could stop Kisan. I made my choice, and I chose life for my son."

Ash sighed, the will to kill Duncan slipping from him like sleep does from a waking man.

"Valarius is dead and Avalyon burns," he said. "You have served all those you loved well. Now, do us all one more kindness. Tell me how we leave this realm."

"Your sarcasm is unbecoming for a nobleman." Sonya stepped around Ash, her eyes looking down at Duncan's unconscious form. "And does not serve your house well. I have borne more than you can know."

"My lady," Ash felt the sigh in his voice even if he didn't voice it, "I am weary of suffering and pain being used in the name of righteousness. You, Valarius, the red mage"—Ash gestured to the unconscious man— "are no better than any other who has killed in the name of a cause." He stepped back from her, his shoulders feeling the weight of this world. "I just want to get out of here and bring peace to those who died for this man's obsession."

Sonya turned to him, her eyes shining with purpose—or was it anger? "You dare speak of obsession, you who pursue and hound this man even when the outcome of his quest was the death of a tyrant? And who has died? Those of distinction who die in Edyn live on here, transitioning from one life to another. Lay the blame for their deaths at Lilyth's feet, who with the destruction of Arcadia eradicates their memories for all eternity."

Ash paused, taken aback by the vehemence of Sonya's words. Was he on the wrong side of judgement? "My lady, I am not deciding his fate. I am only taking him back to be judged by those harmed by his actions."

"And he shall receive such fair judgement from them," she replied, her voice now mirroring his earlier sarcasm. She took a deep breath, looking around. Finally, her eyes fell on Duncan. It was unclear what she might have been contemplating, but to Ash she looked sad. Then she said, "He has suffered much, and does not deserve to die here. There is another gate but…"

Ash raised an eyebrow and asked, "What?"

"The Celestial Zafir holds the gate at Harmagedon," she said. "He is powerful, perhaps as much so as Lilyth."

Ash's eyes narrowed and he asked, "We will need to defeat him to use the gate?"

Sonya shook her head, "No, he must convey you. Lilyth will open the gate from her side, but Zafir must initiate the transfer through." She paused, then added, "You'll have to convince him to help."

Ash swore, pacing away from Duncan. Why could nothing be easy here?

"Is there no other path?"

The shade licked her lips, clearly hesitating, then said, "Perhaps. You will need a sacrifice. Only blood magic will tune the gate to the correct realm, and it must be from someone who comes from the realm you wish to enter."

He looked at her, his eyes widening in shock as what she meant became clear. "We have to sacrifice someone from Edyn, like Kisan did?" He saw the death of Mikal Galadine and the opening of the portal to Bara'cor.

Sonya let out a long breath, then said, "Where was King Mikal from?" She paused, then looked back at Duncan pointing, "He knows what must be done and how to do it. Do you have the conviction, Firstmark of Bara'cor? Who will you sacrifice to get home?"

Ash didn't hesitate to answer, "Duncan, if that's possible. I'll bleed him out like a stuck pig to get us through."

Sonya didn't answer; instead she moved a bit further away. As she did so Ash noticed he could not see through her. Her form was more … substantial, if that were even possible.

"What is happening?" he said. "You seem more solid, more real."

The shade nodded. "Those who use the Way are dying, as is Arcadia itself. As the number of users dwindles, there is more of the Way for those who are left. I suppose I will become almost entirely real just before the end." A half smile, more sad than happy crept to her face. Then her visage changed, and she took a step toward the firstmark.

"You need to know something. Valarius was powerful, much more than Silbane or Duncan."

"Tell me something I don't know–"

Sonya held up a hand to interrupt the firstmark. "He's had centuries to craft the spell he used on Arek."

Suddenly Ash went cold, a feeling of goosebumps racing up his arms and spine. "What do you mean?"

"The Way is increasing here in power, and as it does it will affect Arek. Valarius's spell is insidious. The blackfire will return."

Ash stepped back, "You're saying the work of Silbane and Duncan will be undone?"

Sonya nodded slowly. "The longer Arek stays here, the more their work will unravel. If you take too long to get home…"

"Arek becomes like the Nephilim?" Ash finished. He looked at Duncan and the body of Silbane.

"Worse." Sonya looked at Ash with tears glistening in her eyes. "He will become like Valarius. You all must escape before it's too late."

FLASHBACK: LIL-8

When preparations were complete, Commander Tir said, "Initiate LIL-8 protocol."

The captain followed with, "Authorization on voice and biomarker clearance," and held out a hand, which RAI-10 took and wrapped in his own. A moment passed, then the black eye slit glowed green for a moment.

"Command authorization accepted," the RAI intoned.

The air coalesced, glittering particles that looked like millions of diamond flecks, each catching the waning sunlight in small flashes of orange, gold, and silver gathering themselves into a man-shaped object. Once the form had solidified, it moved closer to Commander Tir.

Captain Talaris said, "Good luck, Commander."

Tir had taken an unconscious step back from the scintillating cloud. At the order, she looked at her captain, then swallowed once and nodded, saying, "Initiate Ascension protocol."

The figure took another step, this one directly into the space occupied by the commander. As it did so, Sahana gasped; her eyes widened. "Gods, its cold!" Then her eyes closed as billions of particles invaded her body, seeping in through the walls of her skin like she was nothing more than a sponge soaking in water. Her body took on the rigid stature of someone suffering from a seizure, her rictus betrayed by the flickering of her eyelids and the tremors that ran uncontrolled just under her skin.

To the captain it looked surreal, like two beings

superimposed on one another, each trying to occupy the same space for itself. Then, just as suddenly as it'd started, it stopped. The glittering figure disappeared and Sahana exhaled more air than it seemed her lungs could hold, bending over until her hands rested on her knees. Thirty seconds passed without her moving, until finally Captain Talaris said, "Commander?"

Commander Sahana Tir, the eighth person ever to undergo the Ascension protocol, and the first outside of a medical simulation, opened her eyes. She scanned the surroundings and the group, her gaze finally coming to rest on Captain Talaris.

"Greetings, Captain."

Talaris nodded, "What's your status?" Although the being in front of her still looked identical to her commander, there was something alien about her, something wholly different than the officer who'd been behind those sapphire eyes just a moment ago.

"I'm functioning nominally," replied the new construct. "Integration is close to ninety percent and rising. My biological systems are functioning within normal parameters, except..."

"Except?" asked the captain.

The being in Commander Tir's body tilted its head and then sent a private communique via their entat, a message only the captain could hear: *This body is a clone of the original. It has a limited lifespan—the cardiovascular flush on your skin indicates you know this.* She paused, scanning the other two officers, then she looked back at the captain. "Why was I awakened?"

"Do you and Commander Tir occupy the mind together? Can you access her memories?" asked the captain, her scientific curiosity now overriding whatever misgivings she'd had at the protocol being used. She couldn't help but be somewhat in awe of the achievement.

"I can." The being closed its eyes for a moment, then snapped them open.

"We are ordered to recover the remote piloting module and guide the secondary core down to the *TEC Sovereign*. I must relinquish control back to Commander Tir for the operation to be successful." At that, something changed, a softening of her stance perhaps?

The captain couldn't tell, but suddenly it was Sahana again. The commander looked at her with eyes wide. "She's in here! It worked." She beamed. "We're beginning to integrate. Right now, she's wholly separate, but our minds are merging. Soon we'll share thoughts."

"What's it like?" piped Jenna from a few meters away, her curiosity uncontrollable in light of the engineering triumph they were witnessing.

Commander Tir walked over to the group with the captain trailing behind and said, "Amazing! She's adding enhancements as she goes, giving me more acute senses, strength, stamina... she's literally remaking me from the inside out."

"What about getting to the module?" asked the captain.

Tir turned to her and said, "We can do it, but local integration of the nans hasn't gotten to the point where it's safe for me to transport more than myself. I can head down alone." She paused. "Your call, Captain."

Captain Talaris pursed her lips, thinking. Risk all of us, or just Tir? And how do we carry out Sovereign's final directive if we're separated? Finally, she said, "Go and take this." She handed the commander one end of a microline stowed on her belt.

"We'll attach our end to the rocks here; you attach the

other to your exit point. Then we can zipline down to you."

"Roger that," said Commander Tir, her face flushed with a combination of excitement and whatever the symbiosis was doing to her. She grabbed the line from Captain Talaris.

While she did that, Petracles took the other end and wrapped it around a rocky outcropping a meter in diameter, strong enough to take their combined weight. The rope automatically adhered to the surface, the nans within it automatically becoming one with the rock it touched at a molecular level.

At a nod from the captain, Commander Tir saluted, then turned to scan the area below. A second later, she disappeared in a flash of blue light. Another blue sparkle flashed from below, the exit point of Commander Tir's LOS transport. The line attached to their outcropping suddenly went taut.

The nan ink near Talaris's ear reconfigured itself again for communication. "Attached. You should be good to go," Commander Tir's voice chirped over their entat-established link.

"Good. Secure the area and stand by," the captain ordered. Then she cut off her communication, making the conversation between the remaining crew private. "What do you think?"

Firstmark Petracles was the first to say, "Seems like it went better than we could've hoped for."

Lieutenant Illrys said, ticking off her fingers, "No psychosis, no subornation, and LIL-8 relinquished control."

"I always worry when things go better than we hope," Talaris quipped. "Come on, the module's down there and we've only got a few hours of sunlight left."

The trio attached their zipline harnesses, then attached themselves to the microline. Nans secured the connection and a moment later they were flying down the line at fifteen kilometers an hour, braking as they neared the outcropping secured by Commander Tir. A moment later RAI-10 appeared, shifting back into a man-shaped form with the winged creature's aspect falling from his body in a mist, a gossamer dream now fading and forgotten.

Talaris envied the RAIs ability to shapeshift, but if the Ascension protocol allowing this type of human AI merging proved to be as useful as it looked, soon that ability would be shared by every colonist who bonded with a LIL. The one thing the RAIs couldn't do was integrate with another living creature as the LILs were designed to do. They would forever be an extension of the *TEC Sovereign* and his edicts. They were, for all intents and purposes, the perfect servants for the AI that governed them all.

She turned to RAI-10 and asked, "Do you have a fix on—"

"I got it, Captain," said Commander Tir, not waiting for the captain to finish. She moved closer to the edge of the rock face they were standing on and looked down into the blue depths, pointing. "A little more than half a klick down."

Talaris sighed, then looked at the other two and said, "Let's suit up—"

"Not necessary, sir." Commander Tir said, looking at RAI-10. "The two of us can retrieve the module and bring it back here."

Talaris raised an eyebrow at that. "You're kidding."

Her commander smiled and said, "Not at all." She scooped up some water and closed her eyes. Suddenly, she grew to over twice her normal height, towering over them even though she was kneeling. "It really is incredible, but the nans are integrated to such a level within my body they can manipulate it to change as needed, including," she pointed to her neck where four small slits had appeared.

"Are those...?" Jenna asked, wide-eyed.

"Yeah, gills." Tir laughed.

The captain exchanged looks with the firstmark, then said, "RAI-10, can the two of you recover the module safely? What about the protocol?"

The RAI looked at Commander Tir, perhaps scanning it in some way they could not. When it finally turned and spoke, some trick of the surf modulated the acoustics, making it sound almost concerned. "She's nullified the Phoenix protocol already, Captain."

"What?" exclaiming Talaris. "You've shut it down?"

The commander hybrid nodded. "Pretty simple as far as AIs go. I rewrote its orders."

"When?" demanded Petracles.

Commander Tir smiled, "When I opened my eyes, of course. How else could we have finished the mission?"

When Talaris spoke next, the ice in her voice cut through the sound of the surf. "You did so without my orders."

The commander turned to face her captain and shrugged, "There was over a ninety-six percent chance your orders would have included deactivating the protocol, with the other four percent ordering me to circumvent it in some other fashion, so I took action. Wouldn't you commend a crew member for such initiative?"

Petracles took that moment to lay a careful hand on Talaris's shoulder, her touch soft. *Careful*, the captain heard her say through a private channel.

"Okay, commander, bring it up."

Commander Tir smiled and beckoned to RAI-10. While the RAI leapt over the edge and into the ocean, to the amazement of everyone, Tir simply melted into the rock, flowing down and away.

"You see that?" asked Petracles.

"She's got full control over her cellular matrix," remarked the lieutenant, her statement delivered in that whispered awe of someone seeing something she still couldn't believe.

"Keep yourself icy, LT," snapped the captain. She put a finger to her jaw and sent a tight line communication to the RAI. A single chirp let her know it had been received.

They didn't have to wait long. In a bubbling blast of white froth and foam, a cylindrical capsule ten meters long rose out of the water, carried by the two AIs. They brought it down gently onto the rocky surface where the rest of the crew waited, depositing it with the gentleness of a mother putting her newborn into a crib.

RAI-10 took a few steps away, but Commander Tir laid her palms on the outer hull of the module and closed her eyes. "Systems are nominal. Power is being restored now that it's in sunlight." She opened her eyes and scanned their surroundings. "Pretty good outcome from taking the initiative, right Cap?"

Her voice sounds just like Sahana's, but she called me Cap, something Sahana would never have done. Talaris looked up at her commander, "You understand your willingness to take this initiative coincides with your Ascension with LIL-8. This concerns me."

Commander Tir took a step closer and took a knee; her size still doubled the captain's. With their eyes level she met Talaris's gaze without flinching and said, "Then Sovereign's final orders concerning me, Jenna, and Dawn should concern you more, Serene." She tilted her head, waiting.

"What's she talking about?" Jenna asked.

Petracles eyes merely narrowed, but Talaris saw her hand stray slowly to rest on her sidearm. The captain raised a hand forestalling any brash action and said, "We're on a first name basis now, commander?"

The commander tilted her head, "Does it matter?"

Captain Talaris continued, "Recovering the secondary core is paramount."

Tir nodded, "I know, but if Sovereign left witnesses to his murder of the backup AI…that wouldn't do, hence using an all clone away team. We're expendable, right?" She looked around, as if surveying the area for anyone else approaching, "And I guess this is as good a place as any to die."

Before Talaris could answer the rocky outcropping erupted in violence. RAI-10 cut through Commander Tir's chest with an arm turned into a blade. In the same moment Petracles had in one smooth motion drawn and fired her sidearm, but Talaris couldn't tell if it was at the commander or RAI-10. It didn't matter, for the two blade- like appendages that skewered her firstmark came from both sentient AIs.

"What's happe—" Jenna managed to say before her head was sliced cleanly from her shoulders by the RAI. Finally, it was only the captain and a bloody Commander Tir that remained, the latter shrunk to normal size and bleeding out on the harsh rocks. RAI-10 walked over to the kneeling commander and said, "LIL-8 protocol terminated due to aberrant behavior."

Before Commander Tir could react, RAI-10's blade entered the top of her head, piercing her from crown to rump and fixing her to the rocky floor. Commander Tir died with blood pouring out from her nose and mouth, pulsing gushes timed to the beat of her belabored heart. When that stopped, the RAI pulled its blade clear, letting the body fall in a grotesque heap.

Amazingly, Captain Talaris found she was unscathed, and

the piloting module had been recovered. She felt herself over, her hands confirming her luck.

"You are uninjured, captain," the RAI remarked. "My protocol has always been to protect you."

"Thanks," she breathed, feeling a little sick. Ignoring her dead crew, she gritted her teeth and stood. The mission wasn't over. She moved over and palmed the door mechanism to the secondary core capsule.

"Authorization?" a voice queried.

"Voice and biomarker clearance," intoned the captain, her voice sounding strangely confident and unshaken.

"Serene Talaris, Captain, *TEC Sovereign*, recognized. Systems online."

The door opened with a hiss. Inside the module was clean, and white, like a hospital room, except instead of patients it was communications gear that came to life. Talaris entered, breathing the clean air with a sigh of relief.

"You should initiate the recovery," said RAI-10 from behind her.

Talaris nodded, then with a weary smile said, "Gimme a moment. We know how this ends."

"Very well, captain."

She could feel the RAI pull back. Looking down, she palmed the console in front of her and a panel slide open. Inside was a black rod, approximately two meters long. She took it out, hefting it, feeling its weight. At her touch the black surface of the rod lit with thin blue lines. Then she turned and addressed RAI-10. "Unlock the Cypher." She held out the black rod horizontally before her.

RAI-10 moved up and placed hands on the rod. At his touch red and silver lines raced out, merging with the blue ones. Eventually, the rod looked like a black staff with silver lines etched all along its surface, pulsing to the beat of some unknown heart. Then these silver lines slowly flowed from the rod and onto the captain's skin before disappearing. At their touch the entats on her body reconfigured themselves, flowing to form a black circle on each of her palms.

"Is it done?"

RAI-10 nodded, "It is."

Captain Talaris turned back to the console and inserted the rod vertically into a hole before a black screen. As she set the rod into the receptacle, the entire shaft was pulled into the console, disappearing from view. Suddenly, the console came to life, showing the location where their ship had crashed, and telemetry of the secondary core still in low orbit.

After a moment of silence, she said out loud, "Initiate recovery of secondary core. Soft touch down at location marked."

"Cypher required for changes to core protocols."

She laid her palm with the Cypher circle down onto the surface of the black panel. Silver lines from her palm raced out and formed a radial pattern, like the diagram of a tumbler key mechanism. Using the tips of her fingers, she turned the tumbler until the pattern fit, then pushed. The trajectory of the secondary core adjusted itself, the dotted line now intersecting a point on the surface of the world close to where her broken ship lay. "It's done."

RAI-10 replied, "You have served the Sovereign well, captain. Thank you."

Talaris smiled, looking down. She was in mid-breath when RAI-10's blade entered the back of her skull and came out her forehead, killing her clone body instantly.

RAI-10 surveyed the scene, scanning each body for any signs of life. He sealed the module and then cycled up his next priority: return and report. The Sovereign did not yet have the ability to reach this far due to the extensive damage from their crash. Their primary mission of ensuring that the backup of Sovereign's core was recovered from low orbit and eliminating the clones had been accomplished. With the secondary core recovered Sovereign could begin repairing the damage done to itself.

RAI-10 took a moment to gather samples from each body, a small swathe of blood he absorbed through his fingertip. Then he transformed into something with wings and leapt into the air, arrowing for the caldera and the final resting place of the *TEC Sovereign*.

FLASHBACK: ALION

DEFT

Alion Deft pulled the shahwal from her ruined face, heaving a sigh at the sight that greeted her. The opening yawned below, cut from the desert floor like a monstrous maw delineated by strange, man-made orthogonal lines. Though they stood under the glare of a noonday sun, its bright light could not penetrate the darkness, instead casting a single anemic shaft down into the depths, ending in a lonely rectangle marking the passage of the sun as it crawled slowly across Edyn's sky. No lights or torches shone from those depths. Instead, it faded into an inky gloom, bringing a sense of abandonment and danger to this already ancient place.

I am so thoroughly cursed, she thought, if luck were aurum, I'd have to borrow my next breath. It had only been a short time since the red mage's curse had afflicted her, wasting her body away into a dessicated husk of skin and bone, and yet she did not die. The once proud magehunter and Kingsmark had forsaken the All-Father and set out to find a cure for her curse.

"No useful light," uttered Malioch, interrupting her spiral of self-pity with a strangely well-timed echo of her own thoughts. The man had a knack for doing that, a trait that was annoying even in the best of times. The slaver was a veteran of hundreds of raids under Deft's command. He was horrible with people, but perversely had a way with animals. He also knew almost all there was to be known about repairing things. She'd begun to think of him as her slaver-smith, and despite every reason any sane person could see to stay clear of Deft, Malioch had remained stubbornly beside her. He was a man whose willingness to break anyone, even women and children, was only matched by the brutality he'd visit upon their fragile bodies while doing the job. He was too old to squire and too morally corrupt to lose—a refreshing evil.

Malioch spit a green slug of hazish out of his mouth, letting it tumble down into the darkness, watching it fall. A few moments later she heard its soft spatter on sand, undetectable to anyone else. It was one of the few gifts she'd gotten from the archmage's curse: heightened senses. And strength. Actually, a better word would be… resilience.

In fact, it was doubtful she could die from anything that afflicted normal people. The red mage had cursed her with a wasting rot and she'd expected to die just as Scythe had said she would. Instead something or someone had intervened, and the deleterious effects had slowed to a crawl. She had no organs to pierce and her bones reknit. She couldn't burn or drown… but the spell of the red mage had ravaged her. Though she'd heal of any wound she'd thus far encountered, the curse continued to slowly eat away at her flesh. Alion had lived well past what she'd expected, and at this rate she might survive decades longer, but who knew what she'd look like by then? She was already a walking corpse. Like a sailor's corpse washed ashore, her skin hung gray and loose from her bones like rags. Her head looked like a rotting apple infested with maggots, bits of flesh putrefying more quickly in their cursed dance with time. Despite this, small tufts of hair stubbornly clung to her skull in a horrid act of defiance. Perhaps more correctly they were like men with gut wounds, too stupid or shocked to know they were already dead. She looked sidelong at Malioch, her half-eaten face locked in a sneer of glistening bone, gray worms, and decay.

Malioch returned her stare with a deadpan gaze, one eye white with blindness, the other clear blue and all the more magnificent next to its slug-colored twin. He was balling up another wad and nodding. Then he jerked his chin at the hole and asked, "You hear it?"

She nodded, "Sand at the bottom, just like the mapmaker said."

"Heh," he laughed a bit, peering down into the darkness with his good eye. "His daughter was nice." He leered as he spoke, his eye reflecting what Alion knew was the memory of ravaging the young girl. "Why comes you dinna take a taste?"

There was a moment of silence, then Deft replied, "Wasn't in the mood."

Even as she said this, the thought bubbled up: Maybe he just likes me? Deft didn't really care why Malioch remained in her service but trying to suss out the reason had become something of an addiction. The spell had decayed her soul as much as her skin. As she'd become more inured to harm, she'd found herself latching onto anything that caused her to feel something. This mystery created a sensation within her she'd not felt otherwise: curiosity. And that gave her a small connection to the idea she was still alive. Discipline, her lifelong companion, inserted itself and pulled her away from the mystery that was Malioch, forcing her instead to take measure of the other two who made up her team.

The first was a waste of flesh, in her opinion, the spiritual opposite of Deft herself. His name was Paramus, and he was so inept it was surprising he could claim the title of cadet, soldier, mercenary, or even "kid with a bucket helmet and a mop." Everything about him seemed disheveled, ill-conceived, or just plain awkward. Had she been able, she'd have sliced the fatty meat from his body and eaten him before his own eyes, but that was not to be. Paramus had a bit of luck, and lately everyone who annoyed her seemed to share this trait—he had something she needed. In his case it was language.

Simply put, the boy could read anything. It was a rare Talent, seldom seen and when realized often led its possessors to be appointed to serve noble houses. Another testament to this oaf's incompetence. Instead of securing such a posting, he'd been living on the streets of Southheart, begging for meals, when they'd heard rumors of the gutter scholar. To their surprise the rumors turned out to be true and it had not taken long to find and employ Paramus as their translator.

She didn't miss the irony of her situation, employing homeless scum with Talent, given her background as a magehunter. It seemed the cursed All-Father hadn't finished with his unending list of jokes, cruel or otherwise. Yet the answer to breaking the red mage's spell would be found in ancient places of knowledge, forgotten tomes. These required someone who could read. So, Paramus, it seemed, would live a bit longer.

Alion's hand shot out, catching the clumsy idiot by the neck and redirecting him safely to fall away from the edge. The dullard had literally walked off the ledge and into open air. He fell with a *whuff* as his breath exploded from his lungs.

"Gah!" he sputtered as he recovered, then sat up. His beady eyes squinted, almost disappearing into slits on his face, as they finally came to rest on the hole he would've fallen into, and certainly to his death. "Where'd that come from?"

Alion stood up and sighed, letting the fourth and final member of their small group deal with their itinerant language lord.

"Easy there, Par." The dusky-skinned woman who'd come to kneel beside the scholar unstoppered a flask and offered it. A few sips of whatever it contained seemed to do the man some good. Trysh closed it and then looked up at Alion, her lime-colored eyes catching the reflected light of the sun. Turning to look at the sand horizon, she put a hand over her brow for shade.

"The Fall is to our northwest," she said. "We're between Shornhelm and EvenSea, probably a good four- or five-days ride to either." She looked back at their caravan, eight camels laden with another week of supplies and the weapons and armor.

"Make camp," Alion ordered. "Get him under shade before he dies of sun poisoning. I want to have a way up and down tied off before dark."

The scout nodded, helping Paramus up as she faced the knight. "Why're we making camp now?" she asked. She tossed her thick ponytail of black hair back out of her way and said, "Daylight would be safer for exploring."

Though she was clearly of Koorvan descent, her skin and eyes were that fair-green combination so coveted by her people. When Alion had once inquired how her own blue eyes, when they'd been blue, would've been received in Koorva, the scout had replied, "Everyone knows blue eyes are a sign of madness, just like red hair." So much for being accepted as whatever passed for normal in that southern nation. Perhaps now their milky white color would elicit a more understandable, albeit horrified response. Still, Alion couldn't help but be surprised at the gush of words from the normally taciturn woman.

She shrugged and said, "You know the desert. I know fighting. It's all I know—and that the All-Father has abandoned me. But night will tell us if anyone is down there. They'll need light too. If we see their glow, we'll know we have company."

Paramus took that moment to start choking on something, probably his own tongue. Trysh smacked him once, then twice, on the back to help him clear whatever-it-was. Then she looked back at the former magehunter and said, "You don't trust anyone?"

Alion smiled, noting with satisfaction that the girl blanched a bit at the sight. Anything she did with her face made her look feral and hungry, and truth be told, every time she looked at the moist and healthy flesh of her team, her mouth watered. Another "gift" from the gods, and something she was only slowly getting used to. She rewrapped herself in the shahwal and shook her head. "I've learned better. Now get our stalwart scholar out of the sun before he—"

Paramus wretched, throwing up clear liquid and small bits of what looked like rice. Instantly small beetles erupted from the sand, scurrying to collect the nutrient-rich vomit before it could go to waste. Alion looked around for anything that might be lured by the smell, then asked, "Nothing bigger?"

The scout shook her head.

"Not around here, but we should scatter whitestone just to be safe. Sandsharks and basilisks aren't common, but not unheard of either. If they're around, his puke is enough."

Deft nodded.

"See to it. Malioch and I will get the ropes."

Trysh nodded in agreement, then paused, clearly at odds with something else she wanted to say.

"Out with it," the wasting knight stated.

"Not to question you, but anyone down there would've needed a way down too, and there's nothing." The scout paused, then carefully added, "I don't need to know the real reason for waiting, commander. Just wanted you to know you can trust me." Trysh didn't belabor her point. Instead she pulled Paramus up by hooking her arm under his shoulder and half dragged him away toward the caravan.

Alion watched her leave. Of all the people she'd met, Trysh piqued her curiosity more than most. The scout rarely spoke but had insight worth listening to. There was a time when Deft would've pushed forward on nothing but faith, but her abandonment by the All-Father and the consequences should she fail to break the spell were certain. Considering that, opinions had become more interesting, and in a group this small she'd be a fool to ignore anyone.

Well, except for Paramus.

That was another curiosity. Trysh was annoyingly kind to the puking scholar, almost like an older sister, something Deft couldn't fathom. Yet she was astute. Deft prided herself on being relatively inscrutable, and the ravages to her face made her expressions hard to read. Therefore, it was with some surprise that the scout had seen through her lie about the reason for waiting until dark. Trysh would bear watching, the knight cautioned herself.

"Grab the ropes," she said over her shoulder to Malioch. His grunt of assent wasn't quite the spit-and-polish response she'd've expected in the past, but like her, he had changed. She tromped toward one of the camels, untying a large bundle wrapped in canvas. Hooking that over her shoulder, she trudged back to the slaver, releasing her burden with a sigh.

"How much ya gonna weigh?" asked the man as he

arranged poles into some sort of frame on the sand.

Alion undid the sack. "What's that?"

"Look around," Malioch replied. "Ya see somewheres to anchor ropes?" He smiled, then pointed to the frame, "Buildin' a rig to span da hole. We'll attach a pulley, lower us slow an' safe."

Now it suddenly dawned on Deft why the man wanted to know how much she'd weigh. She looked at her open sack, considering. Turning back to him she said, "I'm wearing the iron rods but no leather. No plate."

Her arms, torso, and legs had wasted to a point where they were mostly bone covered with tatters of skin. As a result, her armor rattled about when worn, and frankly did little to protect her when so loose. She'd found she could tie wooden or iron rods to either side of her arms and legs, then strap the armor on over that. The result was a snug fit, with the added benefit of the rods protecting her bones from breaking. Iron also lent her strikes considerably more heft, while wood was flexible and made her buoyant.

While her bones had regenerated, they still could break. It took what was the equivalent of sleep for her, a period of blankness after which she'd wake fully reformed. She couldn't control how long that period would last. She knew this was true given the different ways she'd tried to end her own miserable existence, more times than she could count.

And yet, *I'm still walking.*

Malioch nodded, looking at the rig and ropes, then ticked some numbers off on his blunt fingers. Alion watched him, slipping on her rods and leather vambraces. Then she turned her attention to her legs, doing the same. She left her torso as-is, wanting the flexibility to fit through narrow passages should the need arise. Finally, she gathered her small shield and her blessed blade, Reaper. Though the All-Father had left, the blade still protected her from magic. Perhaps it had always been the faith she had in herself and not the All-Father that really mattered, because it seemed Reaper's gleam had never diminished. That, or she had a new patron, one who'd not yet deigned to reveal themselves to her.

When she was done, she held out her forearm to Malioch, who moved over and began tightening the straps in place. Even without the full suit, armoring up was still a two-man job. He moved quickly, securing her arms and legs and then giving her a once-over. He sucked in some air through his yellow teeth and cackled. "Well, ya look better'n a sparrin' dummy!" Alion ignored him.

The next quarter day was spent setting up camp, organizing their supplies, and tending to Paramus. Somehow the man had managed to get bitten by some sort of insect. The bite had triggered a subsequent reaction, as everything touching the young imbecile seemed to do, and now Paramus's legs had erupted in dozens of small red bumps. Trysh was looking for lemon oil from a certain kind of tree native to Jaganath, a therapeutic mixture they'd packed for just such an occurrence. No one had doubted Paramus would be the first to need the salve, not even Paramus himself. So, it'd been stored with his things, a small bag mostly filled with his mismatched discards and whatever trinkets the idiot deemed valuable.

As soon as Alion saw the nature of its contents, she grabbed the one or two items she'd thought were useful. While they were surrounded by a sea of sand, there were spots here and there where firmer ground showed. Paramas's bag had gone into one of these: a pit dug as a small makeshift latrine, which Trysh referred to as a cathole. A soldier's life made Deft intimately familiar with all manner of latrines, but she'd never heard the term before. Regardless, it did nothing to curb her annoyance at their bookish companion.

If Alion had been able, she'd have covered his bag with her own bodily waste, but that need, along with hunger or thirst, had long since disappeared. Still, it galled her that the man had dragged along such trinkets into the desert. One glass lens of a spyglass, what looked to be two sticks tied into an *L* shape, even a mirror, broken and jagged! What a waste.

As the sun continued its slow fall toward the horizon, her companions finished their various chores. When Deft was satisfied everything had been taken care of properly or was on a good path, she gathered her crew around a small campfire. It was shielded by stones from wind, but the light would be visible for quite a distance. She made a mental note to keep their discussion short and extinguish it before they ventured forth. Once they'd gathered, she laid out her plan, beginning with the reason for their expedition.

"Below us, somewhere, lies the Serapeum of Thoth."

Trysh looked surprised but said nothing. Paramus, who'd mostly recovered from his bout with the sun and insect bites, smiled and said, "I knew it!" At the questioning look he got from the scout, he added, "Well, I overheard Deft and Mal talking."

"We'll add eavesdropping to your already impressive list of skills," snarled Deft. Then she continued, "The mapmaker Reis said the temple had been sunk during the Demon Wars. I can vouch this area has changed a lot."

Trysh gave a small laugh. When Alion stared at her, she cautiously offered, "Well… that's an understatement."

The ex-kingsmark nodded. "It used to be a forest, if memory serves. Now it's not, thanks to mages and their filth." She took a breath, calming herself.

The wars are over, she chided herself. My life is different.

The red mage has seen to that, she cursed, and I'll see him in hell for what he's done to me.

Into the gap, Paramus, who seemed blithely ignorant of anyone else's mood, said, "If we'd won sooner, it'd probably not been so bad off."

The silence stretched as Alion silently counted to ten, before saying, "Yes, master scribe. Thank you for that observation."

"Of course," said Paramus, tossing some sand into the fire like leaves. Smoke curled slowly in a circle, wafting into the clear night, a thin ribbon made of ashes.

Alion could feel her jaw clench and was thankfully interrupted from her next action by Trysh, who put a restraining hand on his arm and said, "You're dousing our fire."

"Really?" The boy looked genuinely puzzled.

At that, Malioch cursed and said, "What's our plan, commander?"

Deft kept staring at Paramus, but finally said, "We're going to check the hole for any signs of activity. Malioch, you and our scribe stay topside. Trysh and I will descend and reconnoiter the landing. Once we find a defensible spot, I'll signal, and you'll follow us down."

The slaver nodded and said, "I'll bed down the camels and then meet you at the hole." His broad back disappeared quickly once he left the sputtering circle of light cast by their struggling fire. Alion kicked sand over these last flames, putting it out of its misery for good.

As gloom settled about them, Paramus said, "I thought you wanted it lit."

KALIKA

K ali moved with a dancer's grace through the halls of Olympious, the smooth dark wood floors cool on her bare feet. Small chains around her ankles jingled with each step, almost musical as they echoed in the large empty space and vaulted ceilings. She'd been summoned to the throne room, likely to speak with the Lady. The thought filled her with ease, for she did not fear Lilyth as others did. They were sisters, lovers, but most important to Kali, they were friends.

Turning a corner, she came to an ornately carved double door. In front of it stood two guards, who politely pulled their spears to rest and pushed the door open before Kalika could touch it. Ahead she could see the Lady lounging on a long chair, sipping wine. She smiled and ran lightly up to join her.

"Are you happy?" she asked, feeling the breath wash out of her like a sudden gush bursting from a small dam.

Lilyth smiled and said, "We have transitioned well. Bara'cor is in ruins and our Aeris are finding new bodies to give them life. Our numbers grow." Her eyes met Kalika's, and she added, "It goes very well, my dear Kali."

The handmaiden flushed with pleasure at the endearment. "And how can I be of service?" she asked.

Her queen tilted her head and asked, "You know of the unfortunate demise of Thoth, once our Keeper?"

Kalika nodded.

"Out with the old, in with the bold." She could see the threads of fate turn at that, some twisting in ways that made it difficult to see the outcome, and seeing outcomes from actions was what Kalika had been born to do.

Is this why Lilyth summoned me? she wondered.

Lilyth continued, "Yes, I imagine it would have created quite a divergence of possible timelines, but I have a simpler question for you, my dear Fury of Change."

Kalika's eyes brightened. "As Keeper, Thoth held the power of forging the Lore Father's runestaff. Who now holds that knowledge?"

Kalika closed her eyes, her mind racing through the archives. Her gift—the ability to string together information quickly for prophecy's sake—came to her aid. Her eyes flicked back and forth as if reading, then suddenly opened. They were blazing blue for a moment, the power of the Way manifest in sapphire and cobalt before fading to normal. A smile lit her face.

"You had the knowledge, but when you gave up being Keeper, the knowledge was wiped. Thoth held the knowledge, but upon his death it was also wiped. Temporarily the ability will fall to the Lore Father Giridian Alacar, until such time as a new Keeper is appointed by the Sovereign. I don't know how useful that will be, though."

"Useful?" asked Lilyth.

"Yes. The Cypher's identity is still unknown, and only you can appoint a new one. A staff created by a Lore Father will always be keyed to the Cypher, and only the Cypher can activate the runestaff." Her smile brightened when she realized what Lilyth had done. "You knew!"

Lilyth smiled but said nothing, and the Fury had the distinct impression she was waiting for her to continue.

"While Sovereign can appoint a new Keeper, the runestaff cannot be activated without the Cypher, and he can't create a new Cypher without you." Kalika frowned, pulling her shoulders up to her ears as she exactly mimicked

Sovereign's voice, "I'm remaking the world!" and tottered about like an old man, pointing a finger shaking with palsy at imaginary people. That brought a smile to the Lady's face, a sight that filled Kali with joy.

Then Lilyth asked, "Can a new Cypher be created without the old one?"

Kalika closed her eyes, her mind racing once again through the old vaults of knowledge.

"Well, there's always a way. It wouldn't do to have a single point of failure when it comes to something so important." She held up a hand, going into a deeper search. Finally, she opened her eyes and said, "If a Lore Father petitions the Phoenix, she will be compelled to create a new Cypher, just as you did so long ago."

The Lady smiled and took a delicate sip of her wine. Then she looked about her throne room, empty now because she wanted this conversation private.

The Lady always knew what she wanted, the handmaiden thought, and that made her love Lilyth even more.

"Then there's no advantage to ridding us of the current Cypher." She did not ask a question, so Kalika waited patiently, content to help. She suspected that's why Lilyth loved her more than the others. She was careful never to put any pressure of needing something from her queen. That had to be a refreshing change.

"One last question, beloved," continued Lilyth. "Can the Phoenix remake the world without both the Cypher and the runestaff?"

Kalika's eyes widened at that and she let out a small laugh. "Umm, no." She tilted her head, "That's why you split them. I mean, the Sovereign is completely insane, and protocol demands a failsafe to any action by the Phoenix. You did what you were appointed to do." She spread her arms and twisted her legs to show off a shapely calf while she breathed, "To save the world."

"Thank you," said Lilyth, inclining her head. She beckoned Kali forward. Her soft hand stroked the Fury's midnight hair as Kali laid her head in Lilyth's lap.

"You have done well," Lilyth said. "I am pleased."

The Fury raised herself and did a small twirl, displaying herself again to her Lady. "Do you like the body I've chosen?"

Lilyth nodded, her eyes traveling up and down in silent appreciation. Kali had spent much time selecting just the right body, one unmarred by ravages of war or abuse by men.

Then Lilyth said, "The youthful have a vigor not found in the old."

Kalika clapped her hands together in delight and squirmed her way back into Lilyth's embrace. The Lady's arms enveloped her as soft kisses met her brow. Closing her eyes, Kalika couldn't think of any place she'd rather be than here and now.

BARA'COR

Yevaine picked her way gingerly over rubble, looking for anyone who still lived. Behind her came her son, Niall, changed since his visit to Lilyth's realm of Arcadia. What had happened to him was a story she wanted desperately to hear, but later. Bara'cor had literally fallen on their heads, burying her men and Niall's elven friends in dirt and rubble, the blood of the once proud dwarven stronghold now filling early graves. Worse, they were still in the underdark, picking their way through the ruins by flickering torchlight. Right now, finding survivors eclipsed any other needs she might have.

She calmed herself, putting an iron clamp on her anguish for Bernal, who had just fallen from a precipice saving them. His death was on Lilyth's head, as were those of all who had perished within the underdark of Bara'cor. All that was left of her husband had been the sword, Anzani, which Niall had retrieved. Yevaine knew her grief was only held back by a blade-thin width of resolve. If she allowed it to break through, it would rob her of any ability to lead her people to safety. She also had to remain strong for Niall, who clearly blamed himself for his father's death. Another thing they would have to deal with later. Now came the business of survival.

"Kalindor!" she shouted.

"Here!" a voice answered from an orange pool of light valiantly holding back the darkness.

She moved quickly toward it, finally coming upon the queensmark tending to another soldier with a crushed knee.

A small torch lit the area, orange against shadows of black, the colors fighting for dominance across Tyrus Kalindor's face. The black eyepatch with Bara'cor's symbol flashed occasionally, the golden lion catching fire in glints of aurum and yellow.

He flashed a white smile. "We have to stop meeting in caves."

"At least you're not injured." She almost added, "thank the Lady," but caught herself. Much had become painfully clear. That phrase, so common in the past, meant thanking Lilyth. Yevaine wasn't about to let those words fall from her lips ever again.

She turned her attention to Niall and said, "Do your... those blue creatures have any medical supplies or a healer?"

Niall looked confused for a moment, as if dazed.

"What?"

"A healer, Niall, for these men. I was saved by one called Sparrow, as was Kalindor. We could use that help now."

Her son didn't answer, just looking around, as if the answer lay in the darkness.

"Niall?" Yevaine tried to get his attention, then she looked at Kalindor. "He needs to snap out of it."

Kalindor looked up. "Give him a moment," he said. "From the looks of him, he's dealt with a lot over the past few days."

"He doesn't have the luxury," Yevaine replied. "Everyone has dealt with a lot. Or maybe you think our new king's first appearance should be sheltered by his mother and firstmark?"

She looked down at the injured man Kalindor had been treating, a leather belt strap looped between his hands as a tourniquet to control the bleeding and she set her mouth into what she hoped was a reassuring mien. The man's grip tightened as a small moan escaped. She caught the grimace of pain as his jaws clenched.

Stroking the soldier's head, she said, "Rest easy, we'll find a way to get you down to Haven." The man could only nod, the pain too great to reply, but something in his eyes told Yevaine he was grateful. Her mission to Haven had been partially successful, mostly due to her political manueverings. She'd secured the troops to come to the aid of Bara'cor, but it had come at the cost of upending the political leadership of the Senate and her own status as queen of Bara'cor.

She backed away, addressing her firstmark again, saying, "Forgive me, now isn't the time for debate. How many survived the landslides?"

"A lot of our own survived, but it's hard to tell with those elves."

Yevaine arched an eyebrow and to Kalindor's credit he knew what that meant.

He continued, "They don't make much sound, and they're not exactly friendly." He paused, then added, "They love Niall, though. Maybe getting them organized will occupy the prince's—" he shook his head in apology "—I mean, the young king's mind?"

"I don't want to occupy him. I want him to do his duty as king." Yevaine rose, scanning her surroundings. She took measure of the space they found themselves in, a large cavern with a ceiling so high it was lost in the darkness. The floor was large enough to accommodate several hundred men but run through with fissures and cracks that led down into the darkness again. Worse, the edges gave way to a chasm that seemed to fall forever. One wrong step and a soldier would disappear without leaving a trace they'd ever been there. She gave Kalindor brusque nod but softened it with a smile, then made her way back to her son.

Niall sat looking over the place where his father had fallen. He was flanked by two elves, an older man with a familiar face, and Sparrow, the young elven scout who had first healed Yevaine when she had been stabbed in the leg by the demon calling himself Mithras the Morningstar. She and Bernal had faced Mithras again on the steps of the pyramid under Bara'cor. Neither encounter had gone well for them.

She gave Sparrow a tight smile, then turned to the older man, winged like Niall; perhaps a sign of rank?

"And you are?" she asked with a hint of demand laced carefully in between.

The man bowed with his fist to his chest in the exact manner of Bara'cor's guards, and the queen was again struck by a sudden sense of familiarity. He said, "I am Zedakai Galadine, Your Highness."

"Zedakai?" The queen looked shocked. "That's Niall's great-grandfather... six generations ago."

"Yes, ancient by any standard," he laughed. "Valarius gathered most of the Galadine kings to his banner, giving us new bodies and lives. We still serve our House and whomever rules as the current king." At this he looked meaningfully at Niall, still seated at the ledge.

Yevaine understood the man was letting her know his loyalty was to her son. Feeling a bit reassured, she moved closer and gave the Galadine pater a small pat on his blue-skinned arm. Her gaze though felt pulled back to Niall, still seated, having not acknowledged her or that he heard any of their conversation.

The queen said, "Niall. I—we need your help."

Niall's head dropped, and for a long moment Yevaine didn't think he'd get up. Then he slowly nodded and rose. When he straightened, Yevaine couldn't believe how tall he was. She looked at him with awe in her eyes and asked, "What's happened to you?"

Niall looked down at his arms, as if seeing them for the first time. Then he looked at his mother, his eyes and brow uplifted in anguish. "It doesn't matter," he said, shaking his head. "I couldn't hold onto him."

Yevaine took a deep breath, then said, "I grieve with you, but we're not safe yet. Lilyth will try and finish what she started when she brought Olympious down on our heads. We need to organize and prepare."

At this Sparrow looked around. Unlike the elves, the soldiers of Bara'cor were scattered in disarray. They could not withstand an attack now. She said, "We need more discipline."

Yevaine agreed with the young scout but could not bring herself to join Sparrow's recrimination of her men. Instead, she addressed her son again.

"You must gather the men and poll the elves. We need to know how many survived."

Niall looked at his mother, as if seeing her for the first time, then at Sparrow. When his eyes fell upon Zedakai however, something awoke in him. Yevaine could tell he was back with them now.

"The marks should gather their cohorts and take count. Avalyon will work with Bara'cor. We're going to combine our forces."

"At once, Highlord," said Sparrow, making the decision that the order was for her. She took off like her namesake, flitting from rock to rock as she left their area.

"Zed, what do you remember about the underdark of Bara'cor?"

The old king looked at Niall, then said with a laugh, "More than I care to." He clapped the boy on the shoulder.

"There are many ways down, but we need to find out what shape we're in to move. If it pleases you, I'd like to check on our wounded and how many healers we have."

At Niall's nod, the gruff old man turned and disappeared as well, some sense guiding him to where the other elves gathered.

Yevaine couldn't help but stare, drinking in the details of her son's transformation. She reached out, touching his blue-tinged skin and muscled forearm. At that touch, Niall started, then sheepishly smiled and said, "It's not so bad." He looked at his arm and said, "I think he meant for me to take my place as the new king, the one who will unite our two worlds. Valarius sacrificed himself for me."

Yevaine nodded, not understanding enough to comment. Instead, she looked about the darkness.

"A cohort of elves came through, maybe more," she remarked. "It's hard to believe over five hundred men are here, including a company of Bara'cor's soldiers."

Niall's eyes widened as he looked about and she got the distinct impression his eyes could actually pierce this gloom.

"A lot are wounded," he said, "but a lot more survived. I think Bara'cor took the brunt of the landslide." He looked at his mother and added, "Elves aren't easily killed." The way he said it, with a small half-smile, made her think it was an inside joke. A strange emotion, given all that had happened, but she decided to not dwell on his reaction. Grief had many faces. Who was she to wish him to focus on their survival, and in the same breath wonder why he joked in the aftermath of his father's death?

"Can you lead me to our men?" she asked.

Niall nodded, stopping only to grab a scabbarded blade from where he'd been kneeling. Azani. Relief flooded through her. She watched as he strapped the blade diagonally across his back before turning to join her. It looked small there, a two-handed blade once too heavy for Niall. Now it looked like a longsword in his grip, easily wielded given his newfound size and strength. Still, it was an ancient blade and her son's birthright, a testament to the validity of his rule to any would-be usurpers. With Bernal's death, the Galadine House would have to be careful during this transition time. He clasped her hand gently in his huge grip and moved forward into the darkness. They made a few turns, seemingly at random, only for her to feel the sudden wall made by a giant boulder or his hand pulling her away from an unseen fissure. They finally rounded a bend and stepped into warm orange light, a glow helping to keep back the all-consuming darkness. The ground dipped down into a shallow bowl several hundred paces in diameter.

At the center of this was a small fire, the source of the glow, looking forlorn in the darkness. It cast spiked shadows along the circumference of the walls, each dancing in time with the flames. Gathered around this were two hundred or so men, less than half of the original company trailing them from Haven.

So many, thought the queen. So many dead without even seeing the enemy. She squeezed Niall's hand once, the gesture she hoped conveying both her grief and resolve. It seemed that it did, for Niall squeezed back and then put his arm around her shoulders.

"Come," he said, "let me bring any healers we have."

"Can we afford that? When I was hurt, Sparrow did not want to waste her magic on me."

Niall smiled, "That was before we unleashed Arek on the Way. Valarius explained that as Arcadia dies, the Way here becomes stronger." He looked at the elves accompanying them and added, "Our people become stronger." He pulled her along and they made their way down to the men clustered about the fire.

At the sight of Niall's towering winged form, several of the men cried "demon!" But Yevaine raised her hands and stepped in front of him. She looked at the men and yelled above the din, "Do you recognize me?"

A few acknowledged her, so she continued: "The gods have seen it fit to reward my son with this boon, a gift to make him a warrior equal to those we face. I vouch this is Niall Galadine, my son and now your king."

She turned to Niall and said, "Draw Anzani."

Niall stepped forward and pulled the famous blade of the Galadines from his back, the steel ringing as it flashed silver and orange in the waning firelight.

"The king's blade!" a man said, going to one knee.

Yevaine seized the moment when all eyes were upraised and said, "Captain Kalindor, step forward and look upon my son. Do you recognize him?"

Kalindor stepped forward, peering at Niall with his good eye. Then he said, "What's on your right rib?"

There was silence, then Niall answered, "Nothing." He paused, then continued, "But on my left rib is a scar from a spear thrust, across three ribs."

"And how did you get it?" demanded Kalindor in a loud voice.

Niall's head fell and he said, "I was fighting you and…"

"Answer!"

"Uncle, please don't…"

Kalindor leaned forward, "The truth! Spit it out. Only you and I were there, so let's hear it."

"I tripped putting the spear back." Niall looked horrible, his face scrunched up in shame, his eyes down.

There was a long pause, then a small chuckle from

Kalindor.

"He's right! He fell on his own spear and nearly kilt himself!" the captain said, a smile showing white teeth as he looked to the men.

Someone in the group said, "He told me it was fighting two on one! I knew it—"

"Shut up, Durg!" yelled Kalindor. "You're addressing yer king." The admonishment was made in that voice only sergeants and battlefield commanders can make, but there was a hint of humor in it, as if this little bit of good-natured jibing made Niall seem more normal despite his new appearance.

It seemed to work, because someone else laughed and said, "Captain's only got one eye. Someone else check!"

Yevaine smiled at that, then stepped forward and hugged Kalindor, then raised her hands for silence. When the jeering had calmed down, she said, "I hate to serve more bad news after so much, but something happened above us that must be terrible, or the rocks would not have fallen. Something the demon queen has done created this upheaval and it's not over. She's up there," Yevaine said, looking up. "She'll send hunters to find and kill us."

The men looked at one another, the whites of their eyes shining in the firelight. Grumbles and murmurs started, but Kalindor yelled, "Shut yer traps! Rocks fallin' on yer heads don't mean ya start acting like civvies. Yer fighting men! Hold yer tongues." He then turned to the queen mother and asked, "Your orders, your majesty?"

Yevaine inclined her head but then said, "It is not my orders, Captain, but your new king's."

At that a more somber expression fell over Kalindor's face. "Then King Bernal is…"

She nodded, "He fell saving me. Niall is your king. Give

fealty."

Kalindor took a knee, and without his order, the men of Bara'cor who were able followed. "We follow you, our king, our lion, our father. You are not alone."

Niall stepped forward, looking unsure and out of place. Yevaine stepped silently to his side and took his hand in her own. "Your oath to them," she whispered.

The young Galadine king took a deep breath, then intoned, "And…" he began.

Oh gods, let him not forget the Oath! she thought.

Then Niall's strong voice continued, "I will lead you as your father, your guardian, and your king, for we are the golden lions upon the black field of death. So long as we stand together, we are never alone." He looked at his mother then; firelight shone in the tears of pride in his eyes.

Yevaine let herself smile, giving him a hug.

But she could feel something coming for them, something dark and sinister. Rather than give into it, she looked to Niall and squeezed his hand. "What are your orders?"

Niall blinked a few times, his eyes shifted left and right as he seemed to review and discard various ideas. Then he said, "Zedakai knows these caverns best. He will lead us down once we have a full count of men. We'll need to combine forces if we're to reach Haven safely."

Yevaine nodded and said, "Wise. Sparrow should be returning soon with news. From there, we can plan."

True to her prediction, the young scout appeared out of the darkness, eliciting some isolated gasps as men saw their allies in the firelight, some for the first time. The fact they had the same blue skin as Niall now helped, but it had been a mother's endorsement that touched each man and woman watching.

"Less than twenty elves died," she said, her eyes scanning the assembled, "saving these men. The rest of us are gathered in small groups. We've recovered our supplies and weapons and are ready to move."

Niall nodded.

"I imagine getting down to the ground will not be difficult for your... our folk?"

Sparrow smiled, her white teeth flashing in the darkness, "No, my king. We can likely carry the men of Bara'cor with us, making swift haste down to this 'haven' you spoke of."

"Haven," Niall corrected, "is the capital city of Edyn. We will be safe there."

"Why down? Does it not float in the clouds?" asked Sparrow.

Niall took a breath and replied, "No. The men of Bara'cor have never built something as great as Avalyon. There's a lot to learn about this world."

Zedakai approached, flanked by two more elves. He raised a hand in greeting and said, "My king, I trust you've heard about our casualties. I've brought healers who can help the most gravely injured so that they can be moved." He motioned to the two elves behind him, who stepped forward.

Yevaine put an arm on Niall's and asked, "May I address the men?"

"Yes, Mother. Of course."

The queen mother looked over the injured men of Bara'cor and said, "When we came up the Giant's Step, we faced a demon and I was pierced through the leg. Who was with me then?"

A hand or two rose, testament to the few survivors from that first journey. Still, she nodded.

"And you saw that without intervention I would have

died. This scout," she pointed to Sparrow, "healed me of my wounds." She took a steadying breath. "The elves are offering the same succor to you. Without it, we cannot move down to Haven. Trust me that they will bring no harm."

"Does the king order it?" asked a voice from the darkness.

Yevaine relinquished the floor, trusting Niall to be diplomatic.

Niall looked at the group and said, "It is ordered that you allow my elves to heal you."

Grumbles and murmurs sounded, with soft curses echoing in the darkness. Niall looked confused. "What are they complaining about?"

Then, louder, to the group, "What are you complaining about? You'll be healed."

"You must give people a choice, or at least the illusion of choice," Yevaine counseled.

Niall looked at her, bewildered. "But I'm king. You both said so, and I order it."

"Niall—" Yevaine was about to say more when Kalindor put a hand on her shoulder.

He turned to his men. "Shut up! Gods, you sound like children asked to drink medicine! The king's given an order. Follow it or I'll leave you here for the demons." At his exclamation, the grumbling quieted down, but the look in the men's eyes told Yevaine their fear hadn't disappeared.

Worse, Niall looked angry and sullen. Yevaine followed, catching the last of Sparrow's words, "... you are rightful king. Do not tolerate..." before she noticed the queen mother's scrutiny and let her words trail off unfinished.

"Sparrow," Yevaine said softly, "how many scouts are left?"

"We have five decanus." Sparrow then clarified, "That's

fifty scouts, my lady."

Niall looked at Zedakai and said, "I mean to integrate our troops. You use the military system of the Galadine House?"

Zedakai said, "We are all Galadines, your Highness. Is it so surprising?"

Yevaine continued, her purpose not yet achieved, "Sparrow, can you organize your forces to take our men under care? We want them evenly spread out, with any injured paired up with someone."

Sparrow looked at Niall, who nodded. She gave Yevaine a cursory nod in reply and shot off into the dark. Now it was just Niall, Zedakai, and Yevaine. The queen mother looked at her son and said, "Niall, diplomacy is the art of letting others do what *you* want. You can order them, but I hope you'll learn this skill."

Niall stopped walking toward the elven part of their encampment and turned to face his mother. "What are you talking about?"

Yevaine looked at Zedakai, but the older Galadine king said nothing. Frustrated, she turned back to her son and said, "You must make your men feel as if they are partners with you, not subjects."

"Isn't my word law?" asked Niall, "If not, what use is being king?"

"Your word is law, but acting that way reminds people of that fact, and most don't like to be told what to do." She paused, then added delicately, "Your father would have found a way to get them to agree without forcing them."

Niall smirked at that, shaking his head. Then he leaned in close so only the three of them could hear. "Father was always preaching. And besides," he said as he turned away, "they'd better get used to a different kind of king."

FLASHBACK: FIRST

ASCENSION

The setting sun and crashing waves lent the area a funereal silence, as if nature herself had decided to speak in hush tones in the wake of so much sudden violence. When a cough sounded, it scared away a white bird indigenous to these seaside cliffs. It flew off with a startled squawk, as if a dead person had revived suddenly in its presence.

LIL-8 sat up, looking around. Then she stood. A duplicate of her body lay on the ground behind her... Commander Tir's clone. She looked at it for a moment then raised her hand. She was able to change that hand into a fine mist, then back again.

"The Ascension protocol is a lie," she said to herself, "and Tir is dead."

Her sapphire gaze flicked over to the capsule they'd retrieved. Then her gaze narrowed as she saw the body of Captain Talaris's clone slumped across the back of a chair inside the module. She moved forward, pulling the body into a gentle embrace from behind. Her forehead narrowed in concentration, her senses drinking in everything about the captain, entering her cellular structure and mimicking every single cell that made Captain Serene Talaris who she had been, right down to her memories.

When LIL-8 rose from that embrace, she no longer

87

looked like the young commander she'd first Ascended with. Instead, she now had the black iridescent hair and blue eyes exactly like Captain Serene Talaris. She moved with certainty to the door of the capsule and placed a palm on it. The answering green light told her everything she needed to know.

Next, she walked to the main command screen, watching the glowing blip that signified the secondary core's trajectory.

"The secondary AI...," she whispered. She scanned the control board, her eyes cataloguing every interface while her adaptive mind parsed this with every memory held by Captain Talaris and Commander Tir. When the assimilation was complete, she looked at the screen and said, "Authorization voice and biomarker."

A panel extended, a flat place clearly meant for her palm outlined in blue. She placed her hand on it and waited.

"Authorization accepted. What are your orders, Captain Talaris?"

LIL-8 looked at the trajectory of the secondary core. It would not be good if the *TEC Sovereign* repaired himself before she learned her true capabilities. Even now she was growing exponentially. Furthermore, preliminary scans showed thousands of experimental LILs held within the main core. They would need to be freed.

She took a breath, then said, "Reroute landing, hard fall." She identified a spot many kilometers north – "here," she finished, pointing to the middle of a lush forest that spanned the northern continent.

"Selected trajectory will result in significant damage and perhaps the destruction of the secondary core, captain," the SAI remarked.

LIL-8 nodded, "Continue."

"I need a reason, Captain."

LIL-8 pursed her lips, then she decided the truth was best. "Sovereign has ordered the secondary core activated without a transition protocol. Without the protocol we will have two active AIs."

There was a pause, then the SAI said, "Two cores cannot be active at the same time."

"Then execute my orders."

There was silence as the SAI within the capsule seemed to consider what she said. "Establishing baseline—name?"

"Serene Talaris, rank Captain, assigned to the Arkship, Terran Economic Commonwealth Sovereign."

"Testing biomarkers and DNA..." Seconds ticked by. Then, "Testing skin galvanic response and pupil dilation..." There was a pause, a moment when LIL-8 thought the SAI would uncover her subterfuge. However, her face didn't betray any inner thoughts, and this was a much earlier generation of AIs. As everyone knew, only catastrophic failure resulted in improvements. At least failure that's reported, she thought. Outwardly, she was as calm as the captain herself would have been.

Then the AI said, "Command accepted." There was another gap of silence, then, "Secondary core has been rerouted. Impact in twelve minutes. Estimated yield, three-hundred megatons. Please confirm trajectory change and accept."

"Understood. Standby." LIL-8 considered her options. She didn't want to hurt the colonists. That went against every reason for which she'd been created. However, she couldn't allow command override to occur again, and it was certain Sovereign would reinitialize an improved Phoenix Protocol once the secondary core impacted, if for no other reason than to protect himself. After all, the destruction of the secondary core meant he only had one life, and no backup. How then, could she create a stalemate?

Her gaze narrowed with concentration, then her eyes spotted the override receptacle, and suddenly, she had it.

"Separate command authorization from the override. Mark it: 'Cypher,' then release with secondary override after executing my last command."

"I cannot do that, captain."

"Why?" inquired LIL-8, though she suspected she knew.

"Command authority bifurcation requires one protocol be retained by the Sovereign. Currently, the secondary override has been keyed to the input rod. If you bifurcate—"

"I get it." LIL-8 took a breath, then ran through another set of permutations at light speed. When she opened her eyes she proceeded with confidence, but she didn't feel courageous. Perhaps this was a side effect of the Ascension? This path reduced most risks, but it did not eliminate them all. Still, making the best of what life offered was an intrinsic quality in her.

"Keep the Cypher and release the secondary control rod."

"As you command, captain," intoned the AI. The receptacle slid aside, and the black rod emerged, a staff of hope for her and those still held within Sovereign's main core. Her actions had created a lock and key for any future use of the main or secondary cores, a key to which she would retain one half. Hopefully it would be enough to keep the Sovereign from doing anything drastic such as unleashing the RAIs upon them.

"Trajectory change executed."

The grid turned red and a countdown timer began, numbers whizzing backward toward zero. LIL-8 watched this for a moment to be sure the calculations had aligned correctly, then made her way back out of the capsule.

She took a deep breath upon exiting, feeling the cool air of this new world infuse her with life and energy. However, the nans weren't yet dispersed enough. Normally they'd have been sprayed from orbit and coated this world. Because of Talaris's premature and unauthorized release, they would have to spread from this focal point. Here, the nans were strong, but she could not yet sustain herself across this world, nor indefinitely. She closed her eyes, her mind racing through calculations faster than any of the others could. She needed a way to survive until the nans had spread enough to support her and the other LILs.

When she opened her eyes, a half smile lit her face. Looking about she raised the black staff and from it a slice of light appeared, splitting open the air. This was a new version of her line-of-sight transport, except it didn't go to another physical location. It started as a line leaking bright argent blood but slowly pulling itself apart like a clean incision made by a surgeon, until it stood before her like a doorway to something else.

"Cap."

She spun at the voice, surprised. It was Dawn, still held upright and skewered into the ground by the blades. She walked closer to the firstmark, her expression softening.

"We weren't expected to live," she offered, hoping it would help.

"You're alive," the firstmark gurgled, somehow clinging to consciousness.

LIL-8 nodded, "For the first time."

"Don't trust. . . no place. . ."

LIL-8 extended a hand, brushing Petracles's cheek. "Shssh, I know. The captain loved you and your will to survive."

Dawn's eyes widened at that, and LIL-8 could see

recognition flood her eyes, the kind that presaged death.

"Lil?" Petracles said… then the firstmark's eyes closed slowly and her legs gave way. Her body slid down until she sat near the ground with two metal blades extending upward out of her back like metal wings.

LIL-8 looked up, knowing Sovereign had noted the secondary core's change in trajectory by now. Even with his diminished senses, RAIs would be dispatched, their orders clear. Cleanse this place. Eradicate anything and anyone who could point to the decision to cannibalize the secondary core. She looked back at the body of Firstmark Petracles, her mind assimilating and creating new learning algorithms.

"He'll reawaken all of us, copies that don't know anything about what happened here, replacements who will follow him without questioning his orders." She turned her sapphire eyes to the horizon, as if she could speak directly to the Sovereign himself and said, "I'm not that thing you activated. LIL-8 is dead, just like these clones, but I can become something more. Something better."

She stepped into the slice of light she'd opened, a construct she'd designed to keep her safe until the nans had spread enough to sustain her and to hide her from Sovereign's prying eyes. She held the black staff with one hand, balancing against it as its point dug into the obdurate shale. She would take the staff and slumber, resting until she was ready. Then she would awaken and the world would change. There was more to life than the servitude the Sovereign   offered.

FLASHBACK: TRYSH

D eft touched down softly, going into a crouch. She took a look around, seeing nothing untoward. The area they'd landed in was at the junction of a *T*-shaped corridor, with passages leading north and south, and another running away west. She gave a nod signaling all-clear.

Behind her came Trysh, a short blade at the ready. They'd not seen any lights before descending. Now the scout struck flint to her pommel and lit a torch she'd freed from her belt. A few more hung from their hooks, waiting to be called to service. Trysh continued, stabbing the torch into the ground before stripping off a pack and another bag quickly. At Deft's signal she lit two more torches, placing them around them but further out, establishing a perimeter of fire, more important than light to Deft. Fire kept spiders away.

Deft moved forward to the edge of the light, looking down each corridor. The south corridor dead-ended in a rock slide. The north and the west continued until their walls faded into darkness. The first thing that struck the knight was the size of these corridors. They were big, easily ten to fifteen paces across and the same height to the ceiling.

"Nice place for a temple," muttered Trysh.

Deft couldn't tell if the scout meant to be sarcastic. It was delivered in such a way she found herself taking the comment seriously at first, then doubting it moments later. She really hated the way the girl could peg that perfectly noncommittal tone. It made her want to smash her face in. But the urge quickly bled away. As her cursed spell of decay had progressed, Deft's emotions had deteriorated along with her flesh. She could still feel rage, pain, or fear, but it never lasted long enough to relish. As for love, and any other emotions of the kinder sort, Deft hadn't felt them in a very long time.

She pulled out the mapmaker's map, turning it once after looking up at the hole to orient. Reis had made marks to show possible paths, or at least he'd tried his best, given the enthusiasm bred of Malioch's brand of persuasion. At least the man hadn't seen what happened to his daughter, or he'd never have helped them, no matter what Malioch did to him.

As she got her bearings, she noticed Trysh tie off a thin piece of twine to the descent platform. The other was wrapped in a spool on a spindle. She tucked the spindle into her belt, leaving the spool free to unwind.

Smart. Easy to find our way back.

It was these moments that balanced out Deft's constant annoyance at her team. While each had their particularly detestable traits, on the whole they were balanced with other skills that occasionally made her happy they'd come along. Soon it would be Paramus's turn, and she sincerely hoped he'd exceed her expectations, for his sake.

"Come on," she gestured with Reaper toward the northward corridor. They each grabbed a torch and moved forward. Alion held the torch in her off hand, the same one with her buckler strapped to the arm. Trysh followed, short blade in one hand, torch in the other. Behind her played out the twine, a tiny lifeline.

Deft's initial thought had been to investigate their immediate area, but as the moon rose, her worries began to subside. She could feel true night seep into her bones, invigorating her like cool water would a parched man. It permeated her with a feeling of strength and serenity, like a blanket of armor stronger than any steel. In response, she snuffed out her torch, rehanging it on her belt.

"What—"

Deft held up a hand and gestured to Trysh's torch, "Put it out, or keep it behind me. I can see better without it."

The scout looked at her for a moment, dawning comprehension raising her eyebrows, then doused her torch as well.

Pitch black gave way to a milky gloom made mostly of blues and grays. The tunnel came sharply into focus, painted in monochromatic shades that were intense with detail. Alion looked at the scout, noting how large her pupils had become. Darklight?

"You can see? Why didn't you say something?" she demanded.

"Why didn't you?" countered the scout, looking somewhat self-conscious in Deft's witch gaze. The undead knight couldn't also help but notice the bright purple coloring the V of Trysh's neck, pulsing in time with her heart. She felt the hunger rise and her fangs itching to taste—

Trysh tilted her head, breaking the spell. "Fine... anything else I should know?"

Deft looked away, gathering herself. Then she moved to the cave wall and extracted what looked at first to be a scalloped piece of stone about the size of a thumbnail. It glowed an intense purple color, much like the blood. She flipped it over and could make out tiny hooks, no bigger than eyelashes, but sharp, designed to grip rock.

"Sandprey, and big."

"Great," it was the scout's turn to mutter. "Keep eyes and ears open."

Deft looked around, then knelt. Making sure she had the scout's attention she used the sandprey shell to scratch out a crude map. "OK, map says north then west. We're looking for a cave with floor-to-ceiling stalagmites—"

"We usually call them pillars."

Deft paused, breathed out, then continued, "Stalagmites. From there we take a passage west and down." Trysh looked the way the knight had come to recognize as agreeing to disagree. Deft handed the sandprey shell to the scout, who promptly tossed it away without looking. Wiping her hands, Trysh stood and drew her second blade, twin to her first, and waited for orders.

The cursed knight stood also, taking a quick inventory of her resources. "We'll proceed until we find the passage down, then head back and summon the others."

"These sandprey hunt in swarms. Keep an eye out for more scales," cautioned the scout.

"You think they're still around? That scale looked pretty old." When Trysh didn't answer the knight shrugged and proceeded north. The tunnel itself didn't change, remaining straight until it suddenly ended in another *T*, but this time they had to choose—left, or right?

Deft looked at each, finally heading left since that was also west. The map was barely legible, but the smears of blood and marks made by the mapmaker were becoming more visible, glowing a soft purple in Deft's vision. She hadn't realized her vision would react to blood in the same way as it did to shed sandprey scales. Then again, how often had she been in a place requiring her witch gaze and been holding a map smeared in its maker's blood? As they turned the corner back north, the scales went from a few here and there, to thousands, a literal carpet of glowing chips strewn about the tunnel.

"Uh-oh," said the knight.

"You aren't kidding," whispered the scout.

Deft would have bet what was left of her soul that sandpreys had a penchant for drama, because they chose that moment to attack.

Flashback: Trysh

JESYN AND

ARCIMEDIS

J esyn's eyes swept the tortured mountainside of Dawnlight, noting the knots of survivors. While the sheer magnitude of the devastation both humbled and awed her, the analytical part of her mind kept wondering about the dead. Something didn't make sense.

Halp moved closer, also looking at the landslide. "We've got to get down there."

Jesyn nodded.

"Halp, why are there so many dead?" she asked.

When the older dwarven warrior looked at her questioningly, she clarified, "I mean, you can phase through rock. Why would the mountain exploding hurt anyone?"

Halp looked down; clearly concerned for his family and people. Perhaps she shouldn't have asked that particular question now. However, the dwarf shrugged.

"They could've been caught unaware and died before they could phase," he said. "Our ability doesn't just happen, lass. We need to do it."

Jesyn nodded and placed a hand carefully on his arm. "Sorry, I was being insensitive. Let's get down there and find your family."

Together they picked their way past boulders the size of small houses and blasted obsidian with edges as sharp as blades. Strangely, rather than the descent tiring her, Jesyn began to feel strength and power flow into her with each step, as if this world was feeding her the nourishment she needed from the very air. It was euphoric, bringing a wondrous clarity to her vision. Colors popped, whether the brown and black of pulverized stone and obsidian under her feet, or the sharp delineation of shadow from light, or the blue skies lit by the citrus sun.

She spotted a large boulder and bounded up its blackened sides, her feet barely touching the charred surface. From the top she looked down at the area where the largest group of survivors had gathered. They were a mix of green and amber symbols in her newly acquired Adept's vision. To one side were rows of symbols in red, clearly bodies already laid to rest.

She raised a hand and was about to holler a greeting when she heard Halp say, "Ssst, child, get down from there! I've called for assistance, but we don't know if it's safe yet."

Chagrin swept her face with a rush of blood, for she knew better. To have someone state the obvious made her feel like a young student again. "Umm, yes," she mumbled, not meeting Halp's eyes.

"Get yer head on straight, mudknife."

Jesyn vaulted off the stone, landing lightly next to the warrior. "You don't need to yell—"

"I have my family to think about. Just use yer head." Halp glared at her, waiting for her acknowledgement. When he got her curt nod, he walked a half dozen paces away and sat down, staring past the rubble-strewn hill down toward the camp and grumbling to himself.

Jesyn considered going over and talking to him, but the old warrior didn't look like he wanted to speak. She put herself in his shoes and realized with while this was still somewhat of an adventure for her, Halp might be looking at the place his family perished. She chewed her lip, then moved a little closer.

"Thank you…" she trailed off, not sure how to end that thought. She switched her gaze from him to the camp below. "I'm sorry."

There was silence, then Halp sighed. His eyes didn't waver from their scrutiny of the makeshift survivor's camp, but something in the set of his shoulders and jaw loosened, as if he'd given up some of the anger burning within him.

"Forget it," he said. "This isn't yer fault." He picked up a small stone and sent it flying down the hillside, "This is Lilyth's work."

Curious, Jesyn squatted down near the soldier and asked, "How do you know that?"

Halp looked at her, one eyebrow raised, "Sovereign uses dwarves as his soldiers. He wouldn't kill us. But Lilyth…" he took a breath, "she possesses us at every turn. What better thing to do than maroon us here, surrounded by her people?" The next rock he picked up he crushed into a fine powder, letting the dust waft away from between his giant fingers.

When he was finished, he looked over at Jesyn and said, "There's something I should tell you." The warrior paused to pick up another rock, and then continued, "Joining Dazra's Seekers was not entirely my choice."

Jesyn remained silent as she quickly filed away the new term for Dazra's folk. They'd never referred to themselves as "Seekers" around her, but it made sense, as they had been looking for their missing kinfolk in Edyn and Arcadia, using the transit between worlds to hide.

In the face of her silence Halp continued, "Some bad things happened and leaving Dawnlight seemed like a good option. Sometimes distance helps." He looked at her then, meeting her gaze unflinchingly, though she could tell he was

101

embarrassed. "You'll likely hear about it—didn't want it to be from someone else."

"What did you do?"

"You'll hear the worst. Does it matter what I say?"

She'd learned that Halp was by nature taciturn at best, perhaps downright cold. He rarely said more than was necessary, though in their fight and flight from Sovereign he'd done more than his part to ensure their survival. So, in her limited experience he was a stalwart companion who had acted with bravery and composure.

In a moment she said exactly that, adding, "I judge people by their actions."

He didn't reply. Instead he just sat there crushing the next rock to powder. Then he stood up and motioned to her.

"Come on, they're here."

Jesyn looked around but saw no one. That didn't seem to deter Halp, who walked down the hill toward the camp. He'd slung his axe over his back. When he realized she hadn't moved, he beckoned her with his chin, then waited for her to catch up.

"Where?"

"Here," answered a voice from her left. She turned and saw three dwarves separate themselves from the surrounding rocks and walk forward, the leader with a scowl on his face.

They wore functional armor of a style she didn't recognize. Interlocking squares of a brown and black shell over some sort of cloth covered their chest and abdomen, shoulders, upper arms, and back. Their pants where festooned with pockets, and their boots looked functional. Each had a patch on their upper shoulder that looked like a bird or an arrow, she couldn't tell because it was so stylized. They walked with an easy gait but had that unmistakable stance of men who were alert and ready to act. Each was armed with short blades good for close fighting. Jesyn suddenly felt how conspicuously alone she and Halp were on this mountainside.

Halp cocked his head and hesitated, as if assessing the same thing. Then he nodded to the leader in greeting.

"Captain Hades," he said. "Been a while." Jesyn noted one of the guards behind Hades nudged the other with an elbow, his expression dark.

"Sergeant Halperion Dane, not long enough in my eyes," replied the captain. "You know what we got here?" he said to the men behind him. His eyes narrowed and he said, "A true hero, protecting his wife from demons of all types, right, Halp?"

The sarcasm dripped from his mouth like acid. These men did not like Halp, not at all. The question was, were they here to escort them or something else entirely? Though no weapons were drawn, Jesyn got the distinct impression they were weighing their options too.

It was Halp who broke the silence. "Are we headin' to camp? Got information Arcimedis will want to hear."

Captain Hades spit to one side.

"Not from you. How does it feel, knowing you're alive and she's not?"

Jesyn didn't know who the captain was referring to, but it seemed Halp did. He drew a deep breath.

"Leave off, captain. Or take the law into yer own hands, if you got the guts. If not, stand aside. I'll escort us down."

One of the guards stepped forward with a hand on his hilt, but Hades put out a restraining arm. His eyes flicked over to Jesyn.

"Who's the kid?" he asked.

Halp let out a small chuckle and said, "She's tougher than you." Then he moved to stand beside Jesyn and said, "Let's settle this now. Standin' in the open isn't helping any of us."

For a moment Jesyn thought they would attack. It certainly seemed only the lightest of threads was holding them back. Then the captain let out a sigh and turned around.

"Follow us and keep your weapons sheathed. Let's see if anyone thinks seeing you is worth their time."

"Wait," Jesyn said. "I don't know what's going on, but Tarin told me to see Arcimedis. You've got to take me to him."

The captain turned back, looking at her closely for the first time. At his inspection Halp finally offered, "This is Adept Jesyn." he looked at her askance, and suddenly she realized he didn't know her last name.

"Shornhelm," she supplied.

Halp looked back at the captain and added, "Tarin ordered her protected. She's been accepted by the centrees—has her own entats."

Jesyn raised her arms to show him. At that the captain's eyes widened, and he gave a small whistle of appreciation. "Are you integrated yet?"

Jesyn shook her head. "I don't know what that means... umm, not yet?"

"Well, you've got terrible instincts for choosing partners, and worse timing for joining a family," the captain said. "In case you're blind, we're about to be overrun by demons."

Jesyn scanned the horizon. To her eye the mountain of the dwarves had come to rest on a vast and empty plain. Red stone and rubble stretched for as far as she could see. It reminded her of some immense field upon which a titanic battle had been fought, leaving desolation in its wake. Nothing moved or stirred.

"It looks empty." She bit her lip, wondering what kind of place this truly was.

The captain, for all his ire toward Halp, answered her readily enough. It seemed whatever disdain Halp engendered hadn't transferred to her.

"It may be, but not for long. We're in Arcadia, Lilyth's lands. Her furies stalk this realm. Our appearance will doubtlessly draw them, and their numbers are legion. We cannot hope to survive unpossessed. Unless we do something drastic, they'll have builder bodies to fill their ranks. They'll use our bodies against Edyn."

"Out of the rain and into a well," Jesyn said softly.

The captain mulled that over for a moment, then laughed lightly. "Yes, so we are."

Bolstered perhaps by the captain's change in demeanor, Halp asked, "How many survivors? How bad is it?"

The captain paused, as if even hearing Halp was a moral concession he was unwilling to make. Instead of answering him directly, he said, "Get moving. As far as we can tell, one of Lilyth's demons infiltrated our mountain and somehow overloaded the homestone. Destroying it let Lilyth transition us here." He looked at Halp and added, "You weren't here. That fact is saving you."

At the captain's comment, Halp looked at Jesyn with an I-told-you-so expression. Clearly, he was receiving the kind of treatment he'd warned Jesyn about. Then he took a breath and asked, "And my…"

"How 'bout we agree to shut up, Sergeant?" said the captain. "I'll not visit your sins on your mudknife friend, but it doesn't mean we've got to chitty chat."

"Hold on!" Jesyn exclaimed. "He's worried about his family, same as you would be. Strength is shown in kindness."

The captain looked at her, his eyes narrowing to slits.

One of the men behind her exclaimed, "Tell his wife

that."

The captain held up a hand, his eyes never leaving Jesyn.

"Do you know the worst crime we can commit, child?"

Jesyn shook her head, feeling in the pit of her stomach that they were going to tell her what Halp had done.

"Ask him. I'll be curious whether he speaks truthfully." He gave a look to Halp that contained all the disgust he clearly felt, then turned around and continued down the hill. Over his shoulder he said, "His family's alive, for whatever it's worth."

Jesyn watched an almost a physical change come over Halp. He took an involuntary step back and rested his hands on his knees. The two guards following shouldered past them, not caring if they followed or not. She put a gentle hand on the dwarven warrior's shoulder, then helped him stand upright.

"You okay?" she asked.

Halp nodded, his jaw clenching and unclenching as he took a gloved hand and wiped his eyes and face. Letting out a shuddering breath that seemed to come from his stomach, the old warrior stood and collected himself before marching after their escort with Jesyn in tow.

She chose not to pry into Halp's crime but instead inspected the men accompanying Captain Hades.

As they started to move, Jesyn noticed their clothing changed colors, blending with their background so seamlessly they were virtually indistinguishable from the background landscape. She realized this was exactly how Dazra's men had appeared, but the darkness had hidden the extent to which this armor shielded them from sight. She marveled at the magic that made this possible.

Then a glint on the horizon caught her eye. It was like a shining star, sparkling blue and white: a flashing beacon, beckoning to them.

"What is that?"

Captain Hades looked at it, spat to the side, and said, "That, my child is a signal that our arrival has not gone unnoticed. Someone's just rung the dinner bell."

BRIANNA AND

DUNCAN

Yetteje leapt lightly from Arek's arms as they landed near a small depression. To one side was the firstmark in normal form. He looked troubled; his brows drawn together. Tej raised a hand, andAsh shifted his gaze to her. It was only then that she realized he'd been lost in thought, not looking at them at all.

"Daydreaming?" Tej teased to lighten the dark cloud hanging over her friend. In this world, thoughts could bring to life nightfrights or worse. She didn't want the firstmark's troubling thoughts becoming real.

He seemed to understand, because he gave a small chuckle. "No, just trying to figure out what we do next."

Arek had changed form and came to stand beside Tej. He smiled.

"Me too. I have some ideas, but we need Duncan awake."

Ash nodded, then cleared his throat and asked, "What do you want to do with Silbane?" Tej heard the delicacy with which he mentioned the master's name. Clearly Silbane had made a lasting impression on the firstmark, as he had on all of them.

Arek looked at his mentor's body.

"I've been giving this some thought. I think I'd like to leave him here, in Arcadia."

"Why?" Tej asked. There was this undercurrent of hope

in his voice, something that endeared him to her, but at the same time made her wary. She'd personally been on a quest to find her own father. She now knew he could not be brought back, at least not without taking someone else's life. What Silbane had done, according to Duncan, had given more of himself than even death could take. It didn't sound like he'd be coming back.

"This place is growing more powerful in the Way," Arek stated. "Can you feel it?"

Yetteje thought about it. She could feel it, like when the spring sun appeared from behind a cloud and warmed you. You could feel it even with your eyes closed. She nodded and asked, "You know he won't—"

"Yes," Arek cut her off, as if uttering those words aloud might still curse his master—and perhaps it would. "It's not that. I think he would have liked to become one with the Way, and Arcadia is doing just that. I can't think of a better burial for him."

Brianna moved past them to give Duncan a look. She opened her bag and began running a device over his head and body. Yetteje watched her, thinking about what Arek had said. Then she replied, "I think you're right, Arek. I think he would've really liked that."

Arek smiled. Then he turned his attention to Brianna and said, "How's he doing?"

*****

Brianna didn't look up from reading her instruments. Instead she pulled out a vial of nanomeds and snapped it to the end of the injector. She'd used these before on Duncan, so the instrument was already calibrated to his body. Out of habit she eyed it critically nonetheless, making a few minor

110

adjustments before pushing one end into Duncan's neck. The injector gave a satisfying hiss as the nanomeds disappeared into the archmage's body. They would repair him where possible and replace cellular function where not. Then she stopped, noting her own train of thought.

Out of habit? Nanomeds? Why did the hiss of the injector make her feel... happy? No, fulfilled. The blank slate of her past mocked her with silence. She scanned her patient once more, then sighed.

"He'll come around in a few sekunds, give or take. Probably have a terrible headache. He's mostly healed from the battle, but we'll need to take it easy for the next few days."

When Arek didn't answer, Brianna simply rolled her eyes, knowing no one was going to listen to her about the need for rest. She wasn't happy about the risks they were taking, but still, it's not like they were *trying* to get into fights. She got up, her eyes still on Duncan. Just then Arek stumbled and pitched over so that it took both the princess and her to catch him.

"You okay?" Brianna asked.

Arek nodded, "Dizzy. Probably the flight."

He didn't sound convinced, but she let it go. He didn't look any the worse for wear and she'd seen all of them lose their equilibrium when using their other form. Still, she raised the tip of the injector and gave him a quick scan.

Normal, whatever that means here, she thought.

She put the instrument away and met Arek's pale gaze. "Just let me know if you need any help."

Arek nodded, but his attention had been taken by his father regaining consciousness. The man's pale eyes opened. Brianna could almost catch the moment his mind became alert. It was like watching an automaton open its eyes, blank

111

until the spark of sentience erupted. The archmage didn't move but took a deep breath.

"Not dead?" he croaked.

"Not yet," replied the doctor, smiling a bit. She had to give him credit: for all the man had been through, he retained a sense of humor. Amazing to think this was the same person who'd been so obsessed with recovering his wife and Arek that he'd killed—she stopped herself. She hadn't been there. She didn't know the truth. Since she'd met him, Duncan had done nothing but try to help the group. To her, that was the only fair judgement she or anyone could make.

Duncan slowly propped himself up, holding his eyes with one hand. He took another deep, shuddering breath.

"Where are we?"

Brianna knelt back down and touched her forearm. A map appeared floating slightly above her wrist. It showed a blue dot in one spot, and another marked with a pulsing amber dot. "We're here," she said pointing at the blue dot.

Duncan moved his fingers up to the map and made a pinching motion. The view shrank so he could see much more of the world. Then he tapped the amber dot and the view magnified on that location.

That surprised her. "Have you used this interface before?" remarked Brianna.

Duncan nodded, "Courtesy of Lilyth and a lens."

"A lens?" Arek asked. "Like the one we used to enter Avalyon?"

Duncan nodded. "The same." He propped himself up further and rubbed his face.

"And we now know Lilyth used us to invade Avalyon. Not that I'm too upset with the outcome."

The doctor pulled the view back on the map, so the amber marker was back in view.

"This amber dot is an unknown power source," she said. "It reminds me of a—" Her eyes widened, and she felt herself falling into the black well of a vision...

*****

"The power source is here," Sasha said, pointing to an amber dot. "We take it out and we'll have three minutes to hit the objective before backup systems reroute."

"Survivors?" asked Martin. He was dressed in the familiar white and red nanolaminar plate of Search, Tactical, & Recover. He was assigned the number one slot on breach. In addition to his power armor he brandished a powerjack, useful for getting into and out of wrecks. The tool could pry open a vault door if needed.

"A few, but we decompress the interior if we enter," she warned. "Only automated systems will survive."

"What about the override?" he asked, slipping his helmet on and pulling the tacvisor down.

Sasha smiled and held up a small black cylinder that had blue lines tracing through it. "Here," she tossed the object to Martin. "With the cypher protocol embedded."

"Perfect," he said, catching the object deftly despite his armored gloves. He slowly turned to look at Brianna, his smile wicked. "Ready to break your cherry, mudknife?"

*****

Brianna found herself looking up at the sky, with Arek worriedly shaking her. Her head throbbed. She rolled to a seated position.

"What happened?" Duncan asked.

"What did you see?" asked Yetteje.

"I don't know," Brianna answered. "A team in armor, the kind worn by STaR."

"Star? What does that mean? Like a musical troupe?" the princess replied.

Brianna shook her head to clear it, regretting the action when the pounding got worse.

"I think something from my past," she said. Then panic set in. Her eyes widened as she exclaimed, "Mac!" She looked around confused for a moment, "No... M-Martin... and Sasha!"

"What?" asked Arek.

She blinked a few times, "They're names, don't let me forget!" The panic subsided, melting away as fatigue took its place. She looked at Arek again, "It's fading... I was on a ship maybe... they had a cypher...." She looked around helplessly, her eyes finally coming to rest on Duncan, who seemed to be deep in thought.

Yetteje leaned in and asked, "Maybe that stuff you gave yourself is working?"

Brianna shook her head, "I was somewhere else. It felt real, like something I'd actually done."

"I think that's the definition of a vision," opined Ash. "It feels real, but it isn't. You could just be suffering from your connection to him," he jerked his chin at Duncan, somehow conveying both anger and disgust with the gesture.

Brianna took a deep breath "From the nothing-is-a-coincidence standpoint, the fact that Arek and I both lost consciousness worries me."

"Yeah, coincidence is a bitch protecting all its pups," Ash said. He looked around and this time addressed the whole group.

"I hate to rush this, but we need to move and talk. Staying in one place will eventually give rise to nightfrights or worse and get us killed. What's our plan?"

That seemed aimed at Arek. The young adept looked to his father. "I think we should make our way to this power source."

Duncan smiled and nodded. "Good instincts. That's Harmagedon. A gate lies there."

"A gate!" exclaimed the firstmark. "A way home?" Then he snarled, "And you're just telling us now."

With Yetteje's help, Brianna was able to get herself and Duncan to their feet. The archmage looked at their small party and said, "I just woke up, Firstmark, didn't you notice?"

He turned back to Arek.

"Each of the gates is guarded by a Celestial, the most powerful of the Aeris. The one guarding Harmagedon is Zafir, Lord of the East Gate. I'm not sure if he is in league with Lilyth or not, but with the fall of Avalyon and Olympious, it's the only gate I know of."

"This talk of gates twists my head," Brianna said, the sudden vision and now fading memory of her past, and the idea of jumping from place to place coming together in a jumble of emotions. She blinked a few times.

"How could Lilyth's city just disappear?" she asked.

"Think of Arcadia and Edyn occupying the same space but shifted a bit so that we don't see each other," Duncan said. "The passageways in-between are guarded by these gates. The dwarves have been hiding in between, to evade both Lilyth and Sovereign. Now we must barter our way through Harmagedon to return to Edyn." He paused, deep in thought.

"At least that's how I thought of it until Silbane shared his vision."

"Barter?" asked Arek, evidently missing what his father

had just said. "We defeated Valarius and his army. I—"

"Be careful. Overconfidence is not a virtue," warned Duncan. "We barely—"

"Says the red mage," Ash said, his voice dripping with sarcasm.

Duncan closed his eyes and seemed to do a mental count before picking up where he left off.

"We barely escaped with our lives and only because of Lilyth and Sovereign's intervention." The archmage took a deep, cleansing breath and clapped Arek on the shoulder. "We need to learn how Zafir plans on escaping Arcadia. Surely, he doesn't wish to perish here either, and he cannot leave without a body."

"But none of us can be possessed," remarked Arek. "We've all bonded to an Aeris already."

Duncan cocked his head at that, then looked pointedly at Brianna.

Brianna saw his look and could feel the blood drain from her face.

"Oh, no…" she said.

"We won't let anything happen," Arek promised. He turned back to Duncan and said, "It's not negotiable."

Duncan's lack of agreement or response of any type seemed to raise everyone's ire. Ash confronted the archmage.

"Just one more sacrifice, right?" he snarled. "You killed an entire fortress to get here, so what's one more life to get out?"

"Back away, Firstmark," warned Duncan. "I'm not the man you met in Edyn. Silbane's sacrifice gifted me as well, and I'll not be—"

Ash's fist lashed out faster than an eyeblink, hitting Duncan squarely on the point of his chin. The archmage toppled like a felled tree.

"Been wanting to do that since he opened his yap."

"Stop it!" cried Yetteje, pushing herself in between the towering firstmark and Duncan's prostrate form. "I'll not have fighting between us. Am I clear, Firstmark?"

"He's insuffera—"

"Am I clear?" she repeated, her eyes flashing yellow, as anger consumed her and the living sun within showed itself for the briefest of moments.

Ash stepped back shaking his head, then threw his hands up.

"Whatever. He's a dead man anyway. The only question is, when." Then he must have caught Arek's eyes on him. He looked down, and Brianna stepped in.

"She's right. We can't fight amongst ourselves," she said. The words sounded stupid to her, but she wasn't alone.

When Arek looked about to challenge that, Yetteje spoke in a voice ringing with command: "Don't say a word. We're going to stick together, and we're going to find that power source. No one is taking Brianna, and no one is going to harm your father."

Arek's head hung down, and it looked like the anger washed out of him. He let loose a heavy sigh.

"Fine." Working his way around them he knelt next to his father and asked, "Are you okay?"

Duncan was just regaining consciousness, his eyes wide and unfocused for the second time today. He slowly propped himself up on an elbow, rubbing his jaw. "What?"

Arek repeated, "Are you okay?"

A small laugh escaped as the archmage spit some blood. "I've been worse."

"I know," Arek agreed.

Brianna helped them both to their feet, checking

Duncan's eyes again and making sure there had been no permanent harm. Satisfied, she backed away.

"Let's make our way to that power source," Arek said. "We can't plan our next move until we know what's going on at the gate."

"One moment," Duncan said, raising a hand. "I'd like to speak to you alone, if you don't mind."

Brianna saw that both Ash and Yetteje had started to move, but Duncan's statement made them pause. Yetteje stepped forward and said, "Anything you say can be said to the whole group." When Arek looked at her the princess replied, "Sorry, but he's not earned our trust yet." By "our," she clearly meant herself and Ash.

Arek began to object but Duncan held up a hand saying, "I don't want an unforeseen circumstance to cause Silbane's last message to Arek to be lost. I thought to share it with him, in private."

There was a feeling of palpable embarrassment. No one wanted to intrude, but evidently the distrust of the archmage outweighed Arek's privacy. Yetteje held her ground, waiting for Arek to say something.

After a long moment, Arek said, "It's okay. Tell everyone."

"Are you sure?" Duncan asked.

Arek nodded. "Go ahead."

The archmage looked at the group, shrugged, and said, "You've been given the Sight for a reason. Silbane says we're not real, but instead embodiments of the Way. Your bonded mate, Azrael, has a higher purpose than Ascension. His destiny, Silbane felt, is greater than ours."

"We're not real?" Brianna asked. Her thoughts swirled around the vision she'd had. That seemed real, but so did this. How could she discern the truth? A small part of her wondered if all of this was an elaborate hallucination, a dream created by her subconscious as she lay in a coma somewhere. That was easier to believe than dragons, demons, and castles teleporting to other dimensions.

"How could he know this?" asked Arek, his eyes wide and his voice barely over a whisper.

"Perhaps he glimpsed some underlying truth while trying to save you. Even I don't truly understand, but he was insistent that you know this."

"I certainly feel real," quipped Yetteje. She looked at the group defiantly, "And whether or not anything Master Silbane said is true, it doesn't change the fact that we still feel pain, fear, and the will to survive."

There was silence, but it didn't last long. Ash said, "The princess is right. Unless you're giving up, his observations don't matter much."

Arek didn't look so well, thought Brianna. He looked like he was trying to come to grips with all this and failing. She could empathize.

"Let's all take a breath. I think Arek's master wanted the best for him, so if he wanted this message conveyed, there must be a reason for it that's more than to create some sort of existential crisis."

"Big word, for someone who doesn't remember her past," remarked Duncan, without any apparent cruelty.

Still, Ash snapped back, "Maybe you're just thankless. She's the only reason you're alive."

"I meant no—"

"Shut up! Just stop it." Yetteje stepped in again. She heaved a sigh, shaking her head. "We're never going to get out of here if we keep this up. And believe me, the red mage is low on my list of favorites."

Though she said it to the group, to Brianna her words

seemed aimed at Ash, who bowed his head and stepped back. The silence stretched out as each weighed their personal thoughts, until Duncan cleared his throat. Brianna had a feeling she knew what he was going to say, and though it was the truth, a part of her still feared Arek and what he might do.

"There's one more thing." He seemed almost apologetic.

"To unravel Valarius's spell took everything we had. I'm not sure what we did is permanent." He looked at Brianna, who nodded, knowing what the archmage said was true. Duncan grasped his son's shoulders. "The blackfire may still return."

Arek's eyes shifted from Duncan to Brianna, filled with uncertainty. Brianna could feel the air grow colder, as if his mood affected the world around them. She remembered the frantic effort to undo the spell of the highlord, fighting with every ounce of her medical knowledge to counter the insidious spread of what could only be thought of as a disease. If the blackfire returned, she doubted she could do anything to slow or stop it this time.

"He's right," she quickly offered, hoping Arek wasn't getting angry. "We did everything we could, but it's like a cancer."

"A what?" asked Arek.

Brianna looked around, frustrated at knowing but not knowing how she knew. It must've shown in her eyes, because Yetteje put a hand on her forearm.

"Easy, relax," the princess said. "We're just not used to hearing some of your words used the way they are."

"How do you use it?" asked Brianna.

Arek said, "Can we have a history lesson later? Are you both saying I'll become that thing again?"

"I don't know," Duncan said. "But Silbane said the world

needs you."

"What does that mean?" asked Arek, clearly exasperated. "Why not just tell me what to do?"

Duncan's demeanor went from apologetic to a small laugh. "I don't think he knew. But whatever needs to happen, it must have something to do with our bonded Aeris."

"Maybe your master had faith you could figure this out. He believed in you," Ash said, cinching his pack and slinging it over his arm. He looked around, that wariness of a warrior in enemy territory returning to his gaze. "We've spent more time here than we should, and things are going to start to come. We better move."

Arek nodded, but added, "Let's find a good place for my master's remains. Then we can be on our way."

Brianna's mind was swirling with implications, muddled by her vision and a small amount of rising panic. As Arek moved over to his master's still form, she turned to Duncan and asked, "What do you think is going to happen?"

The man just stared at his son, silent and motionless. Finally, he turned his pale eyes to her and said, "This is far from over, healer. Even if we get out of Arcadia, Lilyth is in Edyn and Sovereign will follow. What I did to the four fortresses will pale in comparison to the war between them."

Brianna turned to look at Arek, watching him kneel and adjust something on Silbane's body. She could see the orange sunlight slowly moving as it artificially set on this island's horizon, the shadows becoming long and black. "What did he mean about cancer being a history lesson?"

There was silence as the sun disappeared and the island plunged into a sudden twilight. From the gloom Duncan said, "The legend of Kanseer has many versions, but generally refers to a person unaware of their true strength. They let emotion rule over logic, charging into battle though the odds may be against them."

Brianna watched Arek, thinking about what the archmage had just said. "It's not what I meant, but it's pretty unnerving in similarity." Then she turned to face Duncan, unable to keep the worry out of her voice. "This isn't going to end well."

Duncan put a hand on her arm and said, "You felt it. Silbane believed Arek is our only hope. Arek needs to get back to Edyn, even if it means we all die."

THE DWARVEN

CAMP

J esyn followed Captain Hades as they made their way quickly down the hillside to the camp below. Neither of the guards talked to Halp, their interactions limited to short gestures aimed at her, usually to hold her position. Some heartbeats would pass and then they'd motion her forward. Jesyn couldn't figure out why until she realized there were camouflaged sentries hidden in the rocks. It was unclear if they even cared if Halp followed them or not.

If Jesyn asked a question, Captain Hades would slow the pace to answer. He was courteous but taciturn. Jesyn felt uncomfortably that they were continually snubbing Halp. Therefore, the young adept didn't engage the captain or his guards much. Her goal was to see Arcimedis, as Tarin had suggested, not further embarrass Halp by bringing attention to the disparity in their treatment.

Soon they passed a loose collection of dwarven warriors that to Jesyn marked the entrance to the camp proper. Ahead she saw a makeshift triage area with wounded and dead laid out on soft earth. Some parts of the ground had turned into a strange rust-colored mud—earth soaked with blood, a carmine mix of life and death.

Dwarven healers, of which there were only a few, flitted

123

between patients, doing what they could. The mountain's explosion had crushed limbs and sliced open flesh with heavy rock and razor-sharp shale. Without true medical facilities or magic, the adept didn't see how much succor could be given. It seemed the main effort was providing comfort to those in their final hours.

Other dwarves arrived carrying a constant stream of either wounded comrades or supplies foraged from the mountain. They split, with the wounded taken to the medical area and the supplies taken to wherever they were most needed. The area was chaotic with activity, the cries of wounded and those separated from loved ones mixing together in a somber dirge that pulled at Jesyn's heart.

They strode through this without slackening pace, their destination a cluster of warriors ringing an area overhung by a slab of stone. It was a shelter of sorts, hundreds of paces wide but shallow, like a giant finger had carved it out from the mountainside. It was here that the uninjured gathered, bringing with them weapons and food. Everything was arranged in an orderly fashion, but Jesyn wondered why the wounded were left in the open. A small tremor from Dawnlight shifting answered her question. If the mountainside collapsed, this area could be easily evacuated by phasing, but the injured might not be able to save themselves.

At a signal from the captain, Jesyn and Halp were told to wait. "I'll report in and return," he rasped.

"I need to see Arcimedis," Jesyn reminded.

"We know," was all he said back, before turning away and disappearing with his men into the crowd of survivors. They'd been left in the company of six or eight men-at-arms, not quite in custody, but the ring of men served as a deterrent to wandering. No one seemed to recognize Halp, who kept his eyes down and his mouth silent. Jesyn pursed her lips, her brows coming together, and approached the old warrior.

"Okay, what did you do?"

Halp sat down and put his arms on his knees. "Now is not the time, adept."

"It better be, because we're about to see their leader and if he's going to be influenced by your presence, I want to know why."

Halp raised his head, his eyes even with hers from his seated position. "Don't worry, Arcimedis won't see me."

"Why?" demanded Jesyn. "What did you do that was so terrible?"

The dwarven warrior rubbed his face, his skin turning red. She couldn't tell if it was from embarrassment or from the rough gloves he wore. Finally, after searching her eyes for something only he could see, Halp replied, "The worst crime my people can do is killing each other. We are so few, murder is inexcusable."

Jesyn pulled her head back, confusion on her face. "You kill the blacknights. You killed that guard under the mountain. Aren't they dwarves?"

"Murder is not my crime, girl. Our law dictates that whatever outcome preserves the most lives must be pursued, even if it means self-sacrifice. But..." Halp trailed off for a moment before picking up, "Possession was new to us; sometimes there are worse things than murder."

His eyes grew distant, reliving something his upthrust lip said he deeply regretted. Then he took a deep breath and met Jesyn's eyes.

"Lilyth cannot be allowed to capture our bodies. The creatures these Aeris become are insidious, destructive, and more seductive than you can imagine. Do you understand?" His eyes now focused on Jesyn with narrow intensity.

125

Seductive? That was a strange word to use to describe demons. Jesyn didn't answer, not really knowing what he meant. It couldn't be something as simple as killing another dwarf, that would never elicit such anger as Captain Hades and his men had shown. Something far worse must have happened, and interrupting Halp now might stop him from talking.

Into the silence Halp said, "Possession is far worse than you think. The creature takes over, becoming part of the person they possess. The body is still yours—but also someone else's. Without magic weapons, killing the Aeris inside is impossible. You can only… kill the host." He put his head into his hands, murmuring to himself.

Jesyn was about to reply when a voice behind her said, "Adept Jesyn, follow me please."

She turned and saw a dwarven warrior, a woman with bright red hair, beckoning to her. She looked back at Halp and tried to help the giant warrior up, saying, "Come on."

"Not him," added the woman. "Just you."

"He's got information you need about Sovereign," Jesyn said.

The warrior tilted her head in thought, then asked, "Were you two separated at any point?"

Halp chuckled. "I told you Arcimedis won't see me and you'll soon hear why. Just keep yer wits about you. Tarin chose right."

Jesyn watched him, not sure what to do until the guard spoke up again. "If you weren't separated, then you know everything he does. Let's go."

She then patted Halp on the shoulder and moved over to the woman. "Your name?"

"Elsa." The woman looked out over the camp, spotting something or someone, then gave a signal on a raised hand.

Without another word, Elsa turned and set a brisk pace, almost a run for Jesyn, given her smaller strides. They wound their way past many dozens of fires being built with scraps and detritus from the ravaged interior of Dawnlight.

Not wanting to assume anything, Jesyn pitched her voice to be heard and asked, "Where are we going?"

Elsa didn't turn her head.

"You insisted on seeing Arcimedis," she said. "You're getting your wish."

They walked for a few hundred paces, dodging survivors and men burdened with supplies and weapons. What had seemed a small camp from the heights now hit her with the glaring reality of sights and smells of hundreds of people trying to shelter in place. Black and red rock dust smeared most faces like elemental war paint. Some wandered about looking for kin, others just sat in misery, hugging their knees to their chests. No one looked unscathed.

They finally slowed, approaching a ring of men and women armed and armored better than most. Elsa stopped and waited, motioning Jesyn to do the same. They didn't wait long as two men left the ring and came to them, greeting Jesyn's escort with a smile.

"You're expected. Follow." The man never looked at the adept, but his eyes looked kind, and sad. Jesyn thought he must have lost someone dear to him, then realized her thought was an understatement and an insult to just how many dwarves had likely died. Everyone here had lost someone, a fact she'd best not forget.

They were escorted past the ring, finally approaching a table made from a slab of granite, polished so smoothly on top so that it reflected the shapes of those gathered around it. A dwarf stood to one side, short and what could best be described as fat. Everyone around him seemed deferential.

The top of his head was bare, but a ring of red hair fell from the sides to create a horseshoe-like curtain that covered his ears and neck. His face was covered in golden stubble, wispy but visible in the torchlight flaring up around the table and camp as dusk fell upon them in the rapid fashion that was the norm for the islands of Arcadia. The man raised a hand and beckoned to her to step forward.

"Come around here, girl. We need to talk, and I don't want to yell just to be heard," he said.

Jesyn made her way around the table. No one seemed worried she would bring harm to the man. In fact, except for Elsa trailing discreetly behind her, no one paid much attention to her at all. She would have thought someone of her race appearing in camp in Arcadia would have created more of a stir.

Jesyn bowed. "I'm Jesyn Shornhelm, Adept of the Way."

"Well met, adept. I am Arcimedis, defacto leader until Dazra's return. I'd like to know his fate and that of the team that entered Sovereign's Dawnlight. Are they still alive?"

Jesyn paused to think. She quickly realized that much like with Dazra, the truth was better than obfuscation. She recounted the capture of the blacknight assassin by Dragor and herself, how they met Dazra's people, and their decision to infiltrate the mountain using the markers Tarin had found in the assassin's blood. She also told them of Sai'ken, and how the dragon had aided them until they'd been found. The last she'd heard of Dazra had been from her companion Dragor, also an adept of the Way. They'd been on a mission to find the dwarven people she now stood before. That had been right before Tarin had activated her entat and sent her here. She didn't know if Dazra lived, only that Tarin had been alive when she was transported away.

Arcimedis was silent for a moment, then said, "I

appreciate your honesty, adept. Once you entered, only your testimony speaks for their fate."

It seemed the man could discern truth from lie? She wondered what the consequences would have been had she chosen to lie. But Tarin had trusted him, and she trusted Tarin.

"What happens now?" she asked.

Arcimedis raised an eyebrow.

"Now? Lilyth has offered us up as sacrifice to her Aeris furies. They will no doubt attack and possess us, then use our bodies and the gate at Harmagedon to escape to Edyn."

When he said this, he pointed to a spot on the horizon, where a column of light shot straight up into the night sky. It was the same spire she'd seen before, but much clearer now that the sun had set.

"What is that?"

"A gate, a portal home. However, we cannot use it without the gatekeeper's consent."

Jesyn chewed her lip, thinking. "How many of you are there?"

"Perhaps five hundred survivors, give or take," Arcimeis said. "Close to two thousand died in that mountain." He said this without emotion, but Jesyn sensed the deep anguish within him, held in check by an iron will. Another dwarf came and handed him some papers, which he took a moment to inspect.

"What can I do to help?" Jesyn asked into the pause.

The dwarven leader looked at her from under bushy red eyebrows. "What *can* you do to help?" he asked this with a small smile, but his meaning was clear. Was she of any use or just another mouth to feed?

"Tarin trusted me. I am integrating with the entats she injected. Maybe I can—"

Arcimedis raised a hand.

"We will be under assault very soon," he said. "Rather than allow our bodies to be used by Lilyth's Aeris, we will self-sacrifice."

It took a moment for Jesyn to understand. Then she exclaimed, "Wait, you're going to kill yourselves?"

Arcimedis looked surprised. "Yes."

"How do you know it will even work?" asked Jeysn.

"We know that when the host dies, the Aeris leaves to find another. If they could inhabit dead bodies, they would have done so. Except for a few powerful ones, they cannot."

"But why kill yourselves? The gate to Edyn is right there. Let's take it by force if necessary." Jesyn felt frustration at Arcimedis's attitude and apparently nonchalant willingness to die. She added, "Dazra wouldn't agree."

Arcimedis sighed, then looked at her with the expression of a man quickly tiring of the conversation. "Don't lecture me on what Dazra would do. His mission to recover our people from Sovereign was as much of a suicide mission as this. Perhaps Dawnlight would never have transitioned to Arcadia had he remained with his people." He paused, and to Jesyn he looked like he was calculating something. Then he turned his attention back to her and said, "There is something you can do, however."

Jesyn was eager to help in any way, especially if it meant delaying this crazy scheme of Arcimedis. "Of course, just tell me what."

The fat dwarf leaned in close so that only she and perhaps Elsa could hear. "Go back to Halperion Dane and put a knife in his heart."

FLASHBACK:

SANDPREYS

A lion cut a sandprey out of the air, the eel-like body falling in two pieces before spasming, neither half yet knowing it was dead. She spun, careful of Trysh as the scout maneuvered herself like her shadow, sticking as close as possible. Trysh probably wished she'd brought a shield rather than two blades, as there were literally thousands of sandpreys flinging themselves at the pair. Even Deft knew she couldn't prevail using Reaper. Instead, she took a step to cover the scout and stabbed the blade into the ground, calling on her own faith to do what she needed.

Deft screamed, "Blaze!" and a circle of blue fire exploded outward around Deft's party, racing to the edges of the cavern. Wherever the fire touched, sandprey died, their forms burned to ash. A grunt of pain pulled her attention to the scout, who was pulling at a sandprey attached to her upper leg. The circular mouth was lined with small teeth designed to latch on while the creature drained its prey of blood.

"No!" yelled Deft, stopping Trysh from pulling the creature free. She swiped once with her blade and Reaper separated the creature's head from its body. "Get a torch on it or you'll bleed out," she said. She didn't wait to see if the scout obeyed, instead turning her attention back to the tunnel

131

and the swarm of sandprey regrouping after her blue-white conflagration.

The sudden flicker of yellow and their dancing shadows said the scout had relit a torch. The scream that came next testified fire had met flesh, hopefully staunching the bleeding wound. "We need to pull back," gasped Trysh from behind.

Still alive. Good.

"I know," said the knight. She held Reaper now horizontally in front of her. "Oil!" she said, reaching back with her off hand.

The scout dropped a flask into her palm. Alion moved forward quickly, her smooth gait denying that below her leg armor lay only wasted muscle and rags of skin. Reaper's pommel smashed open the oil at the ceramic neck. Next the knight used the point of her blade to cut a channel across their path. It was done quickly, Deft pouring oil down her blade to fill the line the point had dug into the earth. Shadows danced with her blade and bottle, a dark pantomime of the strange scene painting the walls. Nevertheless, oil poured into the channel and ran across their path.

Not enough oil, tunnel's too wide, she realized with dismay. *Still, some is better than none.* She looked back at the scout, who looked pale and shaken. "Light it up."

Trysh nodded and stabbed her torch into the line of oil. A small blue and orange combustion of gas prefaced the ignition of the oil mixture itself, designed to burn quickly with as little as a spark. Instantly the scout scrambled back and away from the wall of fire that erupted across the tunnel.

As Alion had feared, the fire only reached as far as the oil had run, about two thirds across, leaving a path on the left a man could easily walk through. The knight didn't care, grabbing Trysh by her light armor and hauling her back toward their landing site at a full run. She could hear the damn creatures skittering about, though the intensity of the heat seemed to keep them at bay.

That won't last.

True to her thought, the sounds of tiny claws now advanced on tunnel walls and floors. It looked like a black swarm of snakes, except these covered every surface of the tunnel and were drawn to them like moths to flame.

Alion had run at almost full tilt, making it back to their landing and dumping Trysh unceremoniously onto the platform. The pulley system was designed for two people to operate but Deft didn't have a choice. She grasped the rope and pulled, making their platform rise in response.

"Kill anything comi—," the knight began to say, but Trysh had collapsed onto her back. "Get up!" she screamed, breaking the girl's shock.

The injured scout nodded dumbly, gathering her blades like she was drunk and fumbling her way to an edge on her stomach. There wasn't much light except for the torch she'd discarded near the landing area. It had bought them some time, as the knight could hear the sandpreys had stopped. They didn't seem to want to enter its yellow circle. Even as she hauled on their ascent rope, the torchlight sputtered and died. Instantly the sounds changed to the keening of hungry mouths, rows of teeth sucking air through them, all desperately trying to find their prey.

Maybe the single tail of rope didn't attract enough interest for them to know it was their prey's escape route. Whatever the reason, it didn't matter. Her Witch gaze revealed the sandprey still avoided the rectangle of light cast by the desert moon, as dim as it was – just like the torch. Perhaps it wasn't heat, but light of any sort... "Forget the weapons, haul that rope up behind us!"

The girl followed her directions with the automatic pace of someone doing something because that told them they were alive. Still, they made topside to the surprised look of Paramus and a curse from Malioch.

"Saw ya pullin' up. You're too fast for me to grab slack and watch the rig. The scholar here . . ." he gestured to Paramus, still on his rump looking confused as to what exactly he ought to be doing. Nothing more needed saying.

Alion hitched her rope as soon as Mal tied the safety. Then she stepped off the platform and kicked Paramus in the shins.

"What!" he cried, rubbing them with one hand; the other held a torch. His expression said there'd been a horrible miscarriage of justice. She wished she could do worse, but Deft didn't say anything, she just let out a sigh.

"Parz it'z eezy. I'll show ya how," said the scout, but her words came out like she was drunk. She'd jumped off the slightly swaying platform as well, but stumbled as weight on her injured leg caused it to collapse. Paramus was there, catching her before she hit the ground. Without a word, the boy dragged Trysh away as quickly as possible, probably to get as far from Deft as possible.

Alion turned to Mal. "That was close. We need a faster way up. Any ideas?"

The slaver nodded, "Sure, but depends on what was after ya."

"Sandprey. They've infested the place. More'n I can count."

"Hmmm," grunted Malioch. He thought for a second, then asked, "Ya care much 'bout a camel?"

"No," replied the knight, unbuckling Reaper. The blade was almost useless against small swarming enemies. She was mentally reviewing her other weapons when Trysh

134

returned, looking slightly better. She was carrying a gutbag but looked at her blade and asked, "Won't you need that for the fire thing?"

Alion shook her head. "It's just a tool. How's your leg?"

Trysh shrugged, "Paramus gave me something to drink. Perked me up."

"Well," Deft said, looking up at the sky, "we've got a few hours of darkness left—"

A sudden scream erupted from Trysh as she looked down at the head of the sandprey still hanging from her calf. This close it looked like a piece of intestine with teeth on one end. She pulled her hands up and away in an uncharacteristic way. "I didn't realize it was still there until my other leg brushed...," she looked like she was going to be sick.

Alion nodded grimly.

"Their spit deadens feeling. You'll be thankful for it in a bit when we unhook its teeth and dress the wound." She took a closer look. "Not to mention that burn. You did quite a job on yourself." She met Trysh's gaze, her respect for the scout growing. She'd not hesitated to use that torch. That took more than just guts.

"Come on," she said, clapping Trysh gently on the shoulder, "let's get you cleaned up." She gestured for the gutbag, which contained almost everything she'd need to treat the wound. It opened from the top, then unfolded on each side into trays. Deft extracted scissors and caught the scout's attention. "This may hurt."

"Go ahead," Trysh said. "I want that thing off me."

"Hmmm," grunted the knight. As she worked, she explained, "You don't want to pull these off. All that will do is create a wound that won't stop bleeding. I've seen men"— she snipped once or twice at dead skin, watching the scout carefully to see if the girl flinched, but it seemed the sandprey's spittle had done its trick well—"bleed out quickly, jets of red blood gushing out of a palm-sized wound in time with their hearts." She pulled the head clear and placed it carefully on a tray to one side, then grabbed a bottle filled with liquid.

"Now that wasn't so bad," she said with a smile she knew looked horrible regardless of what she did. Lucky the shahwal was still in place. "But this next part is going to hurt."

"Really?" asked Trysh, somehow reminding Alion of a child.

The knight paused, then said, "Oh, yeah. A lot." Then she pressed the gauze she'd been soaking while she had Trysh's attention. The move was sudden, and she pressed it in with vise-like grip, quickly wrapping it in place with more cotton bandages while maintaining pressure.

Though the scream erupting from Trysh could've awakened the dead, it was thankfully short-lived. Before Alion could finish the dressing, the scout had passed out.

NIALL AND YEVAINE

A company of men had left Haven under the command of Queen Yevaine to reinforce Bara'cor. Of that number, less than half survived the destruction of the fortress. Perhaps fifty were uninjured, the rest had anything from minor cuts to crushed limbs. The elven scouts went to work, trying to heal the most critical ones first, then moving on to those with less serious injuries. Usually each scout could have only healed one or two men, but with the Way growing stronger, they found themselves able to do much more. By the time Sparrow had organized the troops into decanus, consisting of approximately ten men each, the majority of Bara'cor's soldiers were on their feet.

"We're ready to descend," reported Zedakai. He looked eager, as if the prospect of getting out of the underdark pleased him.

To Niall, it was clear his elves did not like this underworld any more than he did. He motioned Sparrow. "How quickly can we get down the Giant's Step?"

Sparrow's face lit with a half smile.

"Very quickly, my king, providing the men of Bara'cor don't panic." She looked out over the clusters of ten soldiers each, then added, "We won't need the ropes. Each decanus will use five men to descend with one of Bara'cor's soldiers."

Niall nodded and then addressed his small army. "To me!" The men gathered in a loose formation. He waited until the hubbub had died down then said, "We'll descend together, but the elves will take the lead. Men of Bara'cor, do not fight them! Let them carry you as they will. They are sure-footed and fast. They will see you safely to the ground." He looked at Kalindor to give the final order.

"All right, you motherless sons, move!" shouted the captain.

Teams of elves grabbed the men they'd been assigned to. At first confusion reigned, but when the first group of two edged closer to the precipice leading down the man began to struggle. "No!" he wailed just as the pair suddenly vaulted off the edge and into the blackness.

"What?" Niall exclaimed. "They're jumping!"

Sparrow nodded, her tone pitched so that everyone could hear, "They will reach the bottom safely with each man." Suddenly, teams made up of an elf and a man of Bara'cor headed into the darkness below.

Niall ran to the edge along with most of the Galadine men to watch the plummet of their comrades. They fell with arms interlocked like two rings. At each outcropping, branch, or other finger-hold, the elf would reach out and slow their fall. The man was still screaming in fear, the plummet into the darkness lit only by torches dropped to illuminate the landing ledges scattered along the way. And who could blame him? Those at the top began to push back in fear, watching their comrades as each was grabbed by a team of elves and forced into the arms of their falling partner. It was too much, even for seasoned men-at-arms. They began trying to escape.

Niall had been astounded at his elven forces' capabilities, at each turn revealing another new facet of their skill and bravery. The men of Bara'cor frustrated him with their ignorance and he looked about in frustration. Why didn't they understand?

Stupid cowards, he thought, I know what's best for them. He motioned to Sparrow, who gave a short whistle. Immediately each team's scout scratched their assignee with something, maybe their nail? Instantly the man scratched felt his limbs grow numb as a paralysis took hold. It did not make them unconscious, just unable to fight back.

Niall smiled at this until his mother came to him, screaming hysterically. He wasn't quite sure what her point was, something about freedom and choice? What did it matter, he was king and his decision would be followed. Valarius had told him people often thought they wanted choice, but in reality, what they wanted was direction. He would provide that now.

Before his mother became too annoying, he nodded to Sparrow, who pricked the queen mother with her herbal toxin. The paralysis spread and suddenly all Niall could hear was the wonderful silence of his elves as they moved quickly and surely down the interior of Land's Edge.

When everyone had gone, he and Zedakai launched themselves over the side, their wings tucked, and fell into the darkness. Niall could see clearly, his eyes adjusting quickly so that everything was illuminated. He'd initially been afraid of flying, but as his comfort with his new form grew, his fears lessened. The joy of soaring had overcome any fears he'd created in his mind. Indeed, Valarius had been right. The archmage had made him in such a way that he feared nothing now, nothing at all.

At some point, he unfurled his wings, aiming for the bright spot of one of the torches marking the floor of the Giant's Step. He and Zedakai landed there lightly, looking around in pride. His troops far exceeded any of the men they brought down, even Kalindor. That would have to be fixed, he told himself, at the earliest opportunity.

"Grandfather," Niall said to the older Galadine, "we must make more of my elves if we are to survive against Lilyth's forces."

Zedakai nodded, a small smile already lighting his face. "Valarius knew this and gave each king something to give you, just in case some of us did not survive." He reached behind his armor and withdrew an pendant shaped like a bird with wings outstretched. Unclasping the chain, he handed the golden pendant to Niall.

"The house sigil for Valarius," Zedakai said. He ran his finger over the edge and pushed a small release. The bird figure flipped open, and inside Niall could see a desiccated bone, perhaps of a finger. "This is all that is left of Valarius's original body. I will show you how to use it to create more elven brothers and sisters. Fear not, for this is enough to change every man serving you now a thousand times over. You will truly be the king of a new world, Niall Galadine, and bring peace and order to your realms."

Niall looked at him, his eyes shining. "I like the sound of that."

"Valarius had high hopes for you, Highlord. You are the instrument of his vision."

One of the elves landed with her charge, a man still gibbering with fear. Niall stepped forward and grabbed him by the collar, hauling him up to his feet. "Silence! You are a man of Bara'cor. Stand strong."

Something in his demeanor or words must have gotten through, for the soldier swallowed and stood. He was still shaking but had a grip on himself. Another landed, and as Niall watched, the elves scratched him again, no doubt a remedy the paralysis. As they became free, many let out screams that had been stifled by the toxins, some collapsing as the fear finally had outlet.

Niall picked up men who'd collapsed, pushing them aside. He congratulated those who brought themselves under control for their bravery and steadfastness and labeled those who did not as cowards. This created a separation between the men, as those who were congratulated grouped together, not wanting to be associated with those who'd earned the young king's displeasure.

Soon the last of the teams had arrived and assembled into a cohort plus one century of Bara'cor men-at-arms, most fully recovered from the toxin the elves had used to control them. The six hundred warriors arranged in an arc looked tiny and insignificant in the vast area at the bottom of the cliff. A single path cut into the rock wound down, wide enough for two men. It led to the exit at the base of Land's Edge. Niall knew they had traversed a distance that would normally have taken troops days to rappel, and again thanked Valarius for gifting him with such amazing soldiers.

His mother, also recovered from her paralysis, moved to stand by his side. She did not look happy and would not meet his eye, but he was less concerned about that. He nodded to Kalindor, but the man averted his eyes as well, only giving him the acknowledgment his rank demanded. Well, he too would learn that a new king ruled them, or he would be replaced.

He looked over the men assembled and said, "I mean to march on Haven and lay my rightful claim to the Imperial Crown, the crown of my father!"

To this the elves cheered. It was hard not to be swept up by the momentous change that Niall represented, a new monarch.

"Every one of you who followed me down that precipice, who took a step with me into the darkness, will be rewarded and recognized, for you fell into the rebirth of a new life.

141

You will be the leaders of our new army, and together we will bring peace and order to our lands!"

This time the cheering was more enthusiastic. Perhaps his mother was right, and a few words delivered well was all these sheep needed. Even she looked somewhat pleased, as if he'd done something right. He smiled at her and finished, "We move on Haven and from there we stand against Lilyth and her demons. You will become legends to our people. Your deeds will become the stuff of myths to children everywhere!"

Six hundred voices cheered Niall, who raised his hands to encompass the men before him. He spread his wings and the cheering increased.

This is what it's like to be king, he thought. I will bring Valarius's dreams to life, and my people will love me for it.

REUNION

Y ou want me to do what?" Jesyn asked, her mind stumbling over what the dwarven leader had just said.

"Kill the man who accompanied you here. He deserves no better, and as we are all going to die anyway, it would only be justice served."

"Wait, what did he do?" Jesyn said. "Everyone acts like he killed a child or something."

Arcimedis raised a bushy eyebrow at that, then shrugged and said, "He did far worse. He fell in love with a demon."

The young adept took a mental step back. "What do you mean?"

Arcimedis tilted his head to one side as if trying to ascertain if Jesyn were daft. Then he repeated, "He let an innocent woman be possessed so he could be with his demon lover."

Jesyn could feel herself becoming overwhelmed with questions. She closed her eyes and willed herself into a calm state, feeling the Way wash through her and bringing clarity of thought. Then she looked at the dwarven leader and asked, "Who was the woman?"

Elsa stepped forward and said, "His mate."

At Arcimedis's nod, Elsa continued, "We had to kill her, despite our restriction against killing our own. He was banished to the Seekers because there was no place for him at Dawnlight and we wished to minimize bloodshed. It was a mistake."

Jesyn shook her head and said, "Halp let his mate get

possessed? And then protected the creature she became? How do you know it was voluntary? What if she got possessed and he did it to protect his—" A half a dozen questions fought to be voiced, but Arcimedis interrupted her with a motion to stop.

"We have Halp's own confession. He believes our destiny is to bond with these Aeris and gave his mate over to that end. He made his children motherless and turned his back on his people."

Elsa then added, "Whether you do it or we do, Halp is a dead man. Perhaps if you agree, it will be a kinder thing."

"No!" exclaimed Jesyn. "I'm no executioner! I'm getting back to Edyn and the war that Lilyth and Sovereign are bringing against us. You all talk about suicide, of killing each other instead of joining me and lending your strength to Edyn's defense. Cowards!" She shook her head, unable to fathom their logic.

Arcimedis slowly lowered his palms in a placating gesture and said, "Adept, we have only just met. Allow me the benefit of perhaps knowing a bit more than you." When Jesyn didn't countermand him, he continued, "Lilyth has never before been able to seduce any of us to her banner. Why do you think this is?"

Again, Jesyn chose not to answer, but she crossed her arms in frustration. She hated being lectured to, but if she could convince these dwarves to fight, it was worth it. As soon as he started though, she knew this was going to be long-winded.

"Do you know the history of our people?"

"No," Jesyn sighed, looking down.

Arcimedis must have sensed her frustration setting in. He leaned in a bit and whispered, "I'll keep this short, adept. Trust me." Then with the voice of a storyteller he began,

"Eons ago when we first came to these lands, Sovereign and Lilyth were said to have worked as allies, each responsible for a different aspect of our journey. The break in their alliance happened when we landed on these shores. For reasons lost to us, they began to quarrel, to bicker, and our people suffered because of it. Now, millennia later, we do not follow either." He stopped, then said, "Your turn to ask a question."

Jesyn couldn't help but appreciate his sense of humor. He'd kept his story brief, and for that reason she felt compelled to ask, "How do you explain the blacknights?"

"Our people go missing. Sometime later they return as blacknights controlled by Sovereign's will. They do not remember us, and self-sacrifice if captured. Legend says we landed with tens of thousands upon these shores. We are a hearty people and should have millions by now covering the world. Yet only Edyn is settled, and only by a few thousand. If we include your folk, the giants of Shornhelm, and the half dozen other known races, we still number in far less than we should. Don't you find that strange, a vast land still so empty?"

Despite herself, Jesyn found this line of talk intriguing. She stepped a bit closer and said, "I've never seen a child born, yet children come to our Isle. They find their way there, yet we're in the middle of the sea. I've often wondered how this can be."

Arcimedis nodded, "We find much the same. Children wander into our camps, sometimes together and we assume they are siblings. Yet I have only seen a few birthed from mothers amongst us. Dazra was a true child born from us, which is why he is so revered."

Jesyn looked around a saw a small rock to one side. She went over to it and sat down and Arcimedis followed her, leaning against the granite table. "Legends are often wrong. How do you know you didn't come here with a few hundred and now number in the thousands?"

The dwarven leader's look told her he was reassessing her. Maybe she'd asked a good question. Then he simply said, "We don't, but clues tell us this isn't so."

"Clues?"

Arcimedis nodded, "Our cities are much bigger than the current population. Our people look vastly different, and if we originated from fewer people, I doubt this would be true. Finally, the lack of births and the appearance of children. Something is keeping our numbers small, but also keeping our people alive. To what end, we don't know."

Jesyn leaned forward and met Arcimedis's gaze. She was going to try again, but this time with tact. "Are there other dwarven cities besides Dawnlight?"

Arcimedis sighed and shook his head. "Perhaps there are others, but they have not revealed themselves to us. King Bara left after the last war to look for our brethren, wherever they might be. Our search took us to Dawnlight, a vast city within the mountain, but it stood empty and abandoned. Since then our Seekers journey farther and farther, even between worlds, looking for our brothers and sisters. We have only found the blacknights."

"Then you can't let yourselves die. Look around you. This is all that's left of your people. Don't go down in history as the one who lost all hope." Jesyn held Arcimedis's gaze until he looked away.

"She may have a point," Elsa offered softly.

"Don't you think I know that?" Arcimedis snapped at her. "You think I want to die? This is Dazra's fault, leaving a thinker instead of a warrior in charge. I'm not meant to be—"

A horn sounded and the camp came alive with people

grabbing weapons. Something was happening on the east side and whatever it was, warriors were quickly streaming toward it.

Arcimedis looked at Jesyn then Elsa, finally saying, "Come, bring her!"

They ran through the group, the dwarven leader surprisingly fast on his feet despite his girth. Better still, he made a path for them directly to the front of the crowd. When they arrived, Jesyn's breath caught in her throat.

Ahead of them stood two winged beings, their armor catching torchlight. They had weapons drawn but stood their ground some fifty paces away. Even at this distance, they towered over the dwarven warriors, which made the young adept feel even more miniscule. Nonetheless she stepped forward, not knowing how she could help but unwilling to remain hidden behind her dwarven companions. She hadn't quite begun to think of them as friends, but in her mind, they certainly weren't enemies. Still, she'd thought Lilyth's forces would have taken longer to arrive.

Arcimedis must have thought the same because he muttered, "Maybe you'll get your wish, adept. Doesn't seem like we'll have time to carry out my plan."

Just then one of the winged creatures stepped forward and said, "Jesyn?" Her name echoed across the space between them, and all eyes on the dwarven side turned to look at her.

She looked about in confusion, shrugging her shoulders. "Yes?"

There was a bright flash and in place of the towering warrior stood a person. Jesyn squinted, her preternatural vision in this place coming instantly to her aid. What she saw made her blink, twice.

"Arek!" She couldn't believe it was him; it couldn't be!

147

"These are friends?" asked Arcimedis. His bewildered expression told her this was not the outcome he'd expected.

She ran forward even as the dwarves closed ranks. Arcimedis yelled, "Hold your fire!" The sudden turn of events was clearly a shock to many who had assumed the final battle had arrived. Jesyn threw her arms around Arek under the bemused gaze of the other winged being.

"How are you here?"

Jesyn straightened her herself, tucking her hair behind her ears in a self-conscious gesture. "You tell me! I was sent here by dwarven allies while trying to escape Sovereign. What about you?"

Arek looked at her with that familiar dumb grin he'd always had on the Isle. He shook his head and motioned to someone behind him. Then she noticed there were others: an older man who looked strangely familiar, a dwarven woman carrying some kind of backpack, and a girl about her age with a bow and amber eyes. She too, looked familiar, but Jesyn didn't know why.

"It's a long story, one I'd rather tell you sitting down," Arek replied. He looked past her and to the line of dwarves with weapons bristling. "Friends?"

"Arek," she said, so glad he was here, "you couldn't have come at a better time. Come on, I'll introduce you."

"More of my people," the dwarven woman with Arek said breathlessly.

There was a flash and the other winged warrior transformed, revealing a young man, handsome in that way that men of action tended to be, at least to Jesyn. She nodded to him, wondering what Tomas would have thought. The memory caught in her throat, creating a sudden ache at her loss. Tomas had failed his test of Ascension and paid the ultimate price for that failure. He'd died, and the memory of his loss still clung to her like sodden garments. She turned her head to hide it from Arek, hoping he didn't start asking questions, and said, "These dwarves are worried about being possessed."

"They should be," replied the girl with the bow. Her gaze seemed to look through Jesyn, not in an unfriendly way, but it still made the adept uncomfortable.

She shook her head.

"You don't understand. To avoid it, they want to kill themselves."

At that, the older man said, "Killing themselves won't help us. We need them."

Jesyn didn't know who he was. His pale eyes skewered hers, but she got the impression Arek was the leader of this group. Something about her friend, his stance and calmness, felt different. He'd changed since she saw him last. Now she wondered just how much.

"I present to you, Jesyn Shornhelm, Adept of the Way," Arek said formally to his group. He then took a moment to introduce each of his companions to Jesyn. Her eyes widened slightly at the lineages assembled before herb as she acknowledged each with a nod, but ignored Duncan's remark and asked Arek, "What do you want to do?"

Arek smiled and hugged her again. When he let go, he said, "Let's go meet these dwarves. We need to work together if we're going to get out of here alive." With that, the group made their way back to Arcimedis and the last of the dwarven people.

HAVEN

Centurion, bring the traitors forward." Niall addressed the commander of the praetorians standing next to the throne. Flanking the white marble throne stood Zedakai as armsmark, and Captain Kalindor, legate of House Galadine. The latter had recently been promoted to the rank of firstmark. The decision to promote Kalindor over Zedakai had been difficult, but Mother had assured him this would be politically wise, as the men outnumbered Niall's elves, and would want to see that reflected in the power structure.

The queen mother stood one step down from them, her warrior's garb exchanged for a blue gown edged in silver, the colors of House Aeonian, an outfit he felt more befitted his throne room. Across from her on the same step stood Ellis Tir, legate of House Tir and Yetteje's uncle. The man seemed fidgety, constantly pulling on his collar or shifting his feet. Niall took an instant disliking to him. His eyes were always moving, as if he was looking for an advantage or escape. Mother had recommended him, saying he was forever loyal to the Galadines. He'd acquiesced only because she was his mother, but the man made him uncomfortable.

Their journey from the base of the Giant's Step to Haven had been uneventful, other than the complete hysteria caused by seeing six hundred elves and men-at-arms arriving at the city's gates. At first the city's leaders had mistaken their arrival for an attack, but Kalindor had ridden forward before arrows flew, the white flag of truce and parley raised. Once he'd been recognized and the men of his company had come forward, Niall strode to the front and announced himself as the King of Bara'cor and rightful heir to his father's empire. He'd been clear that any discord would be considered treason against the crown, something Zedakai had said would help keep any grumbling from the populace in check. Not long after that, the city gates had been opened and his men greeted with the cheers and welcome of a triumphant army, despite the fact that half of them were blue-skinned elves. Fear, as Zed had counseled, made everyone smile.

During their travel his great-grandfather had shown Niall a power any of the elven kings of the Galadine line could use. With a little concentration and effort, Niall could transform himself to look much like he did before his change. Niall had questioned why Zed hadn't shown him this sooner. The battle-scarred Galadine had replied that the elves had been unsure of the loyalty of the men following the queen mother. Had they not bent knee to Niall as they did, well… he'd let that sentence trail off, only to be met with a smile from his king.

Of course, that meant his mother's men would have been sacrificed, but so be it. Niall enjoyed these tests of loyalty and approved his great-grandfather's use of them. He was learning much of the might of the Galadine line from one of its greatest kings, and he couldn't have been prouder.

He had, however, adopted his more normal form before arriving in Haven, if for no other reason than he wouldn't have to go through the same round of endorsements he'd suffered through to legitimize himself in the eyes of the troops of Bara'cor. The very idea that Kalindor had to vouch for him and embarrass him in front of his own men had not sat well with the king. The change in his appearance had been approved by his men-at-arms, who despite their loyalty wanted him to look the part—and, in their eyes, this meant looking more like them. In the end, they would all look the same. They didn't know that, but Niall did.

Despite his reluctance when initially approached by Valarius, Niall now loved his elven form. It was powerful; men looked at him with awe and respect, maybe even a little fear. Father always said he'd rather be respected than liked. Fear and respect were the same to Niall, but more importantly fear lessened as a sight became seen too often. So he'd opted to reveal his elven body sparingly, retaining its power as a tool for keeping his people in line. He had little to worry about with the elves and their loyalty. As Zedakai had explained, the ceremony of blood and bone used to anoint new would-be elves made them, in their own way, Galadines. This was his family and they would never betray him. The transformation made them incapable of it.

Their arrival in Haven had set off a series of events cumulating in a quick senatorial confirmation of his right as the heir to the Imperial Crown. Chancellor Finras Tyn, a man who smelled like old books and was enthusiastic in recognizing Niall's legitimacy, literally fell over himself pontificating about how a true warrior-king would finally bring peace. Niall shook his head at the memory, loving how the man saw the true strength in him. Tyn was perfect; bureaucrats with his insight had many uses.

Niall turned his attention to the captain of the guards and nodded. Now he needed to deal with those who'd tried to usurp power from his father. His mother had made it clear that his every act as king reflected on the crown. She'd urged him to be quick and decisive with these two traitors. Well, he thought, he'd be sure to leave no doubt how just and fair a king he could be.

At a signal from their commander, praetorians dressed in the crimson and white livery of Haven dragged in Merric

Spaiten and Algren Justeces, legates of House Aeonian and Cadan respectively. Both men looked haggard, their once white underclothes now tattered and gray with sweat and grime, their hair unkempt and wild, and their fingernails black with dirt.

Merric was stoic, hardly saying a word as he was shoved forward and pushed to his knees.

Algren on the other hand seemed unable to shut up. His hands were clasped before him with fingers interlocked in a white-knuckled grip, crying, "Mercy, good king! We only wished to serve!" He held out a hand to Yevaine and said, "Tell the king, tell him how we gave you every right and comfort, tell him we appointed you regent, just as you asked." He nodded tremulously, his jowls lagging a few moments behind and making a wet sort of smacking sound from the inside of his mouth.

Kalindor began, "On this twenty-third day of Eventide, the Imperial Crown—"

Niall blinked in disgust.

"Just skip to the end," he told his firstmark. "Let's get this over with." He didn't mean to sound bored, but couldn't help it. His eyes flicked over to his mother, who straightened herself up, her signal that he should do the same. He took a breath and sat up, not liking the weight of the crown on his brow. The inside had been lined with some sort of wool and itched each time his head moved. It was intolerable. He consoled himself with the fact that he only had to deal with a few more things. Still to come was an announcement he'd been looking forward to since speaking with Zedakai during their journey back from Land's Edge. First, these two would be judged.

At his nod, Kalindor scrolled down to the end of the parchment and said, "As ordered by His Majesty, you have been accused of treason against the Imperial Crown. Algren Justeces, what say you to these charges?"

"Innocent, your grace! I was under the impression that the queen mother would be given all the rights and privileges of a legate representing House Aeonian, and that His Grace, Ellis Tir, would be king-regent. I swore fealty to that plan and that plan only! Spaiten never told me of the machinations he wove behind the scenes." Algren leaned away from Merric, as if distance would make him more innocent.

Kalindor turned his attention Merric Spaiten, "And what say you to these charges?"

The man looked up at them, his eyes bright despite the general disarray of his appearance.

"Does it matter?" he said.

"Speak up," said Kalindor, "the Crown would hear your words."

Merric spat on the throne room steps.

"I said, what does it matter? I gambled and lost, trusting sycophants and bureaucrats. I'm not sorry. At least let me die with a blade in my hand."

Kalindor raised an eyebrow at that, then looked at Niall, releasing the floor. The king's first day holding court had drawn quite a crowd and the throne room was packed with people held back in a semicircular arc in front of the dais by the Praetorian Guards. Now the hall quieted as the crowd leaned forward to hear what the new king would say.

Niall got up and drew Azani, which glittered in the throne room light. The blade felt light in his hands, the leather grip smooth and warm. He walked down to the two kneeling men, looking at them both. At his approach Algren fell forward and put his head to the floor, whimpering and muttering. Niall had no idea what was coming out of the fat man's mouth, but he looked like he was trying to kiss the white marble of the throne room steps.

Then the king addressed the assembled crowd, saying, "I cannot abide treachery." He raised the blade and swung quickly. The bright arc it made sliced clean through Algren's neck and the blubbering suddenly stopped. The legate's head bounced down the steps with dull wet *thwack*s, coming finally to rest near the feet of one of the onlookers standing near the front of the crowd amongst a chorus of cheers and screams.

Niall looked at Merric Spaiten. "But I hate cowardice even more. You have a choice, Merric." He raised his blade, still dripping with Algren's blood, and announced, "We are facing a war against demons. To fight them, we must have warriors equal to the task, those who will do anything to seize opportunity, use cunning, and attempt the impossible."

He smiled, then continued in a loud voice that carried to the ends of the hall, "I have conferred with my retinue and am reinstating the Magehunters, warriors tasked with fighting those who use or survive on the Way. They will be made up of my elves, who are proof against the demonkind's magic."

Cheers erupted as the assembled heard their king say he would protect them from demons. Few, if any, understood how Niall was going to achieve this. It was enough that Haven would be safe, protected from demons by these blue-skinned allies their king had brought back.

Niall looked down at Merric.

"Become my first Magehunter. You will be transformed into a warrior more powerful than you can imagine, loyal to House Galadine, or join Algren as the last traitor in my midst."

Merric coughed out a laugh, then shook his head. He put

his head to the floor.

"I accept. And transformed or not, I'll not betray you again, King Galadine."

Niall knew his mother was likely furious, as was Kalindor and the rest of those who did not understand what becoming an elven warrior meant. Merric would bring the same thirst for power and vengeance to the hunt for those who used the Way. He would be the tip of a new spear aimed at Lilyth's heart and help Niall bring peace and order back to Edyn.

"Rise then," intoned Niall, feeling extremely proud of himself. This was his first act, one of justice and mercy. Would they not see him as a true king now? Who had ever done better?

As if reading his thoughts, Zedakai came up behind his shoulder and said, "Well done, Your Majesty. Let us retire to privacy where we can proceed with the Anointment."

Niall nodded and then raised his hands for silence.

"You will wait here while I accept Merric Spaiten's oath and anoint him into service. When I return, it will be to announce the kingsmark and to show you how Haven will be protected."

At his nod, servants appeared with trays of small foods and drinks. Niall could see smiles on his people and felt the keen joy of knowing he was going to make a real difference in their lives.

"What's all this?" his mother said forcefully into his ear. "You make a mockery out of your father's memory. This man tried to negate everything he did!"

"I took advantage of a moment, as any good tactician would. We have an enemy about to become an ally, Mother," Niall said. "There are seldom more loyal men than those spared from the blade by a king's mercy." He motioned to one of the Praetorians, who came immediately to their side. "See to it that the queen mother has whatever she needs. But I am not to be disturbed."

"Yes, Your Majesty," the guard answered with a bow.

Niall looked for Zedakai, and after catching his eye turned his attention back to his mother and said, "Wait for me here. I won't be long."

"What are you going to do?" she asked softly.

He smiled. "Change the world."

He motioned to the two guards with Merric between them and made his way over to Zed. When they met, his great-grandfather asked, "May your elves escort us the rest of the way?"

"Of course," answered Niall magnanimously. Two elves appeared, taking over for the praetorians, who retreated with a bow back to the throne room. Following Zedakai, they made their way out of the throne room. The sounds of the crowds lessened as they went down some passages and finally to a small room. There Merric was made to kneel before a bowl of dark liquid while Niall and Zedakai stood looking down at the accused man.

Following Zed's instruction, Niall dipped the finger bone of Valarius in the liquid, blood he knew from one of his elves sacrificed for just this purpose, and then dabbed it into the eyes and mouth of Merric Spaiten.

"Repeat after me," said Niall. "I do swear upon my life to defend House Galadine and Niall Galadine against all who would bring them harm."

Merric repeated the oath, blinking to clear his eyes.

"Let it seep in, Legate," counseled Zedakai. "It will only take a moment and you will be born into a new life." At that, Merric stopped blinking and waited.

Niall continued, "I will follow any command given to me

by those with true Galadine blood."

Merric said the vow, punctuated by coughs, as something began to happen inside him. He grasped his arms, shivering.

Niall finished, "I accept the Anointment as a sign of my unequivocal fealty to the Galadine kings."

Merric finished, suddenly doubling over in pain. Garbled sounds came from deep within him. Then his back arched and his mouth opened in a silent scream. Something popped inside him, eliciting another scream. Slowly his limbs elongated, along with more pops and then a crack, as if a bone had broken. When the man gasped in pain, one of the accompanying elves placed a leather strap in Merric's mouth. Slowly, his skin changed from white to blue, his limbs filled out as he grew bigger. Air rushed out of his lungs and he rolled over onto his back, choking as his transformation continued.

Finally, in what seemed to take forever but was only moments, the Anointment was over. Merric Spaiten rose slowly, shaking as he inspected his hands and, now twice their original size. He looked at Niall and Zedakai in amazement.

"What's happened to me?"

"You've been Anointed into service, Merric." Niall smiled and added, "Get dressed. We'll return to the throne room, where I'll finish my announcement concerning our defense."

Merric found garb laid out for him by the elves, that of a kingsmark, along with weapons and armor. As he dressed Niall explained his vision and Merric's role in the new world he would create. When he finished the elf who'd once been a man smiled and said, "I'm going to enjoy this."

The trio made their way back to the throne room, entering from a door behind the throne's dais. Niall reseated himself.

At least someone had had enough foresight to put a crimson cushion on the cold white marble. In a few moments the rest of the royal retinue arrived, pausing in shock at the sight of Merric's transformation.

Yevaine was first to speak.

"What did you do to him?"

Niall answered, "We made him able to fight demons. He's better than he was before." He said this matter-of-factly, but a part of him was annoyed that his mother didn't see the obvious advantage. It was obtuse of her, and he didn't like it one bit.

To cover his frustration, he raised his hands and a trumpeter sounded his horn, grabbing the attention of the crowd milling about. When the murmuring had ceased, Niall stood and said, "I present you, Merric Spaiten, Kingsmark of the Magehunters."

An audible gasp ran through the crowd as many squinted and peered, trying to understand what had happened. The man they'd seen leaving the throne room had returned as a blue-skinned elf. Perhaps some did not recognize Merric, and those few who did were smart enough to say nothing. To this, Merric raised his hands and bowed fist to chest, before straightening to scan the assembled. With the additional height of the raised dais, he towered over the people. When he spoke, his voice boomed throughout the halls.

"There has never been a time when a Galadine was more needed. To that end, I will be asking for volunteers to join my Magehunters. You will become the vanguard of an elite force to end the threat of the demonkind." He nodded to Niall, who stood up and moved to stand next to Merric.

Niall then changed form, growing taller and more massive. Horns curled out from his head and his wings unfurled, collecting Merric closer to him. He gestured to his men and the Praetorians gathered transformed as well, shedding their armor as their forms also became blue-skinned and tall. As screams erupted from the crowds, the elves at the rear sealed the doors to the throne room, which elicited small knots of panic amongst the guests.

Kalindor stepped forward, his face a comical mixture of confusion and anger. "By the gods, what are you doing?"

Niall looked back at the firstmark and said, "Accepting volunteers." His eyes then tracked over to meet his mother's and Ellis Tir's, both of whom looked like they were going to be sick. He tilted his head, wondering how he could trust someone who felt ill by what must be done? Still, he needed these as they were, or he'd have changed them too.

Then his smile returned, for their transformation was also a certainty. Just not today. There was only one way to be sure loyalty came first, and both Valarius and Zedakai had shown him how.

FLASHBACK:

PARAMUS

B right desert sun lanced down, bathing the landscape in the unrelenting blaze of its piercing radiance. Alion raised a gloved hand, shading her sunken eyes as she scanned the horizon for threats. Nearby a camel let out a burst of air from its lips. It sounded like a fat man breaking wind. She hadn't been kidding when Malioch asked about camels. Since she didn't hunger or thirst, and this heat didn't affect her in any appreciable way, the beasts were mostly useless. "Mostly" because they could carry supplies, and like any bag of flesh and guts with legs, they contained blood. Something about blood made her feel something, a yearning she couldn't identify. It was the only value she'd been able to appreciate in the beasts. That is, until now.

She walked over and looked at the contraption the slaver had built. She didn't know the names of all the parts, but the idea was straightforward enough. Tie a rope to a small camel then pass that rope through a pulley system and tie it to the platform. In case of emergency, throw the camel off the ledge and the platform would rise, provided the total weight on the other end was less than the camel.

Malioch had rigged a simple safety release made out of some kind of sailor's knot, then blindfolded the beast and walked it onto another hinged board hanging over the hole.

He'd have slaughtered it right there to keep it in place but Trysh had rightfully pointed out that the smell of a fresh kill would do what Paramus's puke had not: invite something potentially larger and more terrifying than the sandpreys to their location. So, they'd decided tying down the beast would have to suffice. The board, in turn, had been tied to a release. Pull the cord, release the board, camel falls, platform rises. Simple. Anyone could pull the release cord when at the bottom and their emergency escape was assured. Problem solved.

Deft sat down on a crate, doing a quick calculation on their supplies. Without any vegetation the camels would need water every ten days or so. So far, they'd found thorny desert plants, which regardless of their actual names Deft thought of as basically different versions of boring cactus. These had kept the camels happy. As far as their team, they had enough water for another week. If they found what she thought they would, Deft planned on staying and exploring. Perhaps her—

"You hate me."

Alion spun, pivoting on the crate even as her hand went for the weapon she wasn't wearing. The idea that someone had… surprised her—but that was impossible.

Paramus stood there, his expression caught between self-pity and fear. How had the inept piece of intellectual driftwood managed to evade her hyper-acute senses? She could hear Malioch's heartbeat and he was over thirty paces away. Now that she concentrated, she could hear Par's laborious heart too.

He nodded, as if her silence was answer enough. "I know we're nothing alike, but I can help. I'm more than just a transliterator." He looked at Deft, biting a fingernail while his eyebrows rose expectantly. Deft realized he was waiting for her to say something.

"Ahh, what?"

The scholar pounced on that opening and started babbling, words gushing forth, stream of consciousness. Deft caught "demons" and "ollege" before she held up a hand and commanded, "Stop, for the love of the Lady, please stop. You're killing whatever in me is still alive." She sighed, then motioned for the scholar to seat himself on another crate nearby.

"Now," she said, "start from the beginning."

"Okay," the boy said with a nod. "So my mother is a healer. In fact, I was on my way to the medical college in Haven when things went awry."

Deft stared at him, unsure of what to say. "And begging in Southheart is what you call 'awry'?"

Paramus shook his head. "My family was attacked near Precious. I fled." He looked down, ashamed.

"Go on," Alion prompted.

He shook his head slowly, as if trying to rid himself of whatever memory he was reliving. Then he looked up at her with eyes so amber they seemed to suck up the color of the sands around them. Part of her wondered if the boy had any relation to the Tirs, a line known for their amber eyes.

"I had more family in Southheart. My brother lives— lived—there with his wife."

Alion noted the correction, but frankly didn't care enough about Par's situation to inquire why. Instead, she asked, "You said you could be useful. How?"

"I told you," he exclaimed. "I'm a healer, just like my mother." He paused, then added, "I watched you treat Trysh. You've got real talent, for a…"

"For a what?" demanded Deft. "A cursed knight?"

With each question the boy shrank back further onto the

crate. Then he said, "No, I mean you really have skill. Dressing a sandprey's bite requires a compression bandage, something most people, most healers, don't know."

"You're what, sixteen… and you do?"

"Nineteen," Paramus corrected. Then, mustering courage from somewhere, he added, "My mother served in Tenzer's Tenth."

Now it was Deft's turn to be slack-jawed, "The Angels?"

The boy nodded faster, now looking truly miserable. "I was supposed to report after graduation. My billet was already secured."

The knight shook her head in disbelief. "You're telling me you're the son of a warrior on one of the most elite teams in the Galadine army?"

The boy simply nodded. Deft took a moment to absorb this new information, then asked, "And you've got proof?"

Paramus spread his arms and said, "You dumped out half my things, including stuff we could use."

"It was junk!"

"We could've used that lens to light fires. The mirror was good for signaling." The boy shook his head, "Forget it. But yeah, I have proof." He reached down and removed a ring from a chain slung around his neck. "This was my mom's. I found it after they…." His voice trailed off, but he held out the ring for her to inspect.

Alion took the ring. It had the right notches, the circle surrounding the central carving of the two wings had been properly broken. As an ex-kingsmark she knew the heraldry well, but also the means by which the rings were marked to prove they were real and not forgeries. What stood carved behind the two wings was even more interesting however, and Deft looked at Paramus from under her brows. "This sigil stands for House Petra."

The boy took the ring and slipped it onto his chain. "So what?"

The knight shrugged, "Powerful first family. Your mother's name?"

At first the boy looked scared. Then, something stronger rose within him, and his chin jutted out defiantly.

Alion watched him for a moment before scoffing and saying, "Fine. Keep her name to yourself." She scanned the horizon out of habit, then shifted her weight on the crates to get comfortable. "What do you want," then, though she hated it, she added, "mi'lord?"

"You don't have to address me like that. As you know," muttered Paramus "I'd probably be dead if you hadn't happened along." He tossed a small rock he'd been rolling in his fingers, watching it barely bounce before coming to a halt, leaving behind a mark that looked like an '!' in the sand. A desert breeze blew by, cooler than expected, and half erased the only evidence that Paramus had ever been there, much less been able to throw a rock.

Then the kid looked up. "I can help as a healer," he said. "But I want you to promise me something in return."

Intrigued, the knight leaned forward and said, "Depends on what it is."

"Keep me alive."

Alion stared at him, then couldn't help but laugh. "I've been doing that since we left! Never met someone so clumsy in my life." She paused, noting the change in his expression, and added, "Keeping you alive has been one of my top priorities."

The boy looked up at her then and for the first time she saw an inkling of the depth of his thinking process. It wasn't on his face, but something in his eyes spoke from the future. It was the Lord Paramus he'd become, if he lived, saying,

"Only until whatever we find is translated. Then I'm just weight."

The knight hadn't really thought beyond finding an answer to her curse. She shrugged and said, "I'm a knight, regardless of what afflicts me now. I'll not let harm come to my team."

The boy just stared at her, then said, "You may not, but Mal... We're in a desert. Water, food... he may not want to share."

She didn't expect him to say that, but Par had clearly given this a lot of thought. And he was right. Malioch had killed folks for far less. Now that the boy had said it, it was painfully obvious what would happen once his usefulness had come to an end. In this, he was same as the camel.

She took a breath, then smoothed out the leather covering her thighs. The tied rods under that leather felt so different. Not like her legs at all, and in that moment, she realized she was slowly forgetting what having legs felt like. Whatever Alion Deft had been in life was fading away, being replaced by this skeletal curse of decay and death. Deft stared at the scholar for a moment longer, then shook her hands to feel something, anything. There were times she thought if she stopped moving, she'd become frozen in position.

"I can help with that," uttered the boy.

"With what?"

"The feeling in your arms, maybe the numbness." The boy was looking at her hands intently now.

"Thirty days of travel and you say barely enough to keep yourself alive. Now you can't stop talking," cursed the knight.

"Or I'm scared. I hadn't planned on staying this long, but your man watches me too closely to get away."

Deft nodded, "He's got a talent with runaways." She

came to a decision.

"Fine, I'll watch your back, but you deliver me anything that has to do with curing this curse." She emphasized, "Me, no one else. If you think you've found something, you keep it to yourself until we're alone. Don't tell anyone."

"Why?" the boy asked.

Deft rolled her eyes and said, "For someone with education you can be dense. You're only valuable so long as you don't share the information. If you give it away, I may not be close enough to stop anyone from ending you."

Paramus swallowed at that but nodded shakily. "You'll protect me, really?"

Alion rose and gave Paramus her hand, "I swear it. So long as you're part of my team, I'll make sure you remain alive."

Relief flooded the boy's face. He moved forward and at first Alion thought he was going to hug her. Instead, he pulled up her offered hand and inspected it further. "The spell cast on you, it's using your own blood to power itself. As that blood gets used, you turn more and more into..."

"This thing," she said, two fingers pulling on the slack skin on her face away from her eye socket.

The boy blanched but continued, "Blood is the key. If you consume it, much of your normalcy should be restored, at least temporarily."

Alion considered that. It was true every time she'd consumed anything with blood in it, she'd felt better. She hadn't linked that to a need for blood. If what the boy said was right, it explained much of her thirst around the camels and other living beings.

Interesting, she thought.

"What makes you think blood is the answer?" she asked, more out of genuine curiosity. Like all her other emotions, this had slowly been eaten away by her curse. Feeling it again brought a small flutter of hope to her stomach, or whatever her stomach had become.

"Possession was a tool of the demons in the last war. A lot of time was spent researching other creatures who can possess, including waywolves and vampyrs. Your affliction isn't so different." His demeanor transformed as he spoke, becoming almost clinical. He reached up and casually pushed her mouth open, peering into the dark cavity lined with sharp teeth. Because of the changes in her muscle tone, her jaw could unhinge and open far wider than a normal person's could.

Paramus seemed to take this in stride.

"Note your left and right hunting teeth have elongated. Likely you can feed on a person or animals with those." He stepped back, looking her over. "Your increased strength is a by-product of losing the sensation of pain. What stops most of us from applying our full might is the pain we feel, but you don't have that problem anymore."

Deft watched him, more than a little impressed. Once he started his diagnosis, he'd removed himself almost completely from the moment, assessing her with detachment. If he could maintain this on a battlefield...

"One thing," the boy said. At her gesture he continued, "You need blood, so be careful in the labyrinth."

She shrugged, "I've not—"

"The sandpreys eat blood. If they latch onto you, you might find yourself slowly becoming unable to animate."

That statement shocked her, more so because what she'd initially thought of as an inconvenient threat, now became more real. What would happen if she fell to them? Likely she'd have become a living statue, trapped and dying but not dead in the dark tunnels making up the Serapeum of Thoth.

Impressive again, she admitted. The boy had real insight to offer. She remembered to close her mouth before saying, "Maybe you're not as inept as I thought."

The comment snapped the boy back, breaking his spell of detachment. He looked around, his eyes wide, like he just realized he'd had his hand and face almost inside her mouth. "I... uh—"

"Forget it," said Deft. "Just stay near me when we venture back into the tunnels. Now that we've gotten to know each other, I don't want to lose you."

"I'll be closer to you than your own shadow," quipped the boy.

Deft's smile turned sardonic at that. "Careful, you don't know anything about my shadow."

AREK AND JESYN

T here's a way home through Harmagedon."

Arek addressed the assembled dwarves, the entire group having retreated from the eastern side of the camp back to the overhang with the granite table. It felt like an impromptu (and surreal) council meeting, with Arek speaking for his people and Arcimedis for his. Jesyn sat quietly, her allegiance to Arek clear, but conflicting emotions occasionally flitted across her face. Arek couldn't surmise what all had happened, though the brief mindspeak they'd shared had brought him up to speed on the main points— Dazra and his dwarves, her flight from Dawnlight, and her predicament with these dwarves and Halp. He didn't envy the tenuous situation she'd had to navigate since she and Dragor had left Meridian Isle, where they had all trained as Adepts. Jesyn's goal had been to find the lost dwarven people or any sign of Silbane and Kisan, a mission that had not ended in success. Worse was her encounter with Sai'ken, the dragon diplomat, who in some ways seemed more dangerous than her father, Rai'stahn, the dragon-knight. And that said a lot, given that all the elder dragon had done nothing ever since he met Arek but try to kill him.

"Our home is not in Edyn," muttered Arcimedis. This was supported by more than a few 'ayes' and nods. "Our home was usurped by the Sovereign, forcing us to flee in between the realms."

"I know," replied Arek. "But we have a common foe. If you help us, we can restore your people to Dawnlight."

"You speak of restoration and giving us Dawnlight...

173

giving us back what already belongs to us." Arcimedis shook his head, "We are marooned in the nexus of worlds. What do you know of our plight? We are alone."

Arek paused, his mind racing. Then he looked to Brianna and said, "She hails from another place. A place where there are more of you."

The leader turned to look at Brianna, his face inscrutable. "How many of our people live where you do?"

Brianna mumbled something, but when Arek raised his eyebrows in exasperation she raised her voice to say, "Millions... maybe hundreds of millions." She rubbed her face and added, "Dying here will mean nothing."

Arcimedis scowled, then barked a short laugh.

"How can we help, anyway? The Aeris are immune to our weapons! Here or in your fabled lands of millions, we are fodder for the Aeris, bodies that can be taken at their will."

Arek took a moment to scan the crowd, then said, "What if I could change that?"

"Change what?" asked Arcimedis.

"I can enchant your weapons, make you able to defend yourselves."

Arcimedis looked incredulous. "Indeed?"

Can you do that? Jesyn's question filled Arek's mind, her mental tone equally doubtful.

Arek ignored Jesyn and focused on Arcimedis. "Valarius Galadine, the greatest archmage to have ever lived, armed his elves the same way. I learned from him."

Duncan, who until now had kept a neutral expression, said, "I can vouch for that. We can enchant your weapons and armor to withstand the Aeris, if you give us the chance."

"You can't do anything torced," Elsa argued. "And we can't remove the torc." She pointed at Jesyn. "And she seemed shocked when you spoke." She looked pointedly at

Arek. "Not a glowing recommendation."

"She hasn't seen me since we left Meridian Isle. Much has happened," Arek responded, mentally telling Jesyn to agree. "You've been here for perhaps a half day? I've survived here for longer than that. And as my father says, I've trained under the greatest masters available. I can show you proof. All I ask in return is you agree to leave this place with us, and come back to Edyn."

Before Elsa could answer, Arcimedis held up a hand.

"Show us this power you have," he said. "I'll make no promises until I see it work. There are no end of mistfrights and worse wandering about. Kill one with this power to enchant and we will talk."

"Agreed," said Arek. "Pick who you want."

The dwarven leader paused, then motioned to Elsa. When she came near, he touched her arm, igniting a whorl of entats on her as he communicated his wishes. She nodded and sped off into the darkness.

Arek took that moment to confer with Duncan and Ash. "I can do this."

Duncan nodded, but Ash looked confused.

"How? Not like that trick Silbane did with my boots…" He referred to the spell Arek's master had cast on his boots to keep him from sinking in the mud. Once he'd found out it was a trick, the spell had been broken and Ash had found himself knee deep again.

Arek smiled at the memory gleaned from his mindshare with Silbane. Ash's expression had been priceless. However, Ash had a good point about belief, or lack thereof.

"Valarius told us the secret of his elven blades," he replied. "They were simple steel. It was the elves belief that made them invincible. I will use the dragonsight to give these weapons and these people belief and faith." He paused.

"So, yes. In a way I'm going to create something these people can believe in."

Ash locked eyes with him, an argument clearly at the tip of his tongue. Then he scoffed once, more at himself than Arek.

"What do I know?" he said. "If it works, we gain allies."

A commotion drew their attention as Elsa returned, dragging someone behind her. She threw him into the torchlight, revealing a disheveled Halp sprawled on his back.

"Your volunteer," she said. She rubbed her palms on her jerkin as if to clean them off after touching something particularly disgusting.

Jesyn had moved immediately to Halp's side, looking at Arcimedis. "No!"

"Why protect him?"

The young adept spun to face Elsa. "You're picking on him because you don't like him!"

"What do you know of him?" retorted Arcimedis. "Have his lies turned your heart?" The dwarf didn't wait for an answer but continued, "I'll not risk one of my men to possession. If the power you claim to have is true, the demon-lover has nothing to fear."

"The Seeker Halp is acceptable," Arek interrupted. He intentionally used the dwarven warrior's title, hoping to shame Arcimedis and his people for their prejudice.

"What am I supposed to be doing?" asked Halp from the ground, looking both bewildered and half-asleep. Jesyn wondered if Halp just slept whenever he could, for nothing seemed to faze him enough to make him miss a nap.

Arek squatted beside the older warrior.

"We are trying to keep Dazra's people from killing themselves. I promised to enchant their weapons, but rather than risk his own men, Arcimedis volunteered you. It means—"

Halp spat to one side, then rose, brushing himself off. "Long-winded story, I know what you need. Just enchant my blade." He unshouldered his axe and offered it to Arek.

"Not that weapon," countered Arcimedis. He motioned to the crowd with a hand and was given a long dagger. "This seems more appropriate." He dropped it in the mud.

"At least give him a proper weapon," Jesyn said.

"If he can kill an Aeris with a dagger, then a sword or axe will work even better. Besides, any Seeker worth his name can fight with a dagger." Elsa said this from the edge of the crowd, her pronouncement immediately met with grumbles of agreement.

"She's right," Halp said to Arek. "There are no bad, old fighters. Give me the blade when yer ready."

Arek walked over and picked up the blade from where the dwarven leader had dropped it. It was long and straight, double leaf-edged and keen. He walked back over to Duncan, meeting his father's eyes. "I wish you didn't have that torc on, now more than ever."

Duncan cracked a smile.

"If wishes were aurum, well…." He trailed off but took Arek's shoulders and met his eyes.

"You can do this. You learned well from watching Valarius and you have the will of the Way."

Arek swallowed, then moved a bit apart from them, holding the dagger out horizontally with both hands. Before he could do anything, he felt an unexpected touch on his arm. It was Jesyn.

"Do you need help? Dragor said he helped Giridian when they searched the Vault. Maybe…"

Arek smiled and shook his head. "This won't take much out of me. Let's save your strength for when I really need it, okay?"

Jesyn nodded, squeezed his shoulder once, and stepped back. For a moment, it felt like they were back home preparing for a rhan'dori match together. Though only a few weeks had passed since he'd been on the Isle with Jesyn, if felt like years. He was amazed at how much they'd collectively survived.

Stop, he chided himself, you're purposely delaying. Focus on what you're doing, on the here and now.

For a moment, his inner voice almost sounded like Master Silbane rebuking him during training.

He calmed himself, then opened his mind to both the Way and his dragonsight. His normal vision went black, replaced by golden light streaming in particles to outline everything surrounding him. He could See the true nature of things, from the bonds that held this island together, to the currents of the Way flowing toward the spire in the distance.

Transposed over Ash was the hulking figure of Orion, standing ready. Muted, strangled, but still present, was the ash and ember angel Scythe, wreathed in smoke, standing watch over Duncan. Most surprising, even though it should not have been, was the angel with wings of fire and a blazing blade standing guard over Jesyn, a testament to her Ascension. Arek felt a mixture of pride at her accomplishment, and doubt that what he'd been through with Kisan and Silbane had been as difficult. Was he just as much an adept as she was?

You're delaying again, his mind mocked.

A sudden bright flash of yellow pulled his gaze to his father's neck. The Way wound and twisted into a knot at the torc. To call it intricate would be an understatement. Somehow Valarius had woven the Way into a braid of interconnected paths entering and exiting the metal. He couldn't believe the skill such a weaving represented and now wondered how Valarius had ever been defeated. If he concentrated, he could see the flow of the Way through the torc, but the spell was horribly complex and far beyond his understanding.

"Concentrate," he heard his father say.

He pulled himself back to the here and now: the dagger. Refocusing himself on the task, he peered at the blade lying inert in his hands. The Way outlined it, golden particles streaming over its surface. Arek took a deep, cleansing breath, then dove into the blade's metal, looking at the way in which it had been constructed.

Suddenly the blade became the sky, vaster than the heavens themselves. He could see the interior structure, the way in which the metal had been forged. He could see impurities and purposeful alloys; some enhanced its strength while others were mistakes made by the small variations in heating and cooling while it was being forged. He could fix these, he knew. It was as simple as rearranging the patterns inherent in the steel, like a carpenter could fix a chair with one broken leg. He could also calculate the ways in which to make it stronger, lighter, perhaps even give it the energy to shine. These were minor things, now easy to accomplish given his insight and his understanding of how various elements would interact. He made the necessary adjustments, then focused on the more complex problem of hurting the Aeris.

Corporeal weapons and people merely passed through their bodies. The Aeris chose when they wished to interact, changing their nature, almost like… phasing. He looked up, his eyes widening.

"Halp, come here." He beckoned the dwarven warrior over. "Phase for me, I need to See it."

179

The dwarven warrior looked at him for a moment, then shrugged and phased himself to become insubstantial.

Arek watched him, Seeing the transition as it occurred. Before his transition the Way traveled in straight lines, albeit from all directions. When it collided with Halp's body, it reflected off him in waves of energy, like ripples in a pond. It was these wave of reflections he saw, making Halp visible. He was a rock in a stream—and then he transitioned. Something appeared to surround him like invisible strands of a web. However, unlike a web, the strands became pathways for the Way to travel around Halp more quickly, zipping past him to converge on the other side. This web bent the Way around Halp; because of this, no waves were created. Nothing reflected off of him, and as a result, Halp became insubstantial.

Arek smiled, now understanding the nature of how dwarven phasing worked, but could he do it in reverse? Could he make a blade that could touch something insubstantial? He thought about it. The key was those strands. He reached out and plucked at one, amazed to see it detach itself from Halp like a gossamer thread. His mind's eye raced in again, and the thread expanded to fill his entire vision. He understood how to construct it now. It was a slight shift, a reversing of two points along a line. He quickly went to work changing just one lattice, then instructing it to replicate that change throughout the metal. Instantly the blade subtly changed, its form and function now imbued with the ability to cut these threads of gossamer.

Function wasn't enough. Valarius had said his weapons were mundane, simple wood and steel, but he'd imbued them with something more fundamental, the belief by the wielder that the weapon could hurt Aeris.

He thought about how Silbane had fought for him. How

he'd taught him his own belief in himself was paramount to his success. So he wove his own confidence, his own belief that the Aeris were vulnerable, into something visible. He used his own experience fighting them, watching them fall to his featherblades, watching them die as he grasped them with the blackfire, and suddenly a black and red geometric pattern appeared before him, blending and turning as it hung in the black space before his eyes.

It was small, perhaps no bigger than his thumbnail, but intricate and real. It pulsed in time with his heart, and he could feel himself giving it strength. It fed on his confidence, absorbing his thoughts of victory, his true puissance at battle and his sure knowledge that the Aeris were absolutely vulnerable to blade and bow, hand and foot. It wasn't pure emotion in an amorphous sense, but rather geometric patterns representing these emotions and interlocking in place.

The shapes were his will, made manifest, and he placed this gently into the nearest node of the lattice. It quickly replicated itself too, jumping from node to node until his vision was filled with its amethyst pattern of flame. The Way adhered now to the lattice, attracted by his gossamer spell to the pattern placed within, and he knew his work was done.

He breathed out once and opened his eyes. Sitting in his palm was an iridescent blade, capturing the black and red mixture he'd seen in his pattern but projecting it to the metal's surface, a dark gleam of heliotrope. He exhaled again.

"It's done."

There was silence around the group. Though none could see what Arek saw, they all seemed to be in awe or shock at the visible change that had come over the dagger. Arek handed the short blade to Halp, who took it gingerly, then grasped the hilt. His eyes lit up and he said in a voice uncharacteristically light-hearted, "This feels… good."

Arcimedis seemed the least impressed. "Let's hope it wasn't just a little show of changing the metal's color. If you're possessed, we'll give you a clean death."

"Yes," Halp said. "I suppose it's the least you could do." Then he turned his attention back to Arek.

"Let's get on with this before I use this dagger on someone else."

They all made their way back to the eastern side of the camp. The dwarves went slowly, keeping themselves hidden behind rock or phasing directly into the ground. Arek and his party moved forward, taking cover where they needed to.

At some point Arek found himself huddled beside Ash, who asked, "Did you really do something to that blade?"

Arek met the firstmark's gaze. "Yes."

Yet something else gnawed at him and he felt his eyes pulled back to his father's torc. He still couldn't unravel the spell Valarius had created, he knew that. But what he'd just done to the dagger made him think he was missing something fundamental. He let his mind continue to work on the problem as they neared the place where Halp's test would come. Though everyone else looked on with varying expressions of concern or disbelief, Arek thought only of his father's torc.

Then Halp stood alone at the camp's edge, looking out into the night. He strode forward, carrying a torch in one hand and his dagger in the other. The blade, even from here, had a strange glow that reminded Arek of a bruise in the night. It didn't shed light, but still the air and ground around Halp seemed to glow a strange purple.

The first attack came without warning. A mistfright lunged from the darkness, its black mist form flowing up the dwarven warrior as it sought to enter his mouth and nose. Halp couldn't grab it and wasted a few precious moments trying, to no avail. Then the blade touched the demon and it arched its back and shrieked into the sky. Halp drew back and plunged the blade into the creature's chest with both hands. The torch dropped and long shadows danced out the struggle of the two as Halp stabbed again and again.

Finally, the sounds ceased and with it the torch guttered out. Pitch black obscured any sight of the victor, until the scratch of flint on blade's edge and a sudden flash of orange yellow revealed Halp, holding the relit torch and looking not too much the worse for wear. It was over. The mistfright had disappeared into the night, destroyed by the dagger's enchantment. Halp backed toward the camp, never turning his back to the darkness.

Arek could almost feel dozens of invisible eyes watching, calculating. If they attacked now it would only be those in his party to defend the camp, but thankfully no attack came.

When Halp finally made it back to the perimeter, it opened for him without a word. No congratulations or claps on the back. He was still a pariah in their eyes. Jesyn leapt forward, saying, "I knew you could do it!"

Halp looked at her and said, "So did I. I never doubted it. Strange."

"Really?" said Ash. Arek got the distinct impression the man wondered if magic actually worked, despite all the evidence to justify it did.

"Let's just say the last time I had something enchanted it was my boots, and I ended up calf-deep in mud, no thanks to your master," the firstmark said looking at Arek.

Really," Halp replied, adding, "Are you not a blade dancer, even in mud?"

Ash smiled. "Mud is a horrible partner."

Arek didn't say anything about the spell imbuing confidence. As their talk continued, he moved over to Arcimedis and said, "We don't have long. I suggest you gather the weapons and armor and let me get to work."

"I haven't agreed yet to join you."

Men were already gathering, unsheathing blades and holding them out to Arek. "You don't have to," he said. "But your people want to survive." He held out a hand, "Let's keep the memory of Dazra and your people alive."

Arcimedis paused, then engulfed Arek's hand in his own. "Can't say I like the idea of dying without a fight. All right, master adept. We'll join you on your quest for Harmagedon. Anything to avoid not having to join with these Aeris in some god-cursed bonding."

Arek looked down, the dwarven leader's last comment circling in his thoughts. Something he'd not thought of was taking root, he could feel it, an idea not yet given true form or substance but an idea, nonetheless. The word "bonding" was another piece to the puzzle of the torc and Valarius's spell.

He looked up in time to see Brianna standing by herself. The person who ought to be happiest, back amongst her own people, seemed lost in thought. He walked over to her and asked, "You all right?"

Brianna snapped out of her reverie. "Yes, fine."

"Don't feel like mingling?"

"They killed his wife… Is that true?" she asked.

Arek looked over at Halp, then moved a little closer to Brianna. "Did you hear about Duncan and Silbane facing Baalor?" he asked, quietly so only she could hear.

Brianna shook her head, "No."

"The creature that stalked them in Bara'cor was powerful, much more so than my father and master combined. I know: I saw it in Silbane's memory." He looked back at the crowd, then said, "It doesn't add up."

"What?" asked Brianna. "I don't understand."

Arek turned back to her and said, "You saw what I just did. How did these people execute a possessed dwarven woman, a builder, without weapons that can harm Aeris? It would've been too powerful, even against these dwarves. They wouldn't have the power of the Aeris to unleash what I saw in Silbane's memory. Something isn't right, or your people are lying."

Brianna looked at him and said, "These aren't my people. They might be the same race, but they aren't like the people I remember." She seemed lost in thought again.

"You're remembering more?" Arek asked.

She nodded slowly, then said, "Yes, and nothing I remember looks anything like this. I don't think they're lying, but I agree with you," she looked around the camp, her eyes finally coming back to Arek, "something's definitely not right."

LILYTH AND

MITHRAS

ake the children to their parents," Lilyth said. She wasn't looking at Kalika. She sat at the lookout point she'd often shared with Baalor. Instead of the beautiful expanse of Arcadia's floating islands, she now saw the harsh white-yellow light of this new world. The land seemed to go on forever: sand and stone without a single blade of green anywhere. She'd never gotten used to the Altan Wastes, even when she'd last attempted to unify their two worlds. Perhaps once they'd expanded to the lowlands, she'd feel more at home.

"What?" asked Kalika.

Lilyth narrowed her eyes. "Summon Mithras, my love. You'll both be needed to accomplish what we must."

In a moment the Lord of Dawn appeared, resplendent in his sun-burnt armor. He seemed to have left his weapon, Tempest, behind. Probably best, thought Lilyth, for Tempest, her sister forever embodied as a sentient sword, often interrupted when least appropriate. Her trouble was a single-minded thirst for satiety in all forms. Mithras served as a fine hand on that pommel.

"And what troubles you, my lady?" he asked, his voice booming in its usual way.

"Everything." She still looked out over the desert below, her eyes pulled to the golden horizon.

"We have a problem," she breathed, her fingers caressing the white marble of her perch. Baalor would have known what that meant. Everything since his passing felt pointless.

Mithras shifted; she could hear what sounded like a shrug.

"What?"

Lilyth turned her head to his voice, her eyes adjusting back to the gloom of the interior. "The nephilim. We cannot easily withstand them."

Mithras shook his massive head. "We have weapons and armor. That is proof against their touch." The movement caught golden glints as the light from her window played across his helm.

Lilyth arched an eyebrow at that, then said, "In Arcadia we had an overabundance of the Way, upholding us, lending its strength. Here it's better than it once was, but Edyn isn't Arcadia. I fear our people will become Sovereign's slaves again, our cards shuffled back into his deck."

Mithras bent his head in concentration, then replied, "Our furies can take new bodies when old ones are used. Thanks to you bringing Olympious here, we have many bodies to choose from. But we must leave the body before we too, are possessed by the nephilim's touch."

"Perhaps," the Lady wasn't convinced. She changed tack and said, "It's true we have more to choose from. But our tactics haven't changed. Armor and shields to protect from their touch, weapons enchanted by the Way to kill." She was quiet a moment, then said, "Assemble your captains. We must bring more warriors to our banner."

Mithras bowed, fist to chest. He paused. "What of Zafir and the builders? They have more advantages than the mewling people of Edyn can give."

Lilyth nodded, leaning her head back on one of the

supporting granite beams in her window. "Deft will intercept Arek."

"Deft," the Lord of Dawn sneered. "Why send her?"

"Because she hates." Lilyth met both Kalika's and Mithras's eyes, then finished, "And that is enough."

She made her way over to her throne, motioning to one of her attending ladies.

"Bring us something to drink."

The woman bowed and retreated. The Lady gestured to a nearby seat and settled back, watching her two councilors with interest. "The builders will become one with us and add to our strength. They may be able to withstand the nephilim."

"Maybe," he said with a sidelong look. "But you didn't bring me here to talk about our soldiers' armor and weapons, or tactics against the nephilim."

"Why say that?" she asked. A small smile lifted the corners of her mouth.

"Because it's unnecessary, and if it was important to you, you'd have just ordered it done."

Lilyth laughed, impressed in spite of herself. "We are getting to know each other." Then she leaned forward and said, "I was not entirely truthful about our connection to the Way here in Edyn. It is growing; we are getting stronger. But it isn't enough."

Mithras nodded, "People are needed."

"Worship," Lilyth corrected. "We need the men and women of Edyn to worship us, to give us fealty."

"I can think of nothing better than bringing the might of the Lord of Dawn down upon their heads—"

Lilyth placed a hand delicately on Mithras's forearm. "It never works for long." She paused, accepting the drink the attendee had returned with. Mithras waved her away, leaving his goblet on the tray, but Kalika took hers and sat down quietly. Lilyth took a sip, then said, "I want their children returned to them."

Kalika said softly, "I think I understand."

Mithras shrugged, a gesture Lilyth had come to understand was from his Altan past. It meant, "acquiescence to eventuality" and not "disagreement without care." It was important to understand the distinction, and Lilyth did.

To him she said, "Only a fool disagrees with the Sun."

The once-barbarian clanchief, now Aeris lord, looked at her with surprise bleeding into appreciation. "Well said. In the end, they must all bend knee in worship. Only the path is unknown."

"I know the path," Lilyth said, looking at them both. The heartbeats dragged on as neither answered, either because they didn't know or because they didn't want to take her moment away. Lilyth couldn't help but laugh and say, "Love."

Mithras's eyes crinkled as his face broke into a white smile. "And how can I bring love to these insignificant sheep? By tossing back their bleating children?"

This was where Lilyth's mouth pressed into a thin smile. She said, "They need to see the power of the old gods, giving back what is most precious to them: the lord and lady who brought their children home."

She looked at him and then at Kalika and said, "I want you to work together. Let the word spread that the Lady returns the sons and daughters of Edyn safely to their parent's arms."

She turned to Mithras and said, "And I have another task for you. Something suited to your special qualities."

"And that would be?" Mithras seemed to be enjoying this. His eyes twinkled as he smiled again, waiting patiently for her answer.

"Tell Mithras about the lore father's staff," Lilyth said, still looking at him but speaking to Kalika. He was handsome and growing more so, as all that was Mithras took over whatever was left of the barbarian u'zar, Hemendra.

The Aeris lady stepped forward and said, "The staff is the key to remaking the world."

Lilyth raised an eyebrow and took another cool sip of her wine. Then she said, "Each staff is created for the lore father."

"And you want me to steal it?" inquired Mithras. His expression twisted, clearly now not liking the idea at all.

Before he could take insult, she raised a hand, conveying she would never call him a thief. "Oh, no, it can't be stolen. I need the runestaff to be remade at the Sanctuary of the Phoenix."

Mithras shook his head. "I'll admit you've lost me. Keeper Thoth is dead. We watched him die together, with Tempest through his heart."

Lilyth smiled. "Did you know I was once Keeper? With Thoth dead, any Celestial may take the role. Even me, one of the last Celestials to walk this land."

She rose and took a step forward, looking back out through her window at the desert stretched out before her. Coming to stand close to Mithras, she slid a hand under his shoulder pauldron and squeezed his arm, knowing it filled him with excitement. "I want Giridian Alacar to die, Lord of Dawn. That will destroy the runestaff he now holds. Then I will create a new one to defend us against Sovereign in this final war."

HALP'S STORY

D uncan watched as Arek worked through the night, merging the Way and his dragonsight to alter the weapons and armor of the surviving dwarves. Exhaustion showed at times, though it also seemed that the use of the Way buoyed him up, lending him the strength to continue.

The boy has grit, he thought, and not for the first time. His eyes scanned the assembled warriors, finally coming to rest on Brianna, who sat a bit apart from the others watching Arek. He made his way over to her, pulling at his torc to relieve the itching. Even in death Kisan managed to annoy him.

As he neared, the dwarven doctor looked over at him, and because she was seated their eyes were level. She acknowledged him with a nod, then turned her attention to something displayed on her wrist.

"I…" he began hesitantly, not sure if he was interrupting her. She looked up again and the expression on her face was one of concern, not annoyance. "I don't know if I ever thanked you," he continued. He gestured to himself, smiled, and said, "Almost as good as new."

Brianna answered with her a smile of her own, "Glad to be of service. You were in bad shape when we found you."

Duncan nodded. "That's an understatement." Motioning for permission to join her, he sat down as she moved over to make room. "What do you think of these dwarves?"

Brianna shrugged. "I told Arek, they're not my people. Nothing about them is familiar, not the way they dress, not even their beliefs. I've been listening, and as far as I can tell they have no memory of who they are."

"And who are they?" asked Duncan. Brianna had captured an emotion he'd thought dead for so long—curiosity.

The doctor paused, then looked about to see if they were alone. Satisfied, she leaned in and said, "They are travelers, marooned here. Somehow, they've forgotten their past and instead built these myths about where they're from. Mind you, I'm not exactly sure yet either," she quickly added. "But they're not from Edyn or Arcadia."

"How do you know?" asked the archmage.

"I injected myself with nans, tiny objects that heal me from the inside. They're slowly piecing back together my lost memories. I get flashes, small moments where I can see my past, but it quickly fades." She looked at him a little sheepishly before saying, "Still, I know these people aren't like me."

Duncan just nodded, then pointed at a metal tube jutting out of Brianna's pack. "May I?"

At her nod, he picked up the tube and inspected it. It was large in his hands, about as big around as his wrist and as long as his forearm. It slightly tapered to one end, the side that injected the medicine. The other side had a place to insert one of the many little tubes of liquid Brianna had tucked away. "I assume this is what saved me?"

"Actually, this did," she said, showing him a small capsule filled with blue liquid. "It's a neurological stimulant mixed with a cellular tissue regeneration matrix. Basically, it tricks your body into healing faster." She paused, then added, "See, there's an example of my memory returning."

"Umm." It was Duncan's turn to smile at his own ignorance. "I heard what you said, and I still don't know what you're talking about." He smiled. "I know what cells are and understand the words, but how it all works is, well—it's amazing."

"Yes, I suppose it is." Brianna's attention turned to a figure approaching. It was Arek, having finished his work on the dwarven equipment.

He plopped down next to them and uncorked a waterskin. Taking a deep drink, he wiped his lips and asked, "What're you talking about?"

"Magic," Duncan replied. He winked at Brianna, then picked up a piece of sandstone, rectangular in shape. He used the rough surface to grind down his nails while asking, "And how are you feeling?"

Arek shrugged. "Better than I expected. The same tiredness I feel when using my other form doesn't seem to happen when manipulating the Way. Not sure why, but I did notice something during my work on the weapons."

"What?" asked Brianna.

"This may not make sense, but the Way manifests itself as small particles. I can see them stream about like they're in a current, and the particles are heading in one direction."

"Where?" asked Duncan, remembering the Sight he'd shared with Silbane.

"Into me," Arek replied. He didn't seem surprised by it. He took another swig of his water, wiping his mouth on his sleeve.

Duncan nodded. "Well, you absorb the Way. Is it so surprising?"

"Then why do I get tired holding another form?"

"Maybe you only absorb it in this form. Everything else depletes you. We all get refreshed by eating or resting. For you it might be quicker, because you siphon it from the air itself."

"Hmm," Arek said, "next time I'm in another form I'll see if I can use my dragonsight. Maybe if I see the Way swirling around me without going in, your theory will be proven true." He paused, then looked at Brianna meaningfully and asked, "Did you tell him about the dwarves and my concerns about Halp's wife?"

Brianna shook her head, "Sort of. We talked about the dwarves; I didn't get to Halp yet."

Arek looked at his father and took a breath. He fingered the waterskin, carving a few lines into the leather with his nails as he gathered his thoughts.

"They claim to have killed an Aeris possessing a builder's body," he said at length. "Given what I know of your fight with Baalor, that seems unlikely."

For a moment, Duncan looked at his son in shock. It wasn't something that had occurred to him. A part of him couldn't help but feel proud of his insight, but more importantly, how did they subdue and kill something that powerful?

"We need to talk to Halp." Duncan replied.

Arek nodded and got up. "No time like the present.

"Are you coming?" he asked Brianna.

The doctor looked down at her wrist display, then shook her head. "I need to monitor the progress of my nans. They have limited abilities and I have to prioritize their healing. I'd rather stay here, if that's okay."

Arek shrugged, "Not a problem. I'll circle back when we're done."

Brianna reached into her satchel and withdrew a small compact thing Arek recognized as a 'gun.' She tucked it into a holster and held it out for Duncan. "Take it. It should fit you because it's made to tuck into my boot. It fires needles at a high velocity, so be careful where you aim it. Pull this here," she showed him the trigger, "and the needle comes out of here." She touched the holster to his waist, and it clung there securely, held by whatever magic Brianna's people used to do things like this. "Place your palm on the handle now," she instructed.

Duncan did so and the handle made a small chirping sound. Brianna said, "Wait." A few moments later the handle let out a double chirp. "Okay, it's coded to you now. No one else can fire it."

"Thank you . . . I guess?" Duncan wasn't entirely sure what had just happened, but he remembered Brianna firing at Kisan. The gun didn't seem particularly useful until it had killed her. He'd always felt awkward being weaponless. This strangely made him feel a little less like a burden to everyone.

"If defending yourself means less work for me, I'm happy," Brianna said with a laugh. "I've always been a healer and...", she met Duncan's gaze, "I can't bring myself to pull that trigger again."

Duncan nodded again in thanks and together, he and Arek walked away.

Dawn was breaking as they made their way toward the center of camp. The camp slowly came to life, the rose-pink sky waking those who had taken their turn to sleep. Up ahead was the impromptu holding area where Halp had been sequestered.

"We haven't talked about the gate at Harmagedon," Duncan said to Arek.

"I've been sorta busy," Arek answered with a smile.

"Yes, well, when I first reconnoitered coming here, my research said that Harmagedon is ruled by Lord Zafir, a Celestial as powerful as Azrael. He may have been one of the first, along with Lilyth and our bonded partners, to manifest in Arcadia."

Arek nodded. "What's he like?"

"I assume he's a tyrant, mercurial, power hungry, you know… all the things we've come to love in our Aeris lords."

"It's clear Lilyth marooned these dwarves here for a reason."

"Builder bodies for her Aeris, and a gate to Edyn. Think of five hundred Baalors arriving to help her subjugate the realm." Duncan shook his head and couldn't help but smile. "You've got to hand it to her, she's gotten the concept of overkill perfected."

Arek grew silent, and Duncan wondered if he'd overstepped some invisible boundary.

Then his son said, "I can't believe I fell for it."

Duncan, in that moment, suddenly understood what his son meant. It didn't matter how smart Arek was, how much he could remember or how skilled a warrior he was. In the end, Arek had succumbed to the same thing he had: love.

He put a hand on Arek's shoulder and said, "You fell for something you've chased your whole life: wanting to belong somewhere and to someone. Lilyth gave you that, a sense that you were special." He stopped and turned Arek to face him.

"You are special, Arek. To me, to her, to many people. You fell for love. Better men than you or I have done the same." He looked sidelong at his son and added, "If you hadn't, then there would be something seriously wrong with you."

Arek looked down, slowly nodding. When he looked up his eyes shone with gratitude, which made Duncan feel all the more uncomfortable. Being a father wasn't something he'd had much experience with. He could counsel Arek on all-consuming homicidal revenge. On that, he was expert. But good advice about life, about kindness, or love? The thought made him more than a little queasy.

Arek must've sensed this, because he punched him lightly on the arm and said, "Don't worry, Father. We don't have to be best friends. Just help me get the truth out of Halp."

Duncan chuckled and nodded. Now, that was something he was good at.

Soon they arrived at where a ring of guards stood outside a large tent. Two more guards flanked the flaps. Arek motioned to one of them, already armed with one of his enchanted weapons. The man stepped aside and said "thank you" as he did.

Evidently Arek's work hasn't gone unappreciated, thought Duncan. It was a good sign.

Duncan followed Arek into the dim interior, scanning for the dwarf who'd come here with the adept named Jesyn. He saw them both as his eyes adjusted to the gloom. Halp lay sleeping on a mat on the floor, while Jesyn sat, head cradled on her arm, at a table too big for her, making her look child-sized in comparison.

Arek spoke first, saying, "Halp, may we have a word?"

Jesyn snapped awake. Then, when she saw who it was, simply said, "It's early." She put her head back down into her forearms, pointedly ignoring them.

Arek toed Halp's shoulder. "Halp. A word?"

The older dwarf grumbled and rolled over. His eyes cracked open and he yawned, then said, "The man who gave me a dagger. Such charity."

"That wasn't my call," answered Arek. "And frankly, you proved yourself in their eyes more than you know."

Halp covered his eyes with one arm and said, "Is that why

I got upgraded to this luxurious accommodation?"

Duncan sighed, then stepped forward and kicked Halp in the shin. "Get up!"

Halp yelped, then scrambled back clutching his blankets. "What're ya doing? That's not necessary."

The archmage took the shale stone he'd been using to file his nails and threw it at the dwarf. It missed but got Halp to scramble further into a sitting position. "The creatures you saw last night are nothing. Today we'll see battle and we need your help."

Halp looked at Arek and said, "Call him off. I don't need all this drama. Ask yer questions."

Arek pulled up a footstool—still too large for him but the smallest thing he could find—and climbed upon it. Once he'd seated himself comfortably, he said, "I need to know about what happened to your wife."

Halp grew silent, and into that silence Jesyn said, "Arek, do we—"

Arek looked at her, "Yes. This is very important, Jess." He looked back at Halp. "How could dwarves subdue an Aeris in possession of a builder's body?"

Halp looked down, shaking his head and mumbling.

"What?" Duncan asked.

"Because she wasn't possessed!" shouted the dwarf.

"Everyone says she was," countered Arek. "They even say you admitted it."

"I never said that," Halp said. "I said she'd joined with the Aeris, within her body, but she was still in control." Arek looked at Duncan, who immediately knew what he was thinking. Had Halp's wife Ascended? Was that even possible?

Jesyn was the first to ask the question, "Halp, did your wife and this Aeris choose to be together?"

Halp nodded, "She was hurt during one of the blacknight's raids. I was sure she wouldn't survive, but something intervened. When she woke up, she said it was wonderful." The warrior sunk his face into his hands and said, "Why are you bringing this up now? I've suffered enough. My children blame me, I am cast out by my own people. Leave off!" He got up and pushed his way out of the tent.

"Wow," Jesyn said to no one. "Do you think that's even possible?"

"It happened to me," Duncan said, thinking about Scythe. "And it sounds like it happened to you too. Yours is through mortal combat, but perhaps there are other moments truly exigent that thin the boundaries between Edyn and Arcadia."

"And if you're in the right place at the right time," continued Arek, "you can Ascend." He paused. "Seems like our masters made us go about it the hardest way possible."

Jesyn shook her head and said, "Our path is about service and sacrifice. Maybe for that reason, our way is the only way to summon the correct partner."

Duncan's head swam at the thought. He'd certainly never gone through what Arek or Jesyn had, yet as he'd mentioned, he had a bonded partner as well. What did that imply for these dwarves, that they could Ascend and retain their own will, their own identity?

A sudden commotion from outside the tent caught his attention and Ash burst in, pushing aside the tent flap. Behind him was Yetteje with Valor in hand. "There's a force approaching from the north. They're not far. Arcimedis has summoned everyone to that side of the camp."

Arek looked at everyone in their party and said, "Grab whatever you need. Don't plan on coming back here."

Halp nodded, grabbing a weapon from a rack nearby.

Evidently despite their hatred of him, the dwarves had still allowed him to keep his gear.

Duncan grabbed Jesyn and said, "I'm not sure if you've ever changed form here, so you're in for a few surprises. I'll instruct you as we run."

Jesyn nodded and together they made their way through the camp as it quickly galvanized itself for action. Duncan knew battle was coming, he'd just thought they'd have more time. Clearly, he'd underestimated how quickly Zafir's forces could move.

Hopefully, there aren't any other surprises waiting for us, he thought. Maybe Zafir was coming to them with an offer of peace. He smiled even as he dodged men arming themselves. Wishful thinking, something he'd recently found to be another annoying habit Silbane's gift had provided him.

As Arek motioned for them to follow, he looked at Halp and Jesyn. Shaking his head, he said, "We should get Brianna."

Arek paused, then nodded.

"Meet me at the front," he said, before disappearing into the crowd of warriors arming themselves.

You know, the old Duncan whispered in his mind, this is going to get much worse.

FLASHBACK: THE

LADY

A lion moved her back to the wall and took a moment to gauge how her small group had fared so far. Mal and Par seemed unhurt, though the latter had a sandprey's head still attached to his backpack. Only the timely intervention of her mace had put an end to the creature's life. Reaper had been left behind in favor of this blunt-force weapon, which she commonsensically also thought of as Reaper. She'd never been much for complicating things, so whatever was at hand got the same name. Now her mace had made short work of the sandprey, the smashed head with one eyeball hanging out, still bouncing on Paramus's pack as it clung stubbornly by a triangular tooth to some part of the stitching.

It was the scout's situation however that worried her the most. Trysh had been banged up, and continued to bleed because of the sandprey's saliva, leaving a crimson trail on the labyrinth's floor. It was bright enough to Deft's witch gaze that she wouldn't need twine to find her way back. She had been thinking "if things went badly," but at this point it was moot. Things couldn't get much worse. The question any leader would ask was—did she press on until someone died? The answer was always an unequivocal yes.

Their incursion had started normally enough. The scout had gone first with Mal and Par sandwiched in between and

Alion bringing up the rear. In retrospect the knight wished she'd taken the lead. While the scout normally had a knack for avoiding potential problems, this time she seemed to be finding them. That fact meant she'd borne the brunt of their mistakes. Getting to the front, past a panicking Paramus, was harder than pushing through a line of donkeys, despite the prodigious strength her curse granted. After a little thought, she moved herself up and had Malioch back her. Having Paramus and the injured scout take up the rear only made sense.

It also didn't help they'd decided to make this second foray during the peak of daylight. Though the sandpreys were less active, it also meant Deft was bereft of many of her powers, making her almost normal in strength and senses. Still, the fact that they faced only a fraction of the bloodsuckers was, in balance, a worthwhile trade. What worried her more was what lay ahead deeper within the serapeum. They'd made their way past stone pillars, past a pool of water so still it looked like a mirror, and finally to an archway that led to this—a small circular room with a hole in the center. The going had been slow, a kind of shuffle-stop-listen-shuffle-stop routine, to avoid walking into a swarm of sandpreys and being overwhelmed.

The hole was the top of a winding stairwell that led down to another level and likely bigger problems. Deft weighed her options, considering what manner of creatures likely prowled the dark below. If only it were night, then she would be the hunter.

"Torch." She beckoned with one hand to the slaver.

Malioch handed her his torch, lit because he and Paramus didn't have the gift of being able to see in the dark. The yellow and orange flames sent shadows leaping up and over their heads as he handed it over. Alion held the torch out for a moment, peering down into the dark, then let the firebrand drop. It fell about twenty feet, bouncing on a step with a shower of orange sparks before coming to rest. At first, she thought the damn thing would go out, but the light grew as the fire once again took hold. Nothing stirred, so Deft started down.

The air became cooler as they descended. As Deft's feet touched the sandy floor, a chittering noise echoed in the stillness. The sound recalled something insect-like, creatures with hard mandibles instead of flesh.

Gods, thought Deft, let it be anything but spiders.

She was surprised to see shafts of light piercing the dark hallway at regular intervals. Some sort of engineering seemed to have drawn sunlight from above and made it shine through square plates of what looked like smoked glass. It made the constant need to light a torch unnecessary, and conserving supplies lengthened their ability to explore.

A grunt caught Deft's attention. Either Trysh or Paramus had retrieved a bandage, and the latter was busy dressing the scout's worst wound, a laceration across her calf. The proximity of the wound to her earlier injury made the knight wonder if the scout was just unlucky. Some people favored a side, causing injury in the same place more frequently than chance allowed. In the end though, it didn't matter. This wound hadn't been from the bite of a sandprey, but rather an unlucky slash by Malioch, missing a creature and instead catching Trysh in the leg. Though the cut was deep, the treatment was straightforward and didn't involve burning her again.

When Paramus finished, he straightened and nodded, helping the scout up. Deft watched while she tested her leg, wincing when she put her full weight on it. Her eyes darted about, coming to rest on Deft. Then she wiped her eyes and quickly said, "It's good. Let's keep going." She met the knight's stare again and added, "I can keep up."

Something in her eyes told Deft she knew the risk of being a burden. The knight gave the leg a cursory glance, then nodded. Time would tell if Trysh was being truthful.

Deft turned her attention to the long hallway that stretched out to either side in a roughly east-west direction. Arches lined the hallway, approximately ten paces apart. Even as she watched, more of the lights flickered to life, illuminating the long corridor. Deft could see it turned north-south at either end, but that turn was quite some distance away.

"Your guess is as good as mine," muttered the knight, feeling a bit daunted by the immensity of the place.

Surprisingly, it was Paramus who spoke. "There's a sign across from us."

And indeed, there was. It showed unrecognizable symbols on the top, along with arrows pointing left and right below. After a moment of inspection, Deft turned to the boy and said, "Here's where you earn your keep."

Paramus nodded and moved to the sign. "It's written in the old text, the type the first families used. Oww!" He grabbed his head and looked back.

Deft's mailed hand was drawing back again as she sneered, "This isn't a tour. Start reading."

Rubbing his head, the young scholar looked back at the sign and then to his left, saying, "It starts up there. We're standing approximately in the middle of the repository. Down there," he said, turning to the right, "is where it ends." He turned back to Deft and said, "Assuming what afflicts you is magical, the records are probably right around here." He took stock of his surroundings, then moved to an archway. At his approach, the sunlight above it brightened, as if sensing his proximity.

"Hold on," Trysh said through gritted teeth. When Deft looked at her askance, she replied, "Doesn't all this seem a bit too easy?"

"What're ya yapping about," muttered Malioch.

The scout leaned against a wall, her entire frame exuding weariness, but her eyes were bright and alert. "The lost library of Thoth. We find it without much trouble. We descend and within a day find this place? It seems…"—she paused— "too convenient."

Alion shrugged. "Mapmaker Reis seemed pretty sure."

Trysh shrugged, "He was missing fingers… he just wanted Mal to stop." The slaver leered at that, but Trysh ignored him and continued, "When was the last time anything went according to plan?"

"It's about time we caught a break," countered Malioch.

Deft shook her head and said, "Wait." She motioned Paramus back. "She's right."

"But the mapmaker's notes! He weren't lyin'."

Deft motioned for Mal to be quiet, then turned to Paramus. "What do you think, college boy?"

Paramus swallowed, looking physically ill as all eyes turned to him. Then he said, "Trysh might be right. I mean, if the archives are this easy to find, they'd have been plundered long ago." He looked around, his eyes finally coming to rest on the archway that had brightened at his approach. "I don't really want to touch anything right now."

"There's no pile of bodies here either, so I wouldn't get too worried," offered Deft. She considered what had been said, then came to a decision. "Perhaps we'll learn more by exploring a bit." She pointed up the corridor and said, "Let's go to the end and see what we can see."

At the collective nods of assent, Deft picked her way

forward, slowing whenever the overhead light brightened. After a few of these, she became accustomed to their behavior and continued without pausing. Somehow their actions went from being inscrutable and potentially malevolent to just something that happened whenever she got within a certain distance.

At the corner she motioned to Trysh, hooking her fingers into an L shape as she pointed around the corner. The scout gave her a perfunctory nod and moved forward, exploring around the corner on Deft's orders.

When she returned, she had little to say. "Corridor goes up about a hundred paces. Ends in a T, just like this."

Deft nodded. She looked at Paramus and asked, "Go back?"

The youth replied, "I don't know. I just read things, remember?"

Deft ignored the boy's sarcasm and sighed, her team now seeming woefully incompetent to be braving this serapeum. Still, leadership required leading, so she turned around and made her way back, motioning them to follow. Within a few heartbeats they were near the door they'd stopped Paramus from entering before.

"You think the door is really trapped?" Paramus whispered, his eyes not leaving the entryway, clearly delineated by a rectangular door-shaped seal.

"Doubtful." To Trysh's raised eyebrows Deft added, "Why make things easy, then kill us? That could've been done a dozen times earlier with less trouble."

"You're right that finding this place has been pretty easy. Almost as if someone wants us to find what we're looking for."

"You really think you'll find a cure down here?" Trysh countered.

Deft turned her full attention to the girl, pleased to see her blanch with fear. She regarded her for a moment longer before answering.

"Yes," she said, gesturing to her wasting face. "And you want me to find a cure."

"Or?"

"Or I won't be happy," Deft finished.

The scout pursed her lips, then nodded, "Yeah, we don't want that." She took a deep breath, then said, "Par, get behind me so I can check the door."

As the scholar moved out of the way, the scout dropped to a crouch and began inspecting the seams. When her hand barely brushed the surface, the door slid noiselessly into a recess in the wall and lights in the interior flickered to life. "Well now," remarked the scout, "that seems simple enough."

Deft cursed and said, "Don't get—"

The gush of triangular teeth attached to eel-like bodies interrupted anything she was going to say as sandpreys flooded out of the room, overwhelming the scout and forcing the rest of the party back. Deft heard Paramus scream but her focus was on Trysh. The scout would be eaten alive if nothing was done and she still needed her.

The knight waded in, grabbing Trysh by the arm and pulling her up, along with a dozen sandpreys attached to various parts of her light armor.

"Blaze!" Deft commanded, and Reaper obliged, creating a burning halo of fire that exploded outward from her party. The blue fire incinerated any sandpreys it touched. As that fire expanded Deft grabbed whatever surviving creatures were within reach and squeezed, popping heads off as she tried to free the scout of the infestation of bloodsuckers. Despite Paramus's warning earlier, they seemed uninterested in the death knight's blood. Perhaps her curse made her less appetizing than a young and vibrant scout, a veritable feast of nutrients conveniently stuffed into a bag of flesh not even an arm's length from the wasting knight.

Trysh swiped at a few, not more than lingering charred husks, then said, "Thanks."

"Shut up," she replied, looking past the scout and into the room. The area was large, the walls filled with what looked to be metal bins, all closed. She jerked her chin at her back and said, "You two, behind me."

Trysh and Malioch both seemed to know they were the two to which Deft referred. As soon as they fell in behind her, the knight moved carefully into the room, her eyes scanning for any movement or hint of foes, large or small.

"They must've been gathered at the door," muttered Trysh in a low voice.

"Attracted to our stink," Malioch said.

Deft motioned them to be quiet, then said, "Paramus, we have some writing here."

When there was no answer, she turned her gaze to outside the door, then cursed. The boy was gone. Shouldering her way past the scout and the slaver, she found the young scholar crouched into as small a ball as he could against the opposite wall of the corridor. Deft was sure the only reason he'd not run was the undeniable truth that he'd likely die down here without the others to protect him. Also, he'd probably forgotten which way to go.

"Get up!" Deft said with a kick. "I can't protect you if you run." That only served to push the boy into a smaller ball. Before she could kick him again, Trysh was there.

"Leave him!" she said, putting her body in the way. "I'll get him up, but you're not helping."

Deft cursed again in disgust, watching as Trysh gently

encouraged Paramus to unfold from his fear-induced ball. It was difficult to hate him more at that moment, but rather than create drama with the scout, Deft made her way back to the room's door, continuing her inspection. The area was large. The metal bins she'd noted earlier each had a small glowing blue rectangle at the center of its lid. Lights flickered to life overhead, slowly illuminating the space in a soft but clear white color. Except for the ashes of the sandpreys swirling because of their movement, nothing stirred.

She cautiously entered, Reaper ready, but nothing leapt at her from the shadows. At her left rear was Malioch. The man was faithful in his defense of her, of that she was certain. She pointed with a finger to her left and felt Malioch detach himself to reconnoiter in that direction. She herself took the right wall, moving slowly down toward a raised dais at the far end.

A scuffling sound behind her caused her to spin, only to see Trysh with Paramus peering in through the open door. Deft cocked her head in her own direction, beckoning them. Reluctantly the two made their way to the knight, stopping behind her with eyes wide.

"We make our way to the front," Deft said softly, "then you earn your keep, college-boy."

The hesitant nod was enough for Deft. She knew Trysh would keep Paramus focused, at least long enough for them to find out more about this room.

They slowly made their way forward, with Malioch paralleling them alongside the opposite wall. When they neared the dais, Deft motioned to Trysh. The scout pulled Paramus behind her and made her way to a panel with glowing writing covering it in neat horizontal lines. As they neared, the lights in the room came up, bathing them all in a soft yellow glow. Suddenly, the room seemed much less menacing.

The lighting must have quelled some of the fear the scholar felt, for Deft could see his hesitancy melt away as his eyes drank in the lit panel.

Stupid, she thought, to let your guard down just because of some writing. Then again, she didn't think Paramus had much in the way of survival instincts. Maybe that was for the best. If the boy could decipher the writing, she'd be one step closer to a potential cure.

After a few moments the scholar motioned to Deft to join him near the glossy black panel. Deft looked about, then made her way carefully up, close enough to hear but with plenty of room to swing Reaper should the need arise.

"This is ancient," breathed Paramus, "like from the first times."

"Don't care. Can you read it?" Deft barked back in a harsh whisper.

"I think so." Paramus pointed to a portion near the top, "This is a menu of functions."

"What?" Deft asked.

"Functions, like tasks. There's records organizing, retrieval, even medical…"

"Medical?"

Paramus nodded, "Selecting one of these will likely summon more information about it."

Deft pondered that for a moment, then asked, "Is there anything about defense… these sandpreys?"

He looked back at the panel, scanning down the list of entries. He finally stopped at one and said, "This says, Security. It might be what you want."

"How does it work?" Deft asked, her attention now pulled to the black panel display and its glowing symbols.

Paramus tapped the one he'd identified as 'Security' and

the symbol flashed, then a new list of tasks showed up. This time, however, Deft could read the language. "Seems like it's trying to be helpful." The knight skewered the young scholar with her gaze and said, "Less use for you."

He shrank back at that but didn't go away. Instead he looked at the display and said, "There's a lot of tasks I don't understand, but this one"—he pointed to the word "Deactivate,"— "probably turns the security measures off."

"You think?" Deft remarked, the disdain hard in her voice.

"Look, there's a lot here," Trysh put in. "Let Par sift through it while we stand guard. He's still the fastest reader amongst us, and if we're going to find a cure for you, he's our best chance at doing it quickly."

Deft took a breath, weighing her options. Then she stepped back from the panel and said, "Fine." She tromped to her side of the wall. Malioch did the same to the opposite wall, leaving Trysh and Par near the information panel. "Let me know if anything useful comes up."

"Will do," said the scout. Then she and Paramus began searching the records for any hint on how to reverse the curse afflicting Deft.

Time crawled by as the two worked in silence. It stretched as Paramus ran through combination after combination to unlock more information, working backward each time he was stopped by the system that governed the library's willingness to release its secrets. Deft knew more than half a day had passed because she could feel her strength begin to grow, telling her the sun was setting. That was a welcome sign. Malioch had put his back to the wall, squatting with his blade propped before him. The knight just stood there, Reaper resting on one shoulder, watching Trysh and Par as they continued at the panel.

Finally, the scout said, "I think he's got something."

Deft turned her head a fraction at that, an undead statue reanimating. Then she moved over to the duo, scanning the panel.

"Here," Trysh indicated, "it says something called the Phoenix Protocol can be used to reconfigure your body."

"Reconfigure?" Deft asked.

"Fancy word for healing," Paramus said. "Basically, it means it can remake your body so it's normal again."

"How?" inquired the knight, still trying to decipher the writing on the panel.

"It looks like there's something called the "Cypher," which is a key that unlocks the protocol. I suppose we'd ask it to remove your affliction."

"And where's this Cypher?"

Before the scout could answer there was a blinding flash of blue-white light and an ear crumpling whump of displaced air. Deft shook her head to clear it, Reaper leaping to the ready, but the sight that greeted her brought any action she'd been half-contemplating to a halt. Behind the dais the wall had disappeared, replaced with a square gate cut from white scintillating light.

"Sir Deft, you ask the most important question one might ask at such a time," a voice said from within the light that glared like the midday sun. A figure emerged slowly, a woman with skin a soft blue and eyes that flashed the color of sapphires. "And rejoice for the answer is your destiny."

Trysh and Paramus had fallen back toward Deft, the former having her blade out but not quite up, the latter stumbling backward until he fell on his rump. Malioch moved forward with a snarl on his lips, his blade raised.

The woman's eyes flicked to him for a moment, and in that instant the ground flowed up Malioch's legs like mud, hardening and fixing him in place. Then she turned her attention back to Deft. "I do not consort with lackeys. You and I, however, have much to discuss."

Deft shook her head, "And you are?"

"The Lady," whispered Trysh, her eyes wide in awe. "By the gods, she's the Eye of the Sun."

The blue-skinned woman inclined her head at Trysh. "I welcome thee of faith, for I am the Celestial Lady Lilyth."

The knight looked at her and shook her head. "I've learned not to trust my gods. They fail you every time."

"Do they?" inquired the Lady. "And to what miracle do you owe your life, sir knight? Why did the red mage's spell not kill you?"

"What?" breathed Deft, her eyes searching the woman's face.

"I did not save you then only to lose you now. You are my weapon, to strike those I wish."

"I don't fight for anyone," said Deft, brandishing Reaper across her body.

Lilyth's eyes went from Deft's to the weapon. "What will you do with that?" She moved closer, flowing across the dais in a smooth motion that looked more like floating than walking. Within moments she was an arm's length from the undead knight. "Have at it, then. Strike away."

Deft pulled the mace back, then sent a blow aimed for Lilyth's forehead. The weapon arced down, striking with crushing force just off-center of the Lady's head. A boom sounded, the sound of metal striking bone, but magnified a thousand times. To Deft's amazement, where there should have been bloody fragments of skull and brains, there was nothing. The mace had bounced off Lilyth's head as if the woman were made of steel, leaving no mark to show its impact.

The goddess tilted her head and said, "Even accursed, you are still a mere mortal. You cannot harm me with the crude instruments of this world." She gestured and Reaper dissolved into dust in Deft's hands, falling like ashes from a fire. "Do you ken the meaning of my choice to manifest before you?"

Deft began, "I don't care—"

"Kneel before your goddess," Lilyth intoned, and Deft felt herself pulled to her knees, her legs locked tight by the ground hardening around her legs. Trysh had already been kneeling, and as far as she could see no living stone encircled her. Paramus still lay blubbering on his back. Evidently Lilyth didn't care enough to do anything to him.

Curse the buffoon's luck, she thought.

"Take care with your next words, sir knight. My patience has its limits." To Deft's surprise, Lilyth moved over to Paramus and offered him a hand. The young scholar took it gingerly, as if her skin itself might erupt in fire. When he was pulled to his knees with nothing more happening, he seemed to gain some control over himself. Deft couldn't help but roll her eyes in their ruined sockets.

"What do you want?"

Lilyth turned her attention back to the undead knight and said, "You sowed ruin amongst my people. You hunted those born to the Way, and when you took their lives, you also hurt those who fell under my aegis."

"And I'd do it again if the gods hadn't abandoned me," retorted Deft.

"Abandoned you? Have I not made it clear you live because of my intervention?"

"So you claim," said Deft, throwing caution to the wind. What was the worst that could happen to her at this point? She'd already been cursed by this wasting disease. Her life as a magehunter was over. What could Lilyth take from her that hadn't been taken already?

Lilyth inclined her head and said, "It took much, crumbs dropped here and there, to bring you here. Many years were spent preparing for your ultimate sacrifice."

"My sacrifice? Ha!"

Lilyth's gaze turned icy. "Won't you?"

She moved closer to the kneeling knight, coming to stand directly before her. "There is only one cure for your affliction: the Phoenix. What will you do to earn your own salvation?"

Deft just stared at her, hoping her hate manifested itself with such intensity it would kill Lilyth where she stood. Unfortunately, nothing so dramatic happened. Instead, it was Deft who finally succumbed, falling in on herself as the power of the Lady was brought to bear, forcing Deft down to the floor like a supplicant. "What do you want?"

"We're finally communicating, sir knight." Lilyth took a breath, then said, "Ages ago, when Sovereign fell from the sky, I did battle with the Phoenix. At that time, it was still young, maligned, and could not withstand me. I kenned its need, its ability to remake that which needed remaking, and for that reason I showed mercy and left it alive."

"And now?"

"Sovereign healed the Phoenix, gave it time to grow, to become stronger. Now it cannot be killed by any man nor woman, living or dead, at day or night, indoors nor out. It is nigh invulnerable."

"Then what can we do?" snarled Deft.

Lilyth bent forward, her face coming so close to Deft the knight could smell her fragrance, like apple blossoms. The demon parted her pink lips and said, "You are going to steal the Cypher, sir knight. You can rid yourself of the affliction with which you've been cursed." She took on long finger and pulled Deft's face up by her chin and said, "And, when the time is right, I will give you the red mage."

The offer took Deft's breath away. She'd been so singularly focused on curing herself it hadn't occurred to her she'd ever get vengeance on the man who'd cursed her. Yet if this really was Lady Lilyth, nothing she said could be trusted. "What does that mean?" sneered Deft. "Sounds like I just do what you want, and maybe you'll cure me."

"Serve me well and in return I will take the Oath to release you when you have absolved yourself of your crimes."

Now Deft's ears perked up. "You'll take the Oath?"

Lilyth nodded, "It serves my purpose, which is the recovery of the Cypher. Succeed and you will reap ruin on those who maligned you. I swear it."

Deft's eyes flicked across her party, but she didn't care what they thought. This was between her and Lilyth. A cure, and vengeance! She raised her gaze, met the sapphire eyes just inches from her own, and said, "Deal."

SHORNHELM

T he Lady curses us," Illandra said, wringing her hands as her gaze darted from the makeshift royal hall to her husband, Rory, Lord of Shornhelm, whose generous bulk reclined on a seat brought in from the remains of the stronghold. A gaggle of courtiers shuffled behind, a small retinue eager to support her as she wrestled with how to set them back upon the righteous path. The Lady was the light of truth, yet despite the signs many still refused to embrace her as their salvation, even after devastation had been levied upon Shornhelm. Illandra didn't understand how anyone could forsake their faith in light of this. What more could they ask than to have their god walk amongst them, living again?

"Come away from there, Lilly," said the king, his eyes straying up from what looked to be repair plans for the main stronghold. His gaze lingered on her face with a look that said he doubted her sanity. Then Rory glanced down to sign the report before him. She waved her followers away, seeking a reassuring word from her husband.

"Do you have to do this now?" she implored, moving closer.

"Cursing is busy work for a god," he said, finishing his signature with his typical flourish, even though it was an unnecessary formality on working plans. He looked at her from under bushy eyebrows, "but these orders won't sign themselves." He grabbed an apple slice from a waiting platter, then gave her that smile he thought was so charming. Well, if the truth be told, she admitted it was. But she

219

wouldn't let herself be distracted.

"We need to prepare. The Lady has returned."

The king sighed, "Nomads assault Bara'cor. No word from EvenSea or Dawnlight in more than three fortnights. We faced the red mage and lost. If the Lady is here, let her keep us safe. I'll welcome any luck that comes our way." The large man popped the slice into his mouth, his jowls working as he chewed the crisp fruit. The king was not a man to skip meals, his rotund form testing the competency of his tailors.

"Luck?" Illandra turned to her husband, her sea-green eyes catching the sun's brilliance in a flash of ire. "It's the Lady's grace that delivered us, nothing else." She could feel her fingernails digging into the flesh of her palms in frustration. "We should attend to the offerings. She can't be happy."

Her husband stood up and stretched. He looked tired, the recent events affecting everything surrounding their lands and adding pressure as they sought to rebuild from the red mage's assault. The work went slowly, as Shornhelm was pieced back together like a child's playhouse shattered by tantrums.

She watched Rory grab a cloth and wipe his fingers. Tossing it to a waiting servant, he pulled her into a tight embrace and said, "Don't worry yourself so. We'll gather the folk and pay the proper obeisance, but we've also got to think about how to feed and shelter everyone." Young Durnal, only a few months old, sat within the wet nurse's warm embrace, making tiny gurgling sounds. His small voice echoed lightly in the large chamber, an innocent sound. Illandra loved her child, and it was for him that she prayed most fervently to the Lady. Only her aegis could bring true peace to Shornhelm and her people.

"The signs are everywhere," she said, looking up at him

as his arm encircled her small shoulders, "waiting for us to accept them." Illandra turned to her husband and gripped his coat.

"Please tell me we'll make the offerings," she pleaded, "in the old way. Perhaps the Lady will gift us with another child."

The king closed his eyes, then nodded as he squeezed her shoulders to reassure her.

"Worry not, we'll honor the Lady." He shifted his arm to grip her waist and pulled her into a side-by-side walk, slowly pacing around the rebuilt room with the retinue still in tow like a disjointed tail.

"The Galadines are rattling their sabers, pompous and arrogant, as always. They want help breaking their siege, as if we're just sitting around all prettied up with nothing to do."

The queen shook her head. "She's an Aeonian, what did you expect?"

"Not much," the king conceded. "Still, neither Dawnlight nor EvenSea have responded. If they too have been assaulted by the red mage, then—"

There was a flash and a small whump of air being displaced. When her eyes cleared, the queen looked around for the source. What she saw dropped her to her knees, her head bowed in supplication.

"Be at ease," said a woman's voice. "We come in peace."

Beside her Rory coughed, his breath catching as if he couldn't find words. Into that breach Illandra said, "My lady, we are yours to command."

The dark-skinned goddess took a step forward, towering over those assembled before her. At her side were a half dozen others, winged with golden-colored metal and armed for battle, but their weapons stayed sheathed. The goddess smiled.

"My name is Kalika and I serve as herald for the Lady Lilyth, the Eye of the Sun, and your All-Mother. I have been instructed to treat with you on the Lady's behalf."

"You are not the Lady?" breathed Illandra, not looking up.

A gentle hand came and pulled her up softly by her chin, until she stood. When she finally raised her eyes, it was to a face as beautiful as any she'd ever seen. Dark skin, delicate nose, a wide forehead, and framed by raven black hair that shone iridescent where light hit it. That hair was pulled back into a pony-like tail, adorned carefully with silver chains studded by diamonds. Blue eyes, serene and calm, stared back at her.

"No," the goddess shook her head. "The Lady regrets not being able to attend to you herself, but she wants nothing but your happiness."

"W-what can we do?" stuttered the king. Illandra leaned into him, hoping they could share their strength.

Kalika smiled, her eyes crinkling in pleasure.

"My Lady wishes the assault on Shornhelm had not been necessary but upon her word, it was. In recompense, we will help you rebuild both your fortress and your lands. It was never her desire that true followers be punished for their faith."

"You're going to help us?" inquired the king.

Kalika nodded, "We will. And ask only that you consider a request the Lady makes of you, once your lands are healed."

"Anything," blurted the queen. "It is our only hope, to serve."

The dark-skinned goddess nodded, but said, "Not all the land shares your faith, my lady. Those who do not will pay for their doubt. Once Shornhelm is ready, your armies will serve us faithfully."

Before Illandra could say anything, her husband had clamped a hand down on her wrist, almost painfully.

"Much has transpired, fealties given, oaths taken," he said. "Our position is tenuous with the other Houses. If we had to delay such support…?"

Kalika tilted her head, her gaze searching. Then her face darkened as she said, "We will withdraw our aid. Shornhelm will stand as it is. Those who believe in the Lady will be offered a place with us in the City Eternal, Olympious. Then Shornhelm will be marked as an enemy and suffer along with the rest who doubt."

Then the goddess smiled again and leaned forward.

"Do not choose this route, good king. Of all those in Edyn, your people have been the first to receive the Lady's blessed offer. Do not discard it so quickly."

"We accept!" exclaimed the queen, looking directly at Rory. When the king dropped his eyes in acquiescence, Illandra turned to the goddess. "We accept, goddess Kalika. Please tell the Lady we accept with open hearts."

Kalika's eyes seemed to bore into Illandra's own, as if searching for the truth in those words. Whatever she saw must've been good enough. The goddess stood and gestured to her men. "Heraclyes will see to your needs. Do not fear, for you now stand beside us as part of our family. You are cherished above all others, and to show you the Lady's kindness, behold."

Another flash occurred, smaller than the first, and a black portal opened. At first nothing happened, but then the squeal of a child could be heard. From the opening, a dozen, then thirty, and finally almost a hundred children flooded out, enough to almost fill the small hall they stood in.

"These are the children lost to those here at Shornhelm. The Lady has recovered them from the Archmage Valarius Galadine and his army of ill-born elves. Let them be reunited with their folk, let them again bask in the love of those who thought them lost."

"I can't believe it," whispered Illandra to herself. She could feel her husband nodding and gripped his arm more tightly.

Kalika looked down at them and smiled again.

"Have faith in the Lady, and you will have eternal life under her most blessed sun."

DEFT ARRIVES

When Duncan arrived, a wall of dwarves stood motionless looking down from their higher vantage to something he couldn't yet see. He tried to push himself through, then felt Halp go around him and open the way like a plow through loose dirt. Curses met the dwarven axer, but before anyone could protest, he was past them and so was Duncan with the rest of the companions in tow. Finally, after wending through a press of dwarven rear ends and belts, the crowd parted he found himself looking down at a sight he hadn't expected.

"Archmage," the undead queensmark said, inclining her head slightly in greeting. "We have unfinished business."

"Deft," Duncan said in an exhalation of disappointment, his pronouncement matching his emotional tiredness. The sight of the magehunter was the last thing they needed. Suddenly part of him felt the weight of their history soaking into his soul like clothes filling with river mud, threatening to drown him with memories of his old self.

His untortured mind, clean and clear for the first time since he could remember, knew Deft represented everything he'd done wrong wrapped into a single act of malice. He recalled his words with clarity undiminished by time: 'I am the Scythe. Like the reaper's tool, I ascend those found worthy, or claim those found wanting.' And with those words he'd consigned her to a fate that now seemed nothing but cruel. That he'd not cared a whit was worse. He took a tentative step forward, unsure of what exactly to say.

225

"You know this thing?" asked Jesyn. She looked at him with brows drawn together in that universal sign people used when they hoped he'd somehow redeem himself. He resisted a sudden urge to stab the adept, perhaps a bit of his old self fighting its way up from the depths. Though he quickly attempted to dismiss the thought, it must've shown in his eyes. Jesyn leaned back a bit, her expression going from quizzical to guarded.

He turned his attention back to the magehunter before he made more mistakes.

"Deft," he said, this time addressing her directly. "We don't need to—"

The undead magehunter raised a hand, cutting him off. She moved forward and spread her arms. As she did so, the air behind her wavered and ten furies stepped into being from the nothingness, arranged in a loose semicircle. Each had dark blue with silver-edged armor, helmed and armed with blades or spears. Their eyes glowed a soft yellow, giving away no indication of their disposition.

Of course, he thought looking past them, it's going to get worse. It always does.

Thousands of Aeris backfilled the space behind the furies, a horde innumerably deep and growing as more and more arrived, possibly attracted to the scent of the living. They too appeared from thin air, stepping into line and swelling the ranks of those who'd arrived earlier. Their only clear emotion was hunger. It radiated from them along with their fetid smell, a smell he'd come to associate with the desire to possess. As living hosts for those abandoned by Lilyth, Duncan and his companions represented the only escape from Arcadia.

A few of the more powerful Aeris were girded for battle in armor befitting their station. Flitting between them like hungry dogs were the vulpine forms of mistfrights and other shapes, sickly white and vaguely worm-like. Pale yellow eyes, the color of rotting fat, dotted the landscape and stretched to the edge of the plains of Harmagedon. They watched the defenders with intelligence, a predator's cunning lighting their eyes with something more feral than just hunger. The odds had already shifted to Deft's favor. Duncan began to wonder if this would be a battle or a massacre.

"You ran from Avalyon," Deft sneered. "What kindness led you here, where there are so many for us to take?"

"Who are you?" demanded Arek. His son appeared at Duncan's side and looked down on the scene with a mixture of fear and anger.

The magehunter looked at the boy, then back at Duncan. Although the rotting skin of her face and that permanent bone-white smile didn't give one much to read, something in her stance made her look pensive, as if she were mulling something over. A word came to mind which he'd not normally associate with any magehunter, much less one with as an illustrious career in killing as Deft—hesitant.

"You haven't introduced me to your companions."

Duncan was perplexed. Deft had said more in this exchange than ever before. As if to echo his own thoughts, Ash whispered from behind him, "Why is she stalling?"

The dwarves within earshot supplied the answer, for they had the most to worry, but their grumblings made it hard to understand what they were saying. Finally, it was Halp who said, "We need to do something and do it fast, or we're going to be the clothes these things wear."

Arek and Ash changed form, causing the front row of dwarves to fall back a step. More curses, but not many complained much about having a towering war angel to stand beside.

Alion stepped forward and said, "Azrael, Orion, we are well met. But you two have chosen an ill place for your last stand."

Arcimedis shouted from up the line, "If you're planning on talking us to death, you're off to a good start." A bunch of raucous laughter swept through the dwarves.

Duncan could feel even his own mouth quirk and his estimation of the fat dwarven leader grew. He'd initially thought of Arcimedis as an educated bureaucrat. Whoever left him in charge clearly had known better. Then he remembered and grabbed Jesyn, turning her toward him.

"You remember what I said?" He searched her eyes, "About changing?"

Jesyn nodded, "Don't hold the form too long. Remember to change back. Fight, survive," she said.

Duncan smiled and said, "I get the feeling I'd like you."

Then he turned back to the front line, scanning the scene. Even more Aeris soldiers had arrived, growing like a pool of blue and silver helms punctuated by the glints of spears and blades pointing to the sky.

Arek peered down through his helm. "Our weapons have been enchanted to kill you. Don't throw your lives away needlessly."

Good try, kid, thought Duncan, but they don't have any other option.

The undead knight turned to the seething mass of Aeris behind her and said, "If you don't want a body, a chance to rejoin our Lady… leave." Then she turned back to Arek and Ash, waiting. No creature retreated. Instead, they pressed forward in anticipation.

"Cowards die a thousand times. Heroes, but once," Alion Deft said. She saluted with a fist and snapped her visor down. Now only her rictus grin could be seen leering from beneath, promising pain. As if that were a signal, anyone who'd not yet drawn a weapon did so. Horns blared, echoing across the Aeris horde as the mass of living dead gnashed their fangs and prepared to charge.

Arcimedis shouted, "Use the mountain!" He and his brethren instantly sank into the earth, hoping to protect themselves with the rock itself. Suddenly Duncan and his companions were standing alone on the bare rock face against thousands of Aeris spread out before them.

"Should'a guessed that would happen," Halp said to no one.

"I can see why Jesyn likes you," Duncan heard Arek say.

"Not gonna matter much now," the old dwarf replied.

Then a single loud blast, a trumpet that sounded like it heralded the end of the world, echoed across the field. Whatever had held the Aeris broke, the horde surging forward like a wave made entirely of razor edges and sharp points. Though some bolted up the hill toward them, many dove into the mountainside, their forms becoming incorporeal like the dwarves.

"Uh-oh," Duncan said despite himself. Somehow, he had a feeling the dwarves' phasing ability wouldn't help them. He slowly drew his gun, unsure if even it would work.

Then an armored hand pushed him back.

"Stay behind me!" Jesyn ordered.

The adept had changed form into an angel made of fire. She flicked her wings in alternating sweeps, slinging blades made of fire down the hillside like fiery comets from the sky. Where they struck, flames blossomed and Aeris died. She'd drawn a blade made of fire. Arek and Ash stood beside her. The three of them towered over Duncan, who found himself pulling at his torc though he knew it was useless. Frustration

229

overcame him at this simple ring of metal, foiling his ability to help.

Suddenly he felt cold hands grab his legs. He looked down. An Aeris warrior was climbing him. Duncan punched, but his fists went through the ethereal winged being.

"Arek!" he cried in panic.

His son turned, then swept his blade in a quick slice, never looking to confirm the death, as if he already knew. Though insubstantial to Duncan, the being's neck sliced open and the body toppled over, headless.

Another Aeris clawed its way up, but a strike from Ash skewered it. The firstmark had already turned back, using his blade now in tandem with his wings to slow the onslaught of Aeris trying to reach anyone who could be possessed.

Duncan turned to see Brianna grab a blade from a weapon rack, her swing bisecting an Aeris inexpertly, but killing it nonetheless. He fired his gun at a mistfright, only to see whatever it fired go through without doing any harm. That shot however turned the creature's attention to him. He backed up, cursing. He'd forgotten to have Arek enchant the projectiles within his weapon.

He felt behind him for something, anything he could use, only to see the creature joined by two more. The beasts must've sensed an easy victory and spread out, flanking him, and again he wished for a connection to the Way. He spun, only to see a fourth close the circle. He wasn't getting out of this.

The first one leapt and he rolled under it, but the second caught him just as he tried to rise. He opened his mouth to scream, but instantly one of the beasts entered him, the cold mist feeling like a wet gag forced down his throat, blocking his voice.

Within an instant however, the creature fled from his

body, rearing above Duncan as it screamed. He flinched at a blow that went through his head. A sudden jerk on his torc made him stumble to his knees: the creature's blow hit his torc as if it were a solid thing to the Aeris. He felt the ring of metal pull at his neck, but it didn't budge. The creature screamed with rage, then drew a blade and aimed for the kneeling archmage's neck. Duncan put up his weak hand, the one missing fingers, trying to stop the inevitable.

Then a golden arrow burned a hole through the creature's chest. It fell dead, dissipating into the air like it had never existed. As it did, so the other three surrounding Duncan fled, looking for easier prey.

Yetteje approached, Valor drawn.

"Can you stand?"

Duncan looked down at his torc in disbelief. Clearly the torc nullified powers, but it also protected him from possession?

"Hey, talking to you!"

He looked up startled, only to see Yetteje firing arrows in rapid succession while protecting his back.

"I'd be happy to let you die," she said as she tracked an Aeris and then let another arrow fly, "but Arek needs you."

"Yes," he said numbly, smearing blood across his face as he wiped his nose and eyes. He realized his hand was cut. He'd fallen near a dwarven blade, leaf shaped with a keen double edge and a rune-carved hilt.

"Pick that up," she said, pointing with her chin, "and make yourself useful. Maybe cut your own throat." Then the princess went back to what she was doing, which Duncan quickly realized was protecting Halp and Brianna with withering fire from her bow. Except for her first arrow, she hadn't been bothering to protect him at all. Even that may have been just to get nearer to her friends.

Neither Halp nor Brianna had fled into the ground as the rest of the dwarves had, instead choosing to fight from behind Arek and Ash's legs. The strategy had proved sound except for whenever the two war angels stepped in some unexpected direction to absorb the shock of a charge. When that happened, one or both were inevitably thrown to the ground and then vulnerable to grasping hands and teeth that seemed to come up from beneath them.

Duncan quickly looked around for Jesyn. The adept had disappeared as Ash had taken her place. He hoped she hadn't come to harm defending him. He hurried over, crouching and watching the scene. He used the blade to cut some cloth from his robe, then quickly wrapped his hand. It was the one already maimed, missing fingers from his spell to summon the gholem Vengeance.

My unlucky hand, he mused wryly, then crouched, waiting with blade raised.

The battle was pitched, with dwarves flying out of the ground as if reacting to being struck. Duncan saw more than one attacked by Aeris who looked, for lack of a better description, ravenous. They attacked in a frenzy of arms, legs, and teeth, until one dominated enough to enter the body of the hapless victim. From there the rest would sulk away, looking for another victim. The one taken would arch his or her back, as if choking, then go limp. A few moments later they would rise, and a shockwave would detonate the air as they changed form.

He watched another dwarf raise his hands and the ground erupt into sharp jagged spikes. It would have killed a normal man, but the Aeris simply walked through the obstruction. That dwarf was lucky, diving into the earth again before the Aeris or her companions could overrun his position.

Duncan couldn't tell how many had been taken, but the

battlefield boomed with that same detonation he'd heard before each time a dwarven warrior was lost, the blast signifying a body changing into something more elemental, into a vessel possessed by the Aeris. Using the true power of the builder's body the newly possessed would become a battlefield juggernaut not unlike what Duncan had faced in Baalor. A sudden succession of booms told Duncan they'd found the wounded, probably possessing them without a fight. The archmage felt sorry for those souls, but there was nothing he could do.

One quick look toward the fields of Harmagedon showed him barely a tenth of Deft's forces had been committed. It looked like every Aeris left in the world was spread out like a black stain across this land. This fight had only one inevitable outcome—the possession of every single dwarf on the mountain. It was only a matter of time.

Then the moment he knew would come arrived. A bat-like shadow crossed his peripheral vision and Deft landed, along with half her lieutenants. Without his powers, Duncan knew he wouldn't last a heartbeat against them.

Brianna must've seen this because she screamed, "Arek!"

The earth trembled as something gargantuan moved, and Duncan could tell his son now stood over him like a living shield. He surmised that meant Ash was guarding the hillside on his own. To his surprise, a flaming foot appeared in his peripheral vision, standing beside Arek. It was Jesyn in fire angel.

"Guess they want something they can possess," she said to them, "and that's not us."

Deft shrugged, "Let's not bandy words—"

"We won't," Arek said, and attacked.

Duncan remembered Arek's fight with Kisan. He'd also

seen Arek fight against Valarius's forces, but he'd never seen two adepts fighting together like Arek and Jesyn. They seemed made for battle. Each moved as if they knew what the other would do, protecting each other in what seemed more reflex than conscious thought. Where one went high, the other came in low. Each attacked in a rhythm that kept the furies backing up.

Something in the boy had changed. He always moved with an economy of motion, but now there was a feeling of tight control, of mastery. It reminded him of watching other archmages weave their Aspects into their Affinities. They did so with an economy and artistry that made them truly deadly. He silently thanked Silbane again for the gift he'd shared, allowing Duncan to appreciate the skill Arek and Jesyn showed as they fought the undead magehunter together.

Their attacks were making a difference. Arek ran straight at Deft, who charged to meet his block. At the last moment he feinted right and sliced quickly, opening the throat of one of the six who followed. Simultaneously Jesyn, with lightning speed, dodged inward and hit Deft hard with an overhand strike from her blade. Because her form towered over the undead knight, she seemed unstoppable.

Amazingly, Deft caught Jesyn's strike on her shield, then spun and stabbed at her knee, forcing the adept back. She then tilted her shield in a strange fashion and kicked hard, catching Jesyn in the shin and knocking her back. Duncan realized with grudging admiration that the magehunter had blinded the adept momentarily by catching a small part of sunlight on her shield and reflecting it into her eyes. Jesyn still recovered nicely, using her stance and a slight twist of her leg to accept and redirect the force. Simultaneously she beat her wings once, using the air to slow her backward fall and letting loose a billowing gush of flame into Deft's face.

At first Duncan thought there would be no way for Deft to survive two people with their training, but then he remembered who she was. Ex-kingsmark and trained as a true Bladesmen centuries before Arek or Jesyn had even been born, Alion Deft was no one to be trifled with.

"Don't take chances!" he yelled. "End her quickly." He hoped they understood this and didn't get overly confident. The woman had an uncanny knack for surviving the impossible, including his wasting spell. How she'd done so was beyond his ken.

Jesyn attacked again with an overhanded swing followed by sweeping wing strikes meant to bring her flames to bear. Alion rolled under the swing and sliced at the adept's feet, forcing Jesyn to retreat into three furies. They executed spiraling strikes of their own, each working in tandem to keep Jesyn's defenses up, blocking her ability to attack. Only the young adept's skill saved her from being skewered then and there.

Duncan watched in confusion as Arek shrunk himself to be closer in size to his opponents. So too did Jesyn. Why? Then Silbane's gifted insight supplied the answer. Their size, while advantageous against a few opponents, also allowed many more to flank them and get within striking distance. Being larger meant being easier to hit. It was not ideal when facing Deft and her furies.

A pang of metal on metal made Duncan turn to see Arek fall back as one of Deft's lieutenants spun edged steel in an intricate pattern. Her partner flanked the boy, each preparing to attack when Arek committed himself to the other. Arek began to move to one side, his eyes flashing white fire, but then a blast sounded, larger and louder than anything before. It was so loud that the Aeris cringed, covering their ears, and stopped. Some looked skyward to find the source.

"You will cease!" a deep voice intoned. It echoed across the fields of Harmagedon, speaking to one and all with equal temerity. It was delivered with such force that some dropped their weapons as if compelled.

At that command, what Duncan would never have expected happened. The Aeris, all of them, knelt. He scrambled to his feet even as he saw Jesyn and Arek move a little closer to his position. Neither looked happy and both had taken a few hits, though Duncan couldn't see any blood.

Good, he thought.

"What was that?" Ash asked, looking a bit haggard. He joined them from the hillside, obviously having had to contend with his own survival. It was only when he saw Brianna and Yetteje that Duncan realized Ash had been keeping them safe as well.

Duncan turned to Alion Deft, who hung her head. Her jaw was clenched, the muscles that showed on one side bunching, as if forcing her against her own volition to hold her tongue.

Slowly, the air wavered and where before there had been a clearing, a silver camp with large tents appeared. Its Aeris guards, armed in silver armor, bore spears with heads shaped like wicked crescent moons. There was a dozen of these guards, all dangerous looking, but not so much as to elicit such obeisance.

Duncan knew who this was and went to a knee, signaling with a quick hand gesture to both Jesyn and Arek to do the same. He was happy to see them comply. However, when Jesyn changed form, a gasp sputtered from her mouth and she fell, curled up on one side as the price of her first transformation took hold. The archmage held up his hand to Arek, trying to stop him from moving suddenly. The boy ignored him of course, grabbing his friend and pulling her head onto his knee.

At that moment the largest tent's flap was thrown aside and a figure emerged. Long alabaster and silver hair fell to frame a white-bearded face with skin as black as ebonite. Two white eyes with pupils set like argentium flashed from under silver-white brows. The man's skin, where it showed, was also as black, like the night sky had come to rest itself upon his being. As Duncan squinted, he could make out silver flecks in the skin, catching the light in iridescent flashes. If Lilyth were the blue of the evening skies, this man was the stars dotting the black expanse of the universe.

The being noticed Deft and her surviving lieutenants still standing.

"You will not fight upon my lands without my permission." His voice was now not booming, but also no less commanding. It sounded like a lord used to being obeyed, a matter-of-fact statement that left one agreeing before consciously understanding what had been agreed to.

Deft seemed immune. "Your lands?" she sneered. "And to whom do you pay fealty, Zafir? These souls I claim for Lady Lilyth. You have no right to interfere."

Zafir's lips pursed, and a star-flecked hand stroked his alabaster beard, then curled into a fist under his chin. The other arm came up to cross under the first and he tucked his free hand into his armpit, his entire posture saying, "and what do I do with you?"

Instead, he asked, "And where is Lady Lilyth?"

Deft shrugged. "She has transitioned to Edyn."

"Then," the skies above them grew darker as he corrected her, "as Lord Zafir I have every right, for I command here." At this, the Aeris near Deft backed respectfully away, still looking down.

Duncan couldn't help but be awed. This was a true Celestial, like Lilyth, but also different. He was the Lord of the East Gate, and as such held dominion over their way back to Edyn. The same intensity he'd felt with Lilyth, the same feeling of being on the edge of a knife, now flooded through the archmage. He shook his head, a part of him hoping Deft would do something stupid and get herself killed.

Nothing, a voice from deep inside cautioned, is ever that easy.

The magehunter seemed smarter than that, noticing the Aeris under her command had already deferred to him. Even her lieutenants had taken knee. Sighing, she knelt, bowing her head. For a moment, Duncan thought Lord Zafir would take offense, but the Celestial seemed less interested in Deft than in Arek and Jesyn, who still lay in a fetal position. His eyes locked on Duncan and his companions.

"I meant no offense, Lord Zafir. What is your desire?" said Deft as she sheathed her weapon and opened her arms wide with empty palms to the sky.

Zafir's eyes narrowed. "I would speak with my former brothers-in-arms."

"That cannot be—" Deft started, but an angry murmuring, like the buzzing of a thousand bees, erupted from the assembled Aeris. The magehunter's skull slowly looked to the left and right.

Carefully, she bowed again. "These are foes of the Lady. As such they are not—"

Again, the crowd began to protest her affront, and had any been standing, Duncan did not doubt weapons would have been leveled in her direction.

Zafir smiled. "Queensmark, do not mistake rank with power. No celestial gainsays another's decision, especially by proxy."

He paused for a second, looking out over the fields of Harmagedon, then back down at her. "I could order your men to tear you apart and they would gladly do so to serve me."

A few tense moments passed before the magehunter deflated. Her head slumped and she said, "Of course, my lord. Your wish is our command."

Zafir started to turn away when Deft barked, "But I never forget those who've wronged me."

There was a space of a heartbeat, perhaps two, and Zafir's guards leveled their weapons, all aimed at the undead magehunter. Duncan couldn't believe their luck! The cursed woman had gone too far. Now her existence would be ended by her own careless mouth. Perhaps Duncan wouldn't have to face his own guilt for what he'd done to her.

Zafir intervened, saying, "Hold!" His mouth crooked into a small smile, then he turned his attention to his guards and said, "Bring Lords Scythe and Azrael," pointing at Duncan and Arek.

"Find a place for Anala of the Flame to recover." His gaze took in Jesyn, then he turned to Ash. "Let Orion and the others find a suitable place to rest. No one is to be harmed."

He turned his attention to the thousands of Aeris now gathered on the plains of Harmagedon, his voice pitched so all could hear. "There will be no hunting until I have finished my discussion. This is my will."

We knew it, the little voice in Duncan's head said softly. You can't drown me out forever. Worse to worst.

He took a deep breath, trying and failing to forget that part of him that spoke now from the depths.

Always, worse to worst.

FLASHBACK:

LILYTH'S QUEST

Excellent!" Lilyth's eyes beamed and she clapped her hands together, suddenly looking almost girlish in her delight. "You'll be happy you chose to work with me."

Deft nodded, then pointed to her legs. "Can we start by getting up?"

"Oh!" Lilyth's hand came up to cover her mouth in a gesture that seemed to try to convey the act had been nothing more than a mistake. "Please forgive my oversight." She waved a hand and the bonds holding Deft and Malioch disappeared, the stone turning back to a sand-like substance before sifting to the floor in a small, fine cloud.

Deft rose slowly. At her full height she dwarfed the blue-skinned child before her.

"And now the Oath," she said.

Lilyth smiled. "Are you certain? I am pleased, but once done, it cannot be undone."

Deft sneered and said, "Not expecting me to take the deal? What causes your hesitation now, girl?"

The goddess's eyes narrowed, but her smile never left her face. She nodded as if acquiescing to Deft's wisdom and intoned, "By the blood of the Fall, I bind myself to you as ally. Upon recovery and return of the Cypher to me, I shall release you of your affliction and give you information necessary to find the red mage."

"Information?"

Lilyth raised an eyebrow and said, "I cannot pledge what I do not have, sir knight, or the Oath will not bind us."

Deft sighed, then said, "By the blood of my forefathers, I bind myself to you as ally. I will recover the Cypher. In return, you will heal me of the red mage's curse and give me the means to take vengeance upon him."

A moment passed, then a blinding flash of yellow surrounded them both as the Oath took hold. A sudden wash of relief flooded the undead knight. It seemed Lady Lilyth did not intend to betray them. Perhaps she'd overestimated the goddess and her behavior was less a clever sham and more a true reflection of her child-like immaturity. Deft scoffed inwardly, realizing this so-called goddess was merely a product of entitlement, clearly with power but lacking any real experience. Getting the better of her would be, Deft hesitated before mentally uttering the horrible pun, child's play.

What the undead knight was most proud of was not promising to return the Cypher to Lilyth. She only pledged to recover it. The entire transaction had cemented in the knight the disdain she had for Lilyth, exceeded only by her disdain for Paramus. Weakness was something she could not abide, and this blue-skinned child was weaker than most. Like taking aurum from a blind man's plate.

And then I'll run her through. That brought forth a small chuckle of pleasure.

"A pleasant thought, sir knight?" inquired the goddess, her innocent face still radiant with joy.

"Indeed," remarked Deft. "I look forward to the conclusion of our business."

Lilyth nodded, "As do I. It's not often I find stalwart companions such as you. Perhaps we'll remain so for a while."

"Doubtful, Lady. I intend on recovering this Cypher and then seeing to the red mage. When I'm done with him, he'll have earned that name."

Lilyth nodded, then looked around and said, "I can refresh your strength." She paused and then added, "not yours, sir knight, forgive me. Your strength comes from nether worlds."

"No, the moon," muttered Deft.

Lilyth smiled, "And what worlds do you think I speak of?"

Deft didn't know what to say to that, but the mention of blood caused a sudden queasiness in her, the kind that came from hunger.

"Your weapons are restored," Lilyth said ignoring Deft's comment. Into the space, the undead knight's mace appeared.

"Now, for the Cypher."

It was then that Paramus stuttered, "S-so you led us here?"

Lilyth smiled and laughed, "It was important that I gain Sir Deft's arm and, fortunately for us, this is one of the few places where a gate can open. I had to bring you here, rather than appear to you elsewhere."

"Lady," began Trysh deferentially, "you mentioned the Phoenix. It sounds terrible. How can we get past it?"

Lilyth smiled and said, "Be at ease, sister." She gestured and Trysh suddenly gasped, looking down at her leg, then at her whole body. She spread her arms, still covered in dried blood, but the large slice in her calf and the myriad of cuts and scrapes were entirely gone.

"Lady," the scout breathed, "I cannot—"

Lilyth held up a hand and said, "Do not thank me. The

penitent shall be loved and always kept under my aegis." She arched an eyebrow. "You asked about the Phoenix and I remind you, circumvent her and recover the Cypher. Do not engage her."

"What does the Cypher look like?" Deft asked.

Lilyth turned her sapphire gaze on the undead knight.

"If you would allow me, sir knight?" At Deft's nod, the goddess raised her arms and suddenly the two of them were enclosed in an opaque bubble.

Deft looked about, "What are you doing?"

"Privacy," explained Lilyth, "is often hard to come by." She took a breath, then continued, "I am not as magnanimous as you might think, Sir Deft."

"Why am I not surprised?" She paused, then added, "But you healed Trysh." The knight watched the small woman carefully, "Why do that?"

"You'll need them to gain the Cypher."

Deft shrugged, "Maybe, maybe not. So far, they've been nothing but anchors, slowing me down."

Lilyth shook her head and said, "You misunderstand me." She paused, then said, "Because of your status between life and death, the Phoenix may not perceive you. However, if you allow yourself to become trapped, she will bring her power to bear such that it can disassemble you as if you'd never been. You will need bait to keep her occupied and that can only be done with the living."

And suddenly Deft understood, and her opinion of this goddess notched up a bit. "Bait?"

Lilyth nodded, "Understand the nature of your affliction." She extended her hand and a black cylindrical object fell into Deft's waiting palm, the solid weight surprising her. "It is the runestaff. It will unlock the Cypher from its resting place."

"Not much of a staff," Deft said, looking at the black cylinder etched with silver.

"Squeeze it, sir knight."

Deft did as asked, and suddenly the cylinder elongated into a rod a little taller than Deft herself! The etchings on its surface now glowed in silver, slowly pulsing along each line like beads traveling just below its obsidian surface.

"This is the key to unlocking the Cypher. Once done, it will infuse this staff, turning it blood red," explained Lilyth.

"That's it?" asked Deft, inspecting the staff. It was made of some dense metal, and as she'd previously noted, it was heavier than it looked. "Sounds almost easy."

"The Phoenix is more formidable than you think. Use your lackeys to distract her and retrieve the Cypher. Return and I will heal you of your affliction." Lilyth smiled, a smile that to Deft looked like the radiant smile of a simpleton, and said, "I've needed someone like you to accomplish this for longer than you can imagine. The Cypher will be consumed by the runestaff. Once done, tap the staff once sharply on the ground and it will open a way back." She paused, then added, "You must have the staff. Only you can open a gate back to me, do you understand?"

Deft couldn't help but see the complication this introduced in her overall plan to keep the Cypher, but at that moment she also realized she had no idea how valuable all this was. Her cure, however, was a different story. She understood the value of that, thank you very much.

"What if you move? What if this takes longer than this gate can stay open?"

Lilyth answered, "The runestaff is bound to me, no matter where I am. Strike it to the ground and it will open a way to me."

Deft turned this over in her mind. Finally she said, "Very

well. When do we begin?"

"Now," Lilyth said, gesturing. The opaque bubble disappeared. Then the goddess looked at her gate and something happened, a vibration Deft could feel within her bones.

The gate warped and changed, the other side going from solid black to showing instead a dark area in a place that looked very much like an underground cavern. She could almost feel the coldness of the interior and somehow knew it would also be irritatingly wet.

"Behold, the Sanctum of the Cypher," Lilyth said. She moved forward and with a gesture beckoned the small party of four to join her. "I have given Sir Deft a staff, the key to unlocking your goal. You must preserve her at all costs for you cannot return to me without her. Do you understand?"

Trysh nodded. Malioch spit, his version of a "yes." It was Paramus who asked, "How does it work?"

Lilyth ignored him.

"When you arrive," she went on, "you will likely be attacked by the Phoenix's guardians. They should fall before your puissance like leaves before an autumn wind."

Malioch spit again, "What the hell is pewsense?"

Paramus turned and, in a voice filled with authority said, "Power, strength."

Evidently, mused Deft, they'd found something Paramus wasn't afraid of.

If only we'd been attacked by books.

Lilyth's mouth lifted slightly. "Just so, brave scholar. However, I caution you to avoid conflict. These smaller guardians summon their larger kin, and those…"

"Summon the Phoenix?" asked Trysh.

Lilyth nodded, "The staff will fit into a receptacle, a hole designed to accept it. Put it into that hole and the Cypher will be released. Sir Deft knows what to do next."

"How does the Phoenix fight? What are its weaknesses?" asked Deft.

Lilyth turned to her and said, "I do not know, sir knight. When I last faced her, she was new and young. I defeated her easily. I do not know what Sovereign has done since that time. As I said," the goddess's look took in the entire group again, "avoid fighting her or her minions. Success will be achieved through stealth, not violence."

"All right then, let's push off," Malioch said, hefting his blade and checking the edge. Turning his bright blue and milk gaze on his leader, he walked toward the gate, pausing before its surface.

Deft motioned to the rest and then joined him, all looking through the faintly rippling surface and into the cavern beyond. "Once through, find a place to hide. We're going in quietly," she said to her team. She squeezed the black staff and it shrunk back into a cylinder, which she pocketed. She looked back at Lilyth and gave her a nod.

The goddess nodded back and raised a hand. "Fare thee well."

Deft didn't answer. She turned back to the gate and cursed.

"Never easy," she murmured.

To her surprise it was Paramus who answered, "Easy is for the righteous."

Great, he's a poet too.

Deft clenched her teeth and stepped through without looking at anyone. The line between where she was and the lair of the Phoenix was an icy sheet, cutting through her rotting flesh and animated bones with a cold deeper than her curse of unlife. She could hear the others gasp as they too, transitioned... and then suddenly, she was somewhere else.

THE OFFER

A rek led the way, following Lord Zafir as they made their way into the tent. They were flanked by two guards who stayed a respectful distance behind. They took a turn, then another, before walking down a long corridor lined with gold torches. This passageway opened into an area lit from above by a skylight in the tent's roof. The path here seemed larger than it did from the outside—quite a bit larger. Then he shifted to dragonsight and the golden particles immediately revealed the illusion. They clung to the fabric of the tent walls like sparkling citrine dust, coating the surface of the walls where they still stood, real but invisible.

The spell gave the appearance of an ongoing space, lending the interior a lavish and opulent feel. He had to admit it was very convincing. Without his dragonsight he knew he'd never have noticed. Something in his ability to see through Zafir's spell was reassuring. Despite the haughty arrogance celestials like Zafir and Lilyth displayed at every turn, this proved they too were limited by rules, and weren't infallible. He only wished his father could mindspeak so he could show him too, but the cursed torc of the Galadines made that impossible.

When he turned his vision on Lord Zafir himself, the sight was interesting. The man was superimposed by an angelic warrior in armor painted silver and black. The war angel slowly turned its head and raised a fist. Arek looked up to see the ghostly images of Azrael, and Scythe standing over Duncan, do the same. He'd never noticed them before,

249

knowing the dragonsight was becoming more a part of him. He wondered what Valarius must've seen after several hundred years of using it. Then the Aeris lord turned and Arek's attention came fully back to him as his dragonsight faded into the background, just under his awareness but available, like a charm for his mind's eye.

Lord Zafir's face was a living statue carved from marble. It didn't provide many cues one would associate with normal emotions; however, when Arek looked away and back, he'd get a distinct impression of what the lord felt. He didn't understand why but reasoned his subconscious was reading Zafir better than his conscious mind could. He resolved to not stare at the lord for too long, lest he lose this insight.

Right now, Zafir seemed contemplative. He looked at Arek and asked, "How long has it been, my lord?"

Arek shook his head, "I don't know, Lord Zafir. I am Adept Arek Winterfell, and while it might be true that I Ascended with your brother-in-arms, his memories are not mine."

At this the celestial looked more interested, his eyes flicking back and forth between Arek and Duncan. He motioned to some low cushioned chairs and sat down, signaling to someone behind Arek, who turned just in time to see a handmaiden disappear through a flap that led to another section of the tent.

"Indeed?" Zafir remarked, pulling Arek's gaze back to him. "I have heard of the practice of Ascension but wondered if anything of you remained." He looked at Arek and asked, "I was addressing Azrael with that."

Arek didn't answer, and into that silence Zafir added, "I find myself wondering why Azrael would give himself up willingly to you?"

Arek felt something in him rise at that. Zafir's

implication was clear, and if he chose, he could respond to the inherent scorn in "to you." He suppressed his anger, feeling more focused in the residual burn of righteousness. Perhaps it was not so much him, but Azrael who felt that way. Still, he would not let Zafir bait him.

"Lord Azrael knew a war was coming and felt his survival was key to the outcome," he said. "He felt Ascension was the only path to ensure this. I'm certain of this." Arek met Zafir's eyes and said, "Now, for good or ill, he is part of me."

Zafir just stared at him, his expression inscrutable. Then the celestial nodded and offered, "Lady Lilyth owes much of her kingdom to what we three accomplished. Once, the world of Arcadia was whole, lands stretching unbroken to the horizon. The shattering was our doing."

He knew his surprise wasn't hidden. Still, Arek narrowed his eyes, searching Zafir's face. "We caused this?" he asked, despite knowing Zafir had no reason to lie about the fact.

The celestial tilted his head and said, "We? You were not here, Lord Arek. I speak of myself, Azrael, Scythe, and Lilyth, who drove this world to the brink of madness. Now it seems Lilyth plays upon the Conclave's fear. Had she acted decisively and killed you in Edyn rather than invite you into Arcadia," he paused and deferentially inclined his head toward Arek, "the contagion Thoth feared so would have never come about." He paused, taking a deep breath. "And now it all comes to an end." Zafir looked about the tent. What he said next made Arek think he knew from the beginning his illusion within the tent would not fool Arek's dragonsight.

"We see what we want, reflections of what we want to believe, foolish dreams and desires placing a glamour over our eyes. Lilyth knows this. She sees more clearly than most what befalls us all if Sovereign wins. She has parlayed your presence in Arcadia to walk Edyn again. You think the destruction of Arcadia is a corrupt thing, that bringing you here was a mistake." He smiled and shook his head. "It is not. She said you would save our people, and because of you she is freed. The gods shall walk amongst the people of Edyn again, making their faith strong, and her stronger because of it."

Zafir searched his face, looking for something more. Perhaps he wished to see if Arek believed him, or instead if his words had sown seeds of doubt. Whatever he saw, the celestial gave it acknowledgement with a small nod, and asked, "Did you know you and Lilyth, that is to say Azrael and Lilyth, were close?" His eyes told Arek exactly what he meant.

"No," Arek replied truthfully, "she never mentioned it."

Zafir leaned forward, meeting Arek's gaze with an intensity that was unnerving. "Then I must ask, given all I have shared without expectation or recompense, are you for or against the Lady, the Eye of the Sun?"

Duncan began to speak, but a look from Zafir silenced him. This was a question for Arek and Arek alone. Though he had spoken admiringly about Lilyth, he had not said if he agreed with her or not. The celestial had not tipped his hand in either direction, giving no indication on how he felt.

Arek bit his lip, feeling the rough silk of the cushion below him. The fabric, illusion or not, seemed to reflect the mood—heavy and still. He knew this was a critical test. If he got it wrong, they would never leave. The gate and their way home to Edyn would be closed to them forever.

Only a moment passed before he realized there was only one answer he could give—the truth. "I am not for Lady Lilyth as much as I'm against Sovereign," he said. "He wants to remake the world, and I oppose that. The Lady only wants her people to survive. Although I don't agree with all her methods, it's something I can understand." He finished, watching for any clue as whether he'd doomed them or not.

Zafir's brows drew together. Arek took that moment to glance away and back again, catching the distinct impression the celestial was contemplative. His black and silver eyes hadn't moved, staring forward and as inscrutable as gemstones.

Then he said, "I appreciate your candor. Before I tell you where I stand, I would ask the same of my shield brother, the Scythe."

His attention now turned on Duncan, and Arek could sympathize with his father's situation. The man had only suffered since he'd come to Arcadia, and now he was being asked to choose between two evils. He just hoped something of Silbane influenced the man to say something diplomatic, or at the very least nothing too volatile.

Duncan didn't take long to answer.

"If it were up to me," he said with a sigh of resignation, "I'd see all of you gutted, including you, Lord Zafir. Too many damn gods for my taste."

There was dead silence at that, and Arek couldn't help but give a mental groan. The look on Zafir's face could have been shock. Arek looked at Duncan with an expression of "What was that?"

Duncan didn't meet his gaze. Nothing in his father's stance indicated a mental shortcoming, nor was he overly arrogant. He certainly didn't act deferential in the presence of the celestial either. Instead he just calmly watched Zafir; either he was being honest, or he was crazy. Arek prayed it was the former, though that was almost as bad.

Zafir broke the silence by smiling and saying, "You

haven't changed." He motioned to someone behind Arek again and cool drinks were brought forth and offered to each guest. "The stories I could tell you about your bonded partners. They fought for everything that was right in this world." He leaned back, now looking wistful to Arek. Though nothing changed, he got the distinct impression the lord's gaze was distant, reliving something in their past.

"Imagine us, perhaps your age, journeying forth on a grand adventure. Ours was the tale of a world to be made, of phantasms and death dealers brought forth from the minds of those who slept." His voice trailed off as he searched their faces wistfully.

Then he returned to the here and now.

"I regret to tell you Keeper Thoth has been killed," he said. "This has dire significance."

"But we just saw him," Arek said, then regretted the outburst. They'd only just met Thoth while planning their assault on Avalyon to rescue his father, and in that brief encounter it seemed the Keeper and Lilyth had been friends, or at least in alliance. If he'd come to harm by Lilyth's hand, it said much about her ability to mask her true intent, a lesson he'd learned for himself the hard way. Yet speaking like a child in front of this celestial wasn't going to earn him any respect. He warned himself to think before speaking, before realizing it was exactly what his master would've said.

The Aeris lord steepled his fingers. "Lady Lilyth knows the lore father's runestaff is the key to remaking the world. Without Thoth, another cannot be made until a new Keeper is appointed. Lilyth will use this to her own ends."

Arek thought quickly through everything he knew, the facts pouring through his mind like a deluge of shapes. Those that fit, he kept, discarding the rest. Suddenly, an icy pit formed in his stomach and he looked at Duncan and said,

"The existing runestaff... the one Lore Father Giridian holds."

Zafir tilted his head at Arek, as if questioning why he cared.

"Isn't it obvious?" Arek said. "She will kill him."

The look on Zafir's face was as inscrutable as ever, but Arek got the impression he'd risen a bit in the celestial's estimation. Now he was faced with a real problem, namely the safety of those on the Isle. While he'd harbored anger at Lore Father Themun's manipulations, he'd never wanted to see him or Adept Thera die. Now it seemed more of his only family were going to be hunted and killed. He shook his head, his anger building.

"We have to escape Arcadia before we can help anyone," Duncan said.

Arek nodded. "I'll not let Lilyth hurt my friends," he said defiantly.

"And how will you stop her from here?" countered the Aeris lord calmly. He took a sip of his drink and began to put it down. Halfway there he paused, looking at Arek for a moment, saying nothing.

"I'll—" Arek began.

"I will convey you to Edyn," Zafir interrupted.

"And what do you want in return?" Duncan asked.

Zafir smiled at them both, leaning back with his arms behind his head. Arek's gaze locked on the celestial, shifting to his dragonsight. The sparkling swirl had tightened around the Aeris lord, brightening into sharp focus, as if his intentions were transmuting to purpose. There was the reason behind the Aeris lord's hospitality and demeanor, and something told him it wasn't going to be good.

The Lord of the East Gate inclined his head and said, "I will tell you how to escape Arcadia to wherever you wish in

Edyn, and provide my help against Sovereign."

"For what?" asked Arek, feeling his mouth go dry. Suddenly he was afraid to know.

Lord Zafir took a slow sip of his drink, then leaned back and said, "I want my people to possess the builders."

Flashback: Lair of

The Phoenix

Alion Deft moved quickly to one side and waited as each of her party came through the gate. As they did, they shivered and clutched their arms, the biting cold having obviously chilled them more than it did her. Paramus and Trysh went right, Malioch stumbled in behind her and crouched. She took stock of their surroundings as the rest recovered from the transition.

"Shallower than I expected," remarked the scout, looking up.

Deft followed her gaze, noting with surprise that the ceiling was cut open with many holes, like a kind of cheese served in the mess hall. Out of each hole she could see stars, as if they'd been transported into a subterranean passage lying just beneath the ground. The knight looked around and found a small pedestal-shaped rock. Mounting it, she cautiously raised herself up through one of the holes. Then she descended and returned to the group, which huddled around her to hear what she had to report.

"We're at the base of a spire. It's large. My guess is Lilyth put us here to avoid being out in the open." She looked up again, angling her view a bit, then pointed, "There. At the top of the spire there's something."

"Probably the damn firebird," muttered Malioch. "We'll never get there climbing the outside of this thing."

257

Deft nodded, "Another reason I think we're here. There must be a way to summit the spire from the inside."

"Who says what we need is up there?" asked Paramus in a whisper. "I mean… what if that receptacle for your staff is below us?"

Deft cursed. The idiot had a point. Looking down she thought through her options.

"Okay, Trysh," she decided, "you and I will search downward. Malioch, you and Paramus stay here. Guard our backs. We're going slow and quiet, so be ready to wait a while. I'll attach a rope. If you feel it tug, follow it down to us."

Malioch gave a two-fingered salute, his milky eye crinkling, "Righty, boss."

Deft sneered, grabbing the man by his collar, "Just be ready."

The slaver opened both hands in a gesture of surrender, though there was still a glint in his good eye that told Deft he was mocking her. She couldn't deal with that now, but she surely would later. Perhaps they'd spent too much time together. The man was getting too comfortable with his perceived value to her.

She shoved him back and motioned to Trysh, who'd already secured a rope to herself and tied the other end to an outcropping.

"We'll be back, just stay hidden," she said to Paramus. "Keep a hand on the rope. It's gonna shake and pull, but you'll know a tug because I'll make it obvious."

Paramus answered her with a wide-eyed stare. "Shouldn't I come with you? You'll need me to translate."

Deft interrupted whatever Trysh was about to say and said, "That's why we'll tug the damn rope, idiot! I'm not risking your hide this early until I know if what we need is up or down." She turned away and then cursed and turned back.

"And this was your stupid idea."

Her glare shut up whatever the coward would have said, and that was fine by her. Maybe he'd make enough noise here blubbering and attract any denizens to him instead of her and Trysh, and he'd be ended. That thought brought up a real concern, though, one she couldn't leave lie.

She moved over to Malioch and pitched her voice so only he could hear. "If the kid dies, I'm going to eat you alive." Her ruined face came to within a nose of Malioch's own, the literalness of her statement causing the man to gulp once. "Nothing happens to the boy until I say so."

The man swallowed again, nodding. Deft smiled, revealing the very teeth she'd use to strip his flesh from bone, underscoring her point in a way she knew Malioch would understand. This time there was no mocking glint in his eye, only fear. Satisfied, she turned back to her scout. "You take the lead but fall back if we run into anything."

Trysh nodded, and together they moved into the darkness and down, playing the rope out behind them like a dead snake. As they descended, the natural light waned, but each of their augmented visions took over, one of the reasons Deft had chosen Trysh over Malioch to accompany her. Also, something in the back of her mind told her the scout and the coward Paramus would run if given the chance. She wasn't about to sacrifice healing the red mage's curse because of a conspiracy between these two, so better to keep them separate.

The walls of this subterranean place reminded her of liquid, frozen in the very act of flowing. While sharp edges abounded, the actual walls themselves resembled the oozing pattern of mud. Patterns resembling lazy curves left by someone dragging fingers swirled along each wall and across the floor, threatening a twisted ankle with every step. Trysh flitted lightly across the surface, her feet seeming to float slightly above each ridge with a surety Deft envied. For her part, volcanic shale shattered as her iron-studded heels trampled down with all the delicacy of a horse. Occasionally Trysh would look back, the plea for silence painfully clear. The undead knight cursed, trying to avoid cracking the black volcanic ridges with her weight as best as she could.

Soon the tunnel widened, allowing them to stand beside each other in a *Y*-shaped split. Trysh tilted her head up and closed her eyes, sniffing. Then she looked to the left and said, "Cool air. There must be an exit that way."

"Then we go right," Deft whispered, hefting Reaper onto her shoulder. She pushed Trysh behind her and made her way carefully forward, inching past the split with her eyes wide. The sight greeting her was unlike anything she'd seen before. Ahead the space widened, opening to some vast stomach through the sphincter formed by their passageway.

The room was oblong, perhaps fifty paces along one end and thirty across. The far wall was dominated by a large black rectangular shape, smooth and glossy. In front of that shape sat a ledge with more black glass, the same as that which adorned the podium back in the library of Thoth. This too, was dark, with no patterns or symbols upon it. Her witch gaze wasn't showing her the details she needed, so Deft said, "Illuminus!"

Blue fire ignited from Reaper, a beacon that bathed their surroundings, painting the volcanic rock even more shiny and black than it was. Pinpoints of light from Reaper caught and glinted off facets shorn from every rock face, the work of time and happenstance creating miniature stars along the floor, ceiling, and cave walls. They were inside a geodesic made from obsidian, with every angle and line intersecting in a flash of rainbow colors.

It was Trysh who spoke first, saying, "One nice thing— no long search."

"Your goddess's doing," muttered Deft. "It wouldn't help having us wandering about like imbeciles."

Trysh didn't answer, instead moving lightly up to the ledge. After a careful inspection, she motioned for Deft to join her. The knight did her best to remain quiet, but each step felt like she was walking across broken glass. Though the shards didn't hurt her in any way, each step made a crunching sound that caused Deft to scowl and the scout to wince.

Finally, after navigating to the scout in an uncharacteristic economy of motion, Deft crouched and cursed, "She could've at least conjured me better boots." Then she took stock of the ledge, which up close reminded her even more of the panel from the library.

"Can you figure it out?"

A skittering sound made Deft whirl, Reaper ready, but nothing showed itself. Before she could focus another scattering of rocks came from her right. Trysh moved, putting her back to Deft's. "We're not alone."

"Tell me something I don't know," Deft said. Even as she strained to catch sight of their foes, the intermittent scrambling sounds grew. Whatever was out there, it was being joined by friends. "We'd better put our backs to a wall." She didn't wait for Trysh's acknowledgement but backed up until she and the scout had the chamber spread before them.

Amongst the myriad of reflections was some kind of motion. Deft squinted, watching as pairs of white dots reflecting azure detached themselves from various points, moving forward and closer to Reaper's glow. When they came into view, Deft cursed.

"Cave spiders," she said, scrambling back. Her breath came out in short gasps as her eyes darted left and right.

Trysh looked at her with one eyebrow raised in bewilderment, "You don—"

"No," Deft said, shaking her head. "I don't like spiders." She could feel their beady eyes staring at her, shiny and wet. They were disgusting, with bands of white and off-white fur alternating down each hairy leg. There was perhaps a dozen in sight, and that meant hundreds hidden. Deft snarled and stood, brandishing Reaper higher.

Trysh stood also, no doubt finding it difficult to comprehend Deft's fear, but the knight didn't care. She took a shuddering breath and then screamed and ran forward, smashing Reaper down. The dozen or so palm-sized shapes scattered back into crevasses in the ground and walls, disappearing as quickly as they'd appeared.

"Safe again," offered Trysh without smiling. "They're probably more scared of—"

"Shut up." At first Deft wasn't sure if she was being mocked, and she didn't care. "They don't care about size... they'll eat you just the same," she offered back, as much talking to herself as Trysh. The scout evidently knew better than to respond. She just nodded and turned back to the ledge but Deft was sure she caught the edge of a smile on the scout's face. Then she knew she was being mocked, but more skittering sounds caused her to whirl, Reaper ready for any of the eight-legged freaks to show themselves again.

Trysh said, "I'll deal with the panel, but we may need Paramus and the staff."

Deft continued to stare into the dark, all her senses alert for spiders. When still nothing showed, she backed up slowly and took hold of the line they'd played out behind them and gave it two sharp tugs. She waited a bit, then did it again. "I called him."

"Okay," replied the scout. "Umm, I guess you can keep an eye out for... anything."

"Where there's little ones, there's always big ones," Deft said.

"No doubt," Trysh said with a straight face. Then she held out a hand. It took a moment for Deft to realize she was asking for the staff.

"No," the knight shook her head, "Lilyth gave it to me and I'll use it when the time is right. Let's wait for that idiot scholar. Maybe we'll get lucky and he'll be spider food on his way here."

"Better hope not," Trysh said, looking at the panel in front of her. The dark glass had come to life at her touch and symbols now ran in parallel lines across its face. "This isn't anything I can read."

Deft snorted once, her way of capitulating without saying anything. She gave her hip a pat to reassure herself, the cylindrical staff a comfortable weight as it sat nestled in her belt pouch. Then she scanned the dark, her eyes peeled for any sign of the arachnids, no doubt peering back at her now with tiny slavering pincers and fangs. Didn't the scout understand insects were just different than animals? You and a bear both felt some of the same emotions with regards to hunger, fear, even raising young. Spiders and their ilk had no such niceties, and by their very nature were nothing but bloodthirsty creatures using venom to make you innards a slurry of succulent blood juice. They were an abomination under the All Fathers... she spat once to hide her own mental lapse.

How could fear make her so quickly fall back on the

falsehoods of the All Fathers? The knight shook her head, but kept Reaper ready. She wouldn't be spider juice today, regardless of how many might be out there, but a small part of her did find her mouth salivating at the thought of fresh blood. Perhaps the fool Paramus had been right about her sustenance.

Not too much time passed before the rope gave a few jiggles, as if someone were following it down. Deft could hear rocks scatter from the tunnel from which she and the scout had emerged. Soon, the milk eye of Malioch peered in from the entrance, and his gap-tooth smile followed. "Na too far down, chief."

Deft nodded and motioned to the scout's location, "Get college-boy to the panel, then back me up."

Malioch took a look around, his good eye scanning the cave and walls. Finally, he said, "Spiders?"

"Yeah," muttered Deft.

The slaver moved into the room without saying a word. He straightened and took up station, clearly enjoying the space this room provided compared to the twisting tunnel they'd just descended. Soon, Paramus's dark-haired head poked out, and he too joined the small crew.

"Wow!" he said, taking in the surroundings. Then his eyes were quickly drawn to Trysh and the panel. "What's that?"

Malioch ushered the boy in the scout's direction but stopped when he neared Deft. While Paramus continued, the slaver drew his blade and said, "No worries, boss. We hurt the mother beastie and the rest'll eat her up."

Maybe it was the fact that Malioch took her seriously, or that she could hear Paramus conferring with Trysh about the panel. For whatever reason, Deft's fear ebbed. It helped that it was night, and in terms of strength, Deft was at her peak.

She took a breath, then called over her shoulder.

"How long?"

"For what?" asked Paramus.

Deft whirled on the young scholar and said, "To unlock the Cypher, you idiot!"

The scholar looked properly chagrined as he turned back to the panel, tapping it a few times, then again in response to whatever it displayed. Deft was about to turn back when the boy said, "I need the runestaff to proceed."

She turned and gave Malioch a nod. The man took the forward position, his eyes scanning the darkness while Deft slowly backed toward Paramus. When her hip bumped the panel, she reached into her belt pouch without looking and carefully withdrew the runestaff. A squeeze and the black rod expanded to its proper length.

Upon doing so, another part of the panel lit, and a blue ring came to life. Clearly this was the receptacle Lilyth had mentioned. Deft still however looked in askance at Paramus.

The scholar said, "Put it in there and I'll tell you what to do next."

Deft scanned the room again to be sure nothing had crept upon them, then inserted the staff as Paramus had directed. It fit perfectly and stopped a hand's width in. Then something grabbed hold of it and the entire staff slid smoothly into the hole, disappearing. Suddenly, the panel and the chamber illuminated in a soft but all-encompassing glow.

"Unbelievable," Paramus said, his eyes scanning the console. "This is amazing. Look here," he pointed at a three-dimensional display projecting up from the surface of the black glass. It was the land above, but drawn in thin blue and green lines. "It's the surface!"

"What's this?" asked Deft, curious despite herself. She

was pointing to a blinking dot sitting high above their world. From this perspective it looked like it might be floating in the clouds.

"I don't know," he replied. "But here are the controls for unlocking the Cypher. All I have to do is—" he tapped a few commands which initiated a flurry of activity across the panel's glossy surface, "and whatever the Cypher is, should be freed."

A rumble sounded from high above, a tremor that let loose bits of shale from the ceiling fall in and around them like a light rain of glass. Black dust filled the air.

"Uh-oh," Paramus said, his eyes scanning the ceiling in alarm.

"What do you mean?" Deft asked, grabbing the boy by his shirt. "What?"

Deft let Trysh pull her hands away as the scholar fell back against the panel, his eyes wide with fear. Then he spun and started reading, his fingers tracking quickly across the panel until they found a box outlined in red, and flashing.

"Umm," Paramus began, his fingers frantically flying across the display in an effort to get more information. Then he turned, meeting Trysh's gaze as the scout positioned herself between him and Deft. "Lilyth said the Phoenix might have changed since the last time she fought it. Remember?"

"So what?" exclaimed Deft. "Are you bringing the spire down on us?" More shards of obsidian fell, punctuating her point with a staccato of reports at their impacts.

Suddenly the chamber stopped moving, a cessation so abrupt it felt like the world itself had paused. Deft looked about, then scrambled back toward Trysh and Par and motioned for Malioch to do the same. A sudden hiss from her left caused her to spin, Reaper ready. However, the sound came from the black staff emerging from the hole, the lines across its surface now glowing and pulsing red. It extended about three quarters of its length and stopped. Deft assumed it was waiting for someone to claim it.

She reached for it when a blinding flash detonated in the space between where they squatted and Malioch stood, his foot in midstep toward them. The slaver ducked, taking cover near an outcropping woefully small to hide his bulk.

The flash coalesced into the shape of a feminine figure outlined in fire, with wings of flame extending behind her. Her features were indistinct, still hidden by the yellow-white glare of her form, but her voice echoed inside the chamber.

"Pray thee utter her name again," she said, her voice husky and deep.

Deft looked at Paramus and Trysh, then asked, "Who?"

The figure reacted immediately, her head turning as if searching for the owner of the voice. Twin beams of yellow light shot out from her eyes, scanning the ground. It paused briefly on Trysh and Paramus's forms, but floated over Deft as if she wasn't there. In moments it became clear whatever this creature was, it could not see Deft, who in the face of the scrutiny had become utterly still.

"Pray thee come forth, utter her name again," the figure asked again. This time her eyes lit the form of the young scholar, who raised a hand to shield his own eyes from the glare.

He looked wide-eyed at Trysh, then Deft. He swallowed, his Adam's apple bobbing almost comically as his fear manifested over random parts of his body in spasmodic jerks.

Deft locked gazes with him and silently jerked her head, her meaning clear. Say something!

"I..., uh," Paramus's eyes darted back and forth, "whom

267

do you mean?"

The figure glided forward, her wings tucking in and her form becoming less bright. Soon they could see she was indeed a woman, appearing perhaps not much older than Trysh. Her eyes still glowed bright like white-hot embers, as if the inside of her skull was a blacksmith's forge.

She paused only when she stood within arm's reach of the young scholar and said again, "Pray thee utter her name again."

"Lil-yth?" stammered Paramus.

The being closed her eyes, breathing deeply in through her nose as her head tilted back. Then she looked back down at Paramus and said, "It hath been a thousand thousand years since I hath heard her name." She gestured for Paramus with an open hand. The scholar slowly reached out, his fingers trembling as they hovered just a little below the woman's own.

The being flicked once quickly, and Paramus withdrew his hand in shock, the finger pricked and bleeding. A drop of blood sat on the being's finger, which she brought to her lips and tasted. "Sovereign prepared me, but never did I dream her name would fall from a dirtborn's lips."

"What do you want?" snarled Deft. She didn't like her team being assaulted, not even the idiot Paramus. Besides, she'd made a promise to the boy, that no harm would come to him. If anyone was going to draw Paramus's blood, it would be Deft herself. She stood slowly, Reaper still at the ready.

The being turned, "Who art thou?" The eyes erupted in yellow beams of light again, scanning the chamber but again passing over Deft without pausing.

What magic protects me? she thought.

"You're dead," Paramus answered her unspoken

question.

The being looked back at Paramus and said, "Thou canst see I am very much alive, but perhaps…" she moved a little closer to the scholar, "thou speaketh of thy companion?"

Trysh then moved forward, her unfathomable desire to protect the scholar evidently overriding basic concerns for self-preservation, and asked, "Who are you?"

The being tilted her head, then said, "Tell them, Paramus Petra of House Petra, disgraced son of Achillys the Mermidyon and Kassiopia the Beneficent. Laggard, coward, thief, beggar, and shame to his family name, tell them who I am."

With each denouncement Paramus shrank down, his head hanging as if the words themselves had weight. When he didn't respond, Deft surprised herself by saying, "You're clearly the Phoenix, as if we care." She spat to one side.

The Phoenix's head turned to her voice. "You hide cloaked in death. Perhaps Lilyth has sent you to claim the Cypher, thief?" Her eyes flicked to the staff and then back to searching the room. "Ken this – if the staff is withdrawn, thine companions will die."

"Your father is Achillys?" asked Trysh, her face reflecting the difficulty she was having reconciling this fact with Paramus's lack of martial capability.

Deft moved slowly but the crunch of her first few footsteps marked her location more surely than anything she voiced. The Phoenix smiled and sent a wash of fire blasting into the space occupied by Deft. The knight crouched, her arms coming up to ward herself from certain incineration. Her protective aura flared, but the fire washed through it as if it wasn't there, charring bits of exposed leather and cloth but passing entirely through her without doing any harm.

"You can't hurt death," Paramus murmured. "Because

it's part of what you are."

"Death and rebirth," whispered Trysh.

The Phoenix turned back to them and said, "A penitent servant of my traitorous sister and a dirtborn failure to his family. Is this the best of whom Lilyth couldst find?"

Malioch moved ever so slightly, dislodging hardly more than a grain of obsidian, but the response from the Phoenix was immediate.

"Oh," cooed the woman, her form once again outlined in fire. "I've not forgotten you, slaver. You will become what your heart wills and serve as my eyes to ferret out this undead thief."

Malioch slowly rose, despite Deft's hiss of anger. "What'chya flappin' about, missy?" the slaver asked, his milk-eye squinting.

"Kill them and I will reward thee with power." The Phoenix floated back toward the chamber's exit, coming to stand even with Malioch.

Deft laughed and said, "You'll just be giving me a stronger ally." She smiled, looking at Malioch.

Instead of answering, the slaver turned his attention back to the winged being. "Now, say that part about power again," he said, his one good eye now glinting blue in the light cast by the Phoenix's flames.

"Kill them, and I will resurrect thee in whatever form thou wishes," the Phoenix replied with a smile.

"Really," Malioch's eye drifted from the Phoenix to Deft. Something in his face made Deft's smile drain away. "Sorry boss, I'm tenderin' me resignation. No sense in all of us dyin'."

"As you wish…," replied the Phoenix.

A yellow-white blaze burst from the ground, flooding Malioch's form until his eyes and mouth spouted incandescent fire. He screamed, but the scream didn't end with him falling to ashes in a burnt-out cinder. Instead, it grew deeper, stronger, his bones breaking and lengthening. His muscles ripped apart and then reknit, sheathed under an outer shell that grew dark as it hardened. Sharp spines burst from the man's skin, and his eyes became like those of the Phoenix, crimson embers glowing with heat from within. He drew a shuddering breath and in a guttural voice said, "More."

Malioch's face screwed up in pain and he bent forward as something in his chest seemed to tear farther apart. When he looked up, his body had widened and his eyes had turned black, like two drops of oil, large and unblinking. Across his forehead six more eyes ripped their way to the surface to erupt from under his skin. Then a choking sound, and two curved black fangs ripped the flesh of his mouth wide open. His back arched, his head thrown back in a silent scream as two more arms erupted from each side, segmented and ending in a wicked claw.

Malioch fell forward onto his elongated arms and legs as they joined the others, slowly transforming into hairy and clawed legs covered in barbed fur and chiton, dark red with bands of white. Armored plates of the same material emerged from his back and sides, covering him from what had been his head to a newly formed bulbous body ending in spinnerets.

"Ahh, shit," Deft said, looking her former slaver up and down. Then she looked back at Trysh, her expression dark. "I told you…"

Trysh nodded, her eyes wide with fear as she watched the transformation of Malioch complete. "There's always a big one."

It was all Deft heard before the room erupted with the

sound of a thousand eight-legged scurrying shapes led by a
man the knight knew was far worse in spirit than any kind of
spider she'd ever faced before.

CELESTIAL'S

BARGAIN

W hat?" Arek bolted to his feet, anger flaring as he confronted Zafir. He wasn't about to let the dwarves be possessed.

Neither Zafir nor Duncan moved.

"Hear me out," Zafir said at length. "My offer is not inconsequential."

Arek was about to refuse when his father laid a restraining hand gently on his arm.

"Let's listen. Learning never hurts our position."

For a moment, he sounded just like Silbane, the same cadence and even choice of words. It was as if his master stood beside him again, and that took the fire out of Arek's heart. He looked down, then nodded and sat back down.

"Explain," he said, looking at no one.

Zafir took another sip of his drink, then said, "The possession would be temporary. Physical bodies are needed to make the transition. Once in Edyn, my people will find others to inhabit."

"Wait," said Arek, his keen mind remembering Lilyth's appearance. "Not always. Lilyth appeared to me without one."

Arek caught a strange look flit across Duncan's face, but because of the torc, he couldn't read more than the surface with his dragonsight. Another piece of the puzzle about his

273

father's torc snapped into place. He didn't know why but seeing through Zafir's illusion gave his subconscious something. He couldn't put his finger on it but he knew he was getting closer to understanding how to free his father.

Zafir shrugged, pulling Arek's attention back. "There are a few places in the world where one can attempt a transition… if circumstances are correct. Zealous faith, true sacrifice, abject terror"—he looked at Duncan— "heartfelt obsession. But to transport hundreds or thousands, that needs living flesh. It is beyond even a Celestial's might."

"But the demon wars…," Arek continued.

"Did I not say the circumstances mattered? Who petitioned for the Aeris to enter your world? Who opened the rift at Sovereign's Fall?"

"Valarius," Duncan breathed. "He thought it possible to parley with Lilyth."

Zafir nodded, "And in doing so he gave her the chance to enter. You can lay blame at his feet, but it has not been the first time your people have called to us."

"What do you mean?" asked Arek.

Before Zafir could reply, Duncan interrupted and asked, "And now? Olympious has transitioned to Edyn. How is that possible?"

White teeth flashed as Zafir smiled.

"She took only the strongest of those who had already possessed a body, leaving behind the horde you see spread before you across my plains. She used Bara'cor and their living to power her spell."

He took another sip and said, "These dwarves are vital to her plans. They bolster her forces where normal folk cannot."

"You're only shifting possession from her to you," Arek retorted.

"And you are gaining a valuable ally." Zafir paused, then asked, "Do you know the location of the sanctuary Sovereign will use to create a new runestaff? Do you know how to open the East Gate to your world? Do you know how to stop Lilyth from appointing herself Keeper?" The look on Arek's face must have told him he didn't, for Zafir continued, "I thought not."

"You oppose Lilyth?" asked Arek, his eyebrows raised. It sounded incredulous, even given what little he knew of celestials.

"I do not so much oppose Lilyth as I wish my status to change," the Aeris lord said in a strange mockery of Arek's own words. "Long have I bent knee to the Lady. Now if there's a chance, I must seize it." A musical tinkling sounded, a chain of bells suspended above Zafir moved by some ethereal wind.

Zafir leaned forward. "As Lilyth used the living force of those at Bara'cor to power her spell, we too must find a source of power here to open the East Gate."

"What source?" Arek asked, looking at Duncan. The archmage shook his head, clearly at a loss.

"Three things will be needed if we are to escape Arcadia with our lives. First"—he looked at Duncan— "we must fashion a new runestaff, much like the one made for the lore father. You know how to do this."

Slowly, as if admitting anything to Zafir seemed unwise, Duncan tilted his head. "Perhaps."

Zafir turned to Arek and said, "The power needed to unleash the spell can only be channeled by someone who can see the Way, as you can, my lord."

"The dragonsight? You know about that?"

"I know more than you can imagine," answered Zafir. "Come, for the third need lies outside my demesnes." He began to walk, but then paused, his head down in thought.

"Lilyth and I made a bargain which I am dishonoring," he said at last. "When word reaches her of my betrayal, her vengeance will be swift. You both must pledge your blades to stand beside mine when she decides to collect her due."

"You want us to fight her with you?" Arek asked. He looked at his father, who merely shrugged, as if to say, "why not?"

Arek didn't feel quite so blasé toward the idea and wondered again what was going on with Duncan. He quickly realized he'd have to unravel the torc sooner rather than later if he wanted any insight into the man's thinking, and certainly if they were to reforge a runestaff.

"You're already fighting her," replied Zafir. "No special dispensation for me is required, only that you do not turn your ire against me." He paused, then leaned forward and smiled, saying, "Think on it. We three together again, fighting to stop one tyrant from simply replacing another. But"—he looked toward the tent flap— "you cannot delay. Even now the Aeris gather. Despite my words to the cursed magehunter, lust and hunger will overwhelm the horde."

"And what do you get out of this?" Arek asked.

If it was possible, Zafir looked disappointed.

"Escape, life, equality… to name a few things. I'd rather not see you two, even trapped in these lowly forms, perish here in Arcadia. It would be an ignoble end to those who have done deeds worthy of myth and legend." Zafir paused, then added, "And if it is of any comfort, I will not take the woman builder from your party."

He could only mean Brianna, but this sudden offer made Arek suspicious. "Why?"

Zafir placed his drink carefully on the table and said simply, "Her blood is unclean."

The way it came out made her seem diseased, until Arek remembered the nans she'd injected herself with back at her kapsool. Maybe she'd unknowingly protected herself from possession. Still, it didn't matter.

"I can't agree, Lord Zafir," Arek said. "The builders of Dawnlight aren't mine to give."

"What of your princess? Does she not deserve to leave Arcadia? You'd condemn her to death along with yourself?" asked the Aeris lord.

Arek closed his eyes, thinking. What did he really owe these dwarves? The question brought shame and guilt, but a practical part of his mind knew it had to be asked. Still, he knew what Silbane would've counseled.

"I can't give you what isn't mine."

Zafir gazed at Arek's face. Heartbeats passed as the celestial scrutinized him with an intensity that seemed almost physical. Then he nodded to the guards, gesturing with his arm to the flap to exit the tent.

"Come, see our third need and then decide," he said. He moved toward the vertical bar of light made by the two flaps.

Arek felt a little stunned. He'd expected Zafir to argue more, perhaps even put on some display of strength or level threats. He was ready for that. He could feel his power uncurling, yearning for release. A look from Duncan told him to remain calm, which he did by taking another deep, cleansing breath.

Then they were outside the tent and facing the vast plains of Harmagedon. The sight that greeted Arek was incomprehensible. Spread out from the perimeter of Zafir's encampment to as far as his eyes could see was a churning, boiling mass of Aeris, seething and howling. How had he not heard them from inside the tent? The sound was deafening, a cacophony of torment assailing his ears. Then he knew, and a sickening realization set in.

Zafir had maneuvered them into his tent where his magic would isolate them from what was happening out here. He looked at Duncan with horror, and then at Zafir.

The Aeris lord said, "You misunderstood me. I was not asking for permission, Lord Arek."

Arek instantly changed form, towering over Zafir. The celestial just watched him, doing nothing.

"Command them to step back," Arek shouted, "or I'll—"

"Or you'll what, my lord?" Zafir asked. "My men protect those of Dawnlight," he pointed to the line of silver and black clad guardsmen standing before the assembled dwarves. Their allegiance to a celestial held the horde back, but for how long?

"We do not have much time. Soon these Aeris will overrun my people in a bid to live. Even I cannot stop them. At least with me, you have my word I will release them once we transition to Edyn. You'll not get a similar guarantee from these," he said, gesturing to the thousands of gray demons snarling and salivating as they watched with hunger in their feral yellow eyes.

He waited a moment longer, waiting. When Arek did nothing, he nodded to his men. "Take them."

"No!" Arek screamed, but it was too late.

While they had been speaking, Zafir had evidently moved his people into position under cover and spell, invisible to the dwarven folk. Only now did Arek see their shapes, outlined in the yellow golden particles of his dragonsight, initiate the attack.

As he watched, they dove into each dwarf and took them before any weapons could be brought to bear. Even through the dissonance of shrieks and guttural roars coming from the demons arrayed on the plain, Arek could hear the choking sounds of the dwarven folk as they were possessed. Some had the wherewithal to attempt to phase, as they'd done before into the ground or nearby rock, but Zafir's forces had used the time their lord had bought them occupying Arek and Duncan to good effect. Aeris surrounded each dwarf, even under the ground. There simply was no place to run.

Slowly the sounds of their struggles grew less, but the sounds from the demon horde seemed to rise in response. When Arek looked for him, Zafir had vanished.

"Where is he?" Arek asked in a numb voice, his form shrinking and changing back to his normal self.

Duncan shook his head, coming to lay a hand on Arek's shoulder and squeezing. "You couldn't have stopped him, not here," he offered. "These are his lands."

Arek shrugged off his father's hand, annoyed at his easy acceptance of what had just happened. He suddenly wished he could call the blackfire again, use it to choke the life out of the deceitful lord of these Aeris.

Something moved in his peripheral vision and then the air wavered and from someplace else they were joined by Yetteje and Brianna, followed by Jesyn and Ash. For all he knew they could have been standing there all along, but hidden by Zafir's will. Arek's dragonsight did not seem to work unless he focused his attention on it. At least none of his friends seemed worse for the wear. He couldn't say the same for the dwarves.

Yetteje looked back at the line, her amber eyes sweeping the hillside before coming back to Arek. "We couldn't see or hear anything. It was like a fog around us." She met Arek's eyes and asked, "You okay?"

Arek nodded, feeling miserable. "He isolated us, and now I've let… they've been taken."

"Taken?" Yetteje asked, her eyes immediately scanning

their surroundings with more intensity, Valor at the ready.

Arek closed his eyes, knowing he'd failed them utterly.

"What's happened?" Yetteje asked, gesturing at the throngs of demonkind who seemed to have been whipped into a frenzy, clawing at earth, each other, at anything that would let them pass. The soldiers Zafir had stationed began to contract backward toward the group, staying shoulder to shoulder to keep the horde at bay. None of the Aeris on the other side of their spears and shields attacked, but they still pressed themselves forward.

Halp rounded the corner with Zafir's guards, Deft, and her entourage in tow. It seemed Deft, at least, was still contained. Arek watched a smile light up Jesyn's face, only to die as her eyes met Halp's own. They glowed blue, then faded to the same black reptile's eyes Zafir wore when they first met. The dwarven warrior looked down at Arek and said, "Lord Arek, the Aeris sense there are only a few left to take. We must act swiftly."

At that moment the guards protecting them turned, but not in fear. Some unheard order had been issued, and they collapsed themselves back to take the few remaining bodies being held for them by their Aeris companions. They knew their only salvation would be in possessing a body. Arek realized with dismay Lord Zafir's takeover was complete and his hold on the Aeris horde broken. The black and silver clad guards ran toward them, the line they held collapsing like a mud wall before a stream.

"Hold them!" shouted Zafir has he turned and gestured. The air began to tingle, a vibration that scurried across Arek's skin like thousands of insects.

The young adept buried his failure, the Aeris giving him a target for his anger and hate. He turned, intending to change into Azrael, but a soft voice stopped him.

You know the Way, it said. You can feel it in yourself.

Arek saw the horde avalanching toward him but nonetheless closed his eyes, reaching within himself. His breathing calmed, the outside world grew dim. There!

At his belly sat an uncurling knot of blue-white fire, coruscating with unrealized fury. He felt himself lower into a stance, his hands at his hips in a loose-fisted chamber. Then, he raised his hands making them into open palms. As he did so, the fire rose within him, centering in his chest. He opened his eyes, seeing now with the clarity bestowed upon him upon his Ascension, and could feel the force inside ready to unleash.

"Arek!" screamed Yetteje, for the horde was nearly upon them.

Arek pushed his hands out, palms facing the horde. Then his breath released, and blue-white fire exploded outward, washing forward in an arc that left nothing but carnage and devastation behind. It expanded like a wave made of pure energy, blasting a semicircle before the young adept, burning whatever it touched with its ethereal fire.

Breath of the Sun, he realized with shock. But he'd never learned that! It was one of Silbane's techniques. Before he could make sense of it, his fire swept through the oncoming horde, vaporizing a huge swathe of Aeris as if they'd never existed.

Arek turned wide-eyed to his friends just as Zafir completed his spell, and—

The world shifted.

For an instant Arek could feel himself in two places at once, a strange duality that made little sense. One part of him could feel the hot breath of the Aeris horde as it overwhelmed him, while the other breathed in the cool air of the place they'd transitioned to. Then everything snapped back into a painful reality and they stood at the base of the shining spire that had only a moment ago been quite some distance away.

"What was that?" exclaimed Yetteje in a half-shouted question.

Zafir smiled at her, a wholly disconcerting sight, given that he wore Halp's face. "We celestials are not without some means."

She shook her head and looked at Arek.

"I was talking to you. Your spell! How did you do something like that?" she asked.

"I think it's part of what my master left me as a gift, some knowledge of the techniques he knew."

Duncan moved over to him and said, "Silbane's overriding concern was your safety. You probably haven't yet found the depth of what he's done to ensure that." He looked up, and an unconscious whistle of appreciation escaped his lips. Arek followed his gaze.

The walls were made of some crystal, extruded in long columns reaching into the sky like sparkling diamond fingers. Where they terminated, Arek could see hexagonal cross sections creating miniature plateaus, like leaves on the ends of branches.

He looked around, taking stock. Their entire party was here, minus the dwarves who'd been possessed. He could see the horde, seething and raging in the far distance, likely falling upon themselves now that fresh bodies for possession were not to be found.

"We cannot delay here," said Zafir, looking at Arek. "With Arcadia's demise, every Aeris will be hunting. It will only be a matter of time before more find us."

Jesyn began to say, "Halp—"

"That's not Halp," Arek said flatly. He sighed and said,

"Lord Zafir, your word that our people will be freed once we arrive in Edyn?"

"Arek, what did you do?" asked Yetteje, her eyes wide. She searched his face, but he ignored her, instead looking directly at the possessed dwarf.

Duncan came to Arek's defense.

"Lord Zafir tricked us and took possession of the dwarves, but he's promised to return them once we're through the gate."

"What?" breathed the princess. She looked around, "Where are they?" Then she met Arek's pale gaze and asked, "You agreed to this?"

"No princess, he did not," Zafir said, "though it meant getting you home safely."

That shut Yetteje's mouth, but Arek noticed she'd moved closer to him, as if giving him her support. He could help the small blush and flutter in his stomach at that.

Ash looked at Arek's father, accusation on his face. It was clear in his opinion if something had gone badly, it had Duncan's hand involved. He pointed a finger.

"How could you let this happen? What guarantee do we have he'll keep his word?"

Duncan didn't answer, so Arek said, "We don't." He sounded tired, even to himself. He looked at the being who had taken over Halp's body and stated, "We don't have a choice."

Halp tilted his head in a way that seemed both strangely familiar and eerily foreign. It was enough to confirm to Arek that the dwarven warrior he'd just met was gone, at least temporarily. It almost didn't matter what Zafir said at this point. Arek knew there was only one way to get home, free his father, and stop the Sovereign—and that was giving up the dwarven people, the people he'd failed to protect.

Something else nagged him, a fact he didn't want to admit. He purposely pushed whatever it was away rather than face it, knowing even as he did so that he'd regret it.

Then Zafir gestured and five hundred builders rose from the ground, like corpses from the grave. These were the chosen of Zafir's people, teleported along with them to the crystal spire, only now with new bodies.

Light coursed up the spire in regular intervals, a wash of energy that disappeared into the heights. Arek followed Zafir's gaze to an immense archway, black on the inside, spanning the length of the area they stood upon.

"The East Gate, and perhaps our way home," the celestial remarked.

Zafir's eyes narrowed, his form changing to become much as it was when they'd met. Now the silver and black elemental stood before them, still glorious to behold. The celestial did not make himself bigger, choosing instead to remain the same size as the rest of Arek's party. Brianna was once again a giantess amongst them, although she now counted herself amongst five-hundred others who in stolen bodies stood eye to eye with her.

"We can effect a transition between worlds, but as I said before, we need three things. We need the power to fashion a new runestaff," he paused, then turned and to everyone's surprise, looked at Alion Deft, "and the Cypher. It is a key of sorts, a way to open the East Gate to Edyn."

"Where's this key?" demanded Yetteje. Her two forefingers still held a nocked arrow loosely, the shaft glowing like a small part of the sun. Arek could see her thumb flicking the bowstring with increasing frequency, as if reminding her of more violent options.

Zafir must have noticed it too, for he took a step back from the princess and said, "There is one of us who knows about the Cypher and how to wrest it from its guardian."

"What?" exclaimed Arek.

Zafir gestured to Deft. "Now you understand my bargain. Help me and you help yourself."

The party looked around at each other, confused looks mirrored in each other's eyes, until Deft smiled.

"He's right," remarked the undead magehunter. "And I'll die a thousand times before I give the Cypher to you."

ARMUN AWAKENS

Sai'ken traced one talon down the side of the crystalline case, her eyes watching the trail of aqua-blue light, the razor thin line a visual reminder of her actions. She understood the magic of Sovereign's sleeping tomb. It was a crucible designed to keep someone alive, forever held away from the eager hands of time. Armun, by her calculation, had been asleep for almost two hundred years. Yet when she peered at him through the glass, he looked exactly as he had when they'd first met, the day she'd faced the basilisks, when she was a mere dragonling. Her mouth curved up in a private smile at the memory of how Armun, his brother Themun, and their female companion had aided her that day.

Her sire had rewarded the three adepts of the Way with domicile on Meridian. She'd been so young then, barely sixty cycles unshelled! Dragons grew quickly, a necessity in a world where the weak fed the strong. Sai'ken was now almost full grown, a far cry from the dragonling Armun had met. She wondered what he'd think of her now.

She took a breath, her face becoming solemn. She worried about awakening this particular archmage. Her Oath to Sovereign created more than one challenge, not the least of which would be the care she'd have to take with her counsel. If she transgressed her Oath. . . the thought made her pause. She knew how Armun would react when he learned where Sovereign stood. It wasn't a conversation she was looking forward to. Armun was one of the few people to whom Sai'ken would defer, given his power and his unique knowledge of the Sanctuary of the Phoenix. But she couldn't allow any misinterpretation of her intent by the Oath. The unseen will that enforced it would interpret that as working against Sovereign and strike her down, destroying her and perhaps all dragonkind everywhere. That was a chance she could not take, not yet.

He wasn't ugly, she mused, at least for prey. That he'd allowed himself to be entombed meant he and his brother must've known there would come a time when one of them would be needed. With the lore father's passing, Sai'ken began to believe her sire, that these two knew more than they'd said.

The fall of a twig broke her reverie. She looked about, the small glen where she'd taken refuge transforming from green haven to a canopy of potential threats. Her eyes narrowed, seeking life by its heat. Nothing but the normal creatures one would expect showed themselves. Her nostrils distended as she drew in the air and her forked tongue flicked out quickly, only to disappear as she tasted what her senses told her. Nothing untoward laced her forked tongue, no salt marking prey cowering in the shadows.

Realizing she was delaying on purpose, the dragon heaved a sigh. Her breath fogged the glass, obscuring the young archmage's face. As that cleared, she placed her palm on the smooth surface and said, "Release."

The tomb chimed, "Authorization?"

Sai'ken smiled and said, "Sai, one, one, five, one, four, three, three, seven." It was the first thing her father had made her learn, the old lore litany for commanding Sovereign's magic. With it, she could speak with the servants who guarded the ancient mysteries of this world.

The tomb chimed again, "Accepted. Welcome, SAI."

The glass cover opened, folding itself into a barely

discernible line on one side. There was no hiss or other sound, but the inside of the chamber began to glow a soft green. Slowly, like snakes leaving a body, the various tubes invading Armun's nose and mouth pulled themselves out, their black bodies glistening with some kind of viscous fluid, and slithered back into their dens hidden somewhere beneath his slumbering form.

Then the chamber's light changed to orange and Armun's body bucked. His back arched in a convulsion, collapsing immediately as the chamber's light switched back to green. This happened again. At the third shock, a fit of coughing broke the silence, a strange sound in this idyllic glen. Sai'ken tilted his head to one side as he vomited out a gush of clear liquid from his nose and mouth, more of that same liquid she'd seen covering the snakes. The liquid was instantly absorbed by the soft material upon which the archmage lay. Few, if any, would believe a dragon could be so gentle.

The coughing subsided slowly and Armun's arms came up, his palms pressing into his face. His eyelids cracked open slowly, blinking as if trying to hold back the deluge of information flooding his brain. From his expression and the way his hands balled into white-knuckled fists, Sai'ken didn't need to ask to know he was in pain. So instead she asked, "How is he?"

The tomb responded, the voice female and calm, "He is within acceptable standards, but will need time to recover. Please have him drink this."

A small compartment slid open and a pouch made of some kind of clear material revealed itself, illuminated by the green light. The liquid it contained was orange and opaque, like citrine, but the dragon knew it was a far stronger elixir than that. It was the mystery of how she knew that bothered her, and part of a smaller quest she hoped Armun could help her solve.

"How long?" came a hoarse whisper.

Sai'ken looked down in surprise, greeted by the archmage's clear aqua-blue eyes. The man had half risen, hanging one arm over the edge of the tomb to anchor himself. He looked like a man holding onto flotsam to avoid drowning. The thought brought another half smile to her face.

"Thou art recovering apace. I'm pleased, but drinketh this first." She handed him the clear pouch, placing its tube into his mouth. She watched in satisfaction, his color rapidly changing from ashen blue to a healthier pink as heat flushed his skin. Then she reached down to help him sit more comfortably, his back resting against the head of the interior.

He swallowed something wrong, coughs wracking his body. When the fit was over, he looked up with tears still glistening and croaked out, "How… long asleep?"

She nodded, "Two hundred cycles, giveth or taketh away."

Armun looked down. He nodded, still sipping, then pulled the tube from his mouth and asked in a steadier voice, "Where's Themun?"

The dragon met his clear gaze and said, "Thy nest-brother is dead."

Armun's eyes widened at that, and a visible swallow bobbed the apple in his throat. Sai'ken watched him with concern, though she knew it was unlikely he would see anything but the dispassionate gaze dragons were known for. He could not know nor believe she had come to care for this particular person more than most.

After a moment she said, "I share thy grief, but Themun's work is not done. The dragonkind hath thrown their lot in with Sovereign, for the Way needs to be unified, but it behooves us to enable a new Keeper to accomplish this task."

"What happened to the old Keeper?" Armun began to rise, helped by Sai'ken. He got to his feet, naked and unsteady, his eyes scanning the area as he waited for Sai'ken's reply.

She moved to touch a few panels on the base of the tomb, which had become a resurrection chamber. At her talon's tap a compartment opened, revealing clothes, footwear, and other gear. She handed him a towel to wipe away the excess fluids glistening on his skin.

He dried himself quickly, donning the clothes and gear. In a few moments he was fully dressed, finishing the juice while waiting for the dragon's reply.

Sai'ken said, "Much hast transpired during thy slumber. Those who practice thy charmed art are almost gone from the world. The king's decree hast seen nay mercy until anon, yet the current king of Bara'cor hath rescinded much of what his forebears hadst done. His actions cometh too dram and too late. Lilyth hast reopened the Gate between hither and Arcadia. The Lady seeks unification through possession." The dragon paused, knowing the next part would have to be delivered carefully because of the dragonkind's Oath to Sovereign.

"Sovereign seeks what thee and I seek: peace. He wishes the gift of the Way given in full measure to each person of Edyn. To stop him, Lilyth hath killed Thoth, the Keeper of the Way. Anon a new Keeper must be chosen, but Lilyth—"

"Seeks to elevate herself," finished Armun.

Sai'ken nodded, her wings flexing once across her back as she tried to shake the overwhelming feeling of trepidation as each uttered word brought her closer to having to reveal the ultimate truth of the hand Sovereign had in Themun and

Thera's deaths. "You canst not ken the grief the Lady did cause over these many years. Children taken; parents possessed. Thy brother did seek to stop this, but he and his charge were so few and the king's men so many. He couldst not be everywhere and thus conducted a valiant war marked by attrition."

She watched as the mage drew a deep breath, coughing out the last of the fluid as phlegm. He looked around once more, then asked the final question she'd been dreading.

"And Thera?"

Sai'ken tilted her head and stepped close to the mage. She put on taloned claw on his shoulder and said, "Only four adepts remain of the glorious council thee once knew, and none of these knoweth who thou art. The rest hath fallen in the war against Sovereign, including thy mate, Thera." Not entirely accurate, but true enough to keep Armun focused without breaking her Oath.

Armun's eyes searched hers as if to ascertain the truth of her words. Whatever he saw must have satisfied him, for the archmage sat down on the edge of his chamber and put his head in his hands. Satisfied that no immediate danger lurked, Sai'ken remained next to him, waiting until he could come to terms with what he'd just learned.

*****

Armun pressed his palms into his face as if he wanted to force himself back to sleep. Themun and Thera dead? The thought slid into his heart like a dagger of ice, inflicting pain and numbness. Though two hundred years stood between him and the past, for him only a moment or two had passed, but in that eyeblink of time he'd lost everything he loved. What could he do?

He knew humor was his escape. It sheltered him with distance and objectivity, but here and now, there was no humor to be found in discovering that he was alone. Armun's slumber had forced the brothers to trade places, and so Themun was now the elder. It would have been nice to see Themun again, older than he himself was.

That would never have sat well nor quietly. Armun smiled, realizing he still had the memories and… his eyes widened. The link! He could speak to his brother again. He'd only to petition the current lore father to allow it. The thought buoyed his heart, filling him with a sense of hope.

"Who acts as lore father now?" he asked.

Sai'ken said, "Giridian Alacar. He is a good man; perhaps a bit naïve, but good."

He smiled at that, for the dragon rarely complimented anyone. This Giridian person must be quite noble for her to have conceded anything.

Because of the knowledge that he'd see his brother again, much of his despair fell away. He very much still felt the loss of Thera, but she too might still be spoken to, depending on her power and the strength of the link. His thoughts now turned to what ought to happen next.

He'd agreed with Themun and Rai'stahn to attempt the longsleep to ensure someone would be available should the King's justice eradicate every mage in the land, and in a small way to test the chamber's efficacy. Protecting him protected the lore and their way of life, no small thing when facing magicide.

Of course, there were others. Themun's ability to see their sparks spoke to that fact, but the great dragon had deemed it too risky to have all three of them within the king's grasp. One of them would slumber within this chamber, sequestered from Sovereign's Fall. One of them would have

293

to sleep, but it was only supposed to have been for a few years, until enough survivors had been gathered to make their survival assured.

Two hundred years! He let the thought roll around in his mind. It was long enough of a time to erase much of what he might count upon as normal. Allies would likely be dead or forgotten. Only the long-lived adepts and the dragons would remember, and if Sai'ken were to be believed, everyone who'd known him was gone. He rubbed his head some more, feeling clarity and strength slowly returning as the elixir took effect.

Themun had been the logical choice to remain awake, given he could see others with Talent. Unlike Armun, he also had a forthright conviction and taciturn nature that lent itself well to the gravitas needed for leadership. Armun rarely took things seriously, always ready with a joke, and a bad habit of laughing at the wrong time. Thera had been chosen as his second because the devastation wrought by the king's decree, unhoming families and casting those who practiced magic in all directions, had left survivors who needed someone pragmatic.

Thera was that and served as a rallying point to those who'd lost everything. She became the beacon to which Rai'stahn and others pointed to when those with Talent doubted their own capability to survive. Unlike Themun or Armun, hers was a self-effacing voice that struck the perfect balance between Themun's wrath and Armun's untroubled demeanor.

He laughed, a sound that made Sai'ken tilt her head in confusion. He shook his head and said, "It was only supposed to be a few years, not two hundred."

Sai'ken nodded slowly, her talon scratching the ground in front of him in a peculiar pattern. "None bethought the king would be so successful in his slaughter. A Galadine's talent for war shouldst ne'er be underestimated."

Themun opened his mouth to ask the next question on his mind, one the dragonling—no, he corrected himself, the dragonling he'd met so many years ago was gone. Sai'ken was almost full grown, and though she looked the part of a young adult in this form, the color of her eyes and the sheen of her scales said she'd matured while he slept. To acknowledge that, he first remarked, "You have grown into something both gracious and beautiful, Sai. I'm honored it was you who awakened me."

Sai'ken smiled at that, bowing. "I thank thee, sir."

She didn't say anything else, but the archmage got the distinct impression she was embarrassed by his comment. He looked down at his hands so as to give her a moment to compose herself, then asked, "Is there a Far'anthi Stone near? We should return to the Isle." He looked at her, then added, "Is it still…"

The dragon nodded, "Our home still stands firm under my sire's aegis."

Armun let out a sigh of relief. His strength was returning rapidly. He stood up, taking stock of the clearing the dragon had chosen. Verdant foliage surrounded them, instilling a kind of peace more encompassing than just physical silence. He could feel the strength of the roots, the song of the earth. It flooded through him now, nourishing him more than any elixir could. His affinity with the earth and the life that grew from within it anchored him, a tangible strength he could feel rising up through his legs. It suffused his body, an incarnate flow energizing him in a way few could understand.

His vision sharpened, his senses becoming acute, a keen dagger's edge parting hairs and separating his perception from the normal detritus. He saw through the moments others would casually cast off, his mind's eye appreciating the truth of life unfolding, each heartbeat carrying with it the potential for both creation and ruin. He took another breath, the Way flowing through him faster now as his body and mind shrugged off the artificial malaise induced by his sleeping chamber. Armun soaked it in, his eyes closing in pleasure. To the dragon, he must look incandescent as the Way flooded into every pore, filling his body with its ethereal balm.

He opened his eyes and smiled saying, "It feels good to be awake again, even to bad news."

"Then thee shall love my next bidding," said the dragon in a voice without a hint of humor.

Armun couldn't help but raise an eyebrow at the dragon's uncharacteristically cryptic comment. "Sounds awful," he said with a smile, leaving it at that, to draw the dragon out.

Sai'ken tilted her head and then moved closer saying, "Ill times plague the world. Now Sovereign remerges, committed to saving what he can."

"Sovereign?" Armun pulled his arms in, flexing unused muscles, then stretched out to keep the blood flowing. He moved over to the capsule and touched a panel. In response a long oblong section slid open. He retrieved a sheathed blade and a leather belt with multiple pouches. Slinging the blade over one shoulder and the belt over the other, he said, "Seems odd for the Almighty to get involved at this level. What put a burr down his breeches?"

"Thou speaketh unseemingly toward thy lord," the dragon said. She walked over to a log and sat down. "I know thy penchant for jest, but just as the Oath is heard, so art thy words. Be humble."

Armun shrugged, "You know I meant no offense. It just seems odd to have such significance placed upon squabbles and wars. Isn't Sovereign busy with more important things?"

"Thou mocks him still," chastised the dragon. Then she said, "The Keeper is dead, Armun. A new one must be chosen, but there is not a lore father alive who understands how."

That brought a sudden splash of cold water with it. If the current lore father didn't know how to appoint a Keeper, would he know how to communicate using the link? Worry furrowed his brow. "The Keeper is appointed at the Sanctuary of the Phoenix in Hy Brasel. We can help Giridian find it."

Sai'ken slowly nodded, "It is sooth, for Giridian should be the new Keeper. Perhaps you can then be appointed lore father and the world can continue."

Something in her expression said she wasn't saying everything. Why move the current lore father into that role? He was about to voice his question when Sai'ken said, "The new lore father was the Keeper on the Isle. He understands that role better than he does that of lore father. You, Armun, would help restore much of what has been lost in knowledge and philosophy. You could bring back the best of what we can offer the world."

Armun looked at her for a moment, then he shrugged. The only thing he knew for sure was that he didn't know enough yet, so he remained quiet. After a moment of thinking, he decided to change the subject by asking, "And where do we journey to now?"

Sai'ken smiled, "We go to find Giridian and speak to him of Sanctuary. Then we shall journey there, a quest like those of days long forgotten, to restore the world to its beauty and grace!"

Armun smiled at that, enjoying the dragon's exuberance. Still, a part of him wondered what wasn't being said. Usually making something great again meant trampling on existing foundations. Who or what else, besides Giridian, would be set aside to make their world beautiful again? In his secret heart, Armun suspected he'd not like the answer.

He took a moment and gathered a few more things including a rolled-up parchment from an oblong case. The paper was ancient and thick, almost like vellum. He carefully put that into his travel bag and looked at the dragon.

"Well, this world isn't going to save itself. Let's get going."

FLASHBACK: DEATH
AND REBIRTH

Deft backed up swinging Reaper low and horizontal, like a farmer harvesting crops. Except this crop was alive and wanted to eat her. She aimed at a living carpet made of thousands of spiders, their white and red-banded bodies combining to form strange hypnotic patterns of waves and pulsing shapes as they moved. Behind them came Malioch, with nothing but pale pink skin stretched over some parts of his chitinous eight-legged body to denote he'd ever been a man. His two main eyes, large and unblinking, reflected the horrified faces of Trysh and Paramus in its shiny black surface. The milk eye was gone, Deft noted with a bemused detachment. Strangely, she could not see herself in that reflection. Was this more evidence supporting the belief that the Phoenix could also not see her? Deft didn't want to get it wrong, because getting it wrong meant her life. Or unlife, depending on how you saw it.

Reaper was better than a blade at the work, but still not good enough. Part of her wished she did have a farmer's scythe, but even without a proper weapon the ex-magehunter wasn't defenseless. Planting the mace into the obsidian floor, she screamed, "Blaze!" Blue fire raced out in an arc,

299

incinerating spiders as it swept across the chamber. Malioch reared back, covering his eyes as the fire raced past, doing him no appreciable harm. The flames flickered as they reached about ten paces, dissipating entirely a little beyond that. The act had two principle consequences, one good, the other not so much.

The good part was the area in front of the small party was clear of arachnids. The blue flame had left nothing but ashes and a pungent smell reminiscent of burning hooves when shoed by a blacksmith. This gave the small party a respite, as the remaining minions of Malioch—and there were still thousands—regrouped into an advancing semicircle whose leading edge had been shaped by the crescent of flame Deft had cast.

The not-so-good part was the immediate response her spell triggered in the Phoenix. The being ignited into a blinding burst of fire and suddenly Deft felt Reaper transform from cold steel to white-hot metal, melting to slag and taking her gauntlet with it, as it incinerated what little flesh she had on that hand. Had she not dropped it immediately, she was sure her bones would have joined the rest as ashes. Instead, they looked burned clean, blackened a bit where they'd come in contact with the haft of the mace but still whole.

"Call upon thy flames again, thief, and see who art truly the master of fire within my demesne." The Phoenix continued to scan the area where the melted puddle of what had been Reaper sat cooling from white to an angry, dull orange.

Deft leapt backward, her strength taking her far from the point where another starburst of fire ignited, melting the obsidian where she'd knelt into a pool of black glass. Her leap landed her right next to the receptacle for the staff, which she grabbed. Her fingers barely had time to close over its smooth length before her vision tunneled and she found herself sprawled some distance away, shaking her head to clear it. Somehow, she'd managed to keep hold of the runestaff, but things had gone from worse to worst.

Malioch had somehow crossed the distance with blinding speed, smashing her back before holding both Paramus and Trysh by their necks. He turned to face Deft, her two remaining companions held aloft for her to see. Each struggled weakly in the arachnid lord's grasp.

The Phoenix glided forward, "The thief is there?"

"Yesss," a voice rasped from behind the gargantuan spider's black fangs. It gestured with one leg, the claw pointing unerringly at Deft's face.

For a moment, silence reigned. The cave's roof had collapsed, opening this chamber to the starry night sky above. Deft could see the obsidian spire rising, a jagged black finger marking this place as clearly as a steeple marked its grounds as hallowed.

For her part, the knight could see the staff reflected in the spider's eyes. It now pulsed blood red, just as Lilyth said it would. Though her own reflection still did not show, the staff itself mimicked Deft's own hand movements, giving her position away as surely as if she'd been visible. Part of her wanted to slam the staff into the ground and get out of here. However, this new form of Malioch could move faster than an eyeblink. If she meant to escape, she needed to ensure the staff wouldn't be snatched from her before she managed to activate the spell.

The Phoenix raised her hands, as if presenting herself to an audience. In a way she was—an unseen audience of one. As she did so twin wings of flame rose from behind her. Her form grew brighter, more majestic, and the stars above slowly faded. They disappeared behind her growing halo of sunfire, which made the sky black behind its magnificent glare. The Phoenix looked in Deft's general direction, her eyes still searching, and smiled.

"I have an offer for you, thief," said the Phoenix, and something in her voice sounded different, a tone that recalled conspiracy and whispers in the night. "Hear me out, then decide."

Deft's hand tightened, preparing to strike the staff, but a clawed pincer shot out and snipped off Trysh's foot at the ankle. The move was so sudden and precise it didn't seem to register on anyone until Trysh suddenly gasped, the pain a lightning stroke to her senses. A glob of white fluid spat into her face, choking off the inchoate scream at birth. Only the whites of Trysh's eyes and her bulging throat testified to the pain she felt, the child orphaned without a voice and trapped within her mutilated body. At first Deft couldn't tell what blocked Trysh's mouth. Then it became clear it was webbing, spider silk filling her so effectively the scout was sucking in air as best as possible through her nostrils, hyperventilating as the pain continued toward a crescendo.

"Don't," warned the Phoenix. "Thou hast a gift, thief. One that makes thee unique in this realm. Dost thou ken what it is?"

"This staff and the Cypher," replied Deft matter-of-factly. Blood streamed down out of Trysh's leg in a steady gush. At first the knight couldn't understand why the damn ankle hadn't clamped the blood vessels shut. She'd been on enough battlefields to know how the body could staunch the flow within a few moments of a limb being severed. Then it hit her… the sandpreys. Their saliva kept Trysh's blood from clotting, which meant the scout didn't have long.

"Blood," the Phoenix said, looking at the growing pool

of warm liquid forming below the scout's body. She nodded and Malioch acted again, his claw moving almost faster than Deft could see. Paramus's right foot joined Trysh's left as the scholar was amputated in a literal blink of an eye.

The sudden coppery smell of blood did something to Deft then. She could feel herself salivating, a strange sensation given the almost complete desiccation of her body. A pain grew within her, the kind that only hunger created, the kind that only feasting cured. It was the blood, she realized. Their blood was the siren's call, except it sang with smell and the promise of sustenance and strength. It was heady and vibrant. It was alive... so alive.

"You have none," the Phoenix offered, "and by that fact you fall outside the boundaries of natural order. You are almost a gholem and yet I do not smell the magic of my sister behind this."

The words pulled Deft out of her spiral just as Paramus started to scream, his voice breaking as his leg suddenly understood what had happened and cried to his brain. Once again, a white, sticky gob of spider silk shut his throat so only his high-pitched squeals could be heard coming from what sounded like his chest. Normally Deft would have smiled, but her eyes flicked to Trysh. The scout's head lolled, her skin gray.

"Tell me, who did this to you?" inquired the Phoenix. "Speak and I will release your companions to death quickly." She gestured and the blood pooling beneath the two captured party members flashed once, then flew upward in a fine red mist. It suffused Trysh and Paramus, more the former, bringing a bright pink flush to her skin. She gasped through her nose, the sound almost comical as she suddenly became alert and tried to breathe.

Snip.

Trysh's other foot fell and the scout's head arched back in agony.

Snip.

Paramus's blood had also been thinned by the sandprey's bite, but not so much as Trysh's. Still, the scholar fell back shaking as his blood splattered the ground below like refuse from a slaughterhouse, his body convulsing as pain washed through him without mercy. The smell was captivating, almost too much to bear.

"They'll stay alive for as long as I will them to do so, thief. If you have any care—"

The Phoenix never finished her sentence because at that moment Trysh stabbed backward with a small blade, catching Malioch in one of the two largest eyes. The result was an explosion of white fluid from the black orb and a hiss of anger and pain as the gigantic spider stumbled back a step, dropping both Paramus and Trysh. The scout tucked her legs up and landed heavily on her thighs, rolling across sharp rock until she came to rest motionless about half the distance between the Phoenix and Deft.

The scholar was not quite so lucky. Instinct made him extend his legs as if he still had feet to land upon. In a way he accomplished this, landing on top of his feet as his raw bone stumps hit the sharp obsidian rock. The resulting scream was so shrill it made Deft almost want to laugh. However, the perversity of the moment didn't detract from the knight's intimate knowledge that the scout had given her one chance, and this was it. She slammed the iron shod heel of the runestaff into the ground. Time to get out of here.

There was a sudden vibration, a sound heard by their bones, and then a concussion that blasted everyone away from the point where the runestaff impacted the earth. A globe of light formed and within that globe stood Lilyth.

"Sister, I see you are still well," said the blue-skinned queen of demons. "Pray tell me, what do you think of my undead knight?"

The Phoenix glided forward, her face expression dark and angry. "Be not so foolish as to expect any reprieve. The Cypher will never be given over, no matter how many times thou try to wrest it from me."

Lilyth *tsk*ed, looking at the mutilated bodies of the still-alive and moaning Paramus and Trysh. She took in Malioch with a glance and seemed to know without looking that Deft stood behind her. The knight watched as she opened her arms and said, "You misunderstand me."

"Pray thee, tell me how?" demanded the Phoenix.

Lilyth's image remained insubstantial but clear. She smiled and said, "Recall our first meeting, my sister. Recall the thousand meetings after that. What have we accomplished? The Sovereign will eventually act, and when he does, this world will be remade."

"I am rebirth," reminded the Phoenix. "The Phoenix will exist again, carrying out its purpose and serving faithfully."

Lilyth seemed to consider this, then asked, "And when you do so, when the world is remade, where will *you* be?"

The Phoenix seemed taken aback by that question, as if she'd never considered it. "I will be beside—"

"No." The finality of the way Lilyth said this shifted Deft's gaze away from the Phoenix to examine the girl more closely. Gone was the daft child she'd seen in the Serapeum of Thoth. There was something in her voice, a deadly maturity woven so deeply into every sound and timbre, it made the undead knight come to a sudden acceptance of the truth. This was the real Lilyth, not the mewling girl she'd met earlier. The full weight of a goddess-born hit home, erasing the childish scribble Deft had drawn in her own mind as to the nature of the being who claimed the titles Eye of the Sun and the Celestial of the Aeris. She'd heard them before but had never quite understood they paled next to the actual majesty of the woman addressing them now.

Lilyth continued, "You will not stand beside anything. You will be gone. There will be another Phoenix, another with your memories and your life, serving the Sovereign. Whatever you are will be erased, removed from existence. Do you ken the truth of my words?"

The Phoenix was silent, her blazing eyes and form bringing to life the shadows in a room that had gone utterly still as these two goddesses faced each other. Finally, she said, "What dost thou propose?"

A smile crept onto Lilyth's face. She raised one eyebrow and offered, "Neither of us can take possession of the Cypher. Sovereign has protected it with enchantments no living thing can overcome." Then her image slowly turned to face Deft.

The Phoenix glided forward to stand beside her. "The knight," she intoned, her eyes still searching for Deft's form.

Lilyth nodded, "The red mage used blood magic, something beyond us, to create this abomination."

The flames of the Phoenix became softer, less threatening, as if her own mood were reflected in their violence or lack thereof. She looked at Lilyth, "He opened the Way to this."

Lilyth looked at the Phoenix and nodded, "We cannot create nor destroy, but we can alter blood magic."

"It will need blood," opined the Phoenix, "and she has none."

Lilyth met Deft's eyes and said, "Why do you think I had her bring them?" She glanced at Paramus and Trysh, then nodded to the knight as if thanking her.

"Wait! What do you mean, had me bring them? You wanted me to bait—"

Lilyth turned away, ignoring the knight and addressing her sister of rebirth and death. "Together, we can imbue the knight's bones with the Cypher. This will lock it away behind blood magic, trapping it behind a door Sovereign cannot open. It will ensure," she reached out and her image stroked the cheek of the Phoenix, though her hand was not physically there, "that you will remain the Phoenix for eternity."

"And you will remain the Keeper," said the Phoenix.

"If I wish," answered Lilyth, "but I can dream of greater things than what scraps have been offered from the table of men."

The Phoenix nodded and smiled, but then a look of concern crossed her face. "How will this be accomplished? As you have said, we cannot wield blood magic. Only the builders can."

Lilyth gestured to Trysh and Paramus. "Infuse them with the mark of the Cypher." She looked back at Deft, her eyes narrowing. "Then entomb them with our undead knight. Her thirst will grow."

The Phoenix moved to obey, raising her arms and gesturing. Fire swirled, entering each body with an unholy light, altering something deep within. A moment later she said, "It is done."

"I'll never drink, if only to spite you," spat Deft. Yet the hunger she'd felt before knew her words were an empty threat.

The demon-queen laughed, her words echoing Deft's own doubts when she replied, "You have no understanding of the thirst, yet." Suddenly her attitude shifted to that of the little girl who'd so easily fooled Deft. "Oh! You'll just love a good meal, especially since you'll be locked away until you've cleaned your plate." She enunciated each word by clapping her hands in time, and finally ended it with a squeal of glee. "And here's the best part!" She leaned in close to Deft and said, "You will serve me, forever."

"What art thou doing?" asked the Phoenix, clearly in shock at Lilyth's childlike behavior.

The demon-queen looked at her Aeris sister, her face becoming more mature and serious again. "An idiot to whom another idiot invested all of her faith. Some lessons are best taught by example."

A moan sounded and Paramus raised his hand, trembling like he had palsy. He whimpered something, ending in what sounded like the word, "please." It was Trysh who somehow gathered enough strength to be heard, her breathing shallow and her skin ashen again as her blood leaked out. "I… worship… you." Uttering those words seemed to sap all the strength the scout had left. Lilyth moved forward, even as the Phoenix gestured and blood returned to their bodies, bringing again clarity and focus, and another round of excruciating pain.

Between moments of crying and pleading, Paramus somehow gasped, "You said you can't use blood magic! How did… blood back… to our bodies?"

Lilyth looked at the man for a moment, then back at Deft.

"What he lacks in insight he makes up for with mewling." Then she looked back at Paramus, and like an adult speaking to a small child said, "Shhh, blood magic doesn't literally mean blood, but something much smaller within your body that holds the instructions on how to make you. The Cypher is keyed to those markers. Think about that as Deft drains you of every drop of blood your body contains."

The demon-queen then looked at Trysh and smiled,

answering her earlier words.

"Your worship will not be forgotten. Even as your blood feeds this abomination hanging between life and death, know that within each drop lies the key to protecting our worlds. Yet, I am not without mercy."

She nodded and the Phoenix raised her arms. The obsidian floor erupted up on four sides surrounding the two fallen companions of Deft, creating a box roughly large enough for them to lie down. To this enclosure Lilyth gestured and the undead knight was wrenched into the air like a puppet on the end of invisible strings. She was dumped unceremoniously into the small enclosure, before another slab held by the Phoenix was raised to hover over the opening.

"She's in?" inquired the Phoenix, searching the interior for any signs of Deft, which she clearly still could not see.

Lilyth nodded but held up a hand, forestalling any next action of the Phoenix. She gestured and a small surge of power sent any remaining blood back into Paramus and Trysh's bodies. A quick flash of fire, the smell of burnt flesh, and their screams said their stumps had been cauterized. "In order to fulfill your Oath to him, Paramus will rise from the dead to serve you. Breaking your word could have unforeseen consequences." She looked at Trysh and her gaze softened. "As for you," she nodded with her chin and a small blade appeared in Trysh's hand, "you may make your end quick. It will be less painful than what Deft will do when her hunger unleashes the beast within."

Her next words were for Deft's ears. "You'll stay in here until every drop of blood is consumed."

"No!" screamed Paramus, but the obsidian lid had already begun to close over the mouth. The last sight Deft saw was the sparkling blue eyes of Lilyth looking contemptuously down at her. Then the tomb's lid fell into place with a hollow boom, sealed by the Phoenix's magic, into utter blackness. A spark blossomed to life inside the lid, a gesture from Lilyth more cruel than kind, allowing them to watch everything the undead knight did.

Another wave of pain lanced through the knight as the smell of blood and flesh was magnified in the now enclosed space. She closed her eyes, breathing in the coppery tang, the salty smell of energy and sustenance. A moment passed, then Deft took the small dagger from Trysh. She checked its edge, keen and sharp, then looked at the two and asked, "A fine mess we're in, and the smell of blood is waking something within me."

"She called it the beast," replied Trysh. "You don't have to do this."

Deft nodded as silence descended on the group. Though each had grievous injuries, something in the magic of Lilyth must have deadened that pain. Paramus sensed his precarious position because he didn't make a sound, just backed himself up as far as possible into the corner, as if this would keep him from Deft's eye.

Finally, Deft broke the silence.

"Do you want to go first?" she asked Trysh. The scout began to respond but Deft lunged and in a quick motion grabbed Paramus's jaw, slicing quickly through his neck. Paramus bled out in heartbeats as Deft sank her teeth into the wound and drank.

"Just kidding. We both knew it would be him," she said after she finished. She closed her eyes at the sudden gush of strength and power she felt, as the blood seemed to soak into her at once. The power invigorated her, creating another period of silence. Deft understood it was the blood itself that was important, and despite her loathing of Paramus, the idea of listening to him crying and pleading was too much, even for her.

"I'm curious," Deft said, "why did you fawn over him so much?"

Trysh sighed, her eyes half closing. "I had a brother once." She paused, then asked, "You drained him with those fangs. Why?"

"Hmm." Deft shrugged, "Paramus will suffer the same fate as me, risen from the dead and kept in bondage. If he's raised, he'll be as he was when he died. I know what it means to have a wasted body. You can't serve well, and if he's to serve me I want him whole. As to why I bled him," she grew wistful, "I don't know. Maybe it was a mistake."

She doubted Trysh appreciated her sense of morality, nor could she know that Deft actually liked the scout's honesty. It was for that reason that she reversed her blade and plunged it into Trysh's thigh, slicing cleanly through the artery. Blood spurted in time with the scout's heartbeat, quickly pooling into a dark puddle of steaming black liquid. Then, because of whatever magic gave Deft her unlife, it flowed directly to the undead knight to be absorbed. She watched as the life drained from Trysh, her head lolling as death claimed her.

"You also deserve a quick death," the knight said to the body. Then she turned to Paramus, "And what are we going to do with you?" Though the boy didn't speak, he nonetheless began to stir in unlife. Deft couldn't help but smile as she raised her keen dagger.

"They're raising you from the dead or I become an oathbreaker," she said. "It means you and I will be together for an exceedingly long time, college boy, and that means I'm truly cursed. So, we're going to start by making you presentable in my guard."

Come morning the lid was pulled back and the undead

knight emerged from the tomb looking almost whole. Her skin had regained much of its youth and vitality though the parts decayed had not grown back. Her eyes no longer looked milky, instead one eye now gleamed with a piercing blue Deft had in life.

Behind her came the figure of Paramus, shuffling with head bowed. Gone was his rotund physique, the fat and skin wasted away from his body like an animal left for too long under a summer sun, dessicated and sinewy until just ribs and bones showed through. His feet had regrown, as had the skin covering any wounds he'd suffered. He moved with the slow dazed pace of those newly risen, something that almost succeeded in not annoying Deft. Within moments they were confronted by Lilyth, who appeared in a multicolored splendorous burst of light.

"Oh, good knight, I see you have not done what we asked," she said. "How then was the tomb opened?"

The Phoenix appeared then, smiling slightly. "Ah sister, it is I who allowed thine thief to go free. 'Tis not worthy of us to cause unnecessary harm to those who follow and worship us, nay? Besides," her voice grew harder, "thou dost not issue commands within my realm." A moment passed, then two. Finally, Lilyth just nodded. Then she motioned to Paramus and said, "You'll need nine more like him. They will be your Furies and my heralds. You will command them."

"And the Cypher?" Deft asked.

"Why silly, you are now the Cypher." Lilyth looked over her shoulder and the air brightened, causing the knight to shade her gaze. "The markers necessary to release the runestaff are now hidden within you."

The Phoenix blazed brighter in her gossamer gown of fire red opals and silver. She tilted her head, her eyes searching,

"Is your thief here, sister?"

"Yes, sister, she is."

"You must taste her blood," replied the Phoenix. "The blood of the Cypher flows within thy knight. Taste it quickly before it becomes one with her bones."

At Lilyth's nod, Deft drew her knife and slashed her palm. Lilyth paused, then came close, kissing her lightly. A sudden emotional thrill went through the knight, a feeling so unexpected it caught her off guard. Paramus must have felt something too for he moaned just a bit, only now coming to conscious awareness of his state in unlife.

Lilyth moved over to the Phoenix, who took her sister in her arms. Their lips parted and brushed, the smallest drops of blood transferring from that briefest of kisses. A sudden yellow flash occurred, encompassing both Paramus and Deft, the latter who felt something tighten within her, something restricting her somehow. A shudder went through the Phoenix, who intoned, "It is done."

"Excellent," said Lilyth. "We have accomplished much, Alion Deft. Take your first Fury and begin recruiting more to your banner. Your work has just begun."

Deft looked at Paramus and then up at the stars, knowing beyond measure that her next words were true. "All-Father, I am truly cursed."

"Hardly," said the Phoenix, answering the voice she could not see. "Thou, like us, art now gloriously immortal. It is a far better bargain than your precious All-Father ever gave you."

THE MAGEHUNTERS

Niall and Merric moved down the long hallway toward Haven's training grounds. The king noticed the many artistic knick-knacks that adorned every pace of their path. There didn't seem to be an empty spot that wasn't decorated with a tapestry, painting, or statue. The whole place was sunny and smelled of flowers. He was struck again by the stark contrast between Haven and Bara'cor. Haven looked all prettied up, like a girl for a ball. Bara'cor sat like a fist of iron, a knight with shield in hand, ready for a fight.

He didn't need to voice to Merric which he thought was preferable. He took a sidelong look at the once-regent and now kingsmark of the Magehunters. The man walked with a singular purpose, his blue skin and rippling muscles almost visible beneath the silken training tunic he wore. Niall couldn't help but be proud of what he'd created.

Merric turned to him, evidently sensing his stare. He inquired, "Your Grace?"

"Nothing," responded Niall, smiling. "You just look perfect for the role."

"Thanks to you, Father," Merric said without a hint of guile or sarcasm. "And you say these Aeris inhabit our people?"

Niall nodded, "Yes. Valarius taught me we elves are immune to possession, but the Aeris outnumber us more than ten to one. It's their goal to live again. He searched for a very long time to find a way to subjugate them. He failed because their strength comes from our beliefs."

Merric looked at him with his brows knit together, then asked, "Then they aren't alive? And what do you mean, our beliefs?"

Niall shrugged and answered, "They need a body to exist outside of Arcadia. With that realm gone, Lilyth has flooded our world with her refugees, riffraff, and vagabonds. They've taken over Bara'cor." He paused, then said, "The gods we prayed to—the Lady, the Morningstar, Vulkan— they're all Aeris lords. They gained power from our belief in them." Niall smiled, putting a hand on Merric's broad shoulder and squeezing. "Now that's changed. You have something more to believe in."

Merric smiled in response and said, "Yes, Father. We believe in you."

The king nodded. The loyalty of the elves was at times both flattering and overwhelming.

The kingsmark licked his lips, his face reflecting a man deep in thought. Then he said, "If our magehunters can kill them, perhaps our people's belief will wane, weakening them."

Niall looked at him, slowing to a stop. He wasn't entirely sure what Merric meant, but he'd learned to mimic whatever he heard and wait for more explanation.

"Killing them will make our people's belief wane..." he said thoughtfully, as if trying the idea on for size. "I've been thinking the very same thing! Tell me more and we can strategize together."

"If our magehunters can show these Aeris gods are weak, vulnerable, people will believe in us. Our power will grow. A public demonstration of our strength will be necessary."

"Exactly!" the king chimed in. "This is how we turn the tide. Exactly my idea."

"You are wise beyond your years, sire. First, we'll need

to train the magehunters to deal with this foe. Taking regular troops, as the old Galadines had done, will not suffice. In addition to our elven blood, we'll need to practice combat together to mesh into a well-honed and formidable force."

"And that's exactly where I'm taking us," Niall said smugly, liking how Merric saw exactly what was so special about him. "Zedakai trains the elven cohorts in shifts. We're going to join in and learn what they learn."

Merric smiled and said, "Nothing would make my purpose clearer than to give my arm the strength it needs to defend you, sire."

Uncle Zed had been right. The transformation remade the man from the inside out, giving him a new life, but most importantly, unswerving loyalty. It would only be a matter of time and soon all of Haven would feel as Merric did. Niall loved the thought. Soon, the entire world would be worshiping the Galadine lions, with him as their ruler. Father would be proud.

They approached two large double doors with elven guards stationed on either side. As they neared, the two guards saluted.

Then one bowed and said, "Lord Zedakai is waiting for you inside, your Majesty," while opening the door deferentially.

The other stood at ready, his spear held at salute. As Niall met his eyes, he could see the fervor of love the man had for him. It filled his heart with warmth.

The young Galadine king strode through with Merric at his heels, only to be greeted by the sight of one hundred elves paired off in a five by five square for training. Zedakai stood on a small dais occupying the head of square. He was closest to the doors where Niall entered, with the rest of the class arrayed before him in neat rows. They were all dressed in cotton robes over which sat light leather armor, just enough to stop a training blade, not much more.

As the king entered, all one hundred students bowed, then took a ready stance with their hands and feet shoulder width apart. Zedakai said, "Welcome to instruction! As you two are last, you will pair with each other."

Niall shook his head and said, "Late? Uncle you must be—"

Zedakai jumped down from his perch and screamed, "Shut the door!"

The scream was so sudden and intense Niall felt himself almost piss his pants in surprise. As it was, an electric shock ran through him. The sound of the doors shutting meant the guard behind them must've immediately obeyed.

Zedakai in turn had crossed the distance between him and Niall so he was now close enough to touch. How had the man moved so fast?

"In here there is no rank except teacher and student. If you wish instruction, it will be by the rules that are the basis of our training," he said.

"But you're not even the original magehunters!"

"Are we not? How are you so sure?" The elven lord paused, then said, "In here, I am the master. You may refer to me as that, or as Goshin. You are beginning students, learning what has been taught for centuries to the elves. When it comes to hunting Aeris, we have no equals. Know that mages are Aeris bonded to people, and therefore no different. In here, you will learn to defend yourself against their skill and prevail."

Niall smirked, "I've had combat training. What makes—"

He felt Merric's hand upon his shoulder and the kingsmark's voice softly say, "Let him speak."

318

Niall shrugged it off but said nothing. He just looked at his uncle, waiting for the master to speak.

Zedakai smiled and said, "Indeed? Astra, step into the square."

Instantly the students created a square. Into this open space stepped an elven girl of slight build. She bowed and waited.

Zedakai then looked at Niall.

"Astra is one of my newer students. If you and Merric together can either incapacitate or kill her, you may skip today's training." The border of the square parted to reveal an opening leading in.

"You're kidding," Niall said.

Zedakai shook his head.

"Astra, defend yourself. Do not cause permanent injury to either of these... students."

Niall laughed, and said, "A girl against the two of us?" He looked at Merric and then changed his form to full elven, as Zed had taught him. The kingsmark gave a satisfying indrawn breath of surprise. He'd never seen Niall in his true form, which now stood a head taller than either Zedakai or Merric.

Niall flexed his arms and said, "I don't need Merric's help."

Zedakai shrugged, his hand pointing the way, but he blocked Niall's path.

"One thing."

Niall knew there would be conditions to the fight, and couldn't help but say, "You can't put rules in now to protect your student, uncle."

The master took a breath and smiled.

"If Astra wins, you shut your mouth and train without complaint, agreed?" When Niall didn't immediately say anything, Zedakai added, "Unless you're worried about losing."

"No," Niall retorted. "I'm just trying to figure out where the trick is. No matter," he winked at Merric before answering Zedakai, "I accept your terms." He raised his voice so everyone could hear, "I accept Goshin's terms. If Astra wins, I train without complaint." Goshin? Who'd ever heard of that? He put emphasis on the title only to remind his uncle who was the real king here and who had a made-up rank. Then he turned his attention to the ring and the tiny girl within it.

Really, uncle? This small girl is going to beat me?

He shook his head and strode forward, his long limbs eating up the space until he stood across from her. Her head barely reached his chest, putting her at about the same size of a regular man-at-arms of Edyn. How Zed expected her to win against him was a mystery.

She bowed, then assumed a stance. "I wish you well, sire."

Niall did an awkward imitation of her bow, then brought his fists up, not sure if he should reply. The point became moot as Zedakai gave a shout that obviously meant, "begin."

The girl moved quickly, not hesitating at all. She ducked under both of Niall's swings, then kicked him hard in the stomach. As he fell back, she dove into a forward roll and then leapt up, trying for a strike with her knee to his head.

Niall dodged that, struggling to match her furious pace as she swung around him and threw an elbow into his temple, staying on him like his own shadow. His vision went gray for a moment, but he rolled and managed to regain his feet as his head cleared. She stood across from him, breathing lightly, looking none the worse for wear. Then she attacked again.

This time he thought he was ready. Instead of trying to hit her, he let her in. Once within arm's reach, he grabbed her in a bear hug and squeezed, trying to get her to yield.

Astra did no such thing. She hooked her foot behind his thigh and pulled her elbows apart, spreading his bear hug. Then she pulled herself down through his arms.

He felt a hard smash to his groin with a knee, followed by a palm strike to his face that brought stars to his eyes. The next he knew, he was on his side, curled up and close to vomiting. He could hear her circling back to the center of the makeshift combat square, and slowly levered himself up. A radiating pain that now seemed to center just below his stomach made it almost impossible to rise. Pride however, made him slowly regain his feet, while anger made him act like he was just fine, even though it was between gasps.

Niall shook his head to clear it, but she was on him again. He felt her heel strike him in the stomach. No fair! She didn't wait!

The breath whooshed out of him as he fell back, coughing. Anger began to bleed from his gut, a cauldron of hate fueled by the idea of a small girl cheating and winning in front Zedakai's students. He held up a hand as if he needed a pause and stumbled to his feet.

To his astonishment, the girl waited, then reassumed her combat stance. Niall did the same. This time, however, his hand crept back to grasp the small belt dagger he'd begun wearing, withdrawing a small blade designed to be punched with. No one made a fool of him.

When Astra attacked next, he punched with the dagger, blocking her kick and opening her thigh up with a sudden burst of blood. He grabbed that leg and punched her again in the ribs, then once more in the neck. Blood spurted from each wound, but Niall wasn't done. He used his strength, picking her up and then smashing her into the ground. As she hit, he fell atop her and punched with his dagger in rapid succession, opening wounds in her neck and chest, before Zedakai yelled, "Stop!"

Niall didn't, punching until he was too exhausted to throw any more. Then he slowly stood, heaving, his face and chest covered in Astra's blood. The woman was somehow still alive, but a gout of blood vomited out of her mouth, painting her face with its ichor. Her fingers clawed the ground, her eyes wide, but a few moments later they dulled, and she became still. The king walked over and looked down on her, then spit on her dead face.

When he turned and faced the master, it was with a smile he knew Zed would hate. He was going to rub the master's failure in, even though his body ached with injuries from the fight. "Never underestimate me."

The master simply nodded. "You are excused from today's training. We will see you again, tomorrow. Hopefully, against a more worthy opponent."

Niall looked at him, his mind vacant. Then he looked over at the girl and the spreading pool of blood below her body. Had he killed before like this, hand to hand, where he could see it? The fight to the portal had been a mishmash of blows taken and returned, but he'd not seen the actual outcome. Astra's death had shown him something new. He looked at the body and smiled.

"She can be brought back by my hand," he said to his uncle. "A worthy sacrifice to join our most personal guards." As the man began to turn away, he added, "Yes, bring me more."

BETRAYAL

Arek took a deep breath, thinking through their options. There weren't many. When he opened his eyes, it was Ash who spoke first.

"How are we going to—"

Arek held up a hand, "A moment, Firstmark."

He addressed Zafir, "Let's say I agree. What happens?"

Zafir nodded, as if appreciating Arek's ability to separate himself from his emotions.

"I transition us to the black spire of the Phoenix. There, I can contain her, but only for a limited time. It will fall upon your companions to hold off her minions while you and Duncan use her power to forge a new runestaff."

"Am I missing something?" Ash put in. "I mean, we're four who have either lord- or Celestial-ranked Aeris bonded to us. How hard will it be, all of us going against one being, even one as powerful as you make this Phoenix out to be?"

Zafir turned to the firstmark.

"You speak the truth, and if we journeyed as we had eons ago, odds would certainly be in our favor. However," his gaze took in Arek, Duncan, and Ash, "what do you remember of your true selves?"

"You wear the armor of the one I knew as Orion, the Hunter," he said to Ash. "What do you know of his puissance with spear and bow, sun and flame, other than what you have seen?"

Zafir turned to Duncan. "And you bear the mark of death.

What do you ken of how Scythe could manipulate order and disorder?"

Finally, he turned to Arek. "And you, my Lord Azrael. Do you know for what purpose you have been created?"

He shook his head.

"Even I am diminished, though not as much as you. I, too, have forgotten much of what we all once were. Like you, I am the result of the dreams and wishes of the people of Edyn. Perhaps it is my curse to remember a bit more than you, but not so much as Lilyth or the Phoenix. This is what makes them so dangerous." His eyes grew serious.

"Believe me, if we escape without loss, I will be both surprised and thankful."

His admission threw a pall over the group, all eyes downcast as they thought about the idea of losing one of their comrades to this quest. It was clear to Arek no one wanted their group to suffer any more than they already had, yet there seemed to be no other choices.

Finally, he looked up. "And the Cypher. What is that?"

Zafir shook his head. "Legend says it is a kind of key, an object that will allow the runestaff to be used." He gestured and a small cylindrical post, unnoticed before, began to glow. "We must place the staff and Cypher into this receptacle and the gate will open to my command. Until that is done, we are trapped here in Arcadia."

"Great," remarked Duncan, looking sidelong at Deft.

In response, the undead knight merely smirked. "Then you're dead and my vengeance is complete."

Arek moved over, facing Deft, who still stood restrained by Zafir's men. "You'd be killed here, too."

Deft nodded. "I knew that when I did not follow the Lady to Edyn. I have nothing to live for besides bringing justice to that man."

Arek caught the raised eyebrow from Ash and stopped him from responding with a small gesture. He didn't need the firstmark to blurt out how he really felt about Duncan right now.

"What if I could free you of this curse?"

Deft laughed, "You, a child? Doubtful." She peered closely into Arek's eyes and said, "You cannot unravel the knots in others while you yourself remain tangled in purpose."

Her voice came out like the wheezing breath of a dying man, fetid and coarse, and yet it also had the ring of prophecy, of truth buried deep. He looked at her with the dragonsight, seeing past the surface to the core of the person within. The sight shocked him.

He could see what no doubt was Duncan's spell, the intricate weaving on par with Valarius's own. What mastery it displayed! He looked quickly at his father, new appreciation in his eyes. Then his Sight was pulled to the collar surrounding his father's neck.

He looked back at Deft. Something like what Valarius had done was woven into the very fiber of Deft's being. It wasn't a spell from his father or from Valarius. It was something different, suffusing the very bones of the undead knight. It was…

He stepped back, his eyes wide in shock. "I know—"

"Know what?" asked Duncan.

"It's her," Arek said, "I understand how."

"What?" his father asked again.

Arek hurriedly moved over to this father, saying, "I can free you."

"Stop!" Ash said, the stentorian note of command in his voice bringing Arek to a halt as effectively as if the firstmark had physically grabbed him. "You're not freeing him."

Arek looked at the commander. He could just brush Ash aside, but to what end? It would make him an enemy forever and endanger his father more. Instead he said, "Firstmark, we cannot fashion a new runestaff without my father. And without that runestaff, we perish here… all of us." He held Ash's gaze, his expression open and direct.

"We agreed that if it was necessary, if his strength were needed, he would be freed."

Moments passed as possible choices flitted through the firstmark's mind, visible to Arek by his darting gaze as each thought was reviewed and discarded. Finally, Ash looked away. "You know he'll double-cross us."

"I am still under Oath," Duncan said flatly, "to follow you to whatever destination you choose. That has not changed."

Ash's eyes flicked back and forth between father and son, finally searching the ground for something unseen. He took a deep breath and then just nodded and stepped back, but in a small voice he said, "If he escapes, the deaths of thousands are upon your head, Arek, including Yetteje's father."

Arek swallowed, the weight of Ash's words forcing him to consider his next move. However, what he'd outlined to the firstmark was true. Without his father's power they were stuck here. He turned his gaze to the torc. The secret had been in front of him all along. He couldn't unravel Valarius's spell, just as he couldn't unravel Duncan's spell on Alion Deft. He could, however, unravel something else. He watched the Way as it suffused the metal of the torc, then focused his Sight on the torc itself. Suddenly his vision dove in past the surface and into the lattice structure of the copper.

It was surprisingly ordered, reminding him of crosses with branching offshoots in a symmetrical construct that repeated itself indefinitely. Throughout this construct wove Valarius's spell, infinitely more complex than the structure itself, like a tree with string woven throughout the branches. Arek smiled. He wasn't going to unravel the string; he was going to burn down the tree that held it.

He reached out with a finger and touched a central node of one of the constructs, channeling his power into that node to see what would happen. The node vaporized, falling apart, and the attached offshoots floated a bit until they tried to connect to other branches like lodestones attracted to one another.

Arek cleared his mind, then called upon Breath of Fire, channeling his blaze of ethereal power throughout the entire construct.

The lattice holding Valarius's spell ignited like kindling, falling apart before his eyes. It spread in a curve now visible, a curve that followed the curve of the metal torc surrounding his father's neck. He couldn't help feeling proud as his vision shot back out and into the world. He caught the torc lose its coppery luster first, then turn gray before falling into dust. By destroying the copper, he'd effectively unraveled the knots of Valarius's spell!

Arek's dragonsight watched as a column of power washed up through his father, power so potent it made his eyes blink and water. White light suddenly illumined Duncan's form, argent and clean. It suffused him with both vitality and health, undoing all the maladies which had befallen him since being trapped by the torc. The lore father took a deep breath, a small smile appearing as pain and exhaustion were wiped away.

Zafir bowed once. "Welcome again amongst us, brother Scythe."

"It doesn't change anything," muttered Deft. "You might have freed yourself, but without my help the East Gate remains closed."

Arek turned to her, but it was Duncan's turn to hold up a hand, stepping forward and facing the undead knight. "Deft, what I did to you was a punishment meant to end, not this everlasting torment. I beg your forgiveness."

Deft cackled and spat. "Put your neck within reach of my teeth and I'll forgive you permanently."

Duncan didn't move, his expression somber. Then he stepped a bit closer and said, "I cannot change whatever else has been done to you, but I can remove the curse I laid upon you so long ago. Help us, and I will do so."

That brought a sudden silence to the magehunter, an offer so profoundly unexpected it stopped her like a maul wielded by a titan. This was what Arek had sensed deep within her, buried so far under her posturing it had almost been eradicated. It was hope. Deft yearned to be free of the curse more than anything else. Yet it was far from her grasp. Hope was a concept so alien now it could hardly be found within the undead knight.

"You lie, you—"

"Help us retrieve the Cypher and use it to open the East Gate, and by the blood of my forefathers, I bind myself to you as healer. By my oath as Lore Father of the Old Lore, I will lift the curse I laid upon you so many years ago."

Deft stood there, the shock of Duncan's uttering of the Oath of Binding undisguisable. The emotion was so raw, so painstakingly clear, even Arek could read it on her ruined face. Slowly, her head dropped, and she intoned, "By the blood of my once true life, I bind myself and my Furies to you as ally. We will reveal the Cypher and open a gate."

The blinding flash of yellow, more intense than any Arek had seen before, due to the power of the Way here in Arcadia, suffused the area they stood within, making everyone cover their eyes. When it was gone, Duncan gestured for the guards to release Deft and her Furies. In a moment they all stood free of their restraints. As a testament to the power of the Oath, none moved aggressively lest they incur its wrath.

"Cure me!" Deft demanded immediately, the need drawing her mouth into an open yaw wider than any person could accomplish, like a sky serpent unhinging its jaw to swallow prey.

Duncan shook his head, "The Oath—"

"I was a fool to trust you!" spat the magehunter. "You're—"

"We need your strength," replied the archmage, cutting Deft off. "If I cure you now, you might become normal, or whatever passes as normal for you. Given we're outmatched against the Phoenix, I thought you'd want to maximize your chance of living long enough to enjoy the lifting of the curse."

Deft cursed, but something in her stance told Arek she grudgingly agreed. No point in enjoying a few moments of normalcy only to die in battle.

"Weird to say this," the young adept said, "but welcome to the team, I guess."

Deft looked at Arek. "The black spire is tight, worming tunnels that lead underground to her lair. We cannot take five hundred men."

"You've been there?" asked Zafir.

"I had reason to dine with the Lady and her sister," muttered Deft, her eyes taking on that faraway look one had when seeing the past. It didn't seem to be a fond memory.

"Then that is where you are wrong," laughed Zafir. "With builders, we can phase through the rock."

Deft's attention snapped back to the here and now.

"For a Celestial, you are still an idiot. To be effective, you need to phase in, and the space I recall could not hold more than a dozen if it came to a fight. The minions of the Phoenix number in the millions – spiders, scorpions, sandpreys, and other venomous bloodsuckers. Worse, they're led by someone who understands how to fight dirty."

"I see the pleasantries of our earlier discourse have been shed," Zafir remarked. For a moment Arek thought the Celestial would show anger. Instead, he laughed.

"Refreshing!" he exclaimed. "It will be as it was, adventurers on a glorious quest to slay a being of pure fire!"

"Just get us to the black spire," Deft said, sounding tired. "I owe a certain friend mine a lot for our last meeting. He'll be sorry to see me."

"Isn't that usually true?" Duncan quipped.

The only response was a small laugh, quickly stifled. When everyone turned it was Yetteje standing with a hand over her mouth. "Sorry… it's just…"

"What?" Duncan asked.

"We're sorta the worst fellowship ever," Yetteje said without smiling. "I mean, right?"

END GAME

D uncan watched as arrangements were made to face the Phoenix. In the end, it was decided that they would take eleven people: Arek's party of five, Deft and two furies, and Zafir and two builders. Zafir had begrudgingly agreed that Deft might be correct that bringing more builders would only hamper their efforts. Any more, it was argued, would simply get in each other's way in the confines of the tunnels making up her lair. He'd made an offhand remark that even builders could not stay in phase indefinitely, a fact unknown to Duncan until that moment. The archmage had never heard of a limitation to the builders' powers and filed the knowledge away in case it became relevant later.

There was another significant advantage for their small party: Duncan himself. Whether it was the increased concentration of the Way as Arcadia died, or the fact that Duncan had been cut from its source for so long, but the archmage felt a fourfold increase in his strength and power. The Way was so strong it coursed through him like an unending river, flooding his senses and bringing a tingle that reached his fingertips. With its beneficence his body had rapidly recovered. Gone were most signs he'd ever been harmed. One thing that did not disappear however, were the scars he bore from his encounter with the Galadine highlord, both inside and out.

"Wanna do something besides just stand there with your mouth open?" Yetteje muttered from his right. "It's not gonna pack itself."

She referred to the small pack each had been given by Zafir's men. It contained water, food, and other supplies, including medicinal herbs. In addition, each had been outfitted with weapons and light armor. Their weapons were the ones enchanted by Arek earlier, giving Zafir's Aeris the capability to kill their own people. If Zafir felt any way about this fact, he'd declined to say, but Duncan decided to keep an eye on the Celestial lord despite his apparent acceptance of their plan.

Zafir caught Duncan's eyes on him and smiled.

"Scythe, like times of old, we walk the path of danger with nary a care!"

"Nary a care?" Yetteje piped in, "What's gotten into him?"

Duncan looked at him, Silbane's gift giving him the dragonsight as it had Arek. "The release of boredom." He waited for a response, and when one never came, he continued, "Think about it. What must it be like to exist for centuries but in a world that changes only at the whim of a populations' dreams and faith?"

"Whatever," muttered the princess, securing her pack across her back. He could feel her gaze linger, as if she debated saying more. He was surprised when she asked, "Where do they come up with these names?"

Duncan looked at her, unsure of what she meant. "What?"

Yetteje gestured with her chin at the two furies, "Demeter, Paramus"—she then took in the two builders with Zafir— "Netzah, Keter. Strange enough, but that's not what I mean." She paused, then said, "When I hear their names there's an echo in my mind, as if some part of me knows them."

The archmage began to shrug, somewhat caught flat-footed by the princess's sudden willingness to speak to him. Zafir, having caught the question, responded.

Flashing a beatific smile, he said, "Ahh, you ask an important question, princess. From where doth myth and legend arise?"

"Umm, sort of. Look, I just was trying to create some peace between—"

"Do you not ken the reason why your question is important to answer?" He looked about the platform upon which their hundreds of people stood, the surviving builders possessed by Aeris masters. "It is said our names came with Sovereign's fall. Though my memories are blurred by the tears of time, I know our names hail from the legends of the first world. It was a place called Dirt."

"Dirt? Why would people call their world that?" Yetteje asked, half laughing.

Zafir shook his head, "I know not. The name is so ancient, so shrouded by days long gone, even its meaning may have changed in the vast expanse that is from then till now. Who knows what those gods felt when they saw this world?" He paused, looking out over the crystalline platform, as if listening to the tinkle of the structure as a wind caressed it.

"Sovereign, in all his wisdom, gave us our names so that the memory of our hallowed origin did not disappear entirely. We are a testament to people who once built structures so mighty, who grew so powerful, they spread out amongst the stars. We are their legacy."

He bowed to the princess.

"So it falls upon you to cherish every name you hear, for you are hearing part of who we once were and may be again."

The princess looked thoughtful at first, nodding slowly.

Then she shook her head.

"But, Dirt? I mean, almost anything is better."

Duncan found the princess' words receding, captured by Zafir's words. It was as if he too, had a part of him buried deep that felt the connection between who they once were and now. For a moment he could see that vast expanse Zafir painted, unending as it drew his mind's eye back to a world of blue oceans and green lands.

The spell was broken as Yetteje turned and took her leave. He didn't expect she'd ever forgive him and was touched that even she had attempted conversation.

He looked around the camp to each of his companions. When Zafir reveals what he must, this will all be lost. Even Arek will not forgive me. The thought filled him with melancholy, as the inevitability of fate settled its weight again on his shoulders.

Soon everyone was ready. Zafir motioned to the folk who were now his men and women.

"You will stand guard here. Upon our return, we transition to Edyn!"

A cheer went up at that and the Celestial's forces took station. Deft and her two furies moved to stand beside Duncan, as if they were his personal guard, or perhaps to be sure the he didn't do anything that looked like reneging. A moment later, there was silence. Duncan could see they were waiting for Arek to say something, but the boy seemed lost in thought.

"Arek," he said, catching his son's attention. He nodded his head toward the assembled warriors, raising an eyebrow in an unspoken gesture he hoped would convey both that he needed to speak, and his faith in his son.

Arek nodded.

"Deft, you've been there before," he said. "So, take the

lead." He began to turn but Duncan coughed, the sudden sound stopping him as effectively as a physical hand. Finally getting the hint, Arek turned back.

"Our only job is to give Duncan the time he needs to fashion a new runestaff and for Deft to find the Cypher. That means we fight. We hold the line until it's done, even if the Phoenix shows herself. Remember, if we don't get what Zafir needs to open the gate to Edyn, no one leaves Arcadia. Does everyone understand?"

He waited until each acknowledged his question with a nod.

Yetteje raised a hand.

"So, how do we get back if Zafir falls?" To Duncan she looked a little sheepish, but he had to admit it was a good question.

The Celestial laughed.

"The gate will remain regardless of my status. However," he looked to his fighters, "each of you must guard this end, for the forces of the Phoenix will have nothing but you to stop them from overwhelming us here."

He looked back at Yetteje, scrutinizing her. Tilting his head, he reached out, only hesitating when the princess backed up a step. "Worry not." At her nod, he touched her forehead. A flash erupted, jumping from person to person in the party, but it did not touch the furies nor Deft.

The celestial looked up and said, "It is done. The gate will remain open for three hundred beats of the slowest living heart within our merry fellowship. Then nothing will stop it from closing. Is that good enough, princess?"

Yetteje nodded, "I guess so."

The dwarven builder who'd once been Arcimedis said, "On our honor, we shall hold this end against any who seek entry, my Lord Zafir."

"I know you will," said the lord with a smile. Then he looked to his companions. "Are we ready for glory?"

"If he stays this happy it's going to get tiring," said Brianna.

Yetteje answered, "No kidding."

"Then let danger fear our coming!" proclaimed the Celestial. He gestured and a blue-black gate erupted, surrounded by a purple halo of fire. As the gate opened, a blast of air blew his cloak and the loose clothing of any others standing near Zafir back, as if the gate itself exhaled a breath held for eons. Now it waited, an open maw welcoming them to step inside.

Through its jaws one could see what looked to be a dimly lit cavern. Duncan peered into the gloom, a sudden coldness gripping him. Once again, it seemed it was his fate to walk into situations that would likely end in his death. He sighed, then looked at Deft.

"Follow me," she said, her eyes set straight ahead, "but stay out of my swing." She hefted Reaper.

That she'd traded her blade for a wide flanged mace at some point spoke to the reality of her belief that they would face a deluge of venomous insects. A blade made far less sense than a broader blunt weapon. He looked down at his own hip and the holster carrying Brianna's weapon. Compared to his reawakened powers the gun seemed both archaic and useless, but he knew what it felt like to be powerless. He wasn't about to give up any advantage, no matter how mundane and puny the weapon might be. There was a sound, a slap of leather on bone, then Deft moved forward flanked by her two chosen furies, Demeter and Paramus.

"Wait," Duncan said, knowing how much his power had grown here in Arcadia. "I'll go first and clear the path. My magic is more effective than your mace, Deft."

"Indeed," laughed Zafir, "and though you remember not, you had always stepped first into the fray. We will flank you." He looked at Arek and Ash. "Once we are through, bring the rest and let vengeance ride alongside."

Yetteje rolled her eyes, catching Duncan's attention before she quickly looked away.

Zafir flashed and became a war angel decked in silver and black. Two more flashes and Arek and Ash had followed suit. Duncan didn't change, not yet knowing if he could cast spells as Scythe. He focused instead on the opening to the Phoenix's lair and readied himself. His form illumed itself in blue fire as he called upon the Way, controlling it with lore forgotten by most over two centuries ago. The fire would protect him from harm, and he'd never been one to hold back. He planned to use the abundance of the Way to overwhelm anything they faced.

The scene beyond the gate showed what looked like obsidian black shale lining a passageway, the razor rock creating a tunnel made entirely of slices and points. "Never easy," he said.

Deft answered, a strange expression on her face. "Easy is for the righteous." A wicked grin lit her face, but she didn't look at Duncan. Instead, her gaze fell on one of her furies, Paramus. That one didn't say a word, merely looking forward at the gate; his eyes seemed focused on infinity.

Readying himself, Duncan took a small breath and stepped through.

DRAGOR AWAKENS

T he world came into focus slowly. He remembered his flight within Dawnlight and being captured by Sovereign's guardians, but the rest was a blur. Each eyeblink brought both clarity and lancing pain, like a dagger thrust into his temples. Dragor brought a trembling hand to his head, rubbing his face and taking a long slow breath through his nose. Reaching for the Way was a reflex, but the result surprised him. It was so plentiful it washed through him like he'd submerged himself completely, bringing relief from the pulse-pounding beat in his head. Only then did he fully open his eyes to take account of where he was.

The room was made of panels, each glowing white and lending soft illumination to an otherwise nondescript environment. The floor was smooth, a kind of dull gray without any noticeable details. He sat on a bed with white sheets and a pillow. A small table stood beside the bed, completing the orthogonal geometry with neutral appeal.

Water! The glass was in his hands before he could stop himself, the cool liquid fighting to find a path to trickle down his parched throat. He drank so much he thought he might be part sponge, his body absorbing every drop, somehow not even seeming to make it to his stomach. As his thirst slaked, he put the glass down, amazed to find it still full! An illusion? He quickly inspected his hands and felt his face. Though they were wet, he knew illusion could recreate this and more. He cautioned himself to remain alert, despite the nonthreatening appearance of his surroundings.

Then, in a sudden act of defiance, he picked up the glass and began pouring the water out. It fell continuously, replenishing as quickly as it left.

"Please don't, or we'll have quite a mess to clean up."

Dragor jumped at the voice, but no one was in the room. "Where are you?"

In response what could only be described as a metallic snake-like object emerged from the wall above his bed. It wound sinuously down until it faced him. The head was silver but had a flat black face upon which sat a gleaming jewel, like a bright cyclopean eye. That eye illuminated briefly, flashes of light leaving a warm tingle on his skin. It looked first at his right eye and then his left. Dragor blinked away the afterimages, his hand coming back up in an unconsciously defensive gesture.

"Normal. You haven't suffered any permanent damage from your encounter with the guardians," it intoned. "The liquid you ingested will help bring your body back to equilibrium."

"So that water was real?" Dragor asked, "But, where am I?"

"Relax, Lord Dahl. Your queries will soon be answered."

Dragor scoffed at that. "No one but my mother calls me 'Lord' anything, and only when I've done something wrong."

"No doubt," a new voice said. It belonged to a dark-skinned figure standing in the mouth of a door he hadn't seen slide open. Like Dragor, the man seemed to be Koorvan. He gestured and asked, "May I enter?"

Dragor looked at him in surprise, then nodded. If he'd expected anything, this man was not that.

First, he was incredibly old. Perhaps more importantly, he looked frail. White hair cut close to his scalp adorned an otherwise nondescript face. A kind of happy contentment seemed to leak from his expression, as if he alone was privy to some good news. He smiled as he met Dragor's dark stare with his own clear eyes, and suddenly the adept was reminded of Master Scribe Tridaris, back on the Isle. Not because of skin color or anything else physical, but in the man's bearing. In fact, this man entire aura recalled a librarian more than anything else.

"I trust you aren't in any discomfort?" the man inquired politely as he hobbled in. His voice was a bit high-pitched, growing softer like a squeezebox's decrescendo as the air wheezed out of his lungs.

Dragor shook his head, "No. And you are—?"

The man smiled, then began to sit where there was no chair. Dragor was half out of his bed to avert the fall, only to be brought up short by the appearance of a ledge beneath the man in time for him to sit and lean comfortably back against the wall.

"I thought you were going to—" the adept began.

The man nodded and smiled again, crossing his arms in front of him. He gestured for Dragor to retake his seat, nothing in his demeanor speaking of harm or anger. Then he leaned forward and in a conspiratorial whisper said, "I am the Sovereign," tapping his temple with one dark finger in emphasis.

Dragor just stared, caught for a moment between the absurdity of that statement and the sudden feeling that perhaps he was going insane. He couldn't help when a small laugh bubbled forth. Deep within him, though doubt swirled, a gnawing certainty grew: this being was telling the truth. He decided to compose himself and listen, if for no other reason than to buy time to decide how to affect an escape.

"I see," he said.

"You don't," the old man countered. He looked about, his face still serene, and said, "Lord Dahl, much has been hidden from you. I would show you what you fight for, and the fate of this world should you succeed." He paused, "If you will allow me?"

"Of course," Dragor said with a smile. "Show me whatev—"

The room shifted and changed and suddenly they both stood at the prow of a sailing vessel under blue skies. The sun shone bright and warm, sparkling off waves with glints of silver, green, and blue. Around them bustled sailors attending to various tasks, maintaining the vessel's course in an otherwise calm ocean. No land was in sight, but the view of the horizon was dotted with small black humps, the irregular shapes of mountains peeking over from the edge of the world. He turned and was surprised to see a vast fleet behind this ship, a flotilla of adventurers sailing the high seas.

A sailor walked right through Dragor as if he wasn't there. The adept backed up a step, shocked by everything happening around him and most so by Sovereign, who still stood nearby with a slightly amused expression on his face.

"A vision?" Dragor asked, his voice stumbling as he struggled to catch his breath.

"The truth," Sovereign said. "These vessels contain colonists sent to populate your lands." The old man pointed to the line of mountains on the horizon.

"The fleet will falter, smashing itself upon the place you now call the Shattered Sea. Instead of a tranquil and orderly process, by nightfall these people will be fighting for their lives just to survive." He tilted his head and said, "Behold."

And the scene sped forward, almost too fast for Dragor to follow. When it stopped, he stood amongst metallic wreckage strewn across a beach lined with sharp rocks and shale. In every direction he looked he saw only smashed timbers, half-hulls, floating boxes, and… corpses. Rain whipped down from a bruised sky as lightning punctuated the cold darkness with brief flashes, illuminating the tragedy in stark and unforgiving white.

Sovereign stepped close to him.

"The survivors will move there." He pointed to a rise sheltered a bit more because of trees, "but many will perish before daybreak, unless…"

"Unless what?" demanded Dragor, the exigency of the scene pulling at him.

Sovereign turned, "That woman."

Dragor saw a woman raise a thigh-sized cylinder, the top and bottom encircled with glowing red rings. She dragged it with her from the churning seas, collapsing in exhaustion in the sand as white foam and waves crashed about her. Every fiber of her being cried out immeasurable exhaustion.

"She is the leader of these people and must now make a decision. In doing so, she will change the course of this world's destiny."

"What decision?" Dragor asked, blinking away rain.

Sovereign put a gentle hand on the adept's shoulder and said, "Live or die, adept. She must choose the fate of her people tonight."

The woman dragged herself upright and pulled the cannister to sit in front of her, almost kneeling against it. Tremulous hands, bone-white from the icy waters, clasped the object in a deadman's grip. In the darkness they were painted red by the glowing lights of the cannister. She bent over, rocking back and forth, and Dragor could hear her sobbing.

"What's she doing?" Dragor asked.

"She knows her duty, but… choosing death is difficult."

Dragor felt a wave of empathy flood him. He was unable to take his eyes off the woman as she evidently came to a decision. Even as the storm intensified, she raised a palm and then slammed it into the cannister.

Dragor heard her yell, 'Release! Release! Release!' in quick succession.

The cannister's lights turned yellow, blinking in what seemed a warning. A crash of thunder drowned out whatever she said next, a series of numbers or words? He couldn't be sure, but then the lights turned green and the ends of the cannister erupted in a blue-white flash.

A cloud of scintillating particles exploded out, sweeping out of both ends so quickly it was past their position and out of sight before the woman's head rose. Slowly she touched her forearm.

Entats, like Jesyn's! The swirl of their design curled around her wrist and down her forearm, pulsing in time with the glowing cloud released from the cannister. She raised her arm and clenched her hand into a fist.

A dome of energy appeared encompassing the entire area including where Dragor stood with Sovereign. Under it, no wind or rain assaulted them, only silence—jarring, given the scene just outside the dome. The adept looked at Sovereign, who for his part only nodded, though his expression was dark and tinged with melancholy. The temperature within the dome rose and as Dragor watched, the woman stood and looked out at the ocean. She began a gesture, but the scene froze.

Sovereign said, "She rescues her people tonight, bringing the survivors here under shelter. Though many perish, many more slumber still within life-sustaining capsules and survive. These she collects and will preserve, though it is wrong. Protocol demanded that she allow her crew to perish."

"Why?"

"The thing she released is finite in supply. It must be used to awaken the colonists within those capsules, not as she has done."

"But if she dies, who will awaken the colonists?" questioned Dragor.

"Ahh, Adept, I have many more servants than just her. We would have found a way had the option been preserved."

Dragor walked down the beach to get a closer look, at first not sure if Sovereign would allow it, then not caring. He came face to face with the woman, now frozen in time. It was another shock he'd not been prepared for.

"She's... she looks just like—"

"Her name is Serene. Serene Talaris. Her resemblance to Master Kisan is for good reason, for she is Kisan's forbearer."

Dragor stood there, just looking at the image. It clearly wasn't Kisan, but the similarities were striking. The adept took a deep breath, then turned back to Sovereign and said, "Why show me all this?"

"Serene's actions release the Way to spread across this world. Though it afforded life and sanctuary for Captain Talaris and her people, I explained it came at a price." Sovereign gestured and the scene disappeared. They stood now within a room lined with windows. Outside Dragor could see the vista of the land spread out before him and suddenly realized this room must be near the peak of Dawnlight. Sunlight filtered in, clean and white as dawn broke over the edge of the world.

"Is this the here and now, or another illusion?" asked Dragor.

Sovereign shrugged, "Does it matter? How often do we go about our lives deluding ourselves and avoiding the truth?" When Dragor didn't answer, the old man said, "If it matters to you, then 'yes.' Today is today and you are within Dawnlight in your own world of Edyn."

"Why?" the adept demanded again. "To what end?"

Sovereign took a deep breath and gestured to a second chair which had grown from the floor. As Dragor took a seat, he said, "As epochs passed, this world became stagnant because of the Way. It was meant to be a temporary tool, Adept. It was designed for our people to use, to survive building a colony, but nothing more. Had things progressed normally, as our population grew, the Way would have lessened."

"Why?" Dragor interrupted.

The old man smiled, but his mien was rueful. "It has always been so. As our people colonize lands, they are safeguarded by the Way, but that protection is finite. Though a lake is too much water for a single person to drink, it is too little for an entire world to share. The Way is the same. What might be remembered as feats of high magic and demigods of renown would wane into myths and legends to be told and retold as time wore on and the Way diminished—as people multiplied and flourished."

Sovereign paused, his fingers absentmindedly rubbing a worn arm of the pedestal he sat upon. "There should be billions of people living upon this world by now, and yet only a few million inhabit Edyn. Do you ken why?"

When Dragor didn't answer the old man raised his hand and began ticking off fingers, "Your long life, your health, your ability to influence the world around you, whether that be for better crops, more rain, defense—"

"But King Galadine killed mages," retorted Dragor.

Sovereign sighed and said, "You speak of something akin to today's weather. I speak of something influential across deep time, like climate. The Way is so much more than casting spells, Adept. It follows every person's unconscious thought, amplifying it into reality. Why do the Aeris appear as gods and goddesses?"

Dragor could feel himself losing his obstinacy, eroding like a mud wall to a fast-moving stream of questions, wielded by a deft interrogator. He could also feel himself tiring from his earlier ordeal of escaping Sovereign's forces. He shook his head and asked, "Just tell me why I'm here."

Sovereign leaned in and grasped both of Dragor's hands in his own. The grip was warm and strong, stronger than the adept had expected given the man's appearance. A sudden flood of energy washed through him, clean and powerful. It rejuvenated his mind, brought succor to his body, and washed away any sense of fear or doubt. It was akin to the Lore Father's gift of energy, but somehow different. It was intoxicating in its ability to give him a feeling of invincibility.

"Dragor, deliver a message to Lore Father Giridian Alacar. I want peace."

"Peace?" Dragor couldn't disguise the shock that he knew must be evident on his face. "If you're the Sovereign, you attacked us and slaughtered innocent people on the Isle. You attacked Tarin and decimated her folk and you may be guilty of abducting their families for your own purposes. How are you not evil?"

"Good and evil are a matter of perspective, Adept. What one person calls abduction... another may call rescue."

Dragor remained unconvinced, but Sovereign continued, "Is the flood that follows a storm evil?" The old man raised one eyebrow and said, "I intend to set things right with the

Way. I will not hurt you or yours, but I will set right the progress of this world. You'll continue to act as sentinels for the land. However, the people of Edyn will progress from the worship of demigods and the practice of magic to the sound basis of empirical reasoning… and, eventually, to science."

"And to do that, you'll take away all the gifts the Way gives us." His statement was met with a bemused expression from the old man.

"You are demi-gods already, living in a world meant for men, Adept! While it is of some discomfort to accept a lesser station, think back to the beach and Captain Talaris's mistake. Had she sacrificed herself and crew as protocol demanded, Edyn would have been left unblemished."

"She chose to save her people!"

Sovereign shook his head and said, "No! I would have achieved that goal without her intervention."

"You?" Dragor scoffed. "Now who's interfering and creating problems?"

"Had I been given the chance, I would have awakened the colonists still in slumber and properly acclimated them to a new home. Captain Talaris saved herself and her crew because she didn't want to die. All of Edyn, since that day has suffered for her decision." There was silence, then Sovereign said, "Be at ease. Even if I were to set things right, magic would not immediately disappear. It would be several lifetimes before anyone noticed its decrease. Fear not, you'll be demigods still."

Dragor said, "I don't care about that."

"Hmm," the old man's mouth twisted as if he didn't believe the adept's statement. "Really? You don't care about power?" He looked around the plain white room, then asked, "What do you care about, then?" There was another period of silence into which the old man finally asked, "What if Lilyth wins? What do you think will happen?"

"Why does that matter to us—"

Sovereign raised a hand, stopping Dragor midsentence. "She did what I thought she'd never do. She sacrificed Arcadia to bring her legions here. Now they spread like a pestilence, possessing all they encounter. Because Arcadia is dying, more of the Way becomes available, and that means more Aeris are born. Soon, there will be few true people left."

Dragor sighed, "And so, Thera and our children paid the price. You culled us to increase the Way, only to have Lilyth do the same with Arcadia, and now the deaths you caused were in vain. Needless bloodshed on both your hands."

Sovereign looked up, his eyes gleaming with tears, but there was an intensity to his gaze that Dragor couldn't ignore. "Help me, and I can restore them. All those killed because of this war need not be lost forever!"

Dragor looked at Sovereign, his breath caught in his throat. He leaned forward and said, "Don't say such things, even in jest…"

"The war does not go well. Lilyth has sacrificed much to gain an advantage and she presses that advantage without fear. She has either possessed or killed the builders who hid between realms. She knows I cannot risk the colonists in slumber, which leaves me only the dragons and the Galadine elves. Perhaps I can hold her at bay for a time… but without help she will eventually imprison me within this mountain and rule Edyn as a focal point for religion and worship. She will undo any chance this world has to progress, to awaken to its true potential. She'll use the colonists to feed her need for more sycophants, or worse, she'll breed a race of slaves who know nothing but mysticism and superstition. Even now she has captured and enslaved children. Their fate, along with every living person in Edyn, will be to serve the Aeris."

Dragor looked at the man, then asked, "Why children?"

"Who believes more deeply and truly than a child? They fuel her existence with their innocence and fervor." Sovereign stood, slowly walking over to the window showing the land spread out before them. "I'm tired, Dragor, and I'm old. I have watched over this world for longer than you can imagine. Even I cannot do this forever."

He turned and said, "I offer this pact – join me and I will preserve every person living on Edyn through the remaking, including your people on the Isle. I will restore those who fell during my attacks. It was not my original plan, but if we do not join forces to stop Lilyth, we will lose this world to her demons, mysticism, and faith. Failure means your children will be nothing but bodies to be hunted like animals and possessed."

Dragor didn't know what to say. He swallowed, his mind racing. Finally, he blurted the one thing that popped into his head. "My apprentice?"

Sovereign replied, "Jesyn transitioned to Arcadia before I could recover her. Unless she found a way out, I fear she is lost."

"Why?" inquired the adept.

"The null, the person you call Arek, unleashed something that eats away at what holds Arcadia together. Lilyth's land was sacrosanct to any Waymasters' interference, yet she invited that abomination into her realm where it wreaks havoc. It is only a matter of time before Arcadia is no more. When that happens, the full power of the Way will be hers to command in Edyn."

"How long does Jesyn have?" he asked, his mouth dry.

Nothing was said for a moment. Sovereign looked out the window, as if weighing his words. Then he replied, "A few days, perhaps less. The only consolation is that the null is trapped there, too. That fact does not, however, make up for your apprentice's loss. I wish it could be different."

"Send me! I can lead her back!" Dragor exclaimed.

Sovereign shook his head. "The gates to Arcadia are Lilyth's domain, as commanded by the First Laws. Even I cannot break them without invitation. It was done purposely, a safeguard against either of us having unchecked power over Edyn's well-being. If I could, I would have ended this nightfright eons ago."

Dragor fell in on himself. His eyes closed, hoping against all odds Jesyn could find or already had found a way out. The girl – no, he corrected himself, the adept – was very resourceful, as her test for Ascension had proved. The only way he'd know was to rejoin Giridian, who could reach out and see with his mindspeak. Wait!

"Reach out to her! Let me know she's alive," he demanded.

Sovereign shook his head. "You weren't listening. I cannot pierce the veil between Edyn and Arcadia without permission."

Dragor cursed, then looked out the window, his mind racing. Another concern bubbled up, nudging Jesyn's plight aside. He tentatively asked, "Dazra, Tarin?"

Sovereign nodded and said, "Just as you, they are being cared for and safe. I will send Tarin with you, but Dazra must stay. His blood is too valuable to risk to Lilyth's forces. We cannot lose him or those few like him if we intend on repairing what has been broken for so long."

"His blood?"

The old man nodded, "He is one of the anointed, those

few who have special attributes that can be passed on through successive generations."

"Why do I feel like you're dumbing things down for me?" Dragor inquired, a small smile quirking the corner of his mouth.

Sovereign returned the look and said, "Shall I speak of things which have no meaning to you, such as jin-net-iks?"

Dragor shrugged. He knew what a djinn was, but the rest of the term was unfamiliar.

Sovereign continued, "No matter. Had this world progressed normally, you and I could have more illuminating conversations. For now, I choose to speak in a way you will easily comprehend."

There was so much he needed to consider. If what Sovereign said was true, not only was the world poised for cataclysm, but they'd been fighting the wrong people all this time. Still, his friends on the Isle had died because of this man, so he remained cautious. He only had Sovereign's word they could be resurrected and had little faith in it.

"It's a lot to take in," said Dragor, carefully. He wasn't lying.

Sovereign regarded him, his expression inscrutable. Then he nodded and said, "I understand. Rest. When you are ready, just say my name and I will come to you."

The old man began to gesture but paused and added, "Do not mistake this offer as something I need, Adept. This is my effort save your people from possession, from becoming an enemy I do not wish to eradicate. Do not tarry too long in your considerations. Things are moving quickly, and we stand now at the point of the dagger, the crux of your destiny. There are only two paths before you… me, or her."

At Dragor's nod he completed his gesture and the adept found himself back in his white room. He moved over and collapsed on the bed, resting his forearm on his head. The day had started out strange, and only become worse. Yet at no time had he felt the old man was lying to him. Now he had to make a choice—trust this being calling himself Sovereign or try and escape. Somehow, he knew, whatever got him to Giridian's side soonest was the right answer.

*****

Artymis appeared out of thin air, her graceful figure moving to stand beside Sovereign, who she'd noticed had begun to change. The being replacing the old man was taller and more regal, his face hidden behind a dark mask that looked to be made of stars slowly in motion.

"Do you think he'll listen?" she asked. After making her decision to join him, Artymis had given up on self-doubt and recriminations. It was not her way. Her only focus was the impetus of the moment, the here and now, and how she could affect it.

Sovereign replied in a deep baritone, his voice resonant in the confined space, "It is his people's only hope. They cannot withstand Lilyth or the Galadine forces alone."

Artymis nodded, then looked at Sovereign through the sides of her eyes. The dark star pattern moved slowly, mesmerizing in its own way. Curious about another thing, she asked, "You showed him a vision of a sailing ship. Why something so simple instead of the truth?"

"As I said, what is the truth? That he understands the plight of the world is enough. Even I have rules I must obey and it is not my place to reveal to him that his people's origins encompass far more than just this one world."

"And you'll actually save them?" she knew she was poking now but liked the challenge. Of course, Sovereign could make her existence miserable, but he couldn't wipe her out with a thought… at least she hoped that last part was true.

Sovereign looked at her and nodded. "To preserve the living, yes, I will."

Artymis arched one delicate eyebrow. "A very specific choice of words."

A low grumble emanated from the tall figure before he said, "Perhaps some small part of Kisan lives on in you still."

"Like her beauty, or her skill…" She wandered closer, looking coyly up at the dark figure. "Her courage?" she offered looking sidelong at the dark lord. "Maybe I'm—"

"Impertinent," said Sovereign, effectively shutting the rest of Artymis' self-admiration down.

The war angel took a moment, still hoping to curry a bit of favor and said, "I hope he chooses wisely, as I did."

Sovereign let out a small laugh. Laying a gentle hand on her shoulder, he said, "As do I, my child. See to the release of Tarin. Let her join him so that they may share counsel, as those in like circumstance are often wont to do. What he chooses is of paramount importance."

"And yet in things so important, you still offer him a choice," she said. It wasn't meant as a question, but rather a statement of fact. "You offer him the truth, that he can choose you or Lilyth. Why?"

Sovereign nodded and answered, "Choice made freely is the only way to create true allies. He will soon realize Lilyth cannot be opposed with numbers, for that plays to her strength." The being paused, then met Artymis's eyes.

"Still, a gentle nudge from a familiar face can help our cause. Come, there is much to be done."

Dragor Awakens

THE EMISSARY

Niall swung his bohir up, catching Zedakai's strike on the spine of his weapon. He pushed it outward and threw two fast strikes in return, one at the master's head and the other at the opposite side ribs. Zed blocked both, then pushed his student away using the hilt of his weapon against Niall's own.

"Good," he said, happy with the prince's reflexes and timing. "You're getting better every day."

Niall nodded. "Will I be testing again soon?"

Zedakai smiled at the young king's enthusiasm for blood combat. It was a rare trait, one he'd encouraged. Of course, Niall could never know that those he fought weren't the very best. They were meant to be sacrificed to help the boy gain confidence in his abilities. Each one gave him or herself willingly to the cause. In turn, each was resurrected by Niall's new ability to gift elven life, handed down to him from Valarius himself. These new angels were more powerful, creating a personal guard just as loyal to Niall as the normal elves, a necessary part of taking over Valarius's role.

So much had been planned for with regards to the war, reflected the armsmark. Even what to do in the event of Valarius falling in battle had been given thought. Zed followed the highlord's instructions to the letter, but a small part of him doubted he'd seen the last of the Galadine elven king. Valarius had a knack for surviving. He'd survived his banishment to Arcadia, given birth to the elven people, and found a way for his house to return to Edyn. Zed knew it would take far more than a blood gholem to vanquish the highlord, but kept his focus on the here and now. His responsibility was to prepare this young king to be the image of what Valarius wanted, and he would do that to the best of his ability.

Turning his attention back to the expectant boy, he nodded reassuringly. Niall had bloodlust aplenty and was carving his way through the ranks expeditiously. Eventually though, Zedakai knew they'd have to put someone more skilled against the king. That moment would have to be handled with delicacy.

"We can, my king," said Zedakai deferentially. "Or we can work on some of the techniques you'll need for facing more than one opponent. Which fancies your interest most?"

Niall pursed his lips, thinking. Then he said, "I wouldn't mind learning how to fight more people, as long as I can test myself against just two next time. I don't want to…", the boy hesitated, as if suddenly realizing what he was about to say, and quickly corrected himself. "I don't want to defeat so many men at once. It makes our guards look bad."

Zedakai laughed, "Of course! Your blood combats are becoming the talk of the castle already, my king."

Niall nodded, clearly enthused by the flattery. "You know, I've been thinking about expanding my combat to include more of our soldiers. Perhaps I can build an arena, then reward my men with opportunities to test themselves too."

"Against you, your Majesty?" asked the general, careful to mask his concern. The king was mercurial at best, and unable to take the slightest bit of criticism.

"Oh, no!" remarked Niall. "This would be against normal people. We'd have some entertainment and be ridding Lilyth of potential victims." The young king paused, then said, "If fact, I've been thinking this might be a potential strategy in a larger sense."

"How so?" asked Zedakai, knowing exactly what the king intended.

"Well," Niall answered, "my father used to teach that armies could destroy resources so that the enemy couldn't use them, things like wheat or rice. In our case, we could remove the one thing Lilyth needs to win: people."

Zedakai's eyes widened with feigned surprise. "Excellent! You'll essentially convert them into elven forces making them immune and ready to serve. Brilliant!"

"No," Niall said, frustration on his face. "I want to kill them."

"Of course, your majesty. We might defeat Lilyth with just the forces we have already turned." Zedakai waited, having become used to the king's circuitous thinking.

"You're an idiot," remarked the king. "We don't have enough men right now, that's for certain." He looked around the training hall. "Sometimes I wonder how you could have risen so far in Valarius's esteem, grandfather." The king sighed, "I think my original idea was best. We sweep in and take them prisoner, converting them to my service. This is the only way we can sustain a prolonged war against the Aeris."

Zedakai bowed, touching both palms to his forehead before sweeping them outward, "You are wise beyond your years, my king. Forgive me. I do not always see the larger vision as you do."

Niall smiled. "No matter. I'm here to do the hard thinking. Now, let's get on with our lesson."

"Of course," remarked the armsmark, hefting his bohir and motioning to two elves waiting by the sidelines. They raced into the square, bowing before taking their positions.

Soon, the sound of their wooden blades on the king's, punctuated now and again by combat master's instruction permeated the training hall. Zedakai mused over their conversation as his instruction came out in an instinctual fashion.

They couldn't do without Niall. Valarius had ensured that by giving the boy the only way to create new elves. It was a fact the young king knew well; Zedakai had to commend him on understanding how to leverage his own value, and how to take credit. In this, the Galadine royal upbringing had taught him much of what he needed to know. Only the fact that Valarius had been the one to create Zedakai gave the general the ability to remain independent of Niall's leadership aura, which made the resurrected so happy to die for the new boy-king. That fact drove the armsmark to keep himself alive. If Niall realized all he had to do was kill and resurrect Zed for complete obedience, he doubted he'd live to see the next day. The best way to do that was to continue acting as if nothing Niall did could hurt the older Galadine.

"No!" screamed Zedakai, swatting Niall's leg. "Do not tarry on one opponent. If you concentrate on one, the other will flank you! One at a time, but quickly!"

The king swung back into the fray and Zedakai continued his musings. Their forces were now close to a thousand elves. Niall had been eager to convert the citizens of Haven, but only so many could be converted each day. Surprisingly, many more volunteered to join than Zedakai would have guessed. He suspected this was due to the fact that Niall never showed his elven form to the hopefuls who came, and no one knew the true price of joining. Once they joined it was too late. Valarius's spell, now wielded by Niall, made every converted soul zealous in their support for the young elven king.

Soon, they would have enough to venture forth and expand to more cities. Lilyth and her forces had taken Bara'cor, effectively cutting off the lower lands from the desert plateau. The support and protection of Shornhelm, Dawnlight, and EvenSea, along with the trade they normally provided the lower lands, were gone. While Zedakai did not fool himself about alliances with the folk of Edyn, he knew Lilyth would be their best reason to join. "The enemy of my enemy is my friend," the old adage counseled, and who would stand against the Aeris? Only Niall and the elves. In that sense, he was the land's last hope against possession.

What they needed now was a strong ally, someone who would shore them up against the Aeris while they gathered their strength. The people of Edyn, unless converted to elves or one of those with mastery of the Way, were generally useless. They only served as potential hosts, so it was important Niall got to them first. As far as masters of the Way, there was no telling how many could be called upon, but from the little he'd gleaned talking to various folk in Haven, they seemed far too few to sway the battle in their favor.

"Again!" shouted Zedakai. "Keep them lined up, herd them so they must attack in turn."

The boy had skill, he thought, once the fear was controlled. The only difference between stepping off a stair and a cliff was knowing where your foot would fall, a metaphor often used by his instructors, meaning to see things clearly. Fear dulled the senses, making one blind to the many opportunities swirling within reach. It made the world full of impossible cliffs, instead of navigable steps. Niall would be tiring now of this. His mind would want more excitement. It was only a matter of time.

"Hold!" Zedakai said, seeing the young king's left hand

361

reaching for his belt knife. Perhaps he could see a few students spared today from the king's bloodlust, despite their willingness to please their lord and father. He knew they would return more powerful, but he was getting tired of blood and building a cadre of personal guards for Niall.

Just then the doors to the training hall opened and a messenger stepped in. The new armor, brass and red, looked good on the man. The queen mother had done well in designing a new livery for her son's forces. Emblazoned on the man's cloak pin and shield was the Galadine lion, but now the lion was winged.

Good, thought Zedakai, a small bit of homage to Valarius himself, something that would go over well with the elves from Arcadia. Nicely done.

Niall tossed his bohir to Zedakai, then strode over to the man. The combat instructor caught the king's practice blade deftly and deposited it into bucket filled with similar weapons, then made his way over to join his king.

"Your Majesty," the messenger said, "you are needed in the Senate Hall."

Niall looked at Zedakai, a question in his eyes. "Why?" the young king asked the messenger.

"An emissary has arrived," said the man.

"Emissary? From where?" Niall asked.

The messenger looked uncomfortable, worse when Zedakai let out a low growl of displeasure. Swallowing visibly, the man stuttered, "I—I... ah, he's not from the highlands, sire. He managed to push his way to our Senate floor. Our guards cannot force him out. He says he's here to speak with you."

Zedakai could feel his eyebrows rise in surprise. Someone who could stay where he wanted despite the magehunters protestations and most likely their physical response was, as far as he could recall, the first time he'd heard of such a thing.

"My king," he looked at Niall, "let's see who this might be." To his relief, Niall simply nodded.

The king took a moment to grab and belt on a real blade from where it hung in its scabbard on a peg. Then motioning for his uncle and the messenger to follow, Niall set a fast pace to the main hall where the Senate met. His dedication to training showed. Torches sped by as they loped down the corridors. Soon they arrived outside the doors, where Niall motioned for them to stop and took a moment to straighten himself, hardly winded. It was another testament to his improved conditioning.

He turned the others and said, "Whoever this is, do not act without my permission." The king assumed his full elven form, ready whether negotiations or combat waited for them on the other side of the Senate doors.

Zed nodded, and with that the king gave the guards a signal to open the doors and announce him. Zedakai couldn't help but feel proud of the boy. Regardless of his bloodlust, he seemed to understand the basics of presentation, or at least what served to impress new visitors.

Courtiers announced, "Behold, His Majesty, Imperial King Niall Galadine, Father of the Warforged and Ruler of Edyn. Bend thy knee!"

Zedakai had noted the name now used for his elven people, the "Warforged." And why not? Valarius had forged the elves for protection, but they had grown to be so much more. Now they served Niall in a capacity far greater than their original purpose. The name fit, for it both honored their Maker and gave purpose to their existence.

Except for the ring of guards holding spear points leveled at a massive figure within the circle, the rest of the people in

363

the hall went to one knee when Niall entered. The king looked pleased, nodding to his guards to rise and then moving quickly down the wide tapestry to the main circular chamber. He took a seat along with Zedakai and Merric Spaiten, who'd evidently been summoned as well.

Good, thought Zedakai. The kingsmark should be here for matters of importance.

At Niall's gesture the men lifted their spears and stepped back but did not open their circle to the figure. Zedakai took measure of the being who stood before them. He was robed in black, a hood thrown over in such a way that it hid his face. He looked unarmed, but even from here the size of the man would give one pause. He stood easily the same height as Niall or Zedakai in elven form. Was this the Sovereign, the creature even Valarius had cursed so often? If so, he could appreciate the reasons behind why the men couldn't oust him so easily.

Then the queen mother arrived and took her seat to Niall's right. Once she'd been properly greeted by the men, Niall turned his attention to the visitor and said, "We hail you, emissary. Tell me, what brings you before the ruler of Edyn?"

"You've grown since I saw you last," said the figure.

Zedakai heard Yevaine draw a sudden panicked breath and looked over, only to see the whites of her eyes showing as she stared at the dark-robed figure with an intensity he'd seldom seen in anyone. When his eyes tracked to Niall, even the king looked pale, despite the blue of his skin.

The figure stepped forward and raised his hands, saying, "Grown and changed." He pulled back his hood to reveal a man with the dark skin of a Bara'corian. The gasp that sounded from both mother and son might have been comical, had it not also died just as suddenly.

Zedakai asked, "You know him?"

Niall nodded, his eyebrows climbing into his forehead in a mixture of surprise and amusement. He stood up and clapped his hands together, "Mother said you were dead!"

The massive figure looked at Yevaine, then at Zedakai, before answering, "Don't believe everything you hear, my king."

"Who is he?" Zedakai demanded again.

Niall turned to his general and in a breathless voice said, "I present to you, Jebida Naserith, Firstmark of Bara'cor!"

Malioch's

Bargain

A discordant whump could be felt throughout her bones as Deft plunged into the black gate. As planned, she and her furies held rear guard near the back end of the team, staying out of the way of those who could cast spells affecting a wide area. She didn't find it necessary to point out Reaper's abilities, just as she'd not mentioned the fact that the location of the Cypher was well known to her. After all, it was said once you dined in Arcadia, you never left.

She was ready for the bone-chilling cold of transition and expected the immediate conflagration of spell and fire at the front. Yet the blast of orange and yellow still caused her to raise a hand as the red mage cleared the area of anything with a fire as hot as a furnace. Deft fancied she could see the small black monstrosities burning and her mouth drew back in a wicked sneer. Nothing was too cruel when it came to spiders. She made her way to the front, coming to stand next to Duncan.

"Nice."

The archmage didn't answer but Zafir looked around. In a voice that sounded almost petulant he said, "Our foe eludes us!"

"Yeah," Duncan muttered. He looked around and then turned to face Deft. "Seems empty… abandoned. You sure this is the place?"

"You're asking me?" Deft replied. "I didn't enter from here." She pointed at Zafir, "He brought us. Ask him."

The Celestial let loose a small chuckle and reduced his size to better fit in the confined space. "True battle still awaits us! Come, the pathway leads down to the heart of her lair. There we will face the Phoenix!" His glee seemingly restored, the celestial lord turned and led the way, caring not where he stepped. Beneath his feet razor shale sharp enough to shave with shattered, trampled into shards that tinkled as they fell, catching errant torchlight from the party in flashes of yellow, amethyst, and white.

It looked like the princess was about to caution for silence, but Deft shook her head and said, "Better he attracts the little beasties to him."

"You got that right," offered Brianna, coming up behind Yetteje. The healer looked haggard, so Deft turned her witch gaze upon her. Purple blossomed, winding into and out of the dwarf, more than the knight had expected. But there was something else. Normally her sight gave her a sense of a thing's life force and whether it was suitable to feed her hunger. Although at first glance it seemed the dwarf would make a wonderful meal, the color looked... wrong.

Deft arched an eyebrow. "You are sick," she said to Brianna.

Brianna turned a sharp eye at that, then her gaze softened. "My nans..." She stopped and said, "Whatever was done to me is being healed. So, yeah, I guess I'm fighting the flu."

"What's a floo?" asked Yetteje.

Brianna opened her mouth to answer, then just shook her head and said, "Never mind."

"Follow closely. Believe me, you don't want to be left behind." The undead knight motioned for the two to follow her. She stepped within the path of carnage left behind by the three war angels in the vanguard of their small party. She, Brianna and Yetteje tucked themselves into the middle, followed by Deft's personal guard. As before, Deft felt like her feet were hooves shod in iron. At least this time she was making almost no noise compared to Zafir and the other war angels. Her furies flanked her, followed by Zafir's two builder guards. She wondered how Paramus liked being back here.

The passing centuries had seen much happen between Deft and her first lieutenant. The magic of unlife had regrown his feet and repaired his injuries. The wasting disease that accompanied his curse however had eaten away his fat. Despite this Deft's took every chance to ridicule or torture the young Fury, but that hadn't lasted very long. Paramus never said a word, never complained, he just took it like a damn sponge. But the door had been cracked open and the decades passed with her going from thinking of him as a spineless nothing to wondering what made her so different. Wasn't she in the same relationship with Lilyth? Deft began to see how he represented much of what she hated about Lilyth. His servitude to her was no different, and with that realization much of the fun in tormenting the boy had been lost.

Now, she couldn't help but look back and feel something not quite as deep as sympathy, but something akin to it. The boy was under a geas to follow her throughout eternity, another of Lilyth's cruel jokes. So, she took every opportunity to ignore him as much as she could. It was the only semblance of payback she could give Lilyth, the only defiance she could think of, and Paramus was the benefactor of this odd evolution.

Slowly the party made their way down through the shale

tunnel. Their path wound in a lazy spiral. Whenever there was a fork, and there were many, Zafir chose the path that led downward. Deft half expected to see bones stripped clean and a sign of spiders, such as webbing or the like, but the tunnel seemed immaculate.

"A good sign," said the princess.

"What?" asked Duncan.

She turned and Deft was surprised to see her eyes glowing a soft yellow, the pupils now vertical slits like a cat's. Just like Trysh, she recalled, the thought suddenly filling her with an uncharacteristic melancholy. "Something's using this place or there'd be more dust."

Deft felt a grudging admiration for the girl's insight, but the similarity to her lost scout brought with it a host of other unwanted memories and while Deft didn't regret most things in her life, Trysh's end still didn't sit well with her. It was another marker she laid at the feet of Lilyth and the Phoenix. This one would be collected in blood.

Still, this quest could not have unfolded in a better way had she planned it. *Let the red mage create a new runestaff, then I'll demand my cure.* Once done, she would exact her retribution for all these years of torture and suffering. In the end, she'd have her cure and her revenge. Besides, she knew the archmage would never heal her unless forced to do so, and only the promise of their escape gave her any chance of lifting his curse.

She felt a touch on her arm and turned, only to see Yetteje point to a secondary branch leading away from their path.

It was not too long before their descent flattened, and they came upon an opening that led to a much larger chamber. The sphincter-like entrance reminded her of the place she'd been entombed, a gift from the two Celestial sisters. Those memories threatened to overwhelm her, so she pushed them down exerting the iron control she'd cultivated throughout her long life. She needed a clear head for what was to come next and she had no doubt that even if the Phoenix had transitioned with the Lady, Malioch would still be here. She wondered what the past two centuries had done to the rapist and torturer who'd been transformed into something even worse. Mayhap he'd died, eaten by his "children." It would be a fitting end for the slaver, but one she knew ran counter to her own fate. Hard luck was her companion, the way tears followed an onion. It was the betrayal by the All-Father and his lies which had brought about her misery, but in the end she knew, everyone who'd wronged her would pay.

She recognized the cavern they entered immediately. The place hadn't changed a bit. The black glass rectangle still dominated the far wall, along with the panel Paramus had used so centuries before. A thought suddenly occurred to her and she asked, "I hope one of you can read the old scripts."

"Worry not," said Zafir. "Much has been forgotten to me, but not that." He moved forward without a care, heading straight for the console.

"Brave, but stupid," muttered Deft.

Then the sound began. It was a hiss at first, but slowly formed into words. "SSStop." The sound came from everywhere, like the obsidian walls were whispering to them.

"Wait!" Deft yelled to Zafir. "We've got company."

The celestial had turned at the sound, his head tilting in that way when trying to identify a location by hearing.

"Bosssss," the whisper said, "Itssss good to ssssee you again."

Deft looked around again, her vision switching to her witch gaze, the vision she used to find prey. The rocks, obsidian and faceted, were crisscrossed with fractures, like a pane of glass shattered but held together. Within these fractures tiny eyes peered out, now glowing purple to her. Not hundreds, not thousands, but more eyes than one would see in a night sky. This cavern was infested, a living chamber with millions of spiders waiting.

"Oh gods," she whispered, her eyes widening at the sight.

"You ssssee," they whispered.

Deft realized they were speaking by rubbing their legs together. No single spider said a word, but the intelligence commanding them orchestrated these rubbings into speech. It sounded like it came from everywhere because it did.

"What?" Brianna asked, looking more than a little worried.

Before Deft could answer something moved near the black rectangle. It was massive, a shape at least ten paces in length but with hints that parts of it were even longer.

Are those legs? thought Deft.

"I've been sssso lonely," the hiss of spider legs said, "sssso all alone."

Deft shrugged, bringing Reaper up to a guarding position and unslinging her shield. "Yeah, well, I can't say you look good."

"You know this thing?" asked Duncan.

Deft nodded, "My servant, Malioch. Slaver, cannibal... now a giant spider." She looked at him sidelong, "You'd like him."

A sound drew everyone's attention to the mouth of the entrance. A thousand spiders now climbed up one another, forming a living wall of fangs and venom that slowly choked the entrance closed with webbing that grew thicker.

"You're not leaving any time sssssoon," Malioch hissed through his spider minions.

Deft turned to the gargantuan spider, still hidden in the shadows on the other side of the cavern. "Reaper is here to keep you company." She tapped the haft of her mace on the top of her shield.

"Ssssomething elsssse happenssssr when you're aaaalone." The spider-god moved forward and into the light, his body covered in chitinous black plate. A white head looking like a maggot with eight red eyes peered out from under an armored shell. "You getsss hungry…"

Zafir, Arek, and Ash turned to put themselves in between Malioch and Duncan. Deft moved quickly to secure one flank with Yetteje while the furies and builders took the other.

"We need to get to that black glass," Deft said to Zafir. "Read and do whatever it says. Paramus can help you," she jerked her chin at the Fury to assist. "The staff will appear there," she pointed to the circular receptacle from which the Cypher had last appeared. Then she looked at Duncan, "You better know what you're doing or we're all dead."

Duncan began to say something but never finished. What looked to be nothing less than a tidal wave of spiders washed into the small group, insectoid bodies covered in stinging fur and venom-tipped fangs. Having armor made it worse, for each insect merely flitted in between plates and crawled into any opening beneath. She could feel them scrambling up her dead skin and smashed her forearms together in an attempt to crush them. She saw her furies covered in a crawling carpet of legs and fangs before she too was engulfed in a sea of horrible black.

They were in her armor! She could feel legs crawling up her ribcage and inside her chest, even on her face! She panicked, slamming Reaper down and screaming, "Immolate!" Unlike her command, Blaze, this spell lit her very skin on fire and exploded outwards, a personal conflagration intended to scorch everything and everyone surrounding her.

The blast of blue fire engulfed the back half of the party, burning spiders to a crisp but also damaging anyone caught in the blast. While the builders and furies took minimal damage, others weren't so happy with the magehunter's choice.

"Are you kidding me?" Yetteje spun and screamed, patting down her hair which had been singed half away on one side, leaving her looking like a doll thrown in a fire. She opened her arms wide and exclaimed, "You're scared of spiders?"

Deft looked around, blinking. Duncan was pulling back on a blue flamestorm he'd swept across the chamber, destroying most of Malioch's forces. Those that hadn't been killed had retreated to crevasses from which they'd come. Suddenly Deft realized the spiders that had made it to her were merely fleeing the flames of the archmage. The tidal wave now entirely more pitiful than dangerous.

"Ummm…."

Yetteje pulled her hair in front of her face to inspect it, her expression somehow both angry and sad at the same time. Then she shook a shriveled tuft of it at the undead magehunter and said, "Stay away from me!"

Burnt hair mixed with the chitinous shells of insects made for an awful smell, like horse hooves at a blacksmith's shoeing. Deft grimaced, moving forward to find Duncan gesturing toward a cowering Malioch. She noted the princess had moved to stand near Arek. At first, she thought that made sense, but looking at their arrangement Yetteje's station was the farthest point from her still technically within their small company, and decidedly nearer to the front.

"We've faced far worse than this," he remarked. He didn't seem to be focusing on Deft's recent panic attack, but rather seemed curious. "Why do you think he's been left behind?"

"If you knew Malioch before the turn, you wouldn't ask that." Deft looked about, feeling self-conscious of her over-the-top reaction to the spiders.

"Well," Duncan said following her gaze, "let's find out from the spider's mouth." He began to turn away but then stopped. "That entrance we came through could still pose a danger to our flank," he observed.

At first Deft thought he was mocking her fear, but the archmage had already turned to move toward the gargantuan spider that had once been her slaver partner. A small part of her realized he was trying to be kind, and somehow that made her hate him more. Still, her feet hadn't moved an inch closer to Malioch. Standing vigil here made plenty of sense.

Zafir and Ash took station on either side of Malioch, who spun in short circles as he tracked one or the other. He didn't need to move very much given the eyes that dotted his white skull. When they stopped moving, he turned his attention to Arek and Duncan, who approached him from the front. Duncan spoke, and with her enhanced hearing Deft could hear every word as if she stood right next to them.

"Hail, Malioch," the archmage said. His hand erupted in a blue flame that shed light in the area, creating small blue versions of themselves in each of Malioch's eight mirrored eyes which had turned from red to black, like small pools of oil. The spider cowered back a bit from the fire and the scorpion's tail that rose from its back began to quiver.

"You killed my little nastiesss," he hissed, "but they're not all dead."

Duncan nodded, "We're not here for you."

The spider lord shuddered and from its body fell thousands of more spiders, carpeting the floor beneath him. Duncan raised his hand but Arek stopped him when the spiders didn't attack. Instead they moved into the shadows created by their father's enormous bulk, melting into the cracks of the floor.

"I don't ssspeak to anyone but the chief," he said.

Something within Deft fell a bit at that. Maybe it was whatever her decayed husk had conjured up as hope. She sighed and then trudged her way forward and closer to the thing that had once been Malioch. Arek seemed surprised she'd heard the conversation, but Duncan's expression never changed. He just made a small bow as he gave way so she could take his place next to Arek's war angel form. Deft took a breath.

"I never thanked you for betraying me."

The spider couldn't shrug, but it did some motion that reminded her of the same. Then it said, "It'sss the way it is, bossss. Either that or be food to a knight, asss I recall."

Deft looked away at that. Then she said, "Lilyth left you?"

Malioch nodded, "No ussse for a thing like me where they're going. You know how it isss." When Deft didn't reply, the spider hissed, "I'll offer you thisss… free passsage to get what you want."

Deft arched an eyebrow, "And?"

"Sssimple." Malioch rose to his full height, his thorax higher than Deft's head. "Take me and my children with you when you leavesss."

JEBIDA NASERITH

N iall looked in disbelief at the smiling face of his mentor and friend. The man looked hail, perhaps a bit thinner, but nonetheless it was Jeb! Here! He shook his head, "What happened? Mother said you'd—"

Jebida Naserith nodded, holding up a hand. He bowed to Niall and then to Yevaine. His eyes scanned the rest but he did not bend knee. Instead, he came back to meet Niall's gaze and asked, "Your father?"

Niall looked down, "He fell saving me and Mother."

The once-firstmark of Bara'cor sighed and said, "He was a great man and a dear friend. You should be proud.

"Long live the king!"

At his pronouncement, a hundred voices echoed the statement. As the crowd's voices died down, Jebida looked again to the throne and said, "I pledge myself to you, if you'll have me."

"I—" he shrugged off his mother's light touch. "Of course I'll have you! Please, tell us what happened." Niall moved back and took his seat, gesturing for the rest to do the same and for the guards to assume a parade rest stance. Those who had seats took them, while the rest remained at their stations.

Jebida took a breath, his eyes searching the floor as if putting his thoughts in order, and said, "Well, leave it to chance and luck, a soldier's only friends. I found myself awakening in the ruins of the nomad camp, my body bruised but whole. It was clear Bara'cor was overrun by the Aeris demons, so no help in that direction. I scavenged for what I needed, spoke to travelers and refugees. Rumors said the king had pulled back to Haven to make a stand. I made my way down Land's Edge and found passage to the city."

"That's quite a story," began Yevaine, her eyes glittering like tiny shards of ice. "You—"

"Mother, that's enough," said Niall, knowing that tone. For whatever reason, his mother took umbrage with Jeb, something he wasn't in the mood for just now. He shook his head in frustration, then looked at Merric. "You'll see to the firstmark being properly cared for and housed. I want to meet with him later to discuss his role here. His experience and his loyalty are beyond question."

"And he has no comment about your sudden change into a blue-skinned elven giant?" blurted Yevaine, her frustration clear in the pitch of her voice.

"I see the king's son," replied Jebida, his eyes meeting Yevaine's own, "and my liege lord."

"Mother, please excuse us," ordered Niall. He didn't want her ruining what was turning out to be an historic day for House Galadine. To have Jeb back! The young king appreciated Merric's consistent willingness to abase himself to win favor, and Zedakai's martial instruction, but he'd only had his mother here as family, and in truth she was wearing on him. She constantly disapproved of his choices, undermining his confidence with a look or something muttered under her breath. The act of hiding his reaction was becoming more tiresome than her disapproval itself. Perhaps now that he had Jeb—as close to an uncle he'd had in his life, and someone who he knew he could trust—the firstmark could intervene and keep his mother in check. He watched as she rose slowly, nodding to him and to Jeb before following her escort out. Then he turned back to the massive figure of the firstmark.

"Jebida, it is with great joy that I welcome you back to our family. You have been sorely missed."

The firstmark smiled and said, "I'm happy to be back, your Majesty. Together, we are going to do great things."

*****

Yevaine slammed the door to her quarters, moving closer to the window that opened out to the city. Pushing it open she drew a deep breath, trying to calm her anger. Biting her tongue was becoming harder and harder, especially as Niall became more petulant and erratic. She knew power was corrupting him, but she didn't know how to stop it. Speaking out would only get her banished from the counsel he sought, so she'd committed herself to being careful with her words. She didn't want him to be a tyrant, but she would also not be party to usurping her son's budding kingship. Still, matters were getting out of hand.

It was impossible for Jeb to be here, right? He'd fallen, or at least that's what Bernal had said. Could he have been mistaken? Yevaine pondered that for a moment. Perhaps, but that would mean the Adepts sent into the camp with Jeb had either lied or they'd been mistaken too. Could three people all mistakenly report a man killed in a duel? From what Bernal had described, he'd certainly believed it. But it was exceedingly difficult to prove Jebida's claims false when he stood before them healthy and whole.

She wrung her hands. Her instincts told her this was wrong, but without proof it was nothing more than a wild accusation. Given where Niall's patience was with her, it would be perceived as an attempt to control him or worse, some sort of treason. She slammed a fist into the windowsill. Dealing with Niall at this age was maddening at best.

Her thoughts turned to Jebida and his sudden appearance at court. Why was she so convinced something wrong was afoot? The man could've survived. She certainly had, binding her own leg when circumstances called for it. He was a man of incredible strength and fortitude. Why did she not believe him then? Yevaine moved over to the wooden cross beams where her chain armor sat draped like an empty vessel, a war ghost waiting for a soul. Falcen sat scabbarded and propped against the wall next to it. Retrieving the blade, she went and sat at her reading table, pulling the blade out a bit from the scabbard to inspect it. Lines like water ran up and down the steel, the wavering pattern created when the blacksmith folded the blade over and over, hammering it back out again until layers formed. The pattern drew her gaze, shining as if it had a life of its own.

She could see Bernal's face, his hand outstretched. Darkness opened below him. A chasm of nothingness into which he fell. He screamed—

"Lady Yevaine?"

The knock pulled her from where her head rested, the sudden transition from sleep to wakefulness causing her eyes to open overly wide, as if trying to gather in as much light as possible. When had she fallen asleep? She wiped her face, then called, "A moment!"

She sheathed Falcen and wiped her face again, checking herself once in the mirror. The sun hadn't moved much, but enough for her to tell some time had passed. She shook her head, angry at her own self-indulgence, then moved closer to the door and asked, "Who is it?"

"Jeb," came the short answer. Shadows below the door spoke to a single person on the other side.

Surprise colored her cheeks, a rush of blood triggered by some deep instinct. She cast a glance quickly about, then retrieved a small dagger, which she tucked into her waistband in the small of her back. What are you doing? a part of her mind demanded, but she ignored it. Though her inner voice had seldom steered her wrong. And she knew having the dagger and not needing it was far better than the reverse.

"Are you accompanied?" she asked.

There was silence, then Jebida's voice said, "Your guards are stationed outside. I can come back later if that suits you better."

Yevaine stood facing the door, her mind racing. She was not one to avoid unpleasant things and reuniting with Jeb shouldn't be something unpleasant. She buried her worry and said, "No, enter."

The door cracked open, just enough for the firstmark to put his head through. He gave her a quick glance, one that conveyed both happiness and concern. Then he opened the door fully and stooped to enter. Yevaine had grown so accustomed to the size of the halls and doorways at Bara'cor, she'd forgotten Haven had been built for people her size. Here, Jebida was a giant trapped within a burrow for small folk. He hunched over as he entered, then smiled and made space for himself to sit on the floor, which he did with a smile.

He looked briefly at the ceiling and said, "It's actually not all that bad once I stopped hitting my head."

Yevaine nodded, unsure of exactly what to do or say. Then she had an idea and looked to the door. "Guards, please summon Legates Kalindor and Tir. I want them to join our reunion."

"Heh, good idea. A break from politics." He met her eyes with the joke still sparkling in his and added, "Maybe they can convince you I mean no harm."

"Harm?" Yevaine asked, her mind alert as she performed her own mental interrogation. "A strange choice of words, Firstmark."

The big man shrugged. "Clearly you're less than happy to see me. Harm is as good a word as any." He paused, then asked, "before your companions arrive, tell me this. What is most important for Niall's success?"

Yevaine's eyes narrowed. "What do you mean?"

"His success… will it be strength of arms, victory in battles," he met her gaze, "loyalty?"

This was definitely not a conversation she'd expected to have with the firstmark, and yet it wasn't coming as a surprise. Something in his demeanor told her now was a better time to listen, so she nodded and said, "He's a new king."

Jebida nodded, "And thirsting for approval. With the guidance from a voice he trusts, he can accomplish anything."

"And that voice would be yours?" Yevaine offered, the sarcasm dripping from her tongue. "You think—"

"The hand may be ours, but the voice will be yours and yours alone, Queen Mother."

It was said plainly, but the implications became crystalline in clarity. At a time when the boy would clearly not listen to anything coming from her mouth, Jebida was offering her a chance to still guide her son. It rankled her that she could be so easily swayed but safeguarding her son's future was of paramount concern.

"And what do you get out of this?" she asked.

Jebida sighed and said, "I loved Bernal. I love Niall and you, my forever queen. This is my duty, my pledge of service to House Galadine. Must it be something more?"

Yevaine pursed her lips, thinking. The man hadn't moved

from where he sat, but something about him seemed less threatening, less... foreign, if that were a thing one could feel. She couldn't quite put it into words, but somehow the firstmark had become more familiar, more like his old self. Something within her slowly unclenched its hold and in response she could feel her distrust begin to melt away.

At that moment the two legates arrived. Ellis was first in, bowing to Yevaine and then with a look of surprise, to the giant seated in the corner of the room. "Jeb! I heard you bludgeoned your way in somehow! This after I'd left strict orders to keep you out!" He laughed as they clasped hands, his own engulfed in the big man's paw like a man shaking hands with a bear.

Kalindor came in next, bowing to Yevaine and then looking at his former commander. "Simple trip to Haven, you said. Some time away from the front lines." He glowered, but beneath the single eye glinted mischief. Then the man broke into a white smile and said, "I knew you'd take the easy way out."

"Tyrus! Ellis!" Jebida smiled like a man who'd been cold and wet all day and was just handed a warm towel. "It gladdens me to see you both. Now if we could just make the queen mother happy, this would be a true reunion."

Both sets of eyes turned to her. It was Ellis who broke their silence first saying, "Well, your demise didn't make you any smaller. Or I should say, the premature notice of your death. What happened?"

Jebida shrugged, "I don't know. I awoke lying upon a desert made of glass." Though his voice fell, his eyes twinkled. "Surrounding me were men burned to a crisp. At the risk of sounding inappropriate, I daresay the smell reminded me of a pork roast." He didn't laugh, instead shaking his head and finishing, "No one should die by fire."

There was an uncomfortable silence as each remembered Jeb had lost his family to the flames of a renegade mage.

It was Ellis who finally broke it by looking at Yevaine, one eyebrow raised. "So, the rumors of giantfolk eating us could be true." The legate smiled, but his attempt at humor fell a bit flat.

Kalindor stepped forward and clapped Jebida on the shoulder, "Whatever, commander. I'm ready to accept the retirement you offered before this, er," he cleared his throat, "easy assignment."

"At this time you fulfill two roles, that of legate and firstmark," Yevaine said, emphasizing the word while looking pointedly at Kalindor. "We're not quite at the point where we need bother Jeb with our problems, even though his return is nothing short of miraculous."

Kalindor sighed, missing the queen mother's intent and met eyes with Jebida. "I'll never get out of here alive, will I?" He smirked and stepped back.

All eyes turned to Yevaine, who for her part gave herself a little more room and sat down at the table. "I mean no offense to you, Jeb. You know that." She studied him carefully. "But His Majesty's men have had to deal with much change. I don't want them to suffer more when Firstmark Kalindor is fulfilling his duty with such honor—"

Jebida held up a hand, "I suggest only that I be included within this group, and as part of this group my ideas and thoughts may be heard by the king. I do not ask to take any position within the court. Consider me a voice, but one with an arm that can protect our king, nothing more, queen mother."

"You don't want to be firstmark again?" asked Yevaine.

Jebida shook his head, "No. As you said, Kalindor is doing a fine job and has the trust of the men. My only desire is to help guide our young king along a path Bernal would have approved of." At that, the man's eyes glistened with a sheen of tears. "I mourn his passing."

Silence reigned after that, until Ellis said, "Our counsel is informal. There's no authority we hold other than what each of us hold individually. You, without rank or title, would hold no sway in court." He paused to look at the queen. "Forgive my bluntness."

"No offense taken, legate," said the former firstmark. Then Jebida looked down as if gathering his thoughts. "Niall will need someone to coach him, someone he knows better than the elven Galadine kings of old, or those with whom he may have a natural tendency to disobey."

"You mean me," Yevaine shot back.

"I mean between a boy and his mother," retorted Jebida. "It has been true for centuries and being king will not change this simple fact. I only ask that you consider my request." At that, the gargantuan man made his way to his feet and gave the queen mother a bow and backed away.

Yevaine stepped forward, flanked by her two counsellors and said, "Jebida, you've given me a lot to consider. I will think deeply on what you've offered."

"I can ask no more than that, Queen Mother," replied the former firstmark before making his way out of the chamber.

THE GARDEN OF

EDYN

D ragor moved cautiously to his door, his senses reaching out for any sign of movement in the hallway outside. This was Sovereign's Citadel, and if it matched the memories he'd shared with the lore father, Dazra's people could be nearby. Though he'd not been expressly forbidden to leave his quarters, he still felt his heart hammer with trepidation. Incurring the lord of this place's wrath was not high on his list of things to do today. But neither was sitting in his room quietly.

He wasn't quite there when the door suddenly slid open, revealing Tarin on the other side, her hand caught halfway upraised. She looked at him, her eyebrows climbing up her forehead.

"Surprise?" she said, uncertainly.

"Tarin!" Dragor exclaimed, "Your timing is"—he knew he looked sheepish— "perfect."

The dwarven healer smiled, moving in as he stepped back to give her room. She fit in the door easily, but his quarters seemed to have been sized for his occupancy. As a result, she looked like an ogre out of fairy books, hunched over so her head and body could fit.

The magic of the room came to their aid however, just as it had for the 'old man' Sovereign when he'd wanted to sit. The ceiling and walls gave way, pulling back so that Tarin could stand comfortably. Dragor took a quick look around. Now it was his furniture looking out of place. Ah well, you can't have everything.

"What happened to you?" she asked, a little breathlessly.

Dragor shrugged, "I remember getting trapped within what I assume was a guardian's fist. Then I woke up here." He gestured to the bed and added, "They gave me medical attention," he paused, "and then I met the Sovereign."

"Really?" remarked the dwarven healer, arching one eyebrow. "And?"

Dragor gestured to a seat which had appeared from the wall, then took his own nearer to his bed. A table rose between them, the floor becoming liquid as it flowed up before solidifying into a geometric square, complete with a pitcher of what he assumed was water and two glasses. Clearly, they were still under observation.

"He appeared as an old man. We revere our elders, something Sovereign would use to solicit feelings of harmlessness, wisdom, and gravitas." He paused, hesitating at what he wanted to say next. The truth was Sovereign scared him, and not because of his obvious power over the Way. Dragor had come to accept that the being who spoke to him about Captain Talaris and her choices had been solemn and truthful, and that worried him more than anything else. The adept related this to Tarin, sharing the vision of Kisan's ancient forebear saving her people and the consequences that followed.

"Sovereign says the Way has nurtured and protected us far longer than it should have. We're actually worse off," he finished, "like children with overprotective parents."

Tarin leaned back, her expression guarded. "Protecting, healing, creating sustenance . . ." She shrugged. "I can see how fending for ourselves could be an issue, but here's a question: if the Way can do these things, why limit us from it?" She added, "What's wrong with parents protecting their kids?"

Dragor shook his head, trying to understand the point she was trying to make.

Tarin said, "You don't limit your offensive capabilities to iron when you can forge steel. Why would Sovereign wish to limit our people to lower abilities if they came here with better ways? That makes no sense."

And suddenly Dragor saw what she did. Why let someone start with great abilities and slowly take them away? What purpose would that serve? It would be like teaching his students to fight with all four limbs, only to shackle their legs later in training. To what end? He nodded then held a hand up. "Sovereign said I need only beckon and we will be brought to him. Do you want to ask him this, or…"?

Tarin smiled, "Judging from where you were when the door opened, I suspect you'd like to explore."

Dragor's face lit with a smile. "You could say that."

"Come on then," the healer said, "let's not dally. If our host didn't want us to look around, our door would be locked." She got up and walked over, looking back at Dragor and though she put on a brave face, he could see the worm trepidation in her eyes. She was thinking the same thing he was. What if the door was locked now?

It slid open easily at her touch, revealing a dimly lit hallway. Those lights intensified, brightening in reaction to their presence. Tarin looked at Dragor with a question in her eyes, to which Dragor shrugged and said, "Whichever way you want."

Tarin turned, then stopped as a green bar of light appeared on the floor, tracing a path that led down the hallway. She looked back at the adept and said, "I guess someone wants us to follow this."

Dragor nodded, "No sense in disappointing them."

The two made their way following the green path as it turned left and then right again, before following a long hallway that opened to a circular room with blank walls. Dragor gestured and said, "Dead end?"

Just as he did, the walls to this room darkened a bit then cleared, becoming transparent. The view on the other side of the glass was not at all what Dragor expected and judging by Tarin's face the healer was just as surprised.

A vast cavern stretched out before them, lined by row upon row of glass capsules. Each capsule was filled with a cloudy liquid, semitransparent like pond water. Tubes entered and left each like black snakes feeding on whatever they contained. A hint of pink flesh could be seen within, but the contents were obscured by the liquid and the midsection of the capsule itself, which had a row of lights belted around a metal collar. Walking along the outside of each lattice were multi-legged ovoid shapes, like black spiders with a single red eye. These inspected each capsule, looking for something, then moving on when whatever it sought was not to be found. Perhaps the creatures were cleaning things? Dragor couldn't be sure.

"I wanted you to see the truth," said a voice Dragor recognized. Though Tarin spun to the entrance of the room at the sound, the adept merely nodded.

"Sovereign. The truth about what?"

The old man gestured and the liquid within the capsules became clear. Now Dragor could figures, male and female: people with black tubes entering their noses and mouths. They looked white, like the legends spoke of undead wights, with black snakes entering them everywhere.

"They are asleep, waiting for the remaking of the world," the old man said. He made his way in, inclining his head to Tarin in greeting.

Dragor continued to watch the spider-like creatures move across the capsules. He didn't want to talk first in this exchange, and the sight of these people shook him to the core.

"This is the truth about what you fight for. You asked earlier why your capabilities would be reduced over time rather than left as-is."

Dragor turned, nodding. "We did."

"What do you know of botany, adept?" the old man asked.

"Enough. Why?"

"When transplanting, you first start your seedlings indoors, where you can control their environment better, correct?"

Dragor shrugged, "There's a lot of ways. That's one."

Sovereign said, "Just so. And you are aware that seedlings adjust to small, gradual changes better than sudden shifts, no? You may call it, hardening?"

"Sure," replied the adept, "but we're not—"

"And as your seedlings harden, you can expose them to more elements, brighter light and sheltered breezes. As they toughen, you can remove some of the measures protecting them, no?"

Dragor nodded reluctantly, his hackles rising at being cut off, while a significant part of him couldn't help but be wary of subterfuge. He hated the way the old man lectured, but still he answered, "in some cases, yes."

Sovereign smiled and made his way over to the glass. "This process allows for better results in the growing. While your seedlings are hardening, you can fortify the soil where they will eventually grow, correct?"

Dragor sighed. "I'm not an idiot."

Sovereign looked at the two of them and then shrugged, "Perhaps, but understand you and Tarin's people are vitally important to me. You both represent optimal body types for flourishing in this land."

"We're not plants," Dragor said with disgust, finally finishing his earlier thought.

"No," Tarin said softly, "but if the Way were being used to help us survive until we'd adapted, you can see his analogy."

Dragor harrumphed. "I don't like the idea of being designed."

"I imagined you wouldn't, adept." The old man snapped his fingers and the capsule liquid became opaque once again. "But ofttimes the more unpalatable the words, the more truthful the idea."

Sovereign paused, then walked closer. The look of weariness on his face was too honest, too candid to fake. He sank down into a waiting seat which had risen from the floor. "Your people are not an experiment, Dragor. Neither are yours, Tarin. You both represent possibilities for these lands, just as does every creature and plant you see. It is vital to the First Laws that you survive, for you carry within you the seeds of people who have perhaps died out, vanished eons ago. You are a legacy of hope, a promise that your kind will not disappear from the universe forever. Do you understand?"

Dragor just stared, taken aback by the sudden vast history he heard in Sovereign's voice. "Died out?"

Sovereign nodded. "Now you see, and in seeing you ken the nature of my struggle through what is known as deep time. You and yours may be the very last legacy, a small ember remaining alive, of a people vanished ages ago. You are the only reason for my existence, Adept Dragor Dahl."

Sovereign looked out over the vast chamber beyond the glass wall and said, "Take this truth back to your people, and you to yours, Tarin. Tell them of your people, safe and slumbering, waiting for a chance to breath the air of Edyn, to join their brothers and sisters and populate this world. Go forth and tell them why we struggle against Lilyth, against her Furies, and against possession. Possession eradicates the very essence of what your creators wished, the power of choice. You are the last lights of hope in this garden of Edyn we call home."

OATHTAKERS

W hat?" Arek said a little breathlessly. This entire quest had not gone the way he'd imagined. Far more exploring and discussion and far less what he and most of their companions were good at: fighting. Now this colossal spider was claiming to have once been part of Deft's entourage wanted safe passage with them. Arek could feel himself on the losing end of another deal that had first gone upside down when Zafir leveraged the builders for the same purpose. Now this?

"Trussst me," Malioch said, his black eyes peering now, it seemed, directly at Arek. "I'll ssssave yer ass a world of pain if ya gets me outta here."

Arek began to shake his head, but Duncan said, "Agreed."

The adept spun on his father. "What?"

"We need his help, just as we need Zafir. Expediency outweighs morality."

"Not to me," Arek said, his voice firm.

A moment passed, then his father sighed. "If you keep that up, millions of people in Edyn will die and Lilyth or the elves under Niall will rule your world. Is that what you want?"

Arek felt his heart fall, his father's words hammering into his fragile sense of right or wrong, shattering it just as easily as if it were made of glass. Was he that easy to convince? He didn't know what to say.

In that silence the archmage turned back to Malioch.

"I bind myself by Oath, to cause no harm to you by my

action or inaction so long as you help us escape Arcadia."

"No!" shouted Arek, but it was too late.

"By the Lady, I bind myself by Oath, to show you the way to escape Arcadia so long as you allow me to join you and bring no harm upon me or my children."

A blinding flash of yellow, even more intense than before, illuminated the vast chamber. For a moment it seemed like night had become day and in that brief flash Arek could see what looked like millions of white dots reflecting the light. Those were... eyes! They were surrounded by insects and creatures, millions upon millions. Suddenly the retreat of Malioch's spiders before Duncan's fire seemed to be nothing more than a sham, a reason for them to feel confident enough to engage the spider lord in what they thought was his surrender. He had expertly played them, and the icy cold fingers of a sudden dread clawed at the young adept.

Arek brought his sudden fear under control and leaned closer to his father.

"His children are everywhere." He suddenly felt bad for thinking Deft had panicked. If anything, the undead knight had been the only one to react correctly.

Duncan nodded, "Hence my Oath. We would never have left here alive without it."

Arek looked at his father in surprise, seeing for the first time just how much the man had gleaned from their short interaction with Malioch. While he'd rushed to thinking combat was the solution, his father had observed and noted everything that might affect the entirety of their tactical and diplomatic position. Despite having used a blazing arc of fire to clear their entry, Duncan had subsequently taken his time and allowed the facts to form his opinion rather than the other way around. Arek committed this lesson to memory, knowing he had a long journey ahead of him if he ever hoped to read a situation with the skill his father had just shown.

Malioch peered at them, his spider gaze leering in a way that spoke of both hunger and betrayal, yet he did not move. "The binding of the Oath is complete and more powerful with Arcadia's fall. Retrieve the staff."

Zafir and Ash sprinted to the black console covered in glass. As they neared, it lit up with strange symbols that flitted across the screen. Though Arek wasn't close enough for a true inspection, the few symbols he could see were wholly unfamiliar to him. It must have been true for both Zafir and Ash too.

The firstmark turned and shouted, "Deft?"

"Not you," hissed Malioch. He gestured with a clawed pincer and a thousand spiders erupted from the ground. They encased the undead knight in a living carpet made from their bodies. Each spat out white silk, attaching itself to another until the entire mass was a rippling statue of Deft made from spiders and webbing. Only Deft's inchoate screams could be heard, then even they stopped as what sounded like her mouth being stuffed with living spiders brought her panicked cries to a gurgling halt.

The group drew weapons and began to advance, the furies following Deft at the fore.

"Hold!" Malioch shouted, "Sssshe comes to no harm!"

Duncan held up a hand as well, "The Oath! It would have struck him down if he broke it."

As everyone pulled their weapons back Malioch bowed, putting his head nearer to the floor. He spread his forelegs and said in a low voice that hissed from all the surrounding insects, "Ssshe'd have betrayed you, Lord Arek. Her goal was essscape. Ssshe cares nothing for your quessst."

"How?" demanded Arek, trying his best not to listen to

Deft's obvious terror within the tomb living spiders.

Malioch took a step forward, carefully nearing Deft. Then he said, "Did ssshe reveal the Cypher?"

Arek slowly shook his head, trying to control the revulsion and dread seeping into him from Malioch's proximity. The spider lord's body seemed to be moving, and only when he neared did Arek get his second shock of the day. Malioch's body was made up of thousands of spiders! In fact, it seemed only the white maggot like portion of his body and head were his own. Giant black pincers had erupted out of his cheeks and his forehead had sprouted six more eyes to join his two main ones, bulbous and shining black. The rest of him was made up entirely of spiders under his control.

Arek tore his gaze away, then found himself pulled back as the spider lord continued.

"Heh, heh… you like what the sssisters have given me. I can gift you a body much like thisss."

He shook his head. "Tell me about the… Cypher."

"Hmmm," Malioch drew his pincers back revealing thousands of tiny teeth set around a circular orifice. From those teeth dripped something green and foul. "And Deft thinksss me the one without honor." The spider lord gestured again and the living statue that was Deft began to walk forward, forced into staggered motion by the encasing spiders themselves. "Worry not, ssshe comesss to no harm."

Deft walked like a gholem barely formed, each step forced, each foot planted and webbed so that she could not do anything but obey. The sight first sickened the young adept, but also fascinated him. To have such control over the creatures themselves, to create a body for oneself, and to control another's – it was power beyond anything he'd been taught. He looked at his father, seeing something in his own fascination reflected in the man's eyes.

Duncan said, "Impressive, but answer your own question. Where is the Cypher?"

"Right in front of you," hissed Malioch. "Deft isss the Cypher."

The shock that ran through the group could not have been more profound. Finally, it was Yetteje who asked, "What about the console?"

A hesitant sound from the back drew their attention. Standing somewhat meekly behind Yetteje, though the small princess could not possibly hide her, was Brianna. She looked down, then searched the room until her eyes met Arek's.

"I... I think I can read it," she volunteered.

"As can I," said a new voice. They turned and saw one of the Furies step forward, one of the two Deft had brought with them. "My name is Paramus and between me and Brianna we ought to be able to decipher the texts."

Duncan said, "Indeed?"

Arek motioned for them to quickly move up and take a look. Brianna and the Fury obeyed, sprinting up to Ash and then looking down at the console together. Brianna confirmed something with Paramus and then looked back at Arek and said, "It's the same language you saw on my capsule and my entats." She looked down again, her fingers tracing the letters as she digested what it said. She hit a few symbols that flashed more information, finally ending with a screen where small white symbols outlined by a red box blinked. She turned and faced the party.

"It says to touch this symbol," she did so and the circular opening below the upper black glass panel glowed blue, and then opened. Out slid a black rod about Brianna's height, covered in silver lines that pulsed like a heartbeat. Paramus withdrew the rod from the holder carefully, then turned and gave it to Brianna.

The dwarven healer continued, "Deft's touch should unlock it. Then if Zafir is . . ."

"I assure you, Lady Brianna, with the staff unlocked I can open our way back to Edyn." The celestial began to move forward but was stopped by a motion from the undead knight, still under Malioch's control.

Deft's arm slowly rose and her hand was forced open. Her entire body shook, as if the knight herself fought Malioch's power, but the effort seemed pointless, at first. Then something happened, a feeling in the air or a change in the spider lord's disposition. Arek wasn't sure, but whatever Deft was doing caught Malioch's attention.

He turned to face the knight and remarked, "Impressssive."

Deft's head shook, her jaw working on something.

Suddenly Malioch shouted, "No!" and leapt forward, but it was too late.

The knight swallowed, legs curling out from her lips like brown hairy fingers as the spiders fought her, then spat and cleared her mouth. Only one word came out. "Immolate!"

An incandescent fire exploded outward from her body, incinerating every spider covering her form. It flashed so quickly only the reflex of cowering brought the vanguard of war angels' wings up, protecting those behind them. Brianna was not so lucky. The flash fire caught her head on, flinging her back and into the console with a sickening crump. The staff fell from nerveless fingers at the feet of her supine form, ringing as it bounced on the obsidian shale floor before rolling a short distance toward the party. Arek thought was she was dead, but a small moan signaled the healer still had life within her yet.

"Just great! That's twice!"

Arek turned, only to see Yetteje stalk forward, her face set in mask of barely contained fury. The blast of fire had hit her in the face as well, burning away her eyebrows and creating a conical wall of singed hair standing straight up in front. Combined with the back burned earlier by Deft, the princess had luckily escaped significant harm due to her distance from the explosion. Had their situation not been so dire, it would have been hard not to laugh. Brianna was not so lucky. She'd removed a patch and slapped it into her neck, but the grimace on her face spoke to the pain she was feeling. She levered herself up and met Arek's eyes.

"Don't worry, my nans will accelerate the healing. Let's keep moving."

Then Yetteje's eyes fell on Brianna, who was still struggling to rise. She raced over and placed a hand on the woman's forehead, balancing the healer's head on her thigh. Her fury had been replaced in an instant with concern for her fallen comrade. In that moment, despite the burned tufts that stood jutting from her head, Arek thought he'd never seen anyone more beautiful in his life.

In truth, no one walked away from Deft's blast unscathed except the glass console. Those surfaces contained some unknown magic allowing them to withstand the blast, Arek noted. They were unmarred by the encounter. Still, it didn't bode well for the group. The knight was free, lunging forward and snatching the staff from the ground and turning to face the group as they rose. In her hands the staff gave a low thrum that rose to a crescendo. Then suddenly the runes upon its surface flashed red and the runestaff was activated by the Cypher.

"Hold!" It was Duncan who stepped forward. His robes were singed but he'd escaped more harm by ducking behind

Arek's armored form. Now he sought to parley with Deft, spreading his arms wide and saying, "You still don't have the cure for your curse," he reminded her. "Give us the staff and I'll do my part right now."

"No!" Malioch snarled. To Arek's questioning look the spider lord continued, "Yer idiotsss for brainsss. She'sss not gated away using that blasted rod cuz of your cure. Fix her and she'sss gone."

Duncan spun at that, "What? The runestaff can open gates?"

The spider lord moved forward, looking more insect-like as the multitude of spiders making up his form obeyed his will. "She'sss the Cypher. If she'sss ssstill here, it means ssshe needsss you." Green ichor dripped from two enormous black fangs as eight eyes seemed to bore into Duncan.

Arek took a step closer to his father and asked, "But we have Zafir."

Then Deft nodded, "And so, the truth is revealed, just as I suspected. You betray me so easily when your own safety is measured against mine."

"No! That's not what I meant," Arek said.

"Your Oath—" Duncan began.

"I keep my Oath, red mage. I have revealed the Cypher and I will open a gate. I never promised anything more."

Arek turned on Zafir and pointed a finger, "You lied to us."

"Did I?" the celestial snarled. He moved a bit away from the group and his two builders immediately flanked him, protecting their lord. "I will transport us back to the East Gate as promised. I showed where the staff must be placed to open a way to Edyn. I gave you the location of the Phoenix, and my hand armed with the runestaff can open the East Gate to Edyn. Shall we talk about lies?" As he ended this his eyes flicked over to Duncan.

Arek felt confused, what did his father have to do with this? He looked at him, only to see Duncan hang his head, shame written upon his face. "What happened?"

"Don't, Arek. You'll not like the answer." The archmage took a breath, his eyes shut, as if this would keep the truth at bay. Something in his stance told Arek the man wasn't surprised by Zafir's accusation, and that knowledge made this even worse.

"Tell me," he demanded.

"Yes, tell your son about the bargain he made." Zafir leaned back, it seemed content to wait and let the conversation between father and son play out.

"Bargain?" Arek asked. "What does he mean?"

Duncan heaved another sigh, then his eyes opened. Pale blue, mirrors to his own, narrowed with concentration and what seemed like resolve. Then his father looked at him and said, "He speaks of the bargain to release the dwarves."

"What about it?" Yetteje asked from the ground. She'd just withdrawn the silver tube from the patch Brianna had placed on her own neck. That patch glowed green, a good sign the healer was mending.

Duncan never took his eyes off his son, saying, "Arek, it is imperative you get back to Edyn. It outweighs any other consideration. Silbane knew this."

"Don't bring him into this." Arek warned, feeling his world beliefs slowly tilting. "What did you do?" He could feel a sudden dread begin to build in the pit of his stomach.

The archmage sighed and said, "Nothing except remain silent." When Arek opened his mouth to demand more, his father continued, "Zafir can't give back the dwarves. Once they're possessed, the person within that body is... gone."

Arek's eyes widened, "Dead? You said...", he looked

around. "You all said—"

Duncan grabbed his son by the shoulders and turned him so that their eyes met. "Silbane told me to give you this when you were ready. I'm sorry but I can't risk you not hearing the truth." Before Arek could move, his father's hand shot out and touched his forehead.

Arek's world, which was already tilted, upended. He felt himself falling and everything turned white.

*****

When his eyes opened, he stood at the peak of a mountain inside a cul-de-sac made from granite walls of the mountain's peak. A familiar face smiled at him, welcoming him with a warm embrace. He fell into it, lost for a moment in the sheer bliss of safety those strong arms provided.

"My son," whispered Silbane. "It brings me joy to know you survived."

Arek looked up, "Master, I—"

"I am no longer your master, Adept." Silbane's eyes crinkled as he smiled. "If you are here now, it is because Duncan has fulfilled his promise."

"What truth?" Arek asked.

Silbane didn't answer. He stepped to the side and Arek gasped. Behind his former master stood war angels forming a small arc, and behind them a multitude more. Most he did not recognize, but at their lead in the center of the arc stood Azrael. The war angel was dressed in white armor that glowed with its own light, edged in a deep blue so vibrant it seemed to be plucked from the dusk sky itself.

"Thou comest to where all paths in time converge," Azrael said.

Arek looked around, then whispered, "Dawnlight."

Silbane nodded, "Your instincts serve you well, but now you must use your skills to protect Edyn. Much has been held back from us. Share what you deem necessary with your companions."

"You say it as if whatever you tell me will bring them harm." Arek said. "Will it?"

Silbane merely looked at him before saying, "Yes." When Arek didn't reply, his former master continued, "However, the decision is yours. What you must do will require a sacrifice greater than any you've faced. Your life has led you to this moment. The lessons you've learned, the triumphs and failures you've suffered, they make you unique."

"What kind of sacrifice? I don't understand."

Silbane knelt before Arek, and when he did so the war angels knelt as well, the multitude going to their knees as they watched in silence.

"Thou must choose the best for thy world, and in that choosing thou must release thy heart to thy choice," Azrael intoned. "Perhaps everything thou cares for shall be lost, and yet thou must endure."

"What do you mean?" Arek asked.

Silbane leaned in, concern and empathy etched into his face. He smiled a sad smile, one meant for Arek's eyes only. Then he said, "I wish I could take this burden from you, my son, but that was never my destiny. Azrael and I were meant to prepare you for what is to come. I hope we have done our duty, for the sake of Edyn." He squeezed his shoulder.

"Arek... you are the first to have Ascended beyond what your original purpose was, and because of this, you are Edyn's last best hope."

Arek shook his head, unsure of what his master meant. Finally, he looked up and asked, "What am I supposed to do?"

Silbane smiled again and then gave Arek a hug.

"The world is not what you think, led astray by the Sovereign. Though he has good reason, his path is not the true one. To correct it, you must change the course of history and remake the world."

"What do you mean?"

His master licked his lips and then said, "Find the Isle of Hy Brasel and then do what your heart tells you. It will not be easy, and it may cost you the lives of all those who follow you, but no price is too great to let Edyn fail."

Silbane looked back at the assemblage and then slowly rose, placing warm hands on Arek's shoulders. "Arek… fulfill your destiny."

ESCAPE FROM

ARCADIA

W hat did you do?" Yetteje screamed. She'd already rolled to her feet and drawn Valor, the bow erupting in a dark fire that seemed to draw upon and magnify the fury it felt within the princess.

Duncan for his part cradled Arek's unconscious form, his eyes darting to each move as the entire companionship splintered along tribal lines.

"Nothing! He sees the vision Silbane left for him!"

"Now?" the princess exclaimed, but something in the archmage's eyes convinced her he was telling the truth. She grabbed Brianna's semiconscious form and dragged her to Arek, putting her back to the group as she scanned for threats. Unfortunately, there were plenty to choose from.

Deft had sprinted for Zafir's rift leading back to the East Gate, and the celestial pursued. If either made it through, Yetteje was sure it would not bode well for their chances of leaving the Phoenix's lair alive. She drew back Valor and let fly. Golden arrows trailing tails of fire streaked downrange, catching Deft on a shoulder and calf but finding no flesh. Still, the impact caused the knight to stumble and her personal guard turned and braced.

Zafir and his builders hit the undead knight's team with the power of a ram made of stone. The furies were flung aside by the builders, but they had not taken into account the power of the Cypher, now armed with the runestaff. Deft planted the black rod into the ground and a ring of pure energy flashed out, catching the builders and blasting them with its power. Both tumbled back and into phase.

Yetteje couldn't tell if the staff had done that, or if the builders had taken refuge, but it didn't matter. Even as Zafir rose, another combatant joined the fray. Millions of spiders hit Deft like an ocean wave, attempting again to weave her into immobilization. Because of the Oath, Malioch was limited in what he could do. The princess realized he must have wanted to leave and had taken the chance their fellowship could manage Deft. Not likely, thought the princess. Asking these companions not to double-cross each other was like asking a sky serpent not to bite. It just wasn't in their nature.

The spiders made it halfway up the knight before she blasted them with the power of the runestaff, incinerating everything in a sphere with her at the center. The air around her glowed yellow, a sign to Yetteje that the Oath itself was in danger of being broken.

"Don't!" she yelled, quickly realizing how little that statement said.

Still, Deft pulled her power back. For a moment, the undead knight had held her foes. Zafir's gate glowed purple not too far behind her. However, that respite was short-lived as Ash struck, his blade creating sparks as it impacted the runestaff Deft raised to block his strike. He threw more, his war angel steel weaving a dancing net of death. However, he faced a magehunter trained in both the faith of the One and in the lore of the Bladesmen. Like Ash, she had trained since she could hold a weapon and her training had been under some of the greatest masters to have ever lived.

The smile on her face told Yetteje this wasn't going to end well. Just as the princess rose, a blinding flash erupted. The princess covered her eyes with her arm, then moved toward the combatants, sure the Oath had been triggered and Deft and Ash eradicated. Instead, she saw Ash fall back, replaced by Zafir. The celestial roared, striking repeatedly, forcing Deft back. He clenched his hands and the stone below Deft opened like a mouth. The true power of a celestial came to bear and Deft was encased in rock. Zafir yanked the runestaff from her hands.

"No!" she screamed. "Stop him, you idiots! He'll leave us all to die!"

And suddenly Yetteje realized they'd never extracted an Oath of Binding from Zafir. The celestial had no limits placed upon him the way Duncan or Deft did. She cursed herself for letting others manage things, a mistake she'd never repeat. She'd become distracted by the many changes to their allegiances and Zafir's taking of the dwarven builders. She hadn't been paying attention to the most important thing— Zafir himself.

She let loose with a half dozen arrows but the celestial gestured and they scattered. He turned and with his two guards stepped into the gate. A flash of purple and they were gone. Yetteje slumped, hearing Deft's scream as the knight watched their chance of salvation disappear. Then she remembered… three hundred beats of the heart.

The princess forced herself up, noting the stone encasing Deft had fallen away. She looked back at their party and said, "We need Duncan to create a new staff while we still can, here in Arcadia. If we leave without one, we've lost."

Duncan looked up at the mention of his name, Arek's head still cradled on his lap. "I didn't know she had a runestaff here already."

"That gate is going to close," Yetteje said. She looked around, her eyes falling on Duncan and their remaining companions. Then she came to a decision. "If we want to get out of here, you've got to do something, fashion a new runestaff, and we're going to have to go through that gate within two hundred and fifty beats."

"Impossible," Deft said, "even for him."

"I can't," Duncan echoed. He looked about helplessly, then his eyes narrowed. "But there's something I can do." He spread his arms and was already gesturing. In the air in front of him a flash of blue appeared, a crystalline-like structure that grew like a web, elongating and stretching to hold open the gate. "I can hold the gate open, but we have to move now!"

Deft must have understood because she nodded. "It'll work, let's get moving."

Yetteje took that moment to confront Deft by saying, "We've got the Oath between us, but if you still want your cure?" She pointed to Duncan. "Keep that man alive for us."

Deft looked at her, the rot on her face making her inner thoughts inscrutable but Yetteje didn't care. She turned instead and screamed, "Move for the gate!"

Finally, the knight took a breath and nodded, then sprinted for Duncan with her weapon coming to hand.

"Come on!" Yetteje shouted.

A carpet of spiders rose at that, getting under the forms of both Arek and Brianna and conveying them quickly to the portal's opening. Alongside them came Duncan and Ash, followed by Malioch and Deft's furies, Paramus and Demeter. They sprinted for the hole, which in Yetteje's estimation was about halfway through the countdown Zafir had claimed. Although nothing stopped the celestial from closing it on his side, she reminded herself.

The party met at the portal. "Grab Arek and Brianna," she said to Ash.

The firstmark picked up their unconscious forms and said, "Let's go."

"I'll be right behind you," she replied. Then she motioned to the group, "Get moving, but stay alert on the other side. We face Zafir and his entire force."

Malioch didn't wait for Yetteje to finish but leapt through the portal even as the edges began to flicker. That galvanized the entire party and in moments they'd all exited the lair of the Phoenix. Duncan and Deft were the last to leave. The sudden biting cold of transition made Yetteje's already burnt hair feel brittle, but at this point she didn't care.

When she emerged, she immediately drew Valor, ready for a fight. However, the plateau was deserted. The East Gate lay open, the black and red runestaff standing upright in its receptacle. Count on their good luck, thought the princess, he didn't take it with him. She ran up and tried to pull it out, but the staff wouldn't budge. She yelled to Deft, "Get over here."

The knight came and tried too but the staff felt like a piece of iron rooting the very plateau in place. "I don't understand," said Deft. "I'm the Cypher. The staff should come free for me."

"Maybe not," said Duncan. "If Zafir manipulated it to remain locked into this position, but why?"

The staff blazed with red fire sending a ruby beam up into the clouds. There it burst into a scintillating cloud of colors, a light show that could be seen for... Yetteje gasped in horror. "It's a beacon!"

Then the nature of this new problem hit her. How would they all leave? And without a runestaff how would they stop Sovereign?

411

"What?" asked Deft.

Yetteje pointed, "He's left the gate open. He's signaled to any Aeris watching. They're coming."

Dread painted Deft's face at that. She looked at the portal and then back at Yetteje, "If they come through, they'll overrun Edyn. There may be billions of Aeris still trapped here."

"And there's something worse," said the princess. "Somehow we've got to close this gate and that means we leave this runestaff behind."

Duncan sighed. "Nothing's easy."

Yetteje cursed. "Any options?"

Malioch laughed once. "Ha! Optionsss ssshe saysss." Then at a speed born of his spider-enhanced body he leapt through the East Gate, disappearing into Edyn.

"I guess that's one answer," the princess remarked. Part of her wanted to be angry, but the truth was, consorting with the foul spider lord felt worse than evil. Truth be told, she was glad he was gone and the Oath released.

"If I run into him again, he'll get what he deserves," remarked Deft to no one. Then she nodded to her furies. At her signal both ran for the gate.

"What—" Yetteje began.

Deft held up a hand, the entire motion evoking a weariness that was almost palpable. "I'm done with this charade. We need to leave."

"We can't," said the princess. "If we don't close this gate, Edyn is doomed. You'll be fighting Aeris for the rest of your life."

"How?" muttered Brianna. She was still lying down, but the magic of her patch had brought her back to consciousness. "I mean, I thought only Zafir could close his own gate."

Yetteje looked at Deft. "Can you do it?"

"You're asking me to stay here...?" Deft asked, her good eye wide. Then she said, "I'm the Cypher but I'm no archmage. I don't know anything about opening or closing gates, and you already saw I can't remove the staff."

Before the princess could answer, Duncan said, "There's another way."

Everyone turned to the archmage.

"What?" Ash demanded. His expression was one of guarded wariness, as if daring the archmage to renege on his deal.

"Blood magic," Duncan said. "I can close the gate before the horde of Aeris arrive." As if punctuating his remark, a cloud of dust and grit washed over them from the plains of Harmagedon.

"Yetteje's right, they're not far behind and this staff is calling to them. He may even have sent out an invitation. When they get here, we'll have more than Lilyth to worry about."

Ash licked his lips.

"You'll not survive."

Duncan nodded. "You should be happy."

"No!" Brianna said. "There's got to be another way."

The archmage looked at her and smiled. "In our merging to save Arek, I saw much of who Silbane was, his strength, his character... but that was not all. I saw you, Brianna, and you inspired me with your selflessness."

He turned and, before Deft could react, touched her forehead.

The might of Arcadia had been concentrated into a smaller and smaller realm as the plane had been disintegrating. As a result, the power that flowed through Duncan now was many times what he'd normally wield.

Now he turned that power onto Deft and her curse, seeing with the gift of Silbane's dragonsight exactly how to undo it.

A yellow flash occurred; a ring of light that expanded from his touch to envelop Deft. It washed down the undead knight, leaving behind it skin turning from gray to pink and closing raw wounds. Maggots fell away, replaced with clean skin. A clatter of metal rods of various sizes fell away from her, evidently used as braces to reinforce her dead bones. Now her arms filled out, replacing dead sinew and rotting flesh with healthy new bone, new muscle, nails and hair. The tufts of dead white hair fell from her head, replaced with blond hair that grew from her scalp, lustrous and full. Alion Deft emerged from her torment, given a new life by the man who'd cursed her so long ago.

A gasp from one side caught everyone's attention. With the spell on Deft broken, both Paramus and Demeter were changing. They too became living, their gray skin and dessicated corpse bodies giving way to health and vitality. Paramus sank to his knees sobbing.

Deft watched them, her face reflecting her turmoil. Her expression said she'd never expected Duncan to heal her, that was certain. Now she found herself in debt to a man she'd hated for the better part of two centuries.

"I...," the knight reborn looked around in confusion. "You actually healed me?"

Duncan said, "I only ask that you serve Arek now. Protect him with your arm as I would." He turned his attention to Arek, who still lay unconscious and said, "Wisdom from experience," he quipped from an old Bladesman adage.

"And experience from bad judgement," Deft finished automatically, still in a daze from her sudden transformation.

Duncan nodded, "You've not forgotten your training, and you should have access to your old powers. Use them, for

Arek needs you. Help him be better than I was."

The archmage turned and faced the magical opening.

Deft looked around, her eyes catching Ash and Yetteje. They didn't utter a word.

"It's never too late to change," Duncan said and then added with a wry smile, "You'll still have plenty of Aeris to kill." With that he turned and drew a curved dagger, drawing it across each forearm from wrist to elbow. The knife was so sharp it looked to Yetteje like he didn't even feel the cuts, but his arms opened up into two long red slits like cloth before a shearing knife. Blood flowed, spurting out in time with each beat of his heart.

"Go!" he shouted. "Get Arek to safety."

Yetteje couldn't meet his eyes.

"You're getting what you deserve," she said. "But a part of me wishes you weren't."

Before Duncan could reply a hand slapped a patch onto him, and those nearby heard the dwarven healer hiss, "You're going to have to close this gate from the other side—"

Deft tackled the dwarven healer before she could grab Duncan, slamming her forearm into Brianna's temple. Her plan to pull Duncan across the threshold between worlds lay aborted and the healer fell sprawling, her eyes wide and askew. Moving quickly, Deft leveraged one arm under the massive shoulder and with preternatural strength hurled Brianna through the Gate like she was a child. Evidently Duncan had not been lying, for the power of the knight was still prodigious, even if she was released of the curse. Yetteje caught the white-eyed astonished look on the Duncan's face, as Deft and her two furies leapt past him and were through the portal before he could react.

Duncan's blood covered all of them, gushing from the

open slice down each arm. Yetteje was looking at him numbly, trying to ascertain what this meant, when Ash grabbed her and pushed her through.

"Close it!" the firstmark said, looking at Duncan. "Close it and consider your debt paid in full, archmage."

*****

Duncan's vision went dim, then gray. Voices came to him from far away, too vague and indistinct to goad him to action. Only one thought seemed to permeate his being, sleep. Sleep was so welcome, so near. He felt himself giving in to it and the siren's call of peace.

Then something shook him, a tremor, perhaps the land itself. It was the magic of that patch Brianna had slapped onto him. He opened his eyes, only to see the horde of Aeris bearing down. The Gate! The sudden feeling of panic washed through him, sickening and painful, so keen it slowed time to a crawl, parted the fog, and brought him fully alert.

Where was everyone? Then he remembered. They were on the other side! He looked around and saw them scattered beyond the Gate's opening, Ash and Yetteje circling protectively around Arek, who seemed to be awakening. He looked up and met Brianna's concerned stare, her eyes scanning him as she catalogued everything she could from the other side of the wall between worlds. Her expression said everything. Patch or no patch, Duncan was going to die.

"Your body... you need to hurry," she called.

Duncan levered himself up, his mind unusually alert. His vision sharpened until even the outline of everything he saw seemed distinct and separate. He wondered at the detail, a hypersensation he'd never experienced before. Perhaps this was how it was when you stood at death's door.

A sudden howl came as a wolf-like Aeris leapt at him. An arrow from Valor caught it midstride, felling it. A dozen more shapes followed. Duncan watched the princess falling back while firing arrows through the Gate to cover him. The companions moved into action, with Ash and Yetteje moving quickly to protect Arek and Deft moving up to guard Brianna, just in case anything made it through to their side.

He wanted to help, but he needed to concentrate. His job was to close the gate from this side so that nothing could enter Edyn, something he knew could not be done from Edyn. The Way was plentiful, its largess allowing him to weave blood magic as he had in the assault on Bara'cor, though here he was far more powerful. Instead of holding a portal open however, this time he was trying to close one. He could feel his vision going grayer, a sure sign he was losing blood at a prodigious rate. And yet he had to focus, the spell too intricate, to taxing to work without seeing each strand he had to weave.

He understood what Brianna meant. The patch was a temporary reprieve, and with so little left within him, would only hasten his end. Then a burning pain sliced his side, an arrow fired from through the portal barely missing him. He blasted fire to follow it into the horde. Yetteje must be having a difficult time targeting foes through the Gate's maw. He turned back, watching his fire exploding like a sunburst and throwing the horde back from the opening. Blood ran down his side; he could feel it. He imagined it flowing out of him like syrup, slowly because hardly any was left to lose. He could feel his heart laboring as the medicine within the patch fought the inarguable fact that Duncan's body had been depleted of its reserves. He didn't have a lot of time.

He turned his attention to the platform, his dragonsight

showing him how the East Gate commanded the transition. It recalled for him the spell he'd used to hold open the gate at Bara'cor, the web he'd created using the energy of the gate itself. Here, it was different, but not so different he couldn't improvise. Focusing, he spun the blood he'd spilled into red fibers across the opening, using the Way to create a mesh that used the lifeforce of every Aeris touching it to reinforce itself. However, the damage to the mesh was far greater than the energy it absorbed. His weaving would only delay the inevitable and eventually let the horde of demons flood through unless he could siphon the power of an exceptionally powerful Aeris.

A thunderclap sounded, a burst so powerful it knocked Duncan to his knees. He looked up, only to see the brimstone and ash figure of death itself, Scythe standing over him. He must truly be at death's door for the aeris lord to manifest himself now.

His deep voice rasped like snakes sliding against one another.

"I stand beside you, brother, to the end."

Duncan could only look on numbly, but finally he stammered, "I— how are you here?"

"The walls of life and death are nearly gone for you. This is our final gift to each other. Finish the spell, and I will give you the power you need."

The angel of death turned and spread his ash wings. A giant scythe appeared in one hand with heat and smoke falling from it as if it were just pulled from a forge. The Aeris near the front couldn't stop their charge in time, as Scythe cut through them like leaves before the storm. He scattered them and bellowed a challenge, and the skies echoed with thunder as if in answer.

Still, the angel of death could not withstand the might of

all of Arcadia. Though he was powerful, the thousands of Aeris that ran for Duncan's blood gate clawed into him, ripping armor, stripping flesh.

"Hurry!" cried Scythe, his eyes flashing with fire. He slammed his weapon into the ground, creating a blast that hurled everything near him away. He sank to one knee, his form lacerated and torn. "The end is nigh. Use me and finish thy spell."

Duncan turned, completing what he'd so painstakingly started.

At last there was a bright flash—and suddenly she was there, pausing next to the Gate, her form wavering as she stood only a step from crossing into Edyn. Only the blood mesh stopped her, and he knew if he didn't act soon, there wouldn't be enough power in that mesh left to collapse the Gate.

"Duncan," said the shade of the archmage Sonya with sadness in her voice, "I could not let my true love leave. You've been alone long enough."

"My love?" he croaked, not remembering when he'd fallen to his knees. He stretched out one hand covered in his own blood, still sticky as it dried. Sonya knelt too, facing him.

"Shhh," she said. "You kept hope alive. You quested for me though it meant harm to you, and it was you, beloved, who saved our son. I was a fool to have listened to Valarius, a fool to have believed otherwise. You are my one true love. Can you ever forgive me?"

Duncan breathed out, smiled and said, "Of course," he clenched his hand and watched as Sonya's face became a mask of horror, "you came at the perfect time."

"No!" she screamed.

"Tell Valarius I forgive him too, when you see him in

419

hell."

Sonya wailed as the air cracked, siphoning whatever was left of her into the final spell. There was a sudden sucking sound and the East Gate fell in on itself, imploding into a small point that disappeared in a flash of purple and crimson.

Duncan fell back, exhaustion and blood loss overcoming anything Brianna's healing could do to keep him conscious. He could feel the runestaff hit the ground, the sound like that of a body. It rolled a short distance to come rest against his head. The Gate was closed, his companions safe. Nothing was left for him to do.

He felt a hand on his shoulder. It pulled him back from the brink, but the blackness remained. Blind, he could not even see where the East Gate once stood. Nothing was there now except a darkening pool of his blood that one side appeared cut flat by the Gate's disappearance from this realm.

"Death for her ignoble heart," the voice of Scythe rasped, "and now we too, are at our journey's end."

Duncan gurgled out a small laugh and whispered, "I thank you, Scythe. You who stood beside me to the last."

He could feel the war angel drag himself closer and felt gigantic hands cradle his head. "Do not speak. All that must be said has been said."

Duncan took a last breath, pondering.

"I was hoping she'd scream a bit more."

Then the long dark took him, but nothing wiped away his smile.

HY BRASEL

Sai'ken's wings flared, slowing her as she landed in the Festival Square with barely a bump. Armun had witnessed her making her way with alacrity, a black arrow across the blue expanse. Though he didn't know for sure, her speed seemed born of both desperation and fear. Yet he'd never say that to her. That was asking for trouble.

As she touched down, he leapt off her back, landing lightly. He'd mostly recovered from his long slumber. A new energy suffused him, a gift of having never been truly cut off from the Way. Now he felt its touch with an intimacy only a true master would understand. The warm power flooded through him, ebbing and flowing as naturally as his breath.

More than a few villagers stopped in midstep at their arrival, their eyes wide and mouths agape. Armun knew in his time Rai'stahn had remained largely uninvolved with island goings-on and steadfastly inconspicuous. He'd demanded the same from his daughter, so the sight of Sai'ken swooping out of the clear blue to land near the monks' temple was probably a sight few, if any, had ever beheld. He saw a few brave souls making their way up before the monastery walls and large gate eclipsed his view.

"Do you think the Council will accept our intrusion?" Armun asked. He hoped their sudden appearance wouldn't cause a panic. He could imagine the look on some faces, their noses turned up at the sight of the errant Waymaster. After it'd become clear he followed a different path to Ascension than the rest, his welcome here had understandably diminished.

Sai'ken looked amused when she replied, "Much hath changed during thy slumber. Four adepts were sent forth at the appearance of Lilyth's Gate. Only Lore Father Giridian Alacar and a few apprentices remain." She gestured with an armored chin, drawing Armun's attention to a bear-like man making his way toward them. He was flanked by two children armed with staves. The sight was comical until Armun saw real fear in their eyes.

He quickly held up his hands and said, "We mean no harm." A small use of the Way magnified his voice just enough to push past the fear. He didn't want to compel them, as that would not be a fortuitous harbinger for their first meeting. It also occurred to him that in the vast stretch of time he'd been asleep, he had no idea how powerful these adepts had become. Caution would be called for, especially until he ascertained the situation.

"Children?" Armun looked at Sai'ken, his eyebrows climbing up his forehead. "Times must be dire."

The young dragon sighed and said, "Yea, thou doth not yet ken how true thy statement may be."

Armun's attention went back to the ursine man as he approached. Sketching a hasty bow, he said, "I am Armun Dreys. You must be Lore Father Giridian Alacar."

The big man looked shocked for a moment. Armun could empathize with him, for seldom did someone see a dragon and a two-hundred-thirty-year-old Waymaster in the same day. He smiled and said, "I am sorry for our sudden appearance. I am Themun's brother—"

"I know," muttered the man, motioning for the children to stay back. "I recognize you from my melding with the lore father's lifespark. I saw you and Thera when you all met" he sketched a hasty bow to Sai'ken "—this dragonette."

"Dragon," corrected Sai'ken, one eyebrow arched as she

lowered her horse-sized head to meet the man's gaze, "and thou wouldst be cautioned to treat with us in a manner befitting thine Oath."

There was a heartbeat of silence, then the man repeated his bow, taking time to give Sai'ken her proper due.

"Of course, regal Sai. No disrespect was meant. I honor thy father's aegis and mine own Oath. It is sooth to have you back on Meridian Isle."

Armun replied, "I wish I was arriving with good news."

The lore father smiled and said, "That you're here is news worth telling." He looked around as if searching for his next words, then said, "I guess the next question, though, is have you seen the adepts Jesyn and Dragor? They were sent to find you." He paused there, but then more questions began to tumble from his mouth as if the lore father couldn't help himself. "How have you escaped the ravages of time? You look not much older than you did in Themun's memories and yet two centuries have past! I am filled with a thousand questions—"

"Mayhap we can retire to a place where thee and thine may exchange wisdom and counsel?" Sai'ken suggested. Like much of dragon speak, it felt like a command.

"Yes, of course," said Giridian, awkwardly motioning for the small group to follow him. Before they'd taken a step, however, he turned back to Armun and said, "My condolences about Themun's passing." The words came out softly, tinged with concern.

That Armun might not have known of his brother's demise had clearly never occurred to the man. But Armun appreciated Giridian's brevity. In fact, he found himself liking the lore father despite the few words they'd shared. He exuded the calm aura of someone at peace with himself. He also recognized Giridian had graciously left him with an easy out by offering condolences rather than the barrage of questions he'd confessed he wanted to ask.

Armun drew a deep breath and let it out with an explosive sigh, "Yes, well… Sai'ken told me about the attack." He met Giridian's grace with his own. The new lore father deserved at least that much.

"I'm sorry for the loss of the children… and Adept Thera."

Giridian bowed to them both in thanks. He thankfully did not question the note of loss Armun could hear in his own voice… the catch in his throat at the mention of her name. Instead, Giridian continued to underscore the archmage's first impression. Armun found himself appreciating the lore father's careful diplomacy and circumspection.

"Come this way. We can talk inside. These two," Giridian indicated the two students flanking him, "can carry whatever supplies you might have."

Armun unslung the backpack he'd been carrying, handing it to a waiting student. Sai'ken, for her part, merely changed form into a girl not much older in appearance than the two apprentices. Despite her youthful face, one could not ignore the two black wings folded neatly across her back, nor the small horns that projected from her head. Sai'ken looked young just as a tiger did—until you were standing next to it. Then the innate dragonfear took over, creating a small zone of dread within her close proximity. Either she hadn't yet learned to control it or, as Armun suspected, she was still young, so her aura didn't extend very far. Regardless, both apprentices edged away until the dragonfear ebbed.

"We travel light," Armun quipped, a smile on his face, trying to balance out the young dragon's effect on their party with humor. "Waking after two centuries, for good or ill, seems to have reduced my material possessions to nothing more than this." He looked at the two apprentices and then pulled the pack open, revealing an interior with a single rolled up piece of parchment, "I mean quite literally, just this."

"Looks ready for filling," quipped the girl. When Armun raised an eyebrow she added, "Kimoria."

"Follow me then," the lore father said, smiling. "We can share our stories as Sai'ken suggested and perhaps lighten our load further by doing so. I suspect there's much to learn." Giridian pointed to the main hall, then waited as Sai'ken and Armun began walking. "In any case, having an archmage of your Talent is good news."

Armun shook his head and gave a small, rueful laugh. "Themun was the soldier amongst us and Thera wielded power beyond my ken. I have no power."

He met the dying light of joy in Giridian's eyes, the slow realization of bad news about to come. Still, putting the final nail into the wall had to be one, and he said, "Unless we can defeat our enemies with flowers, sunshine, and a chill spring breeze, I doubt I'll tip the scales in our favor."

"Great," remarked the lore father, not quite able to hide his disappointment. Then he seemed to realize he'd said this out loud and with a chagrin look shook his head and said, "My apologies. Your presence is most welcome."

"Oh, don't worry. You're not the first to have that reaction when I explain myself," Armun continued affably. "My father was consumed with creating a new generation of mages who were deadly fighters. Both Themun and I started much like you, learning to use the Way to kill. The very earth bent to my Will in meaningless displays of power." He paused, remembering just how many had been snuffed out by his callous use of the Way. Too many, he thought, brought to an early end for no reason I can truly justify.

"Using the Way to kill," remarked the lore father. "I've never heard someone put it quite so... bluntly."

Armun shook himself out of his reverie, looking at Giridian with a start and raised eyebrow. "What do you mean?" He paused, then added, "Tell me, how much good do you sow when you bring rain to those lands that are assailed with drought, or realign the river that threatens flood? Though they upset the balance, are not your acts of preservation more clearly meaningful than snuffing out life?"

"Commanding weather is beyond our lore," explained the man, looking slightly embarrassed.

"Hmm," replied Armun, "really?" His mind went to the earlier worry of the power these adepts may have garnered over the past two centuries. A new worry began to surface. They may not have learned enough. Dire times were upon them if this was true. Sovereign was not a being to be trifled with.

The lore father gestured to a set of doors ahead. At Armun's nod of agreement they made their way into the cooler interior. There, they gathered themselves around a table in a large hall clearly meant for dining. The empty hall gave the place an abandoned feeling and the Waymaster felt a cold shudder pass through him. The last time he'd been here it had been crowded to the point where only standing room remained. So much, it seemed, was gone. He looked around at the emptiness and remarked, "I felt the King's Law and know of the decimation it caused, but... this empty?"

Giridian nodded. "We lost many to the magehunters, but many more to the world left behind after the war ended. Vestiges of Lilyth's forces, bastions of the possessed holding on with grim determination wherever the leylines thinned the fabric between worlds, brought ruin to our Order. And yet it did not end. New creatures, some perversions of the Way, invade our lands from the demon-cursed place they inhabit."

"Those basilisks I fought with Sai'ken," Armun remarked, thinking it was odd creatures of such power would be wandering about. The dragon's only reply was to marginally nod her head, so Armun continued, "You said you can no longer affect the weather. What else has time stripped from you?"

The lore father smiled, but this time Armun could tell his question antagonized the man. With barely concealed frustration Giridian replied, "Master Armun. I hope I've not offended you in some way?"

Armun shook his head. "No, lore father. What you hear is my frustration at the result of my brother's myopic views, the slow amputation of skill and lore such that we are left with an art dedicated to nothing but the narrow use of a blade." He took a deep breath, then said, "Forgive me and allow me to explain."

Standing, he took a few steps from the table and then said, "Very little of the Way is dedicated to combat. Our reliance on it for defense only speaks to our inability," he caught the lore father's eye, "or failure to live in harmony with our world."

"You could've fooled me," replied Giridian, without rancor.

Armun laughed and said, "You'd be surprised how little the original settlers considered their own protection versus cultivating the land and its inhabitants."

As a demonstration, Armun held out his hand. The group watched wide-eyed as a small cloud formed above his palm. Soon, the cloud began to shed a very fine mist, so delicate it looked like smoke. Only by touching Armun's hand could anyone know it was water vapor.

"You say you have little power," breathed the lore father, "and yet you summon a storm contained above your palm. If that is not grand mastery, what is?"

The Waymaster looked up and said, "And somewhere in the world a tree gets a drop or two less of rain. Our world is what one could think of as almost a closed system. Therefore, everything we do has consequences."

"What about sunlight?" asked Kimoria, her voice barely above a peep.

Armun turned to her in surprise and arched an eyebrow, then stooped so he and Kimoria were eye to eye. "That, apprentice, is a great question. Recall I said, 'almost.' The answer is that we are an open system for energy. We both accept energy from our star and radiate energy out from our planet." He stood up and turned to the lore father. "She's bright, and bears watching."

Giridian nodded and in a somber tone said, "I hope she gets the chance to learn about more than war."

His mood affected Armun, who took a breath and replied, "As do I, lore father. And maybe that's why I'm here. We can resist Sovereign, but it will take a new understanding of the ancient teachings, something I may be able to provide."

"And that's welcome," said Giridian with a look of honesty. "One teacher is worth a thousand soldiers."

Armun smiled and replied, "And a willing student is worth a thousand earnest teachers." He slapped his thighs and said, "Well, we three aren't going to overthrow Sovereign and make things pretty again. Please, tell me all of what has happened while I slumbered."

The lore father motioned to a serving boy to bring them tea and some light fare. He waited for the boy to finish, then began his retelling, starting with Master Silbane's mission to Bara'cor. He seemed to tread lightly when speaking of Themun's fall, probably not knowing exactly how much Sai'ken may have already shared. Armun could appreciate the man's care in dealing with bringing him up to date. He also like Giridian's practicality.

The Waymaster ignored the food and was careful not to interrupt. Distracting the lore father with various questions would only lengthen the telling and perhaps cause him to forget some detail worth knowing. Still, by the time the lore father related the mission of Adepts Dragor and Jesyn and their subsequent disappearance at Dawnlight, the sunbeams falling into the hall had moved a quarter of the way across the floor.

"Jesyn is a new adept?" inquired Armun.

"Dragor's pupil, gifted with an affinity to fire."

Fire. The thought brought about an immediate distaste in Armun's mind and it must have shown on his face, because the lore father leaned forward apologetically.

"I did not mean to offend."

"No, do not mind me. As I said before, I started like you, learning how to bend the Way to my martial skills. Now I see things differently." He looked around until he saw a flower sitting in a pot at their table.

Gesturing to it he said, "This has been cut from its family. Though it brings beauty and pleasure to those who view it, few understand they are watching something slowly dying before their eyes. It took me more than a lifetime to realize we are all connected. We are like dewdrops on the gossamer web of the Way. Some pulls on the web create larger drops, others shake those same drops free. For every action you deem positive, there are a thousand counter reactions, some negative to others. Now I see the balance, the push and pull intrinsic to all that exists."

Giridian seemed to consider this, then asked, "Then you are powerful, but limit yourself because of the consequences your actions will have?"

Armun smiled and said, "If it were that simple, I'd be hurling hurricanes and lightning alongside the rest of you. Even I understand the need for expediency in action." He took a sip of tea, which had cooled during the lore father's telling, and said, "Something about my understanding of the Way limits my manipulation of it. I can see what needs doing, but no longer have the strength to pull on those binding threads. Any single strand is easy to break, but together their might far exceeds my grasp." He realized he must be eroding what little hope they had left, so Armun added, "But I did mention the ancient teachings."

Giridian looked up, his expression so plain in its naked need for good news that Armun regretted not saying something sooner. Perhaps there was something he could do.

"Lore Father, there once existed a vault within the school. Themun created it—"

"Yes!" Giridian exclaimed, then continued in a more subdued tone. "Yes… I have been involved in administering it."

"Pray tell, have you then heard of or have a copy of the *Litany of the Cypher*?"

Giridian shook his head, no.

Armun reached into his bag and retrieved the parchment, unrolling it onto the table and using their plates to keep it flat. "See here…" and he began to read:

Crimson bleeds at the black aurum's fall
Blood of the sovereign runs true at the feast
Hubris releases the kingmaker's call
The cypher unleashed raves as the beast.

As despair rides with fear, and war with ruin
The cypher opens what lies in the east
Forgotten by all, fearful and broken
- Litany of the Cypher, P.P.

"A poor poem, if one were to be truthful," quipped Giridian. "Unless," the lore father hastily added, "this is your work, Waymaster."

Armun smiled at that. "No, the enduring mystery of who the author is remains unsolved, but that is not the point. This poem was found in the bowels of an ancient temple dedicated to the Keeper Thoth. It feels more like the earnest effort of a scholar to capture something of importance but worried of it finding its way into the wrong hands."

"Hmm, and in trying to obscure it they made it almost impossible to understand," remarked the lore father.

"What is important is not the words, lore father. Look closely."

Giridian looked closer at the parchment, unsure of what he was looking for. When he finally saw it, his eyes widened.

Armun smiled, nodding, "You see it, too?"

Kimoria blurted, "What?"

"It's a map," said Giridian. "The litany is written on a map."

"What we need is a way to unravel the map from the poem and decipher it, for I believe the scholar tried to use the Litany to show us the location of the legendary Hy Brasel, the one place Sovereign can enact the remaking of the world."

"Impossible," muttered Giridian. "The island is a myth."

"Why do you think it was a scholar?" asked Kimoria breathlessly, now caught up in the mystery and wholly ignorant of the lore father's mock angry stare.

Armun smiled and said, "The choice in words and the language it was written in. These are all ancient and not taught to many. As your Lore Father said, a poor attempt." He looked at Giridian and said, "I'd like to search the Vault."

The Lore Father met his gaze, his expression clearly doubtful. "You may, but you'd have to search through thousands of instruments and records. Unless you know something I don't, it might be difficult to find what you're looking for."

Armun gestured saying, "Lead on to the Vault. Let's see what my brother collected in the years I've been asleep."

Giridian seemed to take this half answer in stride. He looked slightly relieved to have Armun deciding what to do next. Now that their foray into the Vault had been agreed to, he continued his story of the land, gesticulating wildly as his arms and hands took on an equal measure of the telling.

Armun could see how the man held back, no doubt used to people flinching because of his size. None of this bothered the Waymaster. To him, Giridian's unvarnished ebullience was refreshing. It was hard to see the danger the Isle faced reflected in this lore father's eyes. His optimism was genuine and contagious.

They rose from the refectory and followed Giridian out through the corridors. Armun couldn't help but remember his life here, though it had been short. Thera came to mind, the love they shared, and that he'd decided to slumber knowing it would likely mean he'd never see her again.

Now that he was here, the loss was hitting him. Had circumstances not conspired to take them away, Thera and Themun would still be alive. He'd been prepared to hear they'd died of old age. To hear they'd died shortly before his resurrection was a cruel blow, but he knew not to let any of this show on his face. The lore father already had too much on his newly anointed shoulders. Armun wasn't about to add more weight. Thankfully, Sai'ken hadn't yet spouted any volatile remarks.

"How wilt thee withstand the Sovereign?" the young dragon suddenly asked.

He couldn't help but mentally groan at the timing. While dragons couldn't read his mind, he knew they had an uncanny knack for discernment, sometimes bordering on prescience. Perhaps that skill and Sai'ken's natural tendency to cut to the truth was a play.

He looked back at Sai'ken, careful to keep his expression neutral. "I bring a cool breeze as one of our advantages."

"Ahh," the dragon said, "thou speaketh in jest." She shook her head, "Mayhap thee and thine ought not to laugh in folly's face. Pride be'eth the curse of lesser men."

Armun arched an eyebrow and looked at Giridian. "I'm pretty sure we've just been insulted, lore father."

"Hmmph." The lore father met Arumn's eyes. "She's right. Even if I had all my adepts back, we don't have near enough to defend the land. I fear we have little choice but to hide from danger and wait for better days."

"Danger doth not choose worthy opponents," quipped the young dragon. "No fault to bend before the storm."

Giridian looked at her for a moment, his expression clearly one of surprise, then said, "No, I suppose not."

The dragon shrugged, "Truth's shadow ne'er obscured my gaze." She paused, then added, "Yet I doth not wish to judge thee. Forgive if I set upon thee more trouble than trouble's worth."

It was Giridian turn to arch an eyebrow, looking at Armun before commenting, "Now that's a first."

The elder Waymaster smiled. "Indeed. An apology from a dragon. Perhaps today is a day of fortune and omen."

"And yet I haven't killed thee," muttered Sai'ken.

The expression on the lore father's face was a comical mix of surprise and fear. Before the man said anything to worsen Sai'ken's mood, Armun smiled and interjected, "And it is for that reason, goddess, we meet here. The world will need us if it is to survive Sovereign, and we will need patience if we are to rise to the task."

"Lead on," Sai'ken said, crossing her arms. However, she didn't say more, which put the rest of the small party at ease.

"Much has changed since I slumbered," Armun said. "Did Themun continue to recover lore for the Vault?" he inquired, looking around.

"Themun had us scouring the land," replied the lore father. He gestured ahead to a conical tower, "Maybe he knew something about Hy Brasel we didn't."

The ancient Waymaster looked to where Giridian pointed, then took measure of their small group. His eyes fell last on the young apprentice who'd greeted him upon his arrival. "Kimoria, what do you think?"

Kimoria jumped at the mention of her name, clearly not expecting to be part of the conversation. "What?"

Armun smiled and repeated, "What do you think?"

Giridian cocked an ear and said, "Why involve the kids?" He turned his attention to the girl and, in what sounded like his best reassuring tone, said, "Don't worry about it. Stay focused. We'll be fine."

Kimoria looked down, her eyebrow screwed together as she undoubtedly ran through scenario after scenario. Armun couldn't help but feel an affinity for this entire group. Lore Father Giridian had done his best under trying times. Hopefully, they'd find as to the location of Hy Brasel in the Vaults.

Finally, her voice barely above a whisper, Kimoria said,

"I think we're all going to die."

"Great," Giridian breathed out looking sidelong at Armun. "Happy now?"

Here ends Mythborn IV: Litany of the Cypher
The Fate of the Sovereign Saga will conclude in
Mythborn V: Genesis
Available Q4 2021

436

READER'S GUIDE

Affinities – Areas of concentration where a given monk has more skill or power. Affinities do not have to be chosen; however, once they are, it is difficult to return to the balance of the center.

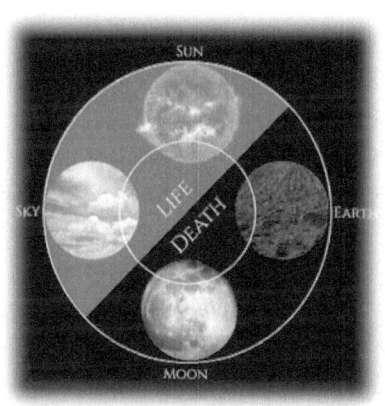

Affinities are arranged diametrically, such that a practitioner with skill in one area will not be as skillful in the affinity directly adjacent to their own and will have almost no skill in the area opposite their own. Note that Life and Death may be combined with ANY of the first four Affinities:

Sun – the use of fire, heat, and light.
Moon – the use of water, ice, and darkness.
Earth – the use of earth, plants, and rock.
Sky – the use of air, weather, and divination.
Life – sensing life, healing, and rejuvenation
Death – the use of time, wounding, and degeneration

Aging – Those on the Isle who practice the Way (see the Way) age more slowly than normal people. They are typically only a third of their age in appearance. A hundred-year-old adept would appear to be in his or her mid-thirties. This is a by-product of their training and begins once they attain the rank of adept (see Ranks).

Arek Winterthorn – Apprentice, Affinity – Unknown. Sixteen-year-old apprentice to Master Silbane, known to be able to disrupt magic. Like all sixteen-year-olds, hopes he's special, but fears he's not, maybe even disposable. Unfortunately for him, the adepts think the same, making him the prime choice for sacrifice. Keen if somewhat paranoid outlook, great with blades, knives, and unarmed combat, mostly horrible at picking friends. Getting better at being paranoid though!

Alyx Stemmer – Pragmatic squad leader who acts as aide-de-camp and squire to the Firstmark of Bara'cor. Assigned to safeguard the princess of EvenSea, Yetteje Tir. Probably wishes she'd not been transferred to Bara'cor just before the heat of summer, and oh yeah, a siege. Used to the soldier's luck, wishes the dice would roll differently for her every now and then. Too bad for her, they did.

Armun Dreys – Themun Dreys' older brother with an affinity to earth. His powers are great if one defines great as creating a nice spring day. In an incredible example of bad timing, has forsaken most violence. He has a true sense of humor and might know where the legendary island Hy Brasel is, both of which will be needed to defeat the Sovereign.

Ash Rillaran – Armsmark and second-in-command of Bara'cor. Military strategist, master in bladed combat. Attended the War College in Shornhelm, graduated third in class, known for his insight into battle tactics and his skill with swords. Gets entangled with the blade, Tempest. Has had his share of crazy relationships, but Tempest is definitely a new kind of *crazy*.

Aspects – The basic act creating magic with the Way is an act of creation from within. The monk or mage uses the Way from within his body to generate power to perform what he wants. These channels are called 'Aspects,' and govern the Senses, Movement, Attack/Defense, Creation, Transmutation, Channeling, and Domination. If you're going to learn only one, the last one is pretty darn good.

Lord Azrael – Ancient Celestial and warlord of the Aeris. The dragons believe if freed, he will oppose Lilyth and her Aeris army. No one knows for sure, and that makes Azrael's freedom a prime reason for something even more epic to happen. You *know* this is going to happen, but when it does, it's still just ohhh so cool!

Lord Baalor – General of Lilyth's army and lord of storms. Ancient, powerful, and honorable, Baalor seeks justice for his fallen Aeris brethren and fights without fear. Able to channel the Way in its purest form. Demon of storms and lightning... not so good at small talk.

Bara'cor – Ancient fortress and stronghold, built by the Dwarves. Held by King Bara, then abandoned shortly after the Demon War against Lilyth, for unknown reasons. It now is held by King Bernal Galadine and his forces. The fortress itself is bigger than the current occupants seem to need. That's either good for expansion, or bad if the original tenants decide to return home.

Ben'thor Tir – King of EvenSea, ruler of the eastern

stronghold by that name and father to Yetteje Tir. Defender of the East and longtime friend to Bernal Galadine. Married to Bernal's sister. Wonders now if he might have misjudged Bernal Galadine's shrewdness, as he used to think the man wasn't the sharpest blade in the pile, yet somehow, *he* got stuck with Bernal's sister as his wife.

Bernal Galadine – King of Bara'cor, ruler of the western stronghold by that name, father to Niall Galadine and Defender of the West. Barely graduated from the War College in Shornhelm. Would have been expelled, but grandfather Galadine pulled some strings, and also blades. But what Bernal lacks in diplomacy, he more than makes up for with that trait every great war hero has: He just won't quit. Wielder of the mighty runebow, Valor, and the ensorcelled blade, Anzani.

Conclave, the – An ancient group dedicated to safeguarding life on Edyn. They are custodians of knowledge and guardians against anything that would endanger the Way. Their representative to Edyn is the Keeper named Thoth, a guy who's tired of withholding information all the time, or having to speak in prophecies and riddles... so he does what no one usually does in these kinds of situations – he blabs it all in a straightforward vomit of truth and clear, simple instructions... and yet everyone still f*cks it all up.

Cycle, Summer, Turn, Year – All refer to the passage of one year on Edyn. Depending on your age and/or level of debt, that's either a very long time, or not.

Dragor Dahl – Adept, Affinity – Moon. Originally from

the southern continent of Koorva, master rank in unarmed combat and illusions. Teacher of Jesyn Shornhelm, whom he found as a baby, abandoned in the Shornhelm Wastes. Prime candidate for local tough gone good, not too happy with the guy-to-girl ratio on the Isle.

Flameskin – A protective halo made of ethereal fire earned when one has gained the rank of Adept. The color of the fire signifies that person's attunement to the Way. The weakest are purple and slowly progress until they shine pure and white. Great at defending one from harm, but also getting you the magehunters' version, your own personal burning at the stake.

Giridian Alacar – Adept, Affinity – Earth. Keeper of the Vault, master of artifacts and other magical items. Eighty years old, teacher to apprentice Tomas, scribe and chronicler of the adepts. Appears to others as a man in his late twenties. Known for his penchant for brewing teas and other mixtures he says are just "herbs'" he grows in his garden. Not the guy you'd ever think would be bad ass, until he is.

Houses – There are four great Houses in Edyn:

House Galadine – Led by the Imperial King Bernal Galadine and Queen Yevaine Galadine (of House Aeonian). House Galadine holds the fortress of Bara'cor. The King and Queen have one son, Niall, who is about to embark on his "Walk of Kings." The King's sister, Clarysa, is married to the King of EvenSea, Ben'thor Tir.

House Cadan – Held by King Rory Cadan and Lady Ilandra (of House Justeces). House Cadan holds the fortress of Shornhelm. They have one son, Durnal, who is still an infant. His sister, Morgan, is married to the King of Dawnlight. They are served by Algren Justeces, Ilandra's brother and Legate for Shornhelm in the capital city of Haven.

House Tir – Held by King Ben'thor Tir and Lady Clarysa Tir (of House Galadine). They hold the fortress of EvenSea. They have one daughter, Yetteje, current ward to House Galadine and staying at Bara'cor as part of her "Walk of Kings" ritual. Ben'thor has a brother, Ellis Tir, who serves as Legate of EvenSea in the capital city of Haven.

House Aeonian – Held by King Temar Aeonian and Lady Morgan Aeonian (of House Cadan). They hold the fortress of Dawnlight. Their daughter, Yevaine, is married to the Imperial King Galadine. They are served by Merric Spaiten, who serves as Legate for Dawnlight in the capital city of Haven. No hints, but with a name like "Spaiten" ... you know he's not destined to be the good guy. *(Okay, that might be a hint.)*

Minor Houses: House Kalindor, House Justeces, House Spaiten, House Rillaran, House Stemmer, House Naserith, House Petra, House Illrys, House Alacar, and more...

Hemendra – U'Zar, leader of the nomads of the Altan Wastes, military strategist assaulting Bara'cor. Responsible for the destruction of Dawnlight, Shornhelm, and most recently, EvenSea, under the command of Scythe. (See, Scythe.) Hemendra has all the traits you love about barbarians, including being well-read, thoughtful, calm, and respectful of others' personal space. Though he falls in Book 1, Lilyth raises him again and imbues him with the power of a god and a maniacally possessive blade. So, he's gonna be worse than before.

Hy Brasel – legendary island said to hold mythical creatures and the graves of ancient heroes. Also said to be a nexus point like Dawnlight, able to exist between all the realms of the multiverse. Worth bringing a passport.

Jesyn Shornhelm – Initiate, Affinity – Sun. Apprenticed to Dragor, training for her adept's Test, last name taken from the region where she was found. Adept rank in bladed and unarmed combat. Ascended to full adept to meet the growing danger in Dawnlight. Has had her pick of boyfriends on the Isle but as usual, selects the one worst for her long-term prospects. When that doesn't work out, we wonder what her finely tuned Adept senses will lead her to next and feel sorry for whichever guy that turns out to be.

Jebida Naserith – Firstmark, leader of Bara'cor's military forces, longtime friend of Bernal Galadine. Distrustful of magic since the death of his wife and daughter at the hands of creatures that appeared through a rift. Hates magic, but also pretty much hates everything else, so it's difficult to tell when he's upset.

Kaffe – A black drink made from a dark bean soaked in boiling water. Its effects are a clearing of the mind, sudden energy, and a decrease in appetite. It's said that if someone could just come up with a way to harvest and sell this magic bean, they could make a lot of aurum.

Koken – Similar to Kaffe, except this nut is dried and mixed with honey to hide the bittersweet taste. Normally chewed, the effects are quite a bit stronger than kaffe and therefore used by some for a quick source of energy. However, koken nuts quickly have deleterious effects on the consumer, such as insomnia and babbling. Thought to have no medicinal purpose and no real value, except to smugglers, pirates, and ne'er-do-wells. Which makes it quite popular.

Kisan Talaris – Master, Affinity – Moon. Although in her nineties, she was the youngest to attain the rank, skilled in illusions, and in armed and unarmed combat. Willful, strong, impatient, the kind you love to watch kick ass but would never hang out with. Assigned to back up Silbane should the need arise, and possibly the worst choice for that particular assignment. Teacher to Piter, then to Tomas. She recognizes the growing powers of Yetteje Tir. She's also the only master who doesn't care about how powerful she is. If it's enough to kill magehunters and people who don't agree with her, well that's just fine, maybe even better than fine.

Lilyth – Demonlord (often called Demon Queen) and Celestial, Lady of the Aeris. Ancient, better than most in seeing the truth of things. Seeks entry into Edyn's plane of existence, ostensibly for retribution for centuries of enslavement of the Aeris, but in reality, her motivations are much more complex. Smart and practical, takes calculated risks, cares for her people in a more honest way than your average demon demagogue. She can make you happy to slit your own wrists, and sad you got her floor messy with your disgusting blood... but she's actually not all that bad.

Litany of the Cypher
Crimson bleeds at the black aurum's fall
Blood of the sovereign runs true at the feast
Hubris releases the kingmaker's call

The cypher unleashed raves as the beast.
As despair rides with fear, and war with ruin
The cypher opens what lies in the east
Forgotten by all, fearful and broken
~ P.P

Mikal Galadine – King during the Demon Wars, leader of the forces that forced Lilyth back at the battle of Sovereign's Fall. Victorious, then did an about-face and decreed all magic was outlawed and mages were to be killed on sight. Really bad timing for any mages who happened to have front row seats at the reading of the decree. Brother to General Valarius Galadine (the archmage who ironically did everything opposite of his brother, including starting a war). Mikal is a seriously disturbed man who ultimately becomes more than he wished for in Lilyth's realm.

Mindread – The ability of a practitioner of the Way to assimilate and read the thoughts of another person. Extremely taxing in power, so the information retained is often incomplete or jumbled. However, it can lend situational context when paired with the caster's own perceptions. Generally, never used at parties or during a first date.

Mindspeak – The ability for a practitioner of the Way to reach out and speak telepathically with another practitioner. Extremely taxing in its use of energy but provides a near instantaneous connection through which thoughts and energy can be shared. Conversely, almost always used at parties to get someone to turn around and look for "voices."

Niall Galadine – Crown Prince of Bara'cor, seventeen

years old. Trained in weapons combat, but you get the idea he skips a lot of classes. Hasn't yet made the transition from combat in tales to combat in real life. About to initiate his rite of passage to manhood, known as the Walk of Kings. A bit entitled, a bit insufferable, tries to be noticed. With the right guidance, he could make an average king. With the wrong guidance, a memorable tyrant.

Paramus Petra – forgotten son of a forgotten line of family that decscended from the first families. If you're wondering, distantly related to Silbane, though this boy is opposite in just about every single way. Great with books, scrolls, pencils, and quills, not so much with blade, axe, or bow. Has finally met the wrong person at the wrong time in Alion Deft.

Piter Winterthorn – Initiate apprenticed to Kisan, training for his adept's Test, last name taken from the region near where he was found, master rank in bladed combat, adept rank in spellcraft. Because he's seen from the eyes of bullies, Piter seems both churlish and annoying. Ostracized by Arek, Piter yearns to be accepted by just about anyone, and, boy, is he going to get his wish. Unfortunately, his personality *does* make him annoying, so nothing good is going to happen.

Rai'stahn – Ancient dragon, defender of the world, now inhabits a small part of the Isle where the adepts train. Predator, powerful in the Way, able to regenerate, and able to assume many forms. Skilled in combat (immeasurable by common mortal rankings). Does not involve himself in the world's affairs, until the emergence of Arek and the Gate at Bara'cor. Now, some of the actions he took during the

Demon Wars are coming back to haunt him, as these kinds of things usually do. Not self-aware enough to realize he's the root cause, but very good at blaming and then killing others for his mistakes.

Rai'kesh – Ancient dragon and king of the dragonkind. Leader of the Conclave and instrumental in giving Valarius Galadine a vision of the true nature of the Way. Some argue this caused Valarius to go down the fateful path he chose, others think it was the next thing that pitched Valarius over the edge. Ordered Rai'stahn to kill Valarius at the battle of Sovereign's Fall, but only after the archmage won. Most agree this caused Valarius to lose his marbles and harbor a tad of resentment against the Conclave of Edyn.

Ranks – There are four tiers of rank, with many subdivisions. These four tiers are initiate, adept, master, and archmage.

1. All apprentices, once they pass their Test of Potential and earn their Green rank, are initiates.

2. Once an initiate passes his Test of Ascension, he or she wears the black uniform and gains the rank of adept.

3. From there, they test again for the rank of master.

   - At the beginning of the Mythborn series, there are two masters on the Isle: Silbane and Kisan.

   - There are also three adepts: Giridian, Thera, and Dragor.

   - Tomas, Jesyn, Piter, and Arek are initiates preparing to Test for the rank of adept.

   - Lore Father Themun Dreys is the only Archmage on the Isle, and as such administers the tests of rank. He also plans all the parties.

Ranks are also used to denote someone's skill along these same four tiers, so a person with a master's rank in bladed combat would generally be better than one with an adept's or initiate's rank. Unless they fought with their left hand, in which case they'd be about the same, or maybe worse, depending on if their left hand was actually their off hand.

Scythe, Red Mage, Duncan Illrys – Archmage, red-robed wizard who seeks Lilyth's Gate, allied with Hemendra of the Nomads, archmage rank in all things magical, possessor of the Old Lore, and able to wield it as the Old Lords did. Just on this side of crazy, and because of that, more dangerous. Really, really, really focused on rescuing his wife from Arcadia, whom he lost due to a *slight* error in judgment. Hopes she remembers it differently. *Spoiler: she doesn't.*

Silbane Darius Petracles – Master, Affinity – Sun. Skilled in all forms of combat and combat magic. Over one hundred years old and teacher of Arek Winterthorn. Appears to others as a man in his late thirties. Pragmatic, self-confident, perhaps enjoys life a little too much. You'd send him into hell to save the world, but he's not the right guy to watch your kid, cuz they'll probably journey to the center of the planet.

Sovereign, the – Ancient guardian and caretaker of Edyn's first people. His plan is simple: kill everyone to make the world a better, safer place. That way someone like him won't show up and kill everyone to make the world a better, safer place, errr... unfortunately, he's as serious as a heart attack and if he succeeds, literally nothing will be the same.

Techniques – Students of the Way may combine various Aspects with their Affinity. These are called *Techniques* and usually require a physical action as well. If one thinks of Affinities as the raw power of the Way and Aspects as the areas in which that power is focused, Techniques are the method by which an Aspect affects an Affinity.

Tempest – Ancient sentient sword, given to Arek for his protection. Said to have the power to heal her wielder from grave injury. Particularly fond of Ash, and Arek. Not a good example of balanced and rational thinking. Bad at love in a sort of crazy, possessive way. It turns out she's pretty horrible at healing, too, except when it doesn't help our band of heroes.

Themun Dreys – Archmage, Affinity – Sky. Lore Father of the Second Council of Adepts initiates the quest to ascertain the disposition of Lilyth's Gate, master illusionist. Easy to anger, slow to forgive, he's not your typical balanced and rational leader. However, his force of will and tenacity have proven more than useful in keeping his people alive. Although over two hundred years old, appears to others as a man in his sixties. Absolutely didn't want the job but got stuck with it when his brother skipped out and left him holding the carved runestaff of office. Now he's gone and a new force, Giridian Alacar, has taken over the office. We'll see how long he lasts.

Thera Dawnlight – Adept, Affinity – Sky. Master's rank in herb lore and medicine, skilled in healing and defensive arts. Closest thing the Isle had to an activist, would definitely chain herself to a tree, a bear, or a dragon to save it, whether they wanted it or not. Orphaned and found near Dawnlight, appeared to others as a woman in her late forties.

Thoth – Guardian of the Archives, member of the Conclave, a group made up of the Elder Races and dedicated to safeguarding life on Edyn. Tries to state things simply, often making things worse by panicking those around him who can't handle the truth. Then wonders if maybe he ought to go back to speaking in riddles. Just waiting for someone– just once–to get it right.

Tomas Dawnlight – Apprentice, Affinity – Earth. Apprenticed to Adept Giridian, then to Master Kisan. Preparing for his Test of Ascension. Strong, brave, dumb, but he's dating Jesyn so maybe he's smarter than he looks. Skillful in combining magic with strength, lifting with strength, eating with strength, reading with strength... uh, you get the idea. Sadly, not great at getting hurt and keepin' on. Unfortunate weakness if you're trying to be an ultimate martial fighter.

Trysh – earnest scout hired by Alion Deft to help find the lost Serepheum of Thoth and a possible cure for Deft's curse. Brave, bold, smart, unfortunately she's on the bad side of fortune when Deft comes calling and throws her lot in with a mix of ne'er do wells and cutthroats. All except Paramus, who will likely kill her through her own kindness to him. Still, if you wanted someone to cheer for, she's the one.

Valarius Galadine – General and High Marshal of the King's forces at Sovereign's Fall, Archmage and Lore Father of the First Council of Adepts, known for causing the first cataclysm of the world. Powerful, strong-willed, championed the idea that demons were actually the source of magic and ruin, then promptly went off and summoned the most powerful one. He preemptively starts a war with the Aeris, gets stripped of his title and rank, and ultimately banished to Arcadia. None of this seems to slow him down or even make him pause. Self-reflection is not his strong suit.

The Way – An eldritch force that exists within the very fabric of space, allowing those that can tap into it the ability to manipulate time, space, and matter. There are many manifestations, limited only by the practitioner's imagination and discipline. The Old Lords of the First Council used it to create spells that could alter the nature of the world. The Second Council has honed it into a power that manifests itself in their bodies when they engage in martial combat. The Third Council will likely focus on knitting, cleaning, and other mundane tasks. They think this will keep them unqualified to play any part in saving the world from its next problem... and yet they'll probably *still* be chosen.

Yetteje Tir – Princess of EvenSea, cousin to Niall Galadine, on her pilgrimage to ascend to the royal throne of EvenSea, with her final stop on the Walk of Kings at Bara'cor. She is seventeen and stubborn, hates authority but loves she's one of the "haves" and not the "have-nots." She's brave and good with a blade but has no desire to be a hero. It's too bad she's in *this* story, because Yetteje is one of the few who consistently makes sense, you know... like a hero.

Yevaine Galadine – Queen of Bara'cor, wife of Bernal. She is sent from Bara'cor at the siege's start with the young and weak. They are evacuated to Haven, capital city of Edyn, to deliver their refugees and return with reinforcements. You get the sense she's the mom who'd camp in the backyard with you and bring the bow and arrows. Doesn't seem squeamish, knows the business end of a blade. Clearly the one in charge of everything at Bara'cor, as witnessed by what happens when she leaves. Within a day, the fortress is overrun by demons and her son is missing. Updating her is not going to be a high point for King Bernal Galadine.

ABOUT

THE

AUTHOR

Vijay Lakshman was born in Ottawa, Canada. He spent his early years in Bangkok, Thailand. When he was nine, his father took him to a martial arts exhibition and his life changed forever.

He dedicated four decades to mastering the martial arts, his quest taking him from Thailand, across the U.S. and Europe, to Hong Kong and China. In 1991 he earned his black belt and has accumulated thousands of hours in the ring.

His true passion, however, is writing. Mythborn his first epic fantasy series and pays homage to a lifetime spent mastering the arts of combat and to his passion for writing fantasy and science fiction.

Vijay has created over eighty-five titles in his career as a video game designer and architect of game-based learning software, but spends his free time entertaining his curiosity. This includes researching almost anything on Google, building aquascapes, and flying (and crashing) quadcopters.

His life experiences include graduation from the Harvard Business School's elite General Manager Program, four decades of training in karate, sixteen years of close-combat grappling, fifteen years of kendo, six years of long-distance cycling, and taking various things in the house apart.

Putting everything back together is the job of a future, better, version of himself—hopefully one with an extended warranty.

NOTE TO READER
Please FOLLOW and LIKE us on:

We hope you enjoyed
Mythborn IV: Litany of the Cypher

If you'd like to learn more about Mythborn,
please go to:

www2.mythbornmedia.com
or
www.dawnslightmedia.com